D0362034

MARK ANTHONY is ⬛⬛⬛⬛⬛⬛⬛⬛⬛ ls and stories set in TSR's ⬛⬛⬛⬛⬛⬛⬛⬛⬛®, and RAVENLOFT® settings. His latest, *Shores of Dusk*—a hardcover due out later in 1997—continues the saga of Drizzt Do'Urden, the popular hero of the *Icewind Dale* and *Dark Elf* trilogies. For his story in this volume, "The Noble Folly," Mark drew on his own experiences climbing mountains in his home state of Colorado (though he has yet to find a dragon atop any of them).

LINDA P. BAKER is the author of the DRAGONLANCE novel *The Irda*, Volume II of the Lost Histories series. Linda contributed to previous DRAGONLANCE short story collections and *The History of DRAGONLANCE*. She lives in Mobile, Alabama with her biggest fan, her husband Larry.

After toiling as a newspaper reporter and copy editor, **SUE WEINLEIN COOK** gave up her Lois Lane aspirations and joined TSR's book department. Currently she works in the games division as an editor for the DRAGONLANCE: FIFTH AGE® line. She and her husband, game designer Monte Cook, live in their hundred-year-old renovated church home with their pet rabbit, collections of dragons, comics, and many, many books.

JEFF GRUBB is an author, game designer, and general nice guy. He is the author of *Lord Toede* and *Knorrman Steel*, *Charonti Bone*, and co-author (with Ed Greenwood) of *Cormyr: A Novel*, and (with wife Kate Novak) the Finder's Stone Trilogy and the newly released *Finder's Bane*. He is currently working on *Tymora's Luck*, a sequel to *Finder's Bane*, and wondering what gnomes would do if they took over the United States Congress.

RICHARD A. KNAAK's novels, including the *New York Times* best-seller *The Legend of Huma* and his *Dragonrealm* series, have sold well over a million copies. His works have been published in German, Italian, Spanish, Polish, Japanese, and soon in Czech and Russian. He has also been a regular contributor to the DRAGONLANCE short story collections. His latest novels include *Land of the Minotaurs*, the modern fantasy *Dutchman*, and a new epic in his *Dragonrealm* world, *The Horse King*.

ADAM LESH, a longtime role-player and aspiring novelist, was first published in TSR's *The History of DRAGONLANCE*. His short story, "Quarry," can be found in the anthology *The Dragons at War*.

TERI McLAREN teaches world literature, writing, and medieval culture at the University of Louisville. She has written "Nature of the Beast" for *The Dragons at War*, and four books for MAGIC: THE GATHERING: *The Cursed Land*, *Song of Time*, and its sequel, *Shadows of Time*, due for publication in 1997. Recently married, she and her husband plan to climb Mt. Kilimanjaro next year.

ROGER E. MOORE, a creative analyst with TSR, has been fascinated with alternate histories for ages. He promises, however, that this will be the only time he ever tinkers around with alternative DRAGONLANCE histories, and he thanks one and all for their forbearance. This story is dedicated to Greg, who will be able to read it in a few more years and might possibly like it.

DOUGLAS NILES is a longtime best-selling author of DRAGONLANCE and FORGOTTEN REALMS fiction. Recently he has described a world of his own creation, the Watershed, in a trilogy of novels published by Ace Fantasy.

NICK O'DONOHOE has written a number of DRAGONLANCE short stories for TSR. He also has written the *Crossroads* novels: *The Magic and the Healing* (selected by the American Library Association as a Best Book for Teens), *Under the Healing Sign*, and *The Healing of the Crossroads*.

JANET PACK, cat-dependent, lives in Williams Bay, Wisconsin. Her musical works appear in *Leaves from the Inn of the Last Home*, *The History of* DRAGONLANCE, and Margaret Weis and Tracy Hickman's *Death Gate Cycle*. Her short stories have been published in *The Dragons of Krynn*, *The Dragons at War*, *Fantastic Alice*, and *CatFantastic IV*. When not writing, she designs jewelry with Margaret Weis for their company, The Medicine Wheel.

CHRIS PIERSON is a longtime DRAGONLANCE fan from Whitby, Ontario. His first short story was published in *The Dragons at War*. He has also published fiction in *Dragon®* magazine and is now working for a computer game company in Boston.

JEAN RABE is a goldfish-keeper and student of World War I aviation who enjoys traveling in the world of Krynn. She is the author of *The Dawning of a New Age* and *The Day of the Tempest* in the DRAGONLANCE: FIFTH AGE line, and the coauthor of *Maquesta Kar-Thon* in the DRAGONLANCE series The Warriors. Her other novels include *Red Magic*, *Secret of the Djinn*, and *Night of the Tiger*.

KEVIN T. STEIN is the author of *Brothers Majere* and short stories in other TSR collections. His other works include *The Fall of Magic* (as D.J. Heinrich) from TSR, *Twisted Dragon* from Ace, and *The Guide to Larry Niven's Ringworld* from Baen.

Husband and wife team **MARGARET WEIS** and **DON PERRIN** live near Lake Geneva, Wisconsin, where they own The Game Guild, a game and science fiction/fantasy bookstore. Weis and Perrin have two new books out: *The Doom Brigade* from TSR, and *Robot Blues* from Roc. Margaret Weis has recently completed work on *The Soul Forge*, the story of Raistlin's early years and his test in the Tower of High Sorcery, scheduled for release by TSR. Visit their web site at www.mag7.com.

Saga

Edited by Margaret Weis and Tracy Hickman

THE DRAGONS OF KRYNN

THE DRAGONS AT WAR

THE DRAGONS OF CHAOS

DragonLance® Saga

The DRAGONS of Chaos

Edited by

Margaret Weis and

Tracy Hickman

THE DRAGONS OF CHAOS

©1997 TSR, Inc.
All Rights Reserved.

All characters in this book are fictitious. Any resemblance to actual persons, living or dead, is purely coincidental.

This book is protected under the copyright laws of the United States of America. Any reproduction or other unauthorized use of the material or artwork contained herein is prohibited without the express written permission of TSR, Inc.

Distributed to the book trade in the United States by Random House, Inc. and in Canada by Random House of Canada Ltd.

Distributed to the hobby, toy, and comic trade in the United States and Canada by regional distributors.

Distributed worldwide by Wizards of the Coast, Inc. and regional distributors.

Cover art by Don Clavette. Interior art by Jacen Burrows.

DRAGONLANCE, FIFTH AGE, FORGOTTEN REALMS, RAVENLOFT, the TSR logo, and DRAGON are registered trademarks owned by TSR, Inc.

All TSR characters, character names, and the distinctive likenesses thereof are trademarks owned by TSR, Inc.

TSR, Inc. is a subsidiary of Wizards of the Coast, Inc.

First Printing: December 1997
Printed in the United States of America.
Library of Congress Catalog Card Number: 96-61029

9 8 7 6 5 4 3 2

8382XXX1501

ISBN: 0-7869-0681-2

U.S., CANADA, ASIA,
PACIFIC, & LATIN AMERICA
Wizards of the Coast, Inc.
P.O. Box 707
Renton, WA 98057-0707
+1-206-624-0933

EUROPEAN HEADQUARTERS
Wizards of the Coast, Belgium
P.B. 34
2300 Turnhout
Belgium
+32-14-44-30-44

Visit our website at http://www.tsrinc.com

TABLE OF CONTENTS

Eyes of Chaos
Sue Weinlein Cook

The last ogre hit the sun-baked ground hard, and he lay still next to the bodies of his companions. After a moment, the dazed creature feebly struggled to crawl forward, away from the carnage.

The blue dragon drew back her claws to take another swipe at her prey, then hesitated. Her eyes narrowed. She had grown tired of this game.

She inhaled deeply, savoring the sharp taste of the lightning breath that threatened to explode from her mouth. The dragon eyed the ogre trying in vain to disentangle himself from the pile of corpses. She held her breath until she could stand it no longer.

A stroke of lightning erupted from the blue monster so violently, it propelled the pitiful ogre back fifty feet through the air, then smashed him into the wreckage of a crude wooden dwelling. He dropped heavily to the ground, his charred body spasming with the massive electrical charges that surged through him. Sparks twined across his blackened, terrorized face. Tendrils of acrid smoke rose from the dry wood, and in seconds the whole structure was awash in hissing, popping flame.

The ogre did not rise again.

Her horned nose raised to the sky, the blue dragon let out a mighty roar. She loved the sound of her own voice thundering across the stricken land. She stepped forward, digging her talons deeply into the pile of ogre bodies, now nothing more than carrion. A few more steps, and the dragon tensed her powerful leg muscles, then catapulted herself into the air.

The dragon beat her wings furiously, accelerating as she climbed into the late summer sky. Clamor loved speed almost as much as she loved sound—velocity and volume consumed her. Faster and faster she flew, fueled by a sudden rush of energy and exhilarated by the flow of cool Khalkist air across her dusky blue hide. Urging her rider to hang on tight, the dragon banked steeply. Clamor dipped her long snout and folded back her powerful wings, then shot toward the ground again like an elven arrow, skimming over the blackened ogre village.

"What did you think of *that*, Jerne?"

Clamor was too pleased with her work to notice that her rider made no reply.

Surveying the destruction, the satisfied dragon rumbled deep in her throat—it was as close as she could come to imitating the chuckle of her Dark Knight partner. She swept her great head back and forth, taking in the remains of rough huts still smoking from the assault of her lightning breath, and crude stone dwellings blasted to rubble. The smell of charred flesh curled around her nostrils and she noted the ogre remains, scorched nearly beyond recognition, lying within the wreckage. Still more corpses were strewn about the center of the village. But these bodies bore no marks at all. Baskets and tools lay next to them, dropped just before their owners themselves fell. The pigs and lizards the villagers raised for food likewise had collapsed in their pens.

"Nothing like the last time we were here, is it, Jerne?" Clamor asked coldly. Was it only a month ago that the two of them, along with the rest of their wing of knights, had swept through the land of Blode to conscript all able warriors for service in the Minions of Darkness? "So much has happened since then. Our invasion . . ."

Lost in her thoughts, the dragon circled around to overfly the village one last time. She spread her wings wide to catch the air and coasted, reliving those weeks of triumph during the hottest summer in even a dragon's memory. The armies of the Knights of Takhisis, made up of fearsome dark paladins and their dragon partners, had swept across the continent in a conquest unparalleled in any of the Great Ages of Ansalon. "Do you remember how we crushed every nation like twigs snapping beneath our feet? We taught them the meaning of true honor—and fear! The entire land bowed before the glory of Her Dark Majesty . . ."

Clamor faltered, not wanting to recall the last chapter of that momentous summer. Instead, her heartbeat pounding in her head, she pumped her wings against the sultry air and climbed again. After gaining altitude, she craned her neck around for one last view of her handiwork. What looked like an ogre hunting party had just entered the village. Clamor smirked as she imagined their amazement at finding their homes—

A knight must not engage in combat with an unarmed opponent.

—nothing more than smoldering wrecks.

One of the hairy creatures looked up and pointed his club at her. The other ogres cowered, looking small standing among the ruins and the dead. "Poor creatures!" she mocked aloud, then shot into the cool whiteness of the clouds.

Poor Clamor!

The dragon winced sharply at a sudden pain in her right leg. The limb—blackened, withered, and dripping with green ichor—dangled limply beneath her. She cursed the ogres far below, knowing that her stop in Blode had aggravated the wound. The pain jerked Clamor's thoughts back to the battle in which she had earned her injury. She felt her heartbeat quicken and her skin grew hot despite the cool southern winds as she recalled the moment she had tried so hard to block from her memory. It seemed like yesterday—no, it *was* yesterday.

* * * * *

Clamor was fiercely proud. She and Jerne had received the rare honor of flying second to the valiant knight Steel Brightblade, who was astride Flare. Their wing had departed from the ruins of the High Clerist's Tower to make its way into the newly formed rift in the Turbidus Ocean. Down, down, down they flew, until Clamor was certain they would come out on the other side of the world at any moment. Finally, they emerged in the Abyss and beheld their foes.

Although few things frightened the great blue, the sight of the giant called Chaos sent waves of terror rippling through her body. The enormous, brutal figure roared like an erupting volcano, laughing at those who had come to battle him.

His ugly visage was enough to make even a dragon hesitate in the attack, and his size dwarfed even the mightiest of the reds. But worst of all were the eyes, Clamor thought. Those lidless holes in his face seemed to suck everything they beheld into their vast nothingness. She believed those horrible dark whirlpools could capture her very soul.

Swooping all about him were fire dragons, terrible minions of Chaos. These creatures of living magma breathed reeking, burning sulphur at their foes as sparks flew from their obsidian scales and fiery wings to singe the flesh of dragon and man.

Steel ordered his knights to attack the riders of these foul creatures, the daemon warriors. Clamor and Jerne, a practiced team from many years of training together and countless battles during that summer's invasion, launched themselves at their foes with a fury echoed by the other blues, as well as the silvers who accompanied them into battle with Solamnic Knights. This was a fight for all the children of Krynn, the dragon knew.

In the oppressive heat of the Abyss, the battle raged on. The shrieks of the attacking dragons mixed with the death cries of the fallen. Clamor and her knight had already destroyed several of the nightmarish daemon warriors when it happened.

Jerne raised his sword, which had been blessed by Her Dark Majesty on the day of his knighting, and urged Clamor to move in just a little closer to the enemy. Though nearly exhausted after her efforts in this endless battle, Clamor gamely acceded. The daemon warrior grinned ferociously at them as its fire dragon mount beat its flaming wings ever nearer.

Wait! the blue thought in alarm. Jerne is not sitting properly in the saddle! She tried to veer off the approach, but it was too late. With one final slap of affection on her flank, the knight launched himself off her back and onto his daemon foe in a suicidal attack, screaming his battle cry and swinging his dark blade in a vicious arc.

Suddenly off-balance, Clamor struggled to right herself. In horror, she watched Jerne topple the daemon warrior from its mount's back, then fall with it to the ground below.

"No! Jerne!" Her cry of despair turned into a howl of pain as the now riderless fire dragon dived beneath her to scorch her right leg. Enraged, Clamor spun in midair and locked her gaze with the fire dragon. Then she belched forth a bolt of lightning at the chaos-spawn. The impact sent obsidian scales exploding outward and the fire dragon speeding backward toward the lance of an attacking Solamnic Knight and his silver mount.

The wounded Clamor had just enough strength left to slow her descent before she hit the ground. Through her pain-clouded vision she saw Jerne lying not far away, unmoving beneath the corpse of the daemon warrior. Wanting to see something—anything—but the lifeless sight of her beloved rider, Clamor looked up. She spied Flare and Steel as they stabbed at Chaos and drew a single drop of blood, which fell to the gray ground near her. Her eyes upon Flare, Clamor cheered weakly at the strike. She hardly noticed the small, silver-haired human who scrabbled frantically with two pieces of shiny rock at the sand where the blood had fallen, then, almost in tears, ran off.

Barely able to contain the throbbing pain of her burned leg, the crippled Clamor managed to rise. She stumbled forward a few paces, trying to get her footing, and placed her injured foot squarely onto the bit of ground stained red with the life-fluid of Chaos.

As the blood of the Father of All and of Nothing mingled with her own, the blue dragon felt herself inexplicably distracted from the fight. Although she remembered Jerne telling her that the very survival of Krynn depended on the outcome of this battle, she could not resist the voice that now commanded her to fly up, up, and out of the Abyss. Abandoned by reason, Clamor thought she saw Chaos looking right at her with those horrible empty holes of eyes. The last thing she heard before leaving the battle far behind her was the giant's volcanic cackle.

Child of Chaos!

* * * * *

Clamor shook her head, trying to clear it of such disturbing memories. "Jerne, how could you leave me?" she whimpered.

You don't remember, do you?

"I don't *want* to remember!" the dragon roared at the clouds.

Almost as if in response, the pain in her leg flared up again. Clamor sucked in her breath sharply, feeling the dark malevolence of the wound creep slowly up her leg and across her belly. She knew at that moment she couldn't hide from the dark truth any longer. It's eating away at me, the panicked dragon thought wildly. The wound is of Chaos himself! It's stealing my life! Jerne, what should I do? The only thing that helps is . . .

A sudden thought stemmed the fear welling within her. Clamor realized how to fuel the ravenous blood of Chaos within her. If it wanted life, that's what she would give it. But not her *own* life.

Flashing exultantly through the air, she blasted out a bolt of lightning that made the clouds blaze with reflected light. A rumble filled her throat. Folding her wings tightly along her back, the blue dragon dropped out of the clouds, surveying the lush forestland below. "I shall conquer all these lands in your name, Sir Jerne Stormcrown!" she proclaimed for the benefit of her absent rider. "All will honor your valiant sacrifice and know you as the greatest of knights!"

honorhonorhonorhonorhonorhonor

Clamor hurtled toward the tree line and skimmed the woods for any sign of civilization. She hadn't visited this area of southern Ansalon in the years since the elves had turned back the Nightmare that had cursed the Silvanesti Forest after the War of the Lance. The dragon breathed deeply of the smell of new growth. Only elves could cultivate anything in the middle of this drought, she thought, amid a pang of homesickness for the cold, arid isle where she and her rider had lived and trained so long.

Clamor's eyes lit on a break in the trees. As she approached, the scene of a tranquil village unfolded beneath her. A lot like the last one, she thought, rumbling with delight as she imagined how furious the elves who lived here would be to hear themselves compared with ogres in any fashion.

The blue dragon circled the village once, then dived. The rush of air around her was like music. "For you, Jerne!" she roared as she unleashed a gout of lightning at the Silvanesti gathered around a small pool at the center of the village. The blast felled half a dozen elves and knocked several others, flailing, into the pool. Other elves scattered, screeching in terror and surprise. Clamor followed a group of the delicate, blond creatures as they sped toward a graceful spire of a building carved from a living tree. The dragon could smell their fear.

As they neared their supposed sanctuary, Clamor's gaze fell upon them, compelling them to turn and face her. She hovered, pinning them with her gaze, and marveled at what happened next. Slowly, thin silvery wisps rose from the elves' bodies to hang lightly in the air.

Strange, the dragon pondered as she willed the silver strands inexorably toward her. The ogres' were bronze. Clamor's relentless gaze drew the elves' delicate life-energies closer and closer, until the silvery light nearly blinded her. The dragon reveled in the infusion of vitality she felt surging through her. She was momentarily taken aback to see on the faces of the dying Silvanesti the same horrified expression she imagined she herself had worn when she first beheld the face of Chaos. Then the elves collapsed like puppets to the ground, and it didn't matter anymore.

Clamor made short work of the rest of the village, alternately blasting the elves and their dwellings with her lightning breath and devouring their souls to feed the blood of Chaos. Taking little notice of the few Silvanesti who escaped into the woods, the dragon flapped lightly back to the central pool. Feeling positively rejuvenated, she lay contentedly down beside the pool and peered at the water.

What she beheld in the smooth surface startled her so, she cringed from the sight. Then, slowly, the dragon leaned closer for another look. In horror and disgust, she stared down at her reflection, at the sick, blackened tinge her hide had taken on from the middle of her chest all the way down to her feet. The entire discolored area was covered all over with horrid pustules and cancerous boils. Her burned right foot had shriveled to nothing more than a misshapen stump. She hardly looked like a dragon anymore.

But worst of all were the eyes. Fixing her gaze on them, Clamor felt fear clamp around her heart. The eyes that stared back at her from the surface of the pool looked like they belonged to a blue dragon even less than did the rest of her hideous body. The lidless holes in her face no longer gave hint of the dragon's intelligence and humor, nor did they offer a glimpse of the dedication and drive she had learned as Jerne's partner. Now they held only a vast blackness. Nothingness.

Like father like daughter.

Clamor screamed and launched herself at the sky. No matter how hard she batted her wings, she could not escape the giant, roaring laughter erupting in her ears.

After what must have been hours of flying headlong, giving no thought to anything but the continued pumping of her great wings, an idea emerged from the frantic dragon's mind. Silvanost! she thought. She was flying straight toward that bright capital of the elves' reclaimed forest. Her otherworldly eyes glittered at the thought. *Thousands* live in Silvanost! Absorbing that many would surely satisfy this hungry Chaos blood!

But the dragon's frenzied pace had begun to take its toll on her. Her wings felt strained from the punishment of the breakneck flight, and her whole body had begun to ache. She would never make it to the elven capital at this rate. "Just a quick rest," she announced to her absent rider, swaying a bit with the effort of staying aloft. "A short nap can't hurt. Then I will win you a shining jewel for the crown of your domain!"

The dragon circled, gliding ever lower in search of a proper resting place. Annoyed at the lack of dry, open places which blue dragons favored, she found a small clearing near a stream and landed. She was surprised at the jolt she gave herself as she roughly met the ground. "Careful, Jerne," she murmured wearily, stretching out carefully on the mossy ground. "I wouldn't want you to fall." The exhausted dragon closed her eyes and succumbed to sleep for the first time since the battle with Chaos.

wouldn't want you to fall fall

fall

fall

fall

fall

* * * * *

Clamor found herself back in the Abyss, once more in the middle of the raging battle against the Father of All and of Nothing. Once more she smelled the horrible sulphur of dragon breath, and heard the shrieks of dragon and man alike. She heard her knight urge her closer to the grinning daemon warrior astride a fire dragon nearby, felt herself respond to his command. She squinted against the light thrown by the flaming wings of the enemy's dragon mount. It was so bright. Where—*No!*

Anxious to avoid contact with her quarry's fiery wing, the half-blind Clamor quickly wrenched herself upward. However, the sudden shift occurred just as Jerne was readying his attack and knocked the knight off-balance. With only a futile swipe to find some purchase, Jerne toppled from his saddle, crying "Clamor!" He twisted his body as he fell and managed to land right atop the startled daemon warrior, sending both of them falling from the mount to the hard ground below.

"No! Jerne!"

* * * * *

Clamor jerked awake, panting from the exertion of the dream. "I wanted to make you a hero!" If only the rush of words could dam the flow of unwanted memories. "I was going to tell everyone about your bold suicide attack."

You know it was no suicide.

"You'll be known as the greatest of the knights! They will speak your name in honor! But first I have to get to Silvanost . . ." The crippled dragon tried to stand, wincing as she pulled her pustulant hide off the ground.

You remember nothing of honor, Clamor.

"I'm doing this for you, Jerne!"

Are you?

"But, don't you see, it's *killing* me!"

A sudden noise from the edge of the clearing made Clamor turn her head. A group of elves—and ogres?—came charging from the undergrowth at her. Hanging back, the elves nocked their bows, while a half dozen ogres rushed forward, clubs raised. What could make allies of such mortal enemies? she wondered.

You.

Just as Clamor was trying to figure out how the creatures could possibly have caught up with her—she would never be so careless as to leave a trail, would she?—the first salvo of arrows hit. The dragon roared in pain and disbelief. Her tender scales, victim already to the cancerous blood flowing through her veins, could not turn back the devastating elven points. She leveled her gaze at the approaching ogres, ready to sacrifice their life-forces to the beast inside her.

When will it end, Clamor?

The blue shook her head, trying to clear her muddled mind of the familiar voice that confused her so.

First them, then Silvanost, then what? Will you make all of Ansalon your prey?

The weary dragon paused. She had grown so tired of fighting the death force within her. "I want to live!"

This is not the way. To save ourselves, we must fight Chaos, not feed it.

As the ogres drew near, Clamor laid her head down quietly and gazed into the stream before her. Out of the clear flowing water, an image resolved itself before her eyes—the familiar face of a man with close-cropped red hair and green eyes. Jerne smiled at her, and when she heard him chuckle, she knew she'd been forgiven. Clamor didn't even feel the ogres' clubs come crashing down on her, didn't feel the second, then the third round of arrows bite into her chest and head and legs. The stream washed away everything except Jerne. "Everything's going to be fine now," he said and beckoned to her.

As though from far, far away, Clamor heard the tiny voices of her attackers rise in triumph. Then their babbling became meaningless as the dragon dashed forward to meet her knight.

The Noble Folly

Mark Anthony

I came to Redstone seeking power.

At least, that was what I told myself. I think, in truth, that I really came seeking death. Yet it is an axiom of life that a man never finds the one thing he seeks—or perhaps never seeks the one thing he finds—and in those last hours I found neither power nor death on the blasted crags of Redstone. But I see now that there is only one way to explain. Very well, then. I will tell my tale. And even at the start it is strange, for it begins not with a beginning, but an ending.

Krynn died.

Fire, thunder, darkness. Then somehow, impossibly, a new crimson dawn. In the first, terrible days after the Second Cataclysm, those who had survived stumbled through the smoking ruins that had been their homes, their cities, their lives, and searched for an answer. Who? they cried out. Who had brought this destruction upon the world? But it was a meaningless question. Through the dust, through the blood, I laughed at them. The answer was so simple because there was no answer. Who had caused the Second Cataclysm? We all of us did, we none of us did. It didn't matter. Everything had changed—that was all that was important now. It was not the first time the world had died.

Before the Second Cataclysm, I had fallen in with powerful forces. Like so many others, I had not chosen them so much as they had chosen me. But they had given me a place and a purpose, a sword for my hand and food for my stomach, and I had believed myself safe with them, and on the path to great things. So strong they had seemed, so glorious, so indomitable. At the end of the Chaos War, they had shattered like so much glass.

Now I was on my own. The old ways of doing things, the old rules, were gone, burned to ashes with the parchments

they were written on. There were new rules to be made, and I
knew that those who made them would come out on top in
this changed world. I intended to be one of them. That was
why I had journeyed to this place.

I was nearly upon it before I got my first view.

The scorched wind changed direction and tore a rift in
gritty clouds of dust. There it stood before me, rising five
thousand feet from the barren Estwilde plain, a great heap of
jagged rocks the color of dried blood.

Redstone.

I licked blistered lips with a parched tongue. "Blast me to
the Abyss," I said, and I wondered if I hadn't already been, if
I wasn't already there.

I craned my neck upward, and upward still, but the summit
was lost in haze, and faded into a sky stained red with the
soot of a thousand thousand fires. For a moment I staggered.
I believe I almost fell to my knees. How could I possibly climb
to the top of this . . . this thing? How could I even think to try?

But I had come so far. I was not going to turn away, not
now. I let the wave of weakness pass over me, drew in a
breath, and walked across the cracked plain toward the
tumbled base of the mountain.

I had heard the story first in a tavern not far from Kalaman,
a filthy pub where swine rooted on the floor for scraps, and
got nearly as good as those who paid hard steel. A traveler
from the south—a merchant he called himself, a thief and a
murderer I guessed—told me, for the price of a cup of sour
ale, of the great rock that had been thrust up from the bones
of Krynn by the tremors of the Second Cataclysm, and of the
silhouette he had once glimpsed by moonlight perched upon
its summit: a winged, saurian shape that lifted its wedge-
shaped head toward the sky.

I drank my ale, and wondered.

I heard the tale again in a village at the foot of the northern
Khalkists, told by a band of pilgrims who searched in vain for
signs of the gods. Then once more, among a camp of outlaws,
who pretended to take me in as a compatriot, and would
have slit my throat in my sleep had I not done the trick to
them first. Again I heard it told, in a hovel, in a village, in a

town. One telling I would have discounted, two doubted. But a dozen I believed, and so here I was.

The sun beat upon my armor. Sweat streamed down my brow, into my eyes, and stung them. A hundred times on my journey I had been tempted to cast off the steel that encased me, to toss it into some foul pit or to send it clattering down a cliff face, to be free of its heat and its stench. But my path had led through dangerous and broken lands. I had kept my armor, and kept my neck.

I was picking my way among the mountain's first jumbled boulders when I saw the smoke.

A thin, dark line rose upward, from behind a large spur of stone. I froze. I had assumed the beast would keep to the heights of the peak, but I had not been able to see the summit for the haze. Perhaps it had come down, to prowl among the rubble for food. True, it might decide I was suitable prey before I opened my mouth and spoke a single word to it, as I intended. But at least it would save me the climb. I scrambled over the rocks toward the pillar of smoke.

It was no dragon I saw in the gully below.

At first I thought to slink away through the rocks, to remain undetected, then I halted. Would it not be better to know who it was that climbed behind me? And there was still a part of me that remembered what I had been before, and the oaths of honor I had sworn. Hollow they seemed now, empty. But what didn't in this new world? I hesitated, then stood and walked down the steep slope.

Dust-devils danced around me. They must have blocked his view, or else he was dozing in the heat, for he did not seem to see me until I was no more than a dozen paces from him and his small campfire. All at once he jerked his head up, leapt to his feet, and drew his sword. He held the blade before him, turned to his left, his right, his left again, searching. I frowned. I was plain before him. Did he not see me?

Only then did I notice the dirty rag bound around his eyes, crusted with dark blood.

No, he did not.

I approached, deliberately grinding my boot heel on the gravel. He spun to face me, sword before him. Beneath the patina of dust, I could see the rose embossed upon his wind-scoured armor.

"Are you friend or enemy?" he called out.

"Neither," I said.

He frowned at this, and I might have turned away then, might have left this ruined knight to himself, but for something I saw at that moment among his few things: a large goatskin in a wicker frame. I worked my dry tongue in my mouth. It would be a long climb to the top, and I had precious little water.

He seemed to make a decision, then lowered his sword. "If you mean no evil, then I will count you a friend in this blasted place."

I made no answer. It did not matter to me what he thought.

"I am Brinon," he said, "Knight of the Rose."

"My name is Kal," I said.

He made a stiff bow. "I cannot offer you a feast, Kal, but I have some food still, and you may share it."

He gestured for me to sit, and I did so. He searched through his gear with blind hands. I watched him as he did. We could not have been more dissimilar, he and I, and it was not only our armor that made us so. He was fair, and short, and powerfully built, while I have always been dark, and tall, and lean. Even wounded he was handsome and noble of face. I never in my life have been accused of being comely. The pockmarks of childhood took care of that.

There was little more in his pack than some hard tack and strips of dried meat, but I did not turn up my nose at these. We ate, then I asked if I could fill my water bottle from his goatskin, and he said he would be honored if I would.

Honored. Sometimes I think that word means the same thing as dead. I almost laughed, but there was scant water in his goatskin, and I filled my bottle only half full.

"You will go now, won't you, Kal?"

"Yes," I said.

He nodded. "I cannot fault you. That is why I came here myself. To stand before the monster of Redstone, and to slay it."

"Why?" I asked, although already I had guessed.

For a moment, beneath the bloody rag, his face shone. "After I perform such a glorious deed, how can Paladine and the other gods of good possibly refuse to return to the world?"

So he was a fool then. A noble fool. But then, they were the most dangerous sort.

"Fighting a dragon is a deadly task even if one is blessed with eyes."

Brinon shrugged. "If the will is strong, one can always find a way. I convinced a merchant to bring me here in his wagon. Now I have built this fire. Sooner or later the beast will see the smoke and will come to investigate." He gripped the hilt of his sword. "I was trained to fight in the dark. So now the dark is always around me—there is no difference. I will succeed no matter."

I grunted at this. He had lost his eyes, but not his arrogance.

"You can keep on waiting for the dragon to come to you," I said. "But I'm going to climb Redstone and find the monster first."

"And will you attempt to slay it then?"

Why not tell him the truth? "No, I'm going to talk to it, forge an alliance with it."

The hauteur on his face turned to shock. "By Paladine, why would you do this?"

One word I said. "Power."

Brinon shook his head. "No, Kal. The dragon is a thing of evil. I cannot let you sell yourself to it." He reached for me, but his boot struck a stone, and he stumbled. I caught him before he fell. He gripped my shoulder to steady himself, and his hand found hot steel. His mouth opened in surprise.

"But you are a knight as well! Why did you not say so, brother? From which order do you hail?"

I said nothing. His blind hands touched my armor, froze, then groped along the metal, tracing the hard outlines. I grinned like the death's head on my breastplate. Yes, let him touch me, let him know what I was.

At last he pulled away.

"Now I understand, Knight of Takhisis. You have your path to follow, and I have mine."

His words were not angry, but rather filled with disgust and pity. This bothered me more.

"Thank you for the water," I said.

He said nothing.

Then I left him, and I did not look back.

I started up the sheer slope. I climbed with speed and with purpose, using my hands as much as my legs to scramble over the treacherous rocks. Hot air rose in dizzying waves from the plains below and seared my lungs, but I ignored it. Brinon had been right about one thing—we did each have a path to follow. Only his path led to death, and mine—if I was right, if I was lucky—would lead to mastery. Surely I could find a way to make myself useful to the dragon. If nothing else, I could catch far more meat for it than I would make as a meal. And with such a powerful ally beside me, there was no telling how far I would rise in this new world.

I kept climbing.

Then it happened, so quickly I could do nothing but watch. With my hand I gripped the corner of a boulder to pull myself up. But it was loose, and precariously balanced. It shifted under my weight, tilted, then all at once came free. With a grating of rock on rock, the boulder slid down. There was no time to move. The ponderous block struck my left leg and pinned it against a spur of stone behind it. The steel greave I wore crumpled like paper. I heard more than felt the wet pop of my leg breaking.

A tingling clarity filled my mind. Injury can do that. *You idiot, Kal! You allowed yourself to be distracted by the fool knight, and now you're going to pay for it!*

Then I did, with the first bright shards of pain.

I almost swooned, but I fought to hold onto my wits, and did so, though just barely. I drew my sword, slipped it under the boulder, and wedged it against the spur of rock that crushed my leg. Then I leaned on the hilt. A groan of rock. The boulder shifted, and I could feel the broken ends of my leg bone grind against each other. I paused to vomit, then leaned on the sword again. The boulder lifted a finger's breadth, then two, then three. I clenched my teeth against the pain and started to pull my dangling leg free.

That was when the blade of my sword snapped.

I flew backward. The boulder lurched to the side, rolled over, and tumbled down the slope. My fingers clutched for a hold to stop my fall, but they found only loose stone. The boulder had set the rocks all around me into motion. I shouted a curse to all the gods of darkness. Then with a roar like thunder a large part of the mountain went sliding down the slope and carried my body with it. I might have screamed, but a stone struck my head, and all went black.

I woke to the unfamiliar stars of the new night sky.

For a moment I struggled in disorientation. A shadow hovered over me. The light of the single moon—which shone where two had shone before—glimmered off the steel outline of a rose. Then I blinked in understanding and let the strong hands ease me back to the ground.

"I knew Paladine would bring you back," Brinon said.

I gave a bitter laugh at the conceit of his words. "Does your god often break the legs of people just to get what he wants? He sounds more like a common thug to me."

Now anger twisted his face. "And what of your Dark Queen? Does she not use others for her gain?"

"She did, only she was honest about it, and never disguised it as anything else. But none of this matters. The gods are gone."

"They will return, I know it."

I only grunted. I wasn't so certain I wanted them to.

With a grimace, I sat up and tried to piece together what had happened. He must have heard the boulders fall, must have followed the sounds of my moans, must have somehow dragged me back to his camp. I searched with my hands. He had splinted my leg, and had tucked the hilt of my broken sword into its sheath. Why hadn't he just killed me? It didn't matter.

"I've got to go," I said.

I struggled to my feet. The pain was manageable with the splint. Then I took a step. A moment later I was on the ground again, clutching my leg, spitting and swearing.

He knelt beside me. "You can't walk well enough, Kal."

"Yes, I can." It was a lie. I didn't care. At that moment I hated him.

"No, it's a sign." Again that utter confidence lit his sightless face. "You can see the way, Kal. And I'm strong, I can help you up the rocks. Alone we can do nothing, but together we can make it to the top."

I fell still, gazed at him. "And what would we do once we got there, Brinon? Or have you forgotten our differing intentions?"

He shook his head. "Perhaps it will be decided for us. Perhaps the dragon will be amenable to your talk of alliance. Or perhaps it won't, and then I will slay it. Let us see when we get there."

It was madness. I knew it. The Solamnic Knight could only be trouble. He thought he would be able to convert me along the way, to win me over to his cause. Blast the righteous arrogance. It made me sick. Yet sometimes, in a mad world, madness was the only way.

"Yes," I said at last. "We will see."

* * * * *

We began our ascent at dawn.

The sun heaved itself over the horizon, a baleful eye that glared at the land. In moments a hot wind sprang up out of nowhere and raced over the plain. Its gritty breath stung our hands, our faces. I looked up at Redstone, but I could not make out the crown of the peak. Instead it was sheer slopes of crimson as far as my eyes could see.

"Are you ready?" I asked.

Brinon adjusted the rag that bound his eyes, then nodded. "I am."

"Then we'd better get moving. We'll want to make the summit before sunset if we can. Whether it's to talk to it or fight it, better to face a dragon in the light than in the dark."

I pushed up from the ground with my arms, got my good leg beneath me, and stood, though in the process I drew in a hissing breath of pain.

Brinon must have heard me. He reached out, found my arm, lifted it to the broad slope of his shoulder.

"I will help you, Kal."

I hesitated. I did not like the idea of depending on another, not for anything. And Brinon seemed too willing, almost too eager to help me, as if he enjoyed that I was weaker than him. But, whatever I felt, he was right—there was no way I was going to climb the mountain alone. I clenched my teeth, then looped my arm around Brinon's neck and allowed him to take the weight off my splinted leg.

"Now you must show me the way," he said.

His face was so calm beneath the dirty bandage, so full of pride still. Was he not disgusted with his own deficiency? Was he not furious that he needed another to lead him like a child? But I only grunted and limped toward the foot of the nearest slope, Brinon beside me.

What an absurd sight we must have been—two broken knights, one dark and one light, one crippled and one blind, struggling together up the knife-edged side of a mountain. But there was no one to see us, only the hot, unblinking eye of the sun. Nothing grew or lived on the slopes of this blasted peak. Rock and sand and wind, that was all.

The slowness of our progress was agonizing. Every boulder, every ledge of stone was a battle. I described what the way looked like to Brinon, used words to guide his hands and feet to the scant holds, until he was able to leverage himself up. Then he would reach down and use his powerful arms to pull me after him while I pushed with my good leg. More than once Brinon's blind hands missed their mark, and he skidded back down the slope, scraping his hands and face. And every time he heaved me up, my broken leg was jarred and buffeted, sending sharp knives of pain up through my body.

Our armor was a hot and ponderous burden, yet we were loath to cast it off, knowing we might well need it at the top. And, too, it saved us from the worst of the scrapes and bruises. Still, by midday we were battered, bleeding, and exhausted. We sat on a broad ledge of rough stone. The plains, flat and brown as the skin of a drum, stretched far below us and it made me dizzy to gaze down. I still could not glimpse the summit for the haze, but by my guess we had come at least halfway.

We ate a little food, then I pulled my bottle from Brinon's pack. The water was scalding and tasted like the waste swill from a tanner's shop, but we drank it all the same, and it was an effort to keep from gulping. I carefully replaced the stopper. There was still a long way to go.

For a few minutes more we rested. I gazed into the empty air before us, while Brinon gazed into I know not where.

"Tell me, was it the Vision that led you here?" the fair-haired knight suddenly asked.

I gave him a sharp look, even though I knew he could not see it. "What do you know of the Vision, Knight of Solamnia?"

"Only that it is something each of the Knights of Takhisis has, something that guides them, that leads them onward to their dark purpose."

"No, not something each has. Something each had. There is no Vision anymore. It's dead, gone." My words were harsh, but I did not care.

I would never forget that day—the day I was brought before Ariakan, the High Commander of the Dark Queen's Army, the day he laid his hands upon me. Some said that his mother was a sea goddess, and I believed it. To me he looked like a god should look: powerful, darkly handsome, his eyes compelling, his voice commanding.

Some of his men had picked me up off the streets of Palanthas, which had been my home ever since the war had taken my family and home from me. Ariakan had given me a choice: go back to the streets and live with the thieves and murderers until I became one myself, and ended up swinging from a gibbet; or join his army, become one of his knights, and know honor and glory. His words had made me angry, I remember. Who was he to offer me such a choice? Who was he to tell me what my life would or would not be? But I could not resist the power of his eyes. I had taken his hand, and he had kissed me and welcomed me, and right there a sword was brought for me. I knelt before him, and he laid his hands on my head and spoke a prayer to the Dark Queen, to Takhisis, and that was when the Vision came upon me.

It was like a dream, the Vision, only it was with me every time I closed my eyes, in the dark hours of the night, and in the stillness between every thought. The true magic of the Vision was that it was different for every knight, and revealed to him his own personal destiny, his own path to glory or death.

The strange thing was, I could no longer remember what the Vision had been to me.

When Ariakan was slain, when Takhisis fled the world, the Vision went with them, for it had come through them, and was of them. Now I was left with a gaping hole in my mind, a gap I could not stop worrying over, like a man who has been to the barber and searches with his tongue the empty socket where his tooth used to be. I know that the Vision had filled me with both terror and wonder. But even the memory of it was gone now, and I knew I would never regain it.

"I am sorry," Brinon said at last.

His words infuriated me. Was he sorry for what he had said? Or sorry for me? Even when he spoke humble words such as these it seemed to be with the implication that he was better than I. Yet there had been genuine remorse in his voice, and I knew I was being unfair.

"There is nothing to be sorry for," I said. "I don't need the Vision. I know my key to glory. I'll have it soon enough, once the dragon and I are in league together. With its strength and my brains, nothing will stand between us."

Brinon shook his head. "Enemies we would have been in another place, Kal, and enemies we still may be, but here and now you are my companion, and so it is not my wish to offend. Yet I still say you are misguided in your intentions. What do you have to offer a dragon? What makes you think you can convince it to form an alliance with you?"

"And what makes you think that if you perform some bone-headed heroic deed that Paladine will come rushing back to the world?"

He winced at my words, and I knew they had struck some sore spot deep within him. Good. We did not have time for this. I glanced up at the sky. The sun had passed its zenith and was already starting its descent.

"Let's get going," I said, "if you really want to kill a dragon."

He helped me to my feet, and we started up the mountain once more.

After my fall yesterday, I should have been more wary of the treacherous slope. But as we climbed on, exhaustion dulled our caution. It was only a matter of time before one of us made a mistake.

It was Brinon who did so first.

We stood on a slim ledge, a drop of five hundred feet below us. Perhaps he was too tired to think, or perhaps he had grown overconfident. Either way, he started to pull himself up the rocky shelf in front of us before I had sufficiently guided his hands to the best holds. The crack he had gripped was too shallow. His blind fingers could not dig in deep enough to support his weight. He dropped back roughly to the narrow ledge. His heel skidded on the edge of the precipice, his hands flew out in search of balance. They found nothing. He toppled over backward.

No!

I don't know if I screamed the word aloud or silently. It didn't matter. Much as I hated to admit it, I needed Brinon. I lunged for him. Pain surged up my broken leg, but I ignored it. I stretched farther than I thought humanly possible, so far my joints popped. My fingers just brushed the hot metal of his breastplate—then caught the top edge of the beaten steel. I threw all my weight backward.

The Solamnic Knight sprawled forward, onto the ledge where we had stood. I in turn stumbled, felt my leg twist sickeningly, and fell to the side. Before I could stop myself, I rolled off the edge of the precipice.

I scrabbled for something, anything, to stop myself. Nothing but smooth stone. I fell. Then one hand slid into a crack in the rock, caught, and held. Fire exploded in my shoulder as my body jerked to a halt. I twisted in midair, suspended from the overhang by one hand. Beneath my dangling boots was five hundred feet of emptiness and, beneath that, sharp stone.

Pain sliced at my hand, blood slicked my palm. I could not hang on for long.

A shadow loomed above me.

"Brinon!"

I screamed the word. So much for pride.

The young knight groped along the edge of the precipice in search of me. He had cut his forehead when he fell, and blood streamed down to soak the already-crusted bandage over his eyes.

"To your left!" I shouted. "Farther!"

Hot agony melted my muscles. My blood-wet fingers loosened. Another few seconds, no more. His hand came within an inch of mine, moved away, then, as if guided by impossible instinct, slid back.

Contact.

Just as my hand slid through the crack, he grabbed my wrist, then heaved back with all his weight and dragged me onto the ledge.

For a minute we both lay there, panting. At last he spoke.

"Are you all right, Kal?"

I cradled my battered hand. "I'll live."

The relief on his blind face was clear. Somehow, I don't know why, that eased my pain.

I was still shaken by the near fall, but I sipped some water, and Brinon tightened my splint. After that I was as ready as I would ever be to move on.

We started back up the peak. Soon it became like a game, albeit a deadly one, and each time we avoided a tilting rock, or survived a tumble down a short slope of scree, or dodged a falling boulder, it was like a personal triumph, a victory that affirmed we were smarter and better than this blasted heap of stone. Before long we were laughing as, battered but not beaten, we fought our way up the mountain.

All at once Brinon's laughter fell short. The curvature of the peak in either direction was apparent now. We were almost there.

"I thought you were gone, you know," he said. "Back down there, after you saved me from falling."

For a moment I was silent. Then, to my own surprise, I grinned. "You'll not be rid of me so easily, Knight of Solamnia," I said.

I don't know why, perhaps I was growing used to the pain in my leg, but at that moment I slipped my arm off his shoulder, reached down, and gripped his hand, and we walked those last agonizing steps in this way, together.

* * * * *

We reached the summit just as the sun was dying in a sea of bloody clouds.

At first I could see nothing. Grit swirled around us. Then the wind shifted, tore a rent through the veil of dust, and at that moment I caught my first glimpse of the dragon of Redstone.

It was enormous. I had seen the blue dragon mounts that the elite Knights of Takhisis had ridden into battle in the Chaos War, and at the time they had filled me with awe and fear. But this creature was five times larger than the greatest of them. It sprawled across the entire top of the mountain, as red as the stones for which this place was named. A serrated ridge ran along its spine like a row of rusty knives. The wings were folded tight against the lean, angular body. Its massive head rested on a heap of rubble, and its maw was cocked open, large enough to swallow a man whole.

We came to a halt behind the cover of a boulder. The dragon was no more than thirty paces away. My hand slipped from Brinon's.

"What is it?" the knight asked.

I said nothing.

He drew in a sharp breath and gripped the hilt of his sword. "You see it, don't you?"

"Yes," I whispered.

Fear slithered up my throat. I gagged and tried to swallow it back down. I think a part of me had not believed we would really find it. But this was what I had come here for. I had not gone through the Abyss and back just to turn around now. Besides, any moment the thing would turn its great, wedge-shaped head—any moment it would detect us standing there. Then it would all be over, one way or the other. I took a step forward.

Brinon's hand shot out, groped in the air, then found my shoulder, halted me. "What are you doing, Kal?" he said in a hoarse voice.

"Let me go."

"No, you can't really mean to do this."

"I said let me go, Brinon. I have to talk to it."

"And what are you going to say?" His grip on my shoulder tightened. "What words are you going to use to convince it not to strip your flesh from your bones the moment it sees you? Tell me that before you go, Knight of Takhisis."

I opened my mouth, but nothing came out. For a long moment we stood frozen, silent. Wind hissed over stone. Then, slowly, he shook his head.

"You don't want to make a deal with it, do you?" he whispered. "That's not why you came here at all. You're hoping that it will kill you. Aren't you?"

What could I say in answer to that? Strange, I couldn't remember the Vision, but I could remember the face of every man I had slain in the name of the Dark Queen, each one of them frozen in the moment of terror, or agony, or disbelief when I pulled my dripping sword from his gut. The Vision was no more, but that—that I would always have.

I think, finally, I laughed. It was a bitter sound.

"Ariakan told me he would save me, Brinon. But I think he damned me instead."

For a moment he said nothing. If he had had eyes, I think he would have wept. Then all at once his expression changed. It was anger now. Righteous anger.

"No," he said. His voice rose to a shout that rang off the hard stones all around. "No, I will not let you do this!"

He pushed me aside. Then, before I could stop him, he drew his sword and scrambled blindly up the last remaining slope. I screamed at him, but he did not stop. He stumbled, fell, got up, and fell again. Hands bleeding, he gained his feet and lurched on. I thought for certain the dragon would see him coming, would turn and pounce on him like a cat on a mouse. But perhaps it was sleeping, for it did not stir. I started after him, but my broken leg dragged uselessly behind me. Then Brinon collided with the dragon's shoulder.

He cried out—a wordless sound of rage, of hate, of sorrow— and swung his sword at the beast.

With a bright metallic ring, the blade bounced off the dragon's skin.

Brinon gaped in blind confusion. Then he swung again, and again, and again. Each time his sword bounced back with a loud chime. Through it all, the dragon did not move.

I think we both knew the truth at the same time.

Brinon sank to his knees. Head bowed, he leaned on the hilt of his sword, its blade now notched in a dozen places. At last I limped to his side. I reached out and laid a hand against the beast's neck.

Rock: hard, warm, solid.

The dragon of Redstone. Of red stone. There is always a kernel of truth in the stories people tell. But only a kernel. I should have known. There was no dragon here. Only a heap of rocks that, in silhouette, happened to look a bit like one, enough to frighten wayward travelers, enough to make them tell tales to knights foolish and eager enough to listen.

I eased myself down beside Brinon. "I guess neither of us got what we wanted," I said. "Did we?"

He did not answer. Bent over his sword as he was, it looked almost as though he were praying.

Suddenly I was angry. "So our dragon turned out to be just a pile of rocks. So what? Let someone else worry about the gods, Brinon. Let someone else do the heroic deed."

He gasped the words like a drowning man. "No. You don't understand. It has to be me."

I looked into his blind face. "Why, Brinon? Why does it have to be you?"

He shook his head. No, that wasn't good enough. I balled my hands into fists, pounded on the hard armor that encased his shoulders, and shouted the words.

"Why you, Brinon?"

For a long moment he was silent, and I thought he would not answer me at all. I let my hands fall. At last he spoke in a low voice, his face distant beneath the bloody rag, the expression of righteousness he had worn since I had met him now gone.

"We were in the midst of a battle when it struck," he said. "Just east of Lemish. My brethren and I—mostly Knights of the Rose, a few Knights of the Crown—we espied a troop of Knights of Takhisis. The Dark Knights outnumbered us four to one. We knew that if we engaged them we would almost certainly die. They had not seen us, and the terrain was rugged. It was possible we could have slipped away without them seeing us. But that would have been a cowardly act. Our commander ordered us to engage. Maybe glory is enough when victory is impossible."

No, I thought, it isn't. But I said nothing and let him continue.

His expression became one of remembered fear. "It was the screams that got to me. I guess I never imagined them. I knew there would be shouting, and the clanging of swords. But the cries of the dying were everywhere. I've never heard grown men scream like that."

"It was your first battle, wasn't it?" I asked. He did not answer the question, but he did not need to.

"It was almost like a sea," he said. "The way the battle surged back and forth. Suddenly everything swirled around me, and I was by my commander. He was fighting two knights, and though he was bleeding from a wound in his side, he was holding them back, but only just barely. He saw me then, and called to me to help him. But I just stood there. I couldn't move. It was like I was a statue, made all of stone. Except for my eyes. My eyes still worked, blast them. They could see everything. My commander let out a roar and charged one of the Dark Knights, killing him. But he stumbled and fell to his knees. The other Dark Knight stood above him and raised his sword."

I could not tear my gaze from Brinon. His shoulders were shaking now.

"It would have been so easy," he whispered. "The Dark Knight's side was exposed. All I had to do was thrust with my sword. But I couldn't . . . the fear . . . all of me, stone, except for my eyes, my blasted eyes. The Dark Knight grinned at me. I think he knew I would do nothing. He swung his sword, and cut off the head of my commander. Then, in that moment, I could move again. I turned and ran. The Dark Knight ran after me. I knew any second I would feel his sword drive between my shoulders."

He drew in a rasping breath. "Only then it struck. The sky went dark. The land shook. And in that moment, all of us, all the Knights of Solamnia, we felt the power of our god, of Paladine, leave us. The battle turned into chaos. Men were running in every direction, and I ran, too. I ran until the ground stopped trembling, and I was alone. It was the last time I saw any of my fellow knights."

I shook my head, sickened by his story. I knew all too well the horrors of battle, had seen how they could shatter the spirits of the young, of the innocent who witnessed them for the first time. Men like Brinon. Yet there was something about his tale that bothered me. Something that didn't seem quite right. Then, all at once, I had it.

"But your eyes, Brinon," I said. "The Second Cataclysm began before the Dark Knight reached you. The battle was over, and you ran. So how were you wounded?"

He hung his head. For a moment I stared at him. Then my mind reeled.

It was like I was a statue, made all of stone. Except for my eyes. My eyes still worked, blast them. They could see everything.

I stared at him in horror. "You did it yourself, didn't you, Brinon? Your eyes. By all the gods who are gone, you did it yourself!"

When he spoke again, his voice was barely a whisper. "Don't you see, Kal? It was my fault. It was my act of cowardice that offended Paladine, that drove him from the world. That's why I came here, to prove myself with a deed of glory. I knew that if I could slay the dragon, Paladine would be pleased, that he would return to Krynn." A sob racked his body. "Only there is no dragon, and there will be no glorious deed. I have failed."

He bowed his head once more over his sword. Somehow I gained my feet and stood over him where he knelt. A wave of disgust rolled through me. I wiped the tears from my cheeks and spit out a laugh like a man who has been kicked in the face spits out teeth.

"Poor Brinon. You wanted a dragon to save you, and all you got was me."

For a moment he was silent, frozen. I started to turn away. Then he snapped his head up, and a quiet word escaped him.

"Yes . . ." He heaved himself to his feet, gripped his sword, and turned toward me.

My eyes narrowed. "What are you doing, Brinon?"

He stumbled toward the sound of my voice. "Don't you see, Kal? Paladine has given me a second chance to prove myself. I was a coward, I fled from the Dark Knight I should have fought. But here you are, another Knight of Takhisis. Why didn't I see it before? It's not a dragon I need to fight." He raised his sword and took another step toward me. "It's you."

I swore and drew my sword. It was broken, but it would be more than enough. "Don't be an idiot, Brinon," I spat. "You're blind. If you come at me, I'll slit your throat in a second."

He took another step forward. Beneath the bloody bandage he wore a rapt expression. It was a look of madness. "Do what you have to do, Kal."

In that moment I knew what he wanted. There was only one way he could save himself, one way he could atone for what he believed he had done.

"No," I said in disgust. "I won't help you, Brinon." I threw my sword clattering down the slope. "Strike me down if you want to, I don't care. But I won't be part of your sick little game."

For a moment Brinon stood before me like a statue. Then he whispered in a reverent voice.

"Forgive him, Paladine."

Too late I saw what he meant to do. He reversed his sword, grabbed the blade, and thrust the hilt toward me. On instinct my hands closed around the hilt as it struck my breastplate. In that moment Brinon threw his body forward. He gripped my shoulders, clenched his teeth, and pulled himself toward me until our bodies pressed together in an embrace. For a moment we stood that way, as one. At last he smiled.

"Thank you, Kal," he whispered.

Then blood gushed from his mouth.

* * * * *

The stars faded in the slate gray sky. I gazed at the distant horizon. Dawn was coming.

I placed one last stone atop the cairn I had built for Brinon. He had gotten what he wanted after all. I only hoped there was some peace in it for him, that maybe in death he was finally with his god again. I myself was alone now. Takhisis had abandoned me, and so had the Vision. Yet somehow this no longer troubled me as it had. I did not need the Dark Queen to save me, nor Ariakan, nor even Brinon.

It was up to me to save myself.

Dawn came then and cast its light on the broken landscape below. It would be a long time before Krynn was healed of the wounds wrought by the folly of gods and men. But the gods were gone now, and we who were left still had the power to choose what we would be. It was not the first time the world had died. Maybe, just maybe, it would be the last.

I tightened the splint around my leg and started down the mountain.

Lessons of the Land
Linda P. Baker

In the late spring, Chislev, Goddess of Beasts and Nature,
Bringer of seasons, drew a great breath,
Held it until the air was parched and hot,
And blew it across the face of Krynn.

Silvanesti poem,
written after the Second Summer of Chaos

The dry leaves of the forest floor snapped and crunched beneath Calarran's knee as he settled into a crouch at the side of the patrol leader. He sighed heavily, eased his bow off his shoulder and shifted, trying to find a more comfortable position on the gentle upsweep of slope.

The patrol leader, Eliad, did not acknowledge Calarran's presence. He simply continued his scan of the portion of Qualinesti forest spread out before him, his slanted elven eyes narrowed almost to slits.

Calarran was happy to leave searching the forest for signs of the enemy to Eliad and his patrol. Hot and thirsty after the long morning's walk, he was infinitely more interested in easing the tiredness in his shoulders and back, in taking a sip of tepid water from the waterskin slung across his shoulder.

He shook his head in disbelief as he twisted to pull the waterskin from behind his back. Calarran, son and grandson of senators of the Qualinesti. How his friends would laugh if they could see him now as one of Eliad's patrol members! Skulking about in the great forest, "scouting" for the enemy troops who laid siege to his city of Qualinost.

To most of the Qualinesti he knew, the elves in the patrol and the elves left behind in the camp of the Tessiel were traitors to their own people, renegades following leaders no longer wanted by their own nations.

To Calarran, who had never met an exile before his arrival in a campful of exiles, they didn't really seem too bad. They didn't have horns, warts, or green teeth. And for Silvanesti, they were really very civil. But he supposed living like gypsy renegades, moving from camp to camp like vagrant wanderers, would take some of the arrogance out of an elf.

The Tessiel were a loosely related group of Silvanesti elves who had followed their queen, Alhana Starbreeze, and her husband, Porthios, ex-Speaker of the Sun of the Qualinesti into exile. Exactly why the Qualinesti Senate had agreed to meet with the exiled Porthios, and had sent Senator Idron of the family Estfalas into the wilderness to do so, was not information Calarran was privileged to know, though it had given him a great many hours' thought. To see in the flesh the shunned dark elf Porthios—this was not the type of assignment he'd pictured when he'd been apprenticed to Idron, Senator of the Qualinesti.

Calarran sipped water from his waterskin. It was warm and tasted of the sandy-bottomed stream at the Tessiel camp. Tiredness sank deeper into the layers of his flesh. He shifted again and tried to free a dry twig that had caught in the hem of his tunic. Leaves crunched and crackled under his knee.

This time Eliad did notice him. The patrol leader did not bother to disguise his annoyance as he signaled for silence with a choppy movement of his hand. Then without a word he returned to his scrutiny of the rolling treetops spread out below them.

Calarran's silk tunic clung to his ribs and back, stuck there by a glue of sweat and dust. His tongue was no less gummy, and the water had done nothing to ease it. There was a rock in his left boot, and two leaves in his right. He had been stoic about the inconveniences the whole day, trudging with Eliad in silence, following the orders given him as if he were one of the troops. Eliad's impatient signal was too much. His face burned red hot with embarrassment. "I can't help that the forest is dry as the desert," he snapped.

"Why bother signaling for silence?" a soft feminine voice asked in a stage whisper, just loud enough that Calarran could hear. "They sound like a herd of hobgoblins."

Calarran had not the Silvanesti height of Eliad, and the elf who had spoken was hidden on Eliad's other side. Calarran had to lean forward to see the owner of the voice. Crunching leaves as he moved, his gaze connected with hers, and he was so surprised, he almost drew back.

Her expression was contemptuous; it was obvious she spoke not of the others of the patrol, who were making every bit as much noise moving into position along the ridge, but of him.

He took in her face, from the tan leather of her collar to the roots of her chestnut-colored hair, from one pointed eartip to the other. Every inch of exposed skin, including her slender hands, was painted in colors of gray, green, and brown, with the squiggles and whorls characteristic of the Kagonesti elves. His lip curled. No Silvanesti, not even a renegade, would disfigure his body so.

He had not realized there was a Kagonesti among the Tessiel. The Kagonesti were little better than savages, living like wild animals in the forest. Even the renegade Silvanesti had more respect for themselves.

Eliad cocked his slender head first one way, then the other, as if considering her words. Though the patrol appeared as little more than shadows, flitting from tree to tree as they climbed up the slope, their snaps and crackles were unmistakably footsteps.

Eliad shrugged and addressed himself to the air in front of him, as if he were speaking to neither of his two companions. "They're trying. Everything's so dry, it's impossible to be silent." He touched the ground beside him, and the leaves under his slender fingers crackled.

"*I* can," she retorted with a sauciness Calarran would never have tolerated from a Kagonesti servant.

Before he could rebuke her, Eliad again signaled for silence, and to the Kagonesti, he pantomimed watching the forest below.

With a shrug, she returned to scanning the treetops.

Calarran did not. He touched the leaves with his fingertips, as Eliad had. The sound made him wince. The dryness of the forest was a thing Calarran could feel on his skin. The oppressive summer heat, the worst even the oldest elf could remember, was a weight upon the heads of the great trees and all those who wandered under them.

Even his untrained eyes could see the magnificent forest was suffering. In good weather, the leaves would have been so thick and lush that they would have blocked out even the sky. Today, from his vantage on the ridge, Calarran could see all the way to the arm of the Kharolis Mountains, which hid the elven city of Qualinost. To his untrained eye, there was no sign of movement, of troops.

"Nothing," Eliad muttered under his breath.

"You sound almost disappointed," Calarran said. "Surely you do not wish to see any sign of the Dark Queen's army?"

"No, of course not. I was hoping for some sign of Porthios's patrol. I hoped they would come this way, and our patrol would be the one honored to escort Porthios back to the meeting."

"Is Porthios supposed to come this way?" Calarran wondered how differently Porthios, as renegade leader, would look from the way he remembered him, as Speaker of the Sun. It was difficult to picture the elegant, arrogant Porthios living as the Tessiel did, in rough camps with tents of leather.

Eliad shrugged. "I thought surely he would. Why else would you have been sent with us, if not as envoy?"

Calarran was so surprised at the idea that he had no answer. It had never occurred to him that his assignment was anything so important as that. Surely if it was, Idron would have told him. "I don't think—"

A sudden call, like the chirp of a wild bird, stopped Calarran's whisper. About him, all sounds from the patrol ceased, cut off abruptly as they halted all movement and became as stone. For a moment, only the rustling of dry leaves shifted by hot breeze, was audible. Then the call sounded again.

Eliad's head whipped in the direction of the chirp. He jabbed a forefinger at the Kagonesti and jerked his thumb backward, directing her. Then he motioned to himself and pointed in the direction he would go.

Without a wasted motion, the Kagonesti skittered backward, dipping out of sight to the left. Eliad aped her crouching crawl, skirting to the right around Calarran.

Calarran scanned the treetops, dared to shift enough to check behind him in the forest. He saw nothing, heard nothing. No sign of Lord Ariakan's Dark Knights. No sign of the renegade Porthios's honor guard.

To his left, where the Kagonesti had disappeared, there was a dry, dusty slash that only weeks before had been a trickling stream. Where it passed near a trio of aspens, a thicket of undergrowth was still green, thick with shadow.

Calarran shifted carefully on hands and knees into the trench, back into the thickest grouping of bushes. A coolness like slipping into a mountain-fed pool washed over his skin. The pungent, green fragrance of the leaves was sweet as candy.

He watched Eliad slip out of sight, bent almost double as he ran into the trees. Almost the instant Eliad stepped into shadow, the feet and legs of the Kagonesti woman stepped into Calarran's field of vision. Her steps, light as air on the dry leaves, still seemed loud as thunder.

She stopped at the edge of the streambed and lowered herself to a runner's crouch, poised like a tightly wound spring. She was near enough that he could smell her citrus mixed with loam scent. With the squiggles painted on her skin, the tunic stained the color of pale, new leaves, she was almost invisible against the brown, green, and silver of the forest.

Calarran edged back, knowing that he was easily visible. He was suddenly aware that his sky-blue tunic stood out like a beacon.

As he moved, the leaves against his cheek quivered, then rattled violently. A harsh, dry wind swept away the coolness. Hot, acrid air filled his lungs with the scent of fire. Thunder rumbled just over his head. The sun disappeared.

Not an arm's length from Calarran's face, the leaves curled and shriveled. In the blink of an eye they went from succulent, plump green to brown and brittle, crisped on branches suddenly black and smoking. For a moment, he hung there, too shocked to move, rocked back on his heels, feeling the heat of an unnatural fire on his face.

Then with a cry, he threw himself back from the astonishing

heat. He tore on hands and knees up and out of the streambed.

The world was pandemonium around him: fire, heat, and the high-pitched screams of the patrol. Running feet. Eliad shouting, trying to bring order to chaos. Wind whipping the tall trees as if they were stalks of grain on the open plain.

And the dragons.

The terrible, terrible dragons. Milling and swooping above the treetops. Blotting out the sun. Roaring. Blowing out their terrible breath in great bursts. Darting about so quickly, there could have been five. There could have been fifteen.

The attack was centered on the high point of the ridge to his right. Fear, like something tangible, so thick he could smell it, enveloped him. He wheeled to run, to get far away from the screaming dragons as quickly as possible.

But before he could lift his boot, the Kagonesti grabbed his arm. "To Eliad!" she screamed. Her fingers bit painfully into his forearm; her weight dragged at him.

Calarran followed, too frightened to do other than obey. As he ran in the direction of Eliad's voice, he could see a wall of dragons coming across the treetops, buffeting the aspens, rolling toward him like a thundercloud. The armor of their riders glinted blue and deadly in the sunlight.

Fear as dark as the roiling cloud of dragons filled him. It overwhelmed all sense of right and wrong, front and back, up and down.

He could see Eliad through the trees ahead. The Silvanesti stood his ground as a dragon swept past him. He raised his arms, screamed in shrill defiance. And he died with his arms still stretched to the sky, burned to ash in an instant.

The scream of the Kagonesti scout was snatched up by the roar of the fire and tossed skyward. Calarran could see her mouth, rounded in a cry of horror. Then she wheeled and ran toward another group of elves, drawing her bow off her back as she went.

Every muscle in Calarran's body wanted to follow her, but his feet were frozen to the ground, his gaze glued to the spot where only a moment before a brave elf had lived and breathed.

Fire blasted from above, searing already blackened and

charred foliage. The heat sucked all the air out of his lungs and baked the ground until his feet had to move or be baked, too.

Gasping for air, he ran.

He was blind with fear. Deafened by the roar of fire and of dragons overhead. Terrified by the creak and snap of leather wings.

Branches tore at his clothes, at his arms. Fear plucked at his heart. He leapt a dry ditch and hit the other side running. He mounted a small rise and zigzagged through trees. And still the flapping wings and the rush of dragon wind sounded in the trees behind him.

A branch snagged the sleeve of his tunic, turning him completely around before it ripped loose, taking leather and flesh with it. Blood slicked the side of his tunic. Pain rippled from wrist to elbow, spurring him to greater speed.

He tripped and rolled down a small slope, slamming into the base of a tree. His heart was pounding so hard he could feel blood in his ears. He could see red at the edges of his vision. And still the sound of the dragons tore at him. Closer and closer. Burning and screaming as they came, spreading out to the east and the west and the south.

There was nowhere to run. There was not enough speed. There was no hope. With a whimper of pain, of fear, of shame, he sank to the ground.

The blue dragon arrowed overhead, toward the camp where Idron waited for the meeting with Porthios. Calarran's mind spiraled down into a black madness.

* * * * *

Gaellal, leader of House Tessiel, stood beside Idron, Senator of the Qualinesti, and watched him turn slowly, surveying the camp. She knew Idron was impatient.

Porthios was overdue by two days for their meeting, and each moment that Idron spent outside Qualinost added to the danger for him—danger from the Dark Knights, danger of his absence being questioned by his own people. The delay also compounded the danger for his city under siege by the troops of Lord Ariakan. But Idron covered his impatience well.

Though Idron was Qualinesti, she liked him well. With eyes the color of golden ale and gleaming honey-colored hair tied back with gold cords, Idron was almost too beautiful to be male. Too elegant to be out in the wilderness. And too soft-spoken and polite to be a senator of the Qualinesti.

The camp was in the triangle created by the forest, a sharp, unexpected upsweep of bluff and the muddy leftover trickle of a creek. The tents had been pitched along the shaded edge of the forest, still clustered enough to be called a camp, but out of the broiling heat of the sun.

"Our last camp was deeper in the mountains. The heat had not reached so deeply there."

"Do you move often?" He asked the question politely, but it was obvious that his thoughts were elsewhere. He was a good two hands taller than she, and he gazed right over her head to the south.

"As need dictates." She tilted back on her heels and looked up into his frowning face.

"From which direction will the dark elf come?" he demanded, still not taking his gaze from the forest.

"We do not know."

"*You* do not know!"

"No. The movements of the Speaker are not widely discussed."

Idron glanced at her with a mixture of surprise and pity. "My lady, I thought *Gilthas* to be the Speaker of the Sun," he said softly but firmly.

Gaellal started to retort sharply, but reined in her temper. Idron was a guest in her camp. "The movements of Porthios are not widely discussed for obvious reasons."

"How do you know he will even come?"

"I'm sorry you're having to wait, Senator," she apologized icily, "but you were given Porthios's word. He will be here."

The distracted manner disappeared in a blink, and he bowed politely. "Forgive me my impatience, my lady. I mean no insult. It's just that this meeting is so important, to your people and mine. If Porthios and I can come to some agreement . . ."

Gaellal nodded, returning his smile with a forgiving one of

her own. "There is nothing to forgive. You are right. Regardless of our differences, together we can achieve victory."

Just as she said the last word, the treetops shivered, flashing a brief glimpse of the silver-green underbelly of the leaves.

* * * * *

As Calarran stepped slowly around the trunk of a tree and emerged into the clearing, the metallic hiss of swords and daggers slipping free of scabbards greeted him. Moonlight glinted off the blades of the elven warriors who stood in a circle about a pitiful campfire.

He knew that without the protection of the guard who had found him wandering in search of the Tessiel camp, those blades would have slivered his flesh into ribbons before he could speak.

The guard called out a password, caught Calarran's arm as he wobbled, and led him into the light. Steel whispered against leather as the weapons of the warriors were resheathed. A soft murmur of questions and comments rippled around him, but Calarran barely registered them. He stumbled, and only the elf's grip on his arm kept him upright.

"Where is Senator Idron?" Calarran rasped. The words hurt, pushing their way through his throat, past his swollen tongue. The guard had given him water, but only a sip. Not enough to ease the scorched dryness of his throat.

"It's Calarran, isn't it?" a voice said.

With effort, Calarran shook off the grip of the guard and stood alone. "Where is Idron?" he demanded, forcing his voice to strengthen. "Tell me!"

"Gone."

"Gone?" Calarran looked wildly about, expecting, somehow, to find Idron's patrician face among those huddled at the campfire. Surely he was there! These fools must not realize of whom he spoke. "The senator!" he demanded again. "The senator from Qualinesti."

"Calarran?" Another voice, this one soft and tired. Gaellal stepped forward. Her long, golden hair was disheveled, her silky tunic rumpled and stained with blood.

Whose blood? Was Idron dead? "Where is he?" Calarran whispered, softer this time.

Gaellal motioned, her hand low, but Calarran had no idea what the motion meant. Was it sympathy? Lack of knowledge?

"Your senator is alive, so far as we know."

A hand reached down to give him a cup of water. The water was lukewarm and gritty and tasted sweeter than any he'd ever swallowed. Her words were even sweeter, but confusing. "So far as you know?"

"The camp was attacked by Dark Knights on dragonback. That's why we're so surprised to see you. We thought you dead, as are so many others."

The faces of the elves as they shifted, reforming into a circle around him and Gaellal, were numb and tired.

For the first time, Calarran peered at the camp. Even in the darkness, he could see that it had been attacked and destroyed. The tents were down, campfires scattered, cooking pots overturned and smashed.

"Senator Idron was kidnapped by the knights who attacked the camp," Gaellal said. "Taken away on dragonback by Dark Knights."

A new dread filled his throat until he could hardly breathe. Kidnapped! He passed a hand across his forehead. His face was gritty, oily with soot and ashes. His stained palm brought back the sounds of the attack. Screams of dragons overhead. The remembered heat of burning. He pushed the thoughts away. He must concentrate. He must think.

"You must go after him," he demanded.

Gaellal was already shaking her head before he even finished speaking. "We cannot help—"

"You have twenty warriors here!" Calarran interrupted, sweeping his hand in a semicircle to indicate the ring of male and female elves.

"We cannot," Gaellal repeated firmly. "I understand your desire to save your senator. But our leader is out there somewhere, too. Our first duty is to assure his safety."

"You don't understand!" Calarran insisted. "They have

kidnapped Senator Idron of the Qualinesti! The only better hostage would be Senator Rashas or the Speaker of the Sun himself!"

Gaellal looked at him. "You are correct. But I must find Porthios first. Then we will find Idron."

Calarran spoke firmly, slowly, as if to a child. "I insist you aid me. Idron was here at your behest, and under your protection."

Gaellal sighed. "I know. I cannot express my sorrow at what has happened. Perhaps you are right. We must do something."

Calarran felt the tension in his shoulders ease, became aware of how tightly his fists were clenched. He flexed his fingers and shivered as the blood rushed back into them.

Gaellal turned and searched the group of elves. When she didn't find the face she sought, she motioned and one of the elves at her side trotted off into the darkness. A moment later, he reappeared, the Kagonesti scout from Eliad's patrol at his side.

"You!" The word burst from Calarran's throat as if hurled.

Gaellal held out a hand, motioning the Kagonesti forward. "Daraiel is the best scout we have," she said. "If any of us can find your senator, she can."

The Kagonesti, her face washed clean of the outrageous paint, looked at him with eyes the color of amber, wearing an expression that mirrored every emotion racing through him. Dislike, disdain, refusal—everything except the shame. His face was as hot as the burning forest during the attack. He supposed it must be flushed as red.

"I will go nowhere with this coward," she spat.

"I am no coward!" Calarran's fingers curled back into fists.

The Kagonesti glared daggers at Calarran, and spat at Gaellal. "This coward tried to run from the battle instead of going to the aid of Eliad."

The muscles along Calarran's jaws tightened so that he could feel his teeth grind. Shame threatened to bow his shoulders, but he refused to allow it. He flung his hands out, palm up, in appeal. "Yes, I ran, but I am no coward. I defy any of you to stand fast in the face of dragons bearing down on you, flaming the very air you breathe. I am a diplomat, not a warrior, trained as an envoy and ambassador. I defy the strongest of you, the meanest, to stand in the face of dragonfear."

The Kagonesti drew back her lips so that her teeth were revealed in a feral imitation of a snarl. He knew she had stood where he could not. He remembered her running toward the fight before he ran away from it. But she said nothing to accept his explanation.

The elves circled around him remained impassive, almost indifferent. There was no hint of sympathy or understanding in their long, narrow faces.

Gaellal glanced from him to the scout, then nodded to herself as if some conversation inside her head was at an end. "You and Daraiel will go," she declared.

Calarran's head snapped up. Anger blazed in him where he had thought himself too numbed, too tired to ever feel any such sensation again. "Us! You will send one Kagonesti servant and one diplomat to aid a senator of the Qualinesti when you have warriors available!"

The Kagonesti stepped toward him, hand on the hilt of the tiny dagger that hung from her belt. "I am servant to no one!" she hissed.

Gaellal put out a hand and stopped her, but her words were directed at Calarran. "Will you fight amongst yourselves while the enemy defeats us? Daraiel is our best scout. Our best tracker."

He glared at the Kagonesti, knowing that her accusations had turned Gaellal from any further offer of aid, knowing that his own actions had as well.

"Enough of this!" Gaellal snapped: "Daraiel knows the location of the Dark Knights' main camp. It is the largest camp, and their only permanent one. That is the most likely destination for so important a prisoner. Daraiel will guide you there. Idron is, after all, *your* senator."

Calarran knew, no matter how terrifying he found the prospect of facing the dragons again, he could not refuse. He could not stand in a camp of renegades and have less courage than they. With an effort he knew was visible to all, Calarran stepped back and bowed his head.

The Kagonesti sagged and lowered her gaze in sullen defeat.

"When we have found Porthios, we will follow." Gaellal turned her back on them both. The other elves drifted away with her, leaving the two of them standing alone.

* * * * *

There was no hint of sun in the inky murk of the deep forest as Calarran set out, and yet it was as hot as a normal summer at midday.

Calarran looked vastly different than he had the day before, and he couldn't help glancing down at himself as he walked. In place of the blue tunic, he wore a borrowed tunic and pants that were used, slightly trail-battered, and stained the colors of the new earth and aspens. He carried a light bow, a rolled blanket across his back, and waterskins at both hips.

The clothes and the trail gear sat awkwardly on his body. The leather tunic was stiffer than his silken garments and tugged at his arms when he raised them. The weight of the bedroll pulled on his shoulders, and the boots had not molded to the shape of his feet. Yet the alien feel of the leather on his back and the heaviness of his burden excited him the way a trip to the Senate chambers had excited him when he was a boy.

The Kagonesti scout, looking much the same as she had the day before with her face painted in squiggles of gray and green, set out ahead of him at such a pace she was soon out of sight.

He had to run, the bedroll banging against his hip, to catch up with her. "We will stay together," he ordered firmly, but kindly.

"You do not command me. And I'm trying to stay far enough away that whoever hears you coming will not find me, too," she snapped.

He glared at her, but let her walk away.

She did slow her pace enough so that he could see her threading her way through the trees. That seemed as deliberately calculated to annoy him as moving had. She was close enough that he could see how lightly she walked. He could hear—or rather, not hear—her footsteps in the dry, brittle ground cover.

And he could hear his own. He did not sound, as she had said the day before, like "a herd of hobgoblins." But he did sound like perhaps one hobgoblin. A small one. Despite his irritation, he passed the morning trying to walk like her. He was determined to discover what it was exactly that she did that hid her footsteps on the crunchy leaves.

He was so busy trying to emulate the skill that he almost bumped into her when she stopped abruptly at the base of a tall aspen. He could feel his heartbeat in his throat as he froze and searched about him, peering into the shadows of the forest. "What is it?" he whispered.

Without answering, the Kagonesti circled the tree slowly, looking up and down. Then she took a chunk of soft, white rock from the pouch on her belt and drew a line at eye level on the tree.

Calarran grabbed her wrist just as she was scratching the lines at the tip that made the mark an arrow. "What are you doing?" This time, he made no effort to keep his voice low.

"Marking our direction. Or did you think Gaellal would find us by magic?" She glared at him, then at her wrist where he held her.

With a jerk, she tore loose from him, turned, and stomped off down the slope. He could follow her progress by all the noise she was made, crushing dead leaves and twigs under her boots, crashing through low-hanging branches.

She definitely sounded like more than one hobgoblin. The sound was infinitely pleasing, and Calarran set off behind her, moving as quietly as he could.

They reached the site of the attack just as day broke, and Calarran stopped so suddenly that the bedroll slid forward off his shoulder.

The Kagonesti cried out softly, her voice a mirror of the pain he too felt as he saw the wounded forest. He might not be as trained to live in it as she, but no Qualinesti, no matter how city-bound, was ever truly apart from the lovely wood that surrounded his home.

The outrage that washed over him at the sight of the charred land was as hot as the breath of the dragons that had destroyed it.

He stopped at the edge of the charred swath, unable to touch the blackened earth. There were no leaves, no bushes, no brambles left, only soot and ash. Where there had been tall, proud aspens, older than the oldest elf, as old as Krynn itself, there were charred stumps, so brittle and lifeless that the slightest breeze blew them away. And in that dust were the ashes of the Kagonesti's friends.

There was no forest scent left here, no smell of life. If a smell could have a name, this one must be called black. Dead. Even the dirt itself was blackened, dried from the heat until it was fine as sand.

The Kagonesti came to a halt at his side as if she, too, were unwilling to touch the destroyed ground. Her shoulder was almost touching his arm.

Calarran knelt slowly and touched a fingertip to the dead soil. It clung to his finger like powder. Gray powder.

As he glanced at her, she turned her face away, but not before he saw that she was blinking back tears. His own eyes clouded over with moisture.

She swallowed and kept her head turned away. "They will pay for this," she said softly. "If I die in the doing, they will pay."

Her anguish surprised him, almost as much as did his own gentleness. "You love this forest as much as the Qualinesti do." For her love of the Qualinesti forest, he might even forgive her for witnessing his cowardice.

"My father taught me the love of the forest. Of all living things."

"I have heard that the Kagonesti live as one with the forest. Of course, there are Kagonesti in Qualinost, but they live as—" He stopped himself before he said "servants." He knew there were many of the Kagonesti who detested the way their brethren had been taken into servitude. "Well, they live in the city. Not in the forest."

"My father was not Kagonesti," she said softly. "He was Silvanesti. My mother was Kagonesti." Without glancing at him, she walked away.

Calarran was so surprised, he remained where he was, crouched at the edge of destruction. A half-breed! How extraordinary. What kind of war went on in her soul, born of a savage Kagonesti and an aristocratic Silvanesti?

He watched the woman until she disappeared between the trees, then looked back at the devastation. The destruction made him forget the woman. He rubbed ash between his fingers and knew that the long, long lifetime stretching out in front of him would not be enough time for the majestic trees to return. "Yes," he agreed. "They will pay."

After a moment he followed the woman. She had chosen a route that led parallel to the burned area but stayed just out of sight of it, up the hillside where they had been when the dragons attacked.

When he caught up to her, she was crouched behind a stand of bushes, looking out over the treetops, just as she had done only a day before. His heart beat rapidly as he joined her and scanned the horizon for signs of dragons.

"The attack came from the north." She pointed. Her voice had a shaky edge to it that brought back the terrifying moment when he had looked up and seen the dragons.

He reached out to put his hand on her arm to stop her from dredging up a memory that was still too new, too raw. She moved away from the touch of his fingers with only the barest hint of distaste on her face.

The expression did not offend him. "I saw them," he rasped, unable to stop himself from remembering. "They appeared as if from nowhere. As if they'd risen from the forest like ghosts. Or smoke." He breathed in audibly, shakily.

"They were not ghosts. They came from the north. The Dark Knights' largest, most permanent camp is north near the White Rage River." She pointed north, but west of Qualinost. "That is where we will go first."

* * * * *

They made good time, despite the treacherous footing downhill into the valley, and even better time once they were on level ground. They ate as they walked—dried fish from the camp, roots, and a handful of pitifully wrinkled berries, almost dried from the heat, that the woman gathered as they walked. And they spoke not one word to each other, but the silence seemed to him somehow easier.

They paused at nightfall near a trickle that had once been a bubbling stream. Calarran dozed, propped upright between the roots of a tree. He suspected that the woman slept no more than he did.

They replenished their waterskins and were up and moving again before daybreak. The heat, which barely eased during the night, grew unbearable as the sun climbed above the trees. The night spent on the ground had left Calarran stiff and sore.

When the sun had climbed past its zenith and was once again casting slight shadows, the woman halted.

"What's wrong?" Calarran asked, as she chose a large sunny spot between the trees and squatted.

Without answering, she stirred the dead leaves that blanketed the ground around her. She picked through the leaves, chose a stick about the length of her forearm, and held it up for inspection. Then she discarded it and chose another.

"What are you doing?" he demanded.

She repeated the gesture once more before answering. "Checking our direction." She emphasized her terse words by stabbing her chosen stick into the ground. She piled through the leaves again until she found a small stone and marked the tip of the shadow with it.

Calarran collapsed nearby in the meager shade of a tree and sipped from his waterskins. "How does it work?"

"What were you learning when the other children were learning woodland skills?" she asked, her tone plainly exasperated.

Her words brought back a pleasant memory of happy mornings spent in the garden with his mother. He grinned. "You wouldn't believe me if I told you."

When he said no more, she unstoppered her own waterskin and settled back against a tree. "When the shadow moves a bit, I'll mark the tip of the new shadow. The line between the two marks will be west to east. The shortest line from the base of the stick to the line will point north. From that I can tell if we're still going directly northwest, as we should be."

He peered at the stick and its shadow, as if it might suddenly move, then realized what he was doing and sat back. Despite himself, he found the trick impressive. "If your father taught you about the forest, what did you learn from your mother?"

She hesitated, searching his face carefully. There was a wariness in her that he suspected came from many, many years of questions from strangers.

She obviously found something acceptable in his expression, because she responded, "Both my parents taught me the love of the land. My mother was . . . the bravest person I've ever known."

Calarran flushed at the reference. Brave. He'd always thought of himself as brave. And still did, he told himself firmly. He looked up to find her staring at him. "Please, go on."

"There is not much to tell. My parents met during the War of the Lance. And they died fighting Lorac's blight in Silvanesti."

Calarran drew in his breath. He'd heard of the terrible things done to the beautiful, ancient land of Silvanost when its ruler tried to use one of the evil dragon orbs to defeat the Dark Queen's army. There was not an elf alive who did not mourn the damage done.

"That is why I follow Porthios and Alhana. Because they fought for Silvanesti. And now they fight to save Qualinesti. I can do no less here."

Calarran lowered his gaze. He was shamed and chastised, but determined to be no less committed than she.

* * * * *

Calarran raised up on his elbows and peered at the camp. For the fourth time, Daraiel pulled him down and signaled that he should keep his head low.

They lay on their bellies on a slight rise to the east of the camp of Dark Knights. The camp, built on the grassy shore of the river, was a busy one, full of troops wearing the gray armor of Lord Ariakan's troops. The camp appeared to be a permanent staging area. Dozens of the big trees had been felled to make room for the tents. The trunks were stretched along the sides of the camp, creating an effective barrier.

While he watched, the sun had almost set, leaving a hot red glow in the western sky.

"Where are the dragons?" he whispered, shifting away from Daraiel so that he had a different view through the trees.

She followed, edging on elbows and knees, careful to stay down. "Probably farther west in the mountains. But that big clear area over there looks like a landing spot. We'll have to be careful of them coming in. They're—"

Daraiel hissed and grabbed his arm. "Look! Over there, near that striped tent. Isn't that Idron?"

Calarran came up on hands and knees to peer down into the camp.

This time Daraiel didn't try to drag him down.

The figure was dressed like Idron and was tall and slender like an elf. He circled the clearing twice, then returned to the striped tent. The two guards took up positions near the entrance.

"That's him!" Calarran whispered. "I know his walk!"

He flopped down on his back, surprised to find that his heart was pounding as if he'd run in circles around the camp instead of crawling. "So now we know they've got him. Now what?"

Through the days they had taken to arrive at the camp, the hours spent reconnoitering, he'd not allowed himself to think of the possibility that they'd find Idron—just as he'd not allowed himself to think that they might find Idron dead.

He bit his lip and stared at the gently moving leaves overhead. What now? He was a diplomat, not a warrior. But he couldn't just walk down there and negotiate for Idron's return.

"Do we wait and watch and hope your people come in time? Do we go back for them? Should you go back for them while I stay and watch?"

Calarran glanced at Daraiel and realized from her reaction that he had spoken all questions aloud. Even through the painted squiggles, her face was set in a determined expression he'd come to know well. "We're only two," he protested. "Do you think we should attack the camp?"

"No, but perhaps we can sneak in and free him."

"What?"

"I can slip into the camp after dark. His tent isn't that far from the forest on one side. We can slit a hole in the back of the tent and have him out of there before they even realize he's gone."

He turned and surveyed the camp once more, his heart pounding with the audacity of the plan. He could see how she might sneak in, through the zigzag pattern of tents, through the shadows.

"Don't you think you can, too?" The words were as much a taunt as a dare.

He couldn't believe he was even considering it. But at the same time . . . what else was he going to do? If he cowered in the trees and waited for her tribe to rescue Idron, he would be doubly damned as a coward. And he was not a coward! He straightened his shoulders, hoping that the strength in his spine would confer strength on his will.

Daraiel laughed without mirth.

He realized he did look ridiculous, sitting tall and proud in secondhand leathers, his face smeared the color of the earth, his long fingers stained with soot and chalk. His city-clean scent was long lost to sweat and dirt. But he would prove her wrong.

He jerked his head in as firm a nod as he could muster. "I can do it."

Their gazes met and held for a moment. She stared into his eyes. Her small face grew solemn. "Why did you run . . . really?"

Calarran sucked in air audibly.

Her gaze, unblinking, assessing, questioning, was so intense he dared not look away. Or fail to answer. "I don't know. There was the dragonfear from the moment I saw the bushes burst into flame. It was like . . . it was like something alive. Like mist come alive. I remember I had to get away. . . . The dragons were screaming overhead, and I could smell the burning. . . ."

He stopped, shuddered, and drew in a deep breath, hoping it would dispel the scent of burned flesh, of dying forest. "I remember that when I came to, I was . . . two arms' lengths from a burned area. The heat was still so great, I could see it, dancing in the air. I don't know why I ran instead of dying. I don't know why they left me. Perhaps they didn't see me. Perhaps the gods have some other destiny in mind for me. I know I prayed to them to spare me."

The strength he had hoped for tightened his muscles, filled his heart. "I won't run this time, Daraiel. I promise." He held his breath as he finally looked up and met her gaze again.

For a long, long time, she didn't speak, but continued to stare into his eyes. Then finally, just when he thought his lungs would burst, she turned and peered over the ridge, down into the camp.

"Look," she said, motioning him to join her. "We'll go in through the tents. If we zigzag through, over there toward the water's edge, we should be hidden from the greatest concentration of guards. You go first. I'll follow."

He started to protest, to tell her that it was safer for him to bring up the rear. Then he picked up his bow and started down the slope at an angle, toward the camp. He didn't look back to see whether she followed.

He circled it carefully, remembering all the things she'd shown him about staying invisible. Moving from shadow to shadow. Flitting, he hoped, like a shadow wafted by a summer breeze.

He made it to the first tent. The second. Tried to move like the flickering shadows cast by the campfires. Past the third. Someone inside was snoring loudly. The fourth. There was no sign of guards. He paused in the deep shadows before beginning his first turn up the rows of tents to look back, to search for Daraiel, following behind.

He had actually started into the camp before the last hint of gray dusk had left the sky. But now the shadows were deep and dark, and there was no sign of his partner. Had she not followed?

His breathing flickered as unsteadily as the firelight. Was he alone in the enemy camp? He took a deep breath to steady himself. No matter. Alone or not, he must go on.

He moved on slowly, carefully, past another row of tents. He turned again in the direction of Idron's prison tent and walked with quiet precision into the arms of a knight who was coming out of one of the tents.

The face of the Dark Knight registered a ridiculous, shocked expression. Calarran could still see it as the man, not as tall as he but twice as wide, grabbed him and shouted to his compatriots for help.

With arms that were as stout as oaks and as big around as young aspens pinning his own arms to his sides, Calarran did not even try to escape. He clamped down on every instinct he had that told him to fight back, to get away. For if he ran, they would search for him and they might find Daraiel.

He drew himself up as best he could, straightened his shoulders and demanded loudly, "I am Calarran, aide to Senator Idron and son of Senator Rodalas. I demand to be taken to Idron." He hoped he was loud enough for Daraiel to hear.

They bound his wrists tightly behind his back with leather strips and boxed his ears when he shouted, demanding again to be taken to Idron. Despite the ringing in his ears from rough handling by one of the guards who captured him, Calarran stood his ground. As the guards hauled him roughly before their commander, he didn't waver.

As he repeated the litany, he felt the guard on his right, the one who had boxed his ears, tense. The guard growled low in his throat and turned menacingly.

"If I hear that one more time—" he spat.

The commander, a smile twitching at the corners of his mouth, waved the guard back. "You are either very brave or very foolish, Calarran."

Heat and color crept up from under Calarran's collar, edging toward his high cheekbones. "I was sent with Idron as his guard, as his aide. My place is at his side. I cannot go back to Qualinost without him."

"So you came all this way, tracked us, evaded our patrols, just so you could offer yourself up as a hostage beside your senator?" The tone of the commander's voice was plainly disbelieving. His last word was so nonchalant it was blatant. "Alone?"

"I did not come to offer myself as a hostage," Calarran said, and was proud of the dignity he managed to convey. "I did not even know if Idron was alive. The elves at the camp said he was taken away. I had to make sure. I had to know what happened to him. And having determined that, my job was to free him." Calarran swallowed. "Having failed that, my place is at his side."

"And what of the others? The elves who were left at the camp?" It was clear from the commander's tone that he hadn't approved of leaving anyone alive.

"They would not come. They pretended alliance to the Qualinesti, but in the end they showed their true colors." Calarran curled his lip in his best imitation of disgust. "Renegades. Exiles," he spat. "They are no friends of mine. And I have word of their leader's whereabouts."

The commander regarded him with an assessing gaze.

"Which I will give only if I am taken to Idron."

The commander's face split into a wide, feral smile. He motioned for the guards to precede him.

Through the rough-trod camp, past cooking fires and tents and groups of guards, Calarran's captors took him. The smells, so unlike the elven encampment, were harsh, of human sweat and animals, of boiling meat, of oiled weapons, destroyed forest, of grass and bushes crushed to dust underfoot.

Despite the ropes binding Calarran's wrists behind his back, the guards who escorted him held his upper arms so tightly his fingers were numb. Knights turned and watched as he was led past, their faces hard and impassive under their gray helms.

His escorts led him straight through the camp to the guarded striped tent and pushed him roughly inside.

Idron leapt to his feet as Calarran lurched into the tent. He had been seated at a rough-hewn wooden table. "Calarran!"

The fright Calarran had been controlling spilled out as he saw Idron. The guards followed Calarran into the tent, grabbing at him roughly as he stumbled.

"That's enough," Idron ordered, his voice level but firm, as of someone who expects to be obeyed under any circumstances.

The guards righted Calarran, then released him and stepped back just as the commander stepped into the tent.

"Commander Haros, what is the meaning of this?"

"We caught this one sneaking into the camp, Senator. He claims to be your aide. He *says* he tracked you, alone, because he belongs at your side."

Idron smiled at Calarran and said gently, "You should not have come." Then he turned to the Dark Knight, Haros, and said proudly, "He is my aide. My staff is very loyal."

Haros's lip curled with disdain. "Obviously." He turned to Calarran. "Now, here is your master. Tell me where the renegade Porthios can be found."

Idron gasped, but before he could speak, Calarran shook his head. "Did you really think I would tell you?"

Haros stepped forward angrily, but Idron intervened, casting a warning glance over his shoulder at Calarran. "Commander . . . let me speak with Calarran. I will not have him harmed."

Haros hesitated, glaring disgust and hatred over Idron's shoulder. Then he saluted, the movement stiff with sarcasm. "I will leave him here with you for a few minutes. Talk some sense into him before I return. His good behavior is your responsibility."

As soon as the door flap of the tent dropped behind the last guard, Calarran surged forward. "My lord, have they harmed you?"

"No. This is not the most elegant of lodgings, but I have not been ill treated. How did you come here?"

For the first time since he'd entered, Calarran paused to glance at his surroundings. Like the camp outside, the tent was much different than it had appeared from the hillside. The canvas sides and domed roof moved slightly in the hot evening breeze, giving Calarran the eerie, claustrophobic impression of being inside the lungs of some striped beast.

The table at which Idron had been seated was near the center of the tent. A book lay open on it. A lamp, glowing warm and yellow, and a tin cup sat beside the book.

In one corner was a bedroll, neatly bound with leather strips. In the other was a lantern, seated at shoulder height upon a tripod of branches that had been stripped bare of bark.

"How did you come here?" Idron repeated.

Calarran brought himself back from his inspection. With one more quick glance around to assure that they were alone, he stepped close to his master. "We have to stall the commander as long as we can. I'm here with a scout from the Tessiel camp. We've come to rescue you."

"So Porthios is not with you?"

Calarran shook his head.

Idron's slender features twisted in a grimace. "You and one scout? Is that the best that renegade trash could do?"

That Idron had so little confidence in him stung worse than nettles. "I thought we would be enough," Calarran lied. "Their camp was all but destroyed. Daraiel and I came ahead to find you. The others follow." Calarran paused, a bit breathless from the hurried words.

"Porthios will be with them?"

"I do not know, my lord. I expect so."

"And this Daraiel?"

"She was to come in behind me." Calarran could not stop himself from glancing back, as if she might be in the tent with them. "I . . . I don't know what happened to her."

Idron hesitated a moment, then moved so abruptly that Calarran was startled. With an apologetic smile he stepped behind Calarran to inspect his bonds. Idron tugged from first one side, then the other.

Calarran winced as the rough leather cut into his wrists.

"I fear I cannot loosen them. I will ask the guards to cut them." Idron strode with sure grace to the tent flap and went out, calling the name of one of the guards.

Though their tones were too low for Calarran to understand the words, he could distinguish first the senator's voice, then a voice he did not know, and then the senator's again. The first tones sounded demanding, the last few persuasive, even cajoling.

Calarran was not surprised when Idron stepped back into the tent and shrugged apologetically. "He says they will release you when Haros returns. Not before."

"What should I tell him when he returns?" Calarran looked to his mentor for advice.

"I hope your friend will come along before Haros returns. If she does not . . . we must have a plan that will appease him."

"He wants to know where Porthios is."

"Yes. The knights were quite disappointed that Porthios was not in the camp." Idron circled around the little table, his pace slowing, stroking his chin with his thumb. "Yes-s-s-s . . ." He drew the word out, long and low, obviously deep in thought.

It was a gesture Calarran had witnessed many times since he had been apprenticed to Idron. He found it comforting now, reassuring. It gave him strength and hope.

Idron stopped, half turned away from Calarran, his long face in shadow. "But *you* do not know, do you?"

"Well . . . not really. I know they were to follow us. Daraiel marked our trail so they could. But where they would be now . . . I don't know."

A smile lifted Idron's mouth. His head snapped up to attention, chin jutting out proudly.

This, too, Calarran had seen many times. When Idron had won a point in a debate, defeated his opposition in a game, or pressed home his opinion in a meeting of the Senate.

"You have a plan!" Calarran said with certainty.

Idron turned on his heel. His eyes were bright, teeth exposed in a grin. Before he could speak, there was a commotion outside the tent opening: loud voices, scuffling sounds, and a loud thump followed by a grunt, as if a fist or a foot had connected with someone's gut. The tent flap flew up and a body, all kicking feet and wriggling torso, was thrust in.

The Dark Knight who had hold of Daraiel half shoved, half tossed her into the tent. She rolled into a tight ball as she hit the ground and came up onto her feet, wheeling, shifting into attack stance on the balls of her feet even though her wrists were bound behind her back.

The guard drew his sword halfway out of the scabbard.

Another guard, hand on his sword, ducked into the tent and joined the first one.

Daraiel tensed as if she would attack anyway. But as she shifted, she saw Calarran and Idron. In an instant, all her fury changed direction. She leapt toward Calarran and the first guard caught her in midstep, wrapping one massive arm around her slight shoulders and snatching her back against his body.

As she struggled to free herself, she cursed in Kagonesti.

Calarran did not understand a word of what she said, but the anger and fury in her eyes left no doubt as to the essence. Neither did her words, when she finally remembered to switch to Silvanesti. "You traitorous coward! You told them where I was, didn't you?"

As Haros stepped into the tent, Idron said sarcastically, "Well, Commander, I see you found her."

Daraiel's voice stopped as if the words had been cut by a knife. Calarran reeled as if he'd been struck. The pain of Daraiel's attack was like a mosquito bite compared to the knife wound of Idron's betrayal.

"Exactly where you said she would be." The big human jerked a thumb to point in the direction.

"Yes." Idron bowed to Daraiel.

She growled, a low, animal sound unlike anything Calarran had ever heard issue from an elven throat, and lunged at Idron.

The guard yanked her back.

She kicked back at him, using his grip across her chest as leverage to lift both feet off the ground.

He swore as her heels connected with his shins. He flipped a glittering dagger out of his belt and jammed it to her throat, beneath her ear. "Hit me again," he growled, "and I'll water this dry ground with your blood."

Daraiel continued to wriggle, but she kept both feet on the ground.

Idron smiled grimly. "I have another errand for your troops, Commander, as soon as there is enough light. My young aide informs me that Porthios and his band are following their trail, looking for me. I believe they will be coming from the south." Idron looked to Calarran as if for confirmation.

Calarran didn't respond. He was too sick to even look at Idron. He was as numb and heartsore as Daraiel was angry. Idron was his mentor, his friend, the elf his father had most trusted to teach his only son. To learn that Idron was in league with the Dark Queen . . . Calarran had almost died in the attack. Then he'd trekked across the Qualinesti forest. And for what? To save the life of a traitor.

Daraiel saw the sickness in his face, the paralysis. She went suddenly limp in the guard's grasp, as if all the fight had gone out of her, too.

Idron saw it and smiled. "Commander, I think you may go now. We'll have no more trouble here."

When Haros and the second guard were gone, and the tent flap once more closed, Idron caught Calarran's arm gently. "Please understand, Calarran, I take no pleasure in what I do."

Calarran snatched his arm free and backed away to the far side of the tent. "You're a traitor to our people! To my family! To me! I almost died in the attack on Eliad's patrol!"

"That was unfortunate. I never intended you harm. What I do, I do for Qualinesti. You saw the damage these troops can do." Idron leaned forward, all sincerity and candor. "Would you have them do that to Qualinost? Would you see your home burned to the ground? With me as a hostage, Lord Ariakan will have leverage with the Senate. The Senate will force Gilthas to deal with Ariakan, to come to some agreement."

Calarran looked into Idron's eyes and saw that he had no sense of the ultimate wickedness of his plan.

"And Porthios?" Daraiel asked, her voice husky. She had been standing so quietly that the guard who held her had lowered the dagger from her neck. "Will you sacrifice him, too?"

Idron shrugged. "There are still members of the Senate who value Porthios. While he lives, he will influence their decisions."

"And afterward?"

"His death is, unfortunately, a necessity. The humans want Porthios dead. That is one part of their price for Qualinost's safety. But I must admit, his death will serve us, too. With Porthios gone, there is much that will be made easier. While he lives, there will always be those who work for his return to the throne."

"You can't do this!" Daraiel protested. She shifted as she spoke, and her captor tightened his grip again.

Idron said simply, "I already have." He turned to Calarran. "Calarran, I want you at least to understand. Do you see that this is the only way to save our city, our people? I am no traitor."

"There is a way!" Daraiel cried. "Porthios has been protecting Qualinost, spreading his followers along a line to the east. With the warriors in Qualinost . . . !" Daraiel stopped, looked from Idron to Calarran as if weighing whether she should continue.

Calarran nodded to her.

"With the warriors from Qualinost, the dark troops could be caught in between our forces and yours. We could squeeze them out of Qualinesti."

"This is the plan Porthios wanted to propose in our meeting?"

"I wasn't supposed to know this . . ." Daraiel glanced back at Calarran, then continued. "I overheard them discussing Porthios's plan."

Calarran held his breath as Idron considered Daraiel's words.

"It would never work." Idron looked at her with pity, as if she were a child or an idiot, then opened his hands, palms up, to Calarran. "There are too many of them. Too few of us. Don't you see?"

After a moment, Calarran nodded reluctantly. "Yes. Yes, I do."

Idron's head whipped up as if he had not heard Calarran's

words correctly. "You agree? Will you bow to me on it?" Idron asked cautiously.

Calarran paled, but acquiesced. "I will."

"No!" Once more, Daraiel lunged. Once more the burly guard held her back.

As Idron moved toward him, Calarran turned his back and held out his hands for Idron to untie him. The wooden legs of the lantern tripod were at his feet. The heat from the flame washed across his face.

Calarran looked sideways at Daraiel, trying to catch her gaze. "Daraiel," he said softly.

He shifted as Idron touched the leather bonds and moved his foot nearer the closest branch of the lantern tripod.

Daraiel gasped as she saw his foot move. He saw her throat move as she swallowed convulsively. Their gazes met and held for so long that Calarran was afraid the guard would notice.

Then she nodded with just the tiniest move of her head. The motion was enough to alert the guard, but he was too late.

The moment Calarran saw her chin move, he kicked the leg of the tripod. As the whole thing toppled, he lowered his shoulder and slammed the lantern toward the wall of the tent. Hot oil arced out from the lantern. Glittering beads like black diamonds sprayed the wall of the tent, the ground, and Calarran's shoulder. Fire exploded into life everywhere the oil touched.

As the guard tightened his grip on Daraiel, she arched her back and leaped into the air. She kicked back with all her might. The guard could not hold on to her and the dagger and avoid her feet all at the same time. His grip across her shoulders loosened as he tried to avoid the kick. She twisted as she fell and tore herself out of his grasp. Before he could right himself, she gained her footing, lowered her head, and powered into him with all her lithe strength.

Calarran saw the two of them falling as he fell himself. He rolled away from the instant inferno of blazing oil, rubbing his shoulder against the ground in case any of the oil on him was also ablaze.

When he came to a stop and pushed himself up on one

elbow, Daraiel and the guard were both on the ground. Daraiel, like him, was using her elbow to lever herself up. The guard, whose head was against the leg of the wooden table, was not moving.

The tent was already beginning to fill with smoke and the smell of burning cloth. Calarran got to his knees, wobbled to his feet.

Idron came at him with his fists raised. "You fool!" he yelled over the roaring of the fire.

Calarran lowered his shoulders and met the attack head-on. He heard the whoosh of Idron's breath leaving his lungs as his head connected with the taller elf's stomach, felt the jolt of the two of them hitting the earth, heard the thump of Idron's head on the ground. Then he heard the whoosh of his own breath leaving his lungs as he fell on the senator's legs.

Daraiel was there as he rolled over this time, offering her thigh as a brace as he tried to rise. She was coughing so hard, she could barely stand.

Unlike the guard, Idron was conscious. He groaned groggily and tried to move, his hands scrabbling weakly at the ground.

Calarran gasped for air and smoke filled his lungs. Fire was crackling all about them now, licking hungrily at the roof of the tent. Not much time.

"We have to get out!" Daraiel choked out.

Idron groaned again.

Calarran shoved his foot under Idron's head and pushed. The elf rolled toward the wall of the tent.

"What are you doing?" Daraiel pushed at him with her shoulder. "Get out! Get out!"

"I can't just leave him," Calarran shouted back. "Help me!"

For the barest fraction of a second, she hesitated.

"I won't kill him."

She joined him and together they pushed Idron through the burning wall of the tent. The moment he was free of the fire, Daraiel ran, bent low. Calarran followed her.

The camp was alive with shouting, running troops, some already carrying buckets. Daraiel ducked away from the thickest group and went behind a tent.

The hot night air was the sweetest, coolest Calarran had ever breathed. The freshness of it sent him into another paroxysm of coughing.

Daraiel was coughing too, but she kept moving down a line of tents, made a quick turn and went down another line. She ducked behind a tent to avoid a group of soldiers, and Calarran was able to catch up with her. "We're running the wrong way," he gasped. "Bear left, toward the forest."

She shook her head, already beginning to move. "Away from the river," she gasped back. "They all . . . be going . . . river. Fire."

Calarran paused to look back. The fire had spread. The bright orange flames were leaping into the night sky as high as the tops of the nearby aspens. Ash was already beginning to float down around him. The night was loud with the shouts of the Dark Knights, the crackle of fire, and the terrified whinnying of horses.

He ran after Daraiel. There were no soldiers in sight, and she had stopped zigzagging through the tents and was making straight for the forest. He caught up with her just as she entered the trees.

He followed the silver-gray of her tunic through the darkness, barely able to see his own feet. They had not gone very far when she slowed to a fast walk, then a slow walk, and finally stopped. She went down a slight rise, and her head slid out of sight as he heard her sit down.

He looked back before he followed her. An eerie glow lit the sky by the lake, but it seemed perhaps smaller. The trees were menacing black shapes, branches silhouetted against the glow like gnarled, misshapen arms reaching for him.

He took two steps down the incline, sank to his bottom and slid down even with Daraiel. "We have to go soon. I think they're getting the fire under control."

He could see her nod in the strange orange light. Not much of the glow penetrated into the forest, but he could hear the moan and crackle of the fire. It sounded like the conflagration from a dragon's breath.

"Have to rest just a minute more. Catch my breath," she gasped.

"Are you hurt?"

She shook her head jerkily. "No. Have to go on, to warn the others. Tell them—about Idron."

The pain of Idron's treachery squeezed at his heart, pushing out the elation over their escape.

Daraiel's breathing was harsh and ragged, and he realized his own sounded just as bad. He shifted closer, pressing one leg against hers. She smelled of smoke and sweat. Her leg was hot and trembling against his, but very comforting.

"I'm sorry I didn't trust you," she said in a small voice. "I'm sorry I called you . . . all those names."

He shrugged in the darkness, certain that she could feel his shoulder move against hers. "It's all right. I understand. You were thinking of the attack."

Her voice was even quieter, even smaller when she spoke again. "You never asked me how I was able to survive the attack."

The words were a surprise. "I guess I just assumed you escaped."

"I ran, too," she said bluntly.

His breath caught in his throat.

"I was afraid, so afraid. But I could hear Eliad. I wanted to go to him. I did go to him, even with the fear pounding down on me. But I . . . I didn't save him. Couldn't save him. There didn't seem to be any reason not to run."

Calarran lay absolutely still, breath barely stirring in his chest, thoughts barely stirring in his mind.

For a few minutes, she said nothing. Her gasping slowed and as he heard her breathing become more regular, the ache in his own lungs eased. As the trembling left her limbs, and she lay pressed against his side, still and quiet, so did the ache leave his heart. "We have to go," he said finally. His voice sounded very loud against the darkness.

With a sigh, she sat up and started to wriggle and twist.

He sat up, too. "What are you doing?"

"Trying to loosen my wrists. I'm not going one step until my hands are untied." She twisted so far sideways, she almost fell over. "I can feel the knot on top. If I could just see it . . ."

Grinning, he shifted away from her. "Perhaps I can help?" He balanced himself on the balls of his feet, took a couple of deep, relaxing breaths, and very deliberately blew them out. Then he rolled gracefully onto his back. Tucking his knees tight into his chest, he brought his bound hands down and to the front of his body.

Triumphantly, he sat up and wiggled his fingers at Daraiel.

"You asked what I was learning when I should have been playing in the forest? My mother was teaching me tumbling and acrobatic skills."

She gazed at him in amazement.

After a moment, she grinned. Then she turned around and stuck her bound wrists as far back as she could. "I hope your mother also taught you how to untie knots."

The Son of Huma

Richard A. Knaak

And the world was death . . .

The darkening sky rippled and the earth below twisted as if molten. The contingent of Solamnic Knights had little time to register the savage disaster, much less save themselves from it. Men and horses screamed as they were thrown into the air or sank swiftly into the liquid earth. The four dragons accompanying them fared no better, the heavens around them becoming a storm so violent that they were tossed about like tiny toys. The gold dragon who led the foursome died first, battered against a mountainside with such force that his spine cracked audibly. The old bronze tried valiantly to stay aloft, but weakness finally sent him plummeting to the ground. Only the two silvers managed to stay airborne for a time, but there was nothing they could do for either their kind or the humans.

Stoddard had just time enough to register Blane falling from his horse and being crushed under a swirling mass of earth before he himself was thrown from his panicked animal. The Knight of the Rose struck the earth with a harsh clang, but then his relief at landing on solid ground gave way to horror.

It was then he saw the rippling darkness take shape. Death had come for them, yes, death in the vague form of a huge dragon. Stoddard knew of the molten dragons of Chaos, but this one was different. Its body was a swirling star field, a living maelstrom. The beast's wingspan was twice that of any of the dragons accompanying the contingent of fifty men, and its jaws could have swallowed two or three warhorses whole, armor included.

The first silver dragon, the female, never noticed the massive form. The chaos dragon's terrible claws ripped through her wings. She roared in pain and tried to turn, but could no longer control her flight. However, apparently not satisfied with simply letting her fall to her death, the chaos monster seized her with its talons and, while she struggled, tore out her throat. Only then did it release the silver's body and turn to the other.

The male, her mate, roared with fury and tried his best to attack, but the rippling waves of air that seemed to surround the chaos dragon made it impossible for the silver leviathan to gain any momentum. His horrific adversary vanquished the valiant dragon as easily as if it were one of the puny humans. It raised its head high, opened its mouth . . . and an ear-shattering peal assailed the injured knight.

Stoddard dared not release his grip in order to cover his ears, although he dearly wanted to do so. Tears ran down his face. The male dragon's head hung to the side, his eyes staring sightlessly into the distance. The monster shook the body once, then released it.

Paladine . . . preserve us, Stoddard thought. It controls . . . all around us! It . . . fifty good men . . . the dragons. Can nothing stop it?

The chaos dragon stretched its wings and surveyed the tableau of destruction. Its eyes seemed to fix on Stoddard.

All thought fled the Knight of the Rose. Never in all his life had he felt so helpless, so . . . frightened.

The leviathan opened wide its mouth and roared . . .

This time the fear was too much. Stoddard blacked out.

* * * * *

A trickle of water coursed down his parched mouth. Stoddard swallowed involuntarily, then eagerly as more liquid followed. A stream of water dribbled down his cheek.

"I'm sorry," someone whispered from the darkness surrounding him. "I was too late. . . ."

Satiated for the moment, the knight ceased swallowing. The flow of water halted shortly thereafter but not before his chin and neck were drenched.

"Who. . . ?" Stoddard could barely recognize his own faltering voice. He coughed, then tried again. "Who?" No better.

Another voice, also whispering. "Move aside, boy. Let me see him. You've nearly drowned him."

Stoddard finally recognized the second person as one of his own men, a Knight of the Sword named Ferrin. He had not realized his eyes were still closed tight. The world slowly swam into focus, revealing the narrow, bearded face of Ferrin and that of a pale young man, handsome, clean-shaven, and with what seemed vaguely elven features. His brown hair was tinged with premature gray.

"How do you fare, my lord?" Ferrin asked in the same hushed tone.

"I am . . . battered, but . . ." The Knight of the Rose gingerly tested his limbs. His left shoulder ached terribly, but nothing seemed to be broken. He gave thanks to Paladine for the miracle. "I appear to be whole."

"Praise be."

"Why do the two of you whisper? Is the monster still around?"

Ferrin grimaced. "I am not whispering, my lord. Neither is the boy."

The dragon's cry—it had impaired his hearing. Perhaps with prayer he might eventually be able to set things right, but Stoddard knew he had neither the strength nor the time to worry about such things now. Too much was at stake. "How . . . how . . . many alive?"

The knight and the young man glanced at one another. That said it all.

"I found only Karis, Crandel, and Marlane, my lord," Ferrin finally responded. "Marlane died in my hands and Karis passed away not an hour ago. I managed to bind Crandel's wounds. Crandel is resting for now."

"No one else?"

"None. I nearly did not find you. You were thrown a great distance." Ferrin eyed the boy. "When I did, this one was already tending to you. That was about an hour ago, my lord." The other knight sighed. "We have only one horse. I had to put down four others I found. I think shock alone killed most of the others."

Shock. Trained warhorses dying from shock. It was

almost unheard of. Stoddard finally found the strength to try to sit up. "And the dragons are all dead?"

"The bronze lives, Lord Stoddard."

The senior knight made him repeat the astonishing statement. "Does he? I thought I saw him fall."

"He can fly only short distances and one leg is twisted, but he is otherwise physically unharmed. His thoughts might come a little slow for a time."

The young man looked down. There were traces of tears in his eyes. "I'm sorry. I tried to follow as best I could, but I underestimated the chaos dragon. I didn't know it could fly so fast."

His rescuer's words made little sense, but Stoddard really did not care at the moment. Fifty men and four dragons. The monster had wiped out an entire contingent meant to protect the port of Aramus, an important link in the supply routes for the armies combatting the forces of Chaos in northern Ansalon. The Knights of Takhisis had stripped the port of most of its original force, thinking the place far enough away from hostilities to be safe. Only belatedly had they realized that Aramus was no more secure than anywhere else, and so Stoddard and his men had been relegated to the task of defending it.

Now we have failed without even reaching our destination, thought Stoddard.

It could be no coincidence that the chaos dragon had struck so near to the port city. Either Aramus already lay in ruins or it soon would. "Aramus. We have to find out—"

"The city should be unharmed," the youth quickly informed him, "but not for long. The chaos dragon would have to take time to recuperate after this attack. But a day has already passed. It won't need much more."

Stoddard had to concentrate to pick up every word. He studied the young man carefully. His rescuer was young—a squire perhaps. "You seem to know more than we do about this monster. Who are you?"

"I am Liam of Eldor, my lord. I have been hunting the creature since first it entered Krynn. I . . . I'm sorry that I could not manage to stop it before it attacked you."

He had intended to stop the chaos beast before it destroyed fifty well-armed knights and four full-grown dragons? The boy must be addled. Stoddard was not terribly surprised. He had met too many like him, victims of war who lived in their own fantasy world rather than face the horrors of reality. A shame. "And why would such a terrible responsibility be yours in the first place, Liam of . . . Eldor, is it? This is war and such tasks belong to warriors." Stoddard could not help shuddering. "And even we fail."

Liam looked skyward. "There was no one else. My father does what he can, but the forces of Chaos are everywhere." The youth shook his head and wiped away the remnants of his tears. "But I can no more leave things be, my lord, than my father could've. I'm also the only one who might stand a chance against such as the chaos dragon."

Signaling Ferrin to help him to his feet, Stoddard politely replied, "I am grateful for your aid, Liam, but this is still a matter best left to us. If indeed you have family left, you should return to them. This is not . . . this could never be your responsibility."

"But you need me! I know I'm not my father, but I've learned so much from him."

Leaning toward his commander, Ferrin muttered, "Ask him who his father is, Lord Stoddard. Ask."

Judging from his tone, Ferrin had already heard the answer and found it wanting. His curiosity aroused, Stoddard followed Ferrin's suggestion. "So is your father a knight, then? What is his name? I might know of him."

The young man stood tall, looking for the moment, admittedly, far more impressive than the senior knight had first imagined. "You may know of him, my lord. His name is Huma of Eldor, also known as Huma of the Lance."

Stoddard was certain his hearing had failed him completely this time. He blinked, then looked to Ferrin for confirmation. The other knight nodded sadly. "That's what he said, Lord Stoddard, 'Huma of the Lance.' "

Stoddard cleared his throat but said nothing aloud. *Addled . . . the boy is definitely addled.*

Liam noted the uncomfortable silence and continued, "Of

course, his mortal form died centuries ago, but both he and my mother were brought up to Paladine, to dwell there with him." His chest swelled with pride. "I am the product of their union. Their son. I've always watched Krynn, always wanted to walk Ansalon. When at last my father did return to the world . . . to help in this war . . . I wanted to go with him, but he feared for me. He forbade me to come." The youth looked a little guilty. "He couldn't have known about this monster, though, because it appeared after he had rejoined the mortal world. I sensed it, and decided that I had to come to Krynn and help."

"Did you . . ." But there was little use in paying any serious attention to the boy's story. With a weary sigh, the Knight of the Rose turned his gaze from Liam and surveyed the landscape. New hills had been formed by the ravages of the chaos dragon. In many places trees lay broken and scattered. Of the human carnage, though, Stoddard could see nothing. "Ferrin, take me to the men."

"You should rest, my lord . . ."

"Take me to them."

The other knight took hold of his arm. Stoddard did his best not to rely on his companion, fighting both pain and weakness. As the two started off, Liam of Eldor suddenly rushed to Stoddard's other side and seized his forearm, no doubt trying to be of aid. Instead, he only succeeded in aggravating Stoddard's injuries.

"Be careful, you dolt!" Had he not been assisting his superior, it is likely that Ferrin would have seized the younger man by the throat.

"I'm sorry, my lord." Liam edged away, but did not abandon them.

"It's all right, lad." Stoddard glanced at Ferrin, telling him by expression alone that he need waste no time berating their deranged companion.

The journey was not a long one, although it did require more strength from Stoddard than he had thought would be necessary. What he saw made him forget such minuscule matters as exhaustion and pain.

The bodies of his men still lay where they had fallen,

some of them half-buried in the earth. An arm thrust out of one hillside, a booted foot out of another. A warhorse lay sprawled not far from the trio, its back clearly broken. One man lay crushed under a huge rock, his horrified expression enough to cause a shiver in the seasoned warrior. The scene was almost surreal.

Liam stumbled beside him. His face was white, his mouth hung open. He stared without blinking at the sight before them, then, in an act that Stoddard could have predicted, the young man turned away, dropped to his knees, and vomited.

"The son of Huma . . ." commented Ferrin wryly, speaking loud enough so that not only his commander could hear him, but the would-be champion as well.

"Do you recall your first experience with battle, Ferrin?"

The other knight quieted. Lord Stoddard stepped away from him, determined to survey the rest of the tragedy under his own power. He had to learn to depend on his own strength again and quickly.

Many of the men had died swiftly. A few had obviously lingered on, something that Stoddard did not care to dwell on. It was one of the worst disasters that he had witnessed during his lengthy career. The men had not even been allowed the opportunity to honorably defend themselves.

And an entire city—Aramus—faces the same danger, thought Stoddard. If what Liam of Eldor said had a grain of truth to it, Aramus is in dire danger from the same beast. We are only three . . . four counting the dragon . . . but we must do something. . . .

Suddenly Liam stood next to him. Stoddard silently cursed his poor hearing. The boy's presence combined with his own dark thoughts had given the knight a start.

"I . . . I'm sorry for before when I. . . . I've never seen such a terrifying sight."

"All part of war, lad. You should know that. It is one of the first things we impress upon those entering the knighthood. War is not a game. Knights do not simply ride around having jousts and sword contests." Stoddard raised his arms, indicating the death that was all around them. "This is what each new member of the Solamnic Orders must learn to anticipate: death in its most ghastly form."

Liam's face grew more pale, but this time the young man seemed to recover his pluck. "My father told me about this aspect of being a knight. I think he did it to scare me from ever trying to follow in his footsteps. But I always thought that if he felt it worth the risk, how could I do any less?"

The boy was so earnest, Stoddard almost wanted to believe that the youngster was who he believed himself to be. However, he could not afford the time to humor him. Perhaps a question the boy could not answer would jolt him back to reality. "Commendable, but why now, Liam? Certainly we could have used both you and your father during the War of the Lance. Why did you not come then? The situation was dire enough. The Lady of Darkness nearly seized control of Krynn."

In reply, Liam mumbled something that Stoddard doubted he could have understood even if his hearing were healed. The knight stared at him until Liam repeated himself. "Father wanted to help then, but Paladine wouldn't let him. It wasn't time, Paladine said. It was the same, I know, during the Cataclysm. Again my father wanted to help, but Paladine forbade it. Only now, only when Paladine himself decreed it possible could my father return to Krynn." Liam looked like a small, guilty child. "And only because he wasn't watching over me anymore was I able to visit Krynn myself."

Liam had sneaked out of whatever celestial realm he had existed in while his parents were busy elsewhere? On the one hand, Stoddard was so amused by the tale that he nearly smiled. On the other hand, the story was so pathetic as to sadden him. Likely Liam was the son of some farmer killed during the present campaign, a survivor who wanted so desperately to make amends that he fancied himself a hero.

Stoddard politely responded, "You've done what you could, son. I thank you for that. But I recommend that you leave the fighting to those who have trained for it."

"But—"

Stoddard could not afford to be too gentle. Each moment they were delayed lessened what little chance they had of aiding the city. They had to hurry, even leave the dead unburied.

And what will we do even if we reach Aramus in time? Stoddard asked himself. Three injured knights and a crippled old dragon . . .

It did not matter. They were Knights of Solamnia. The Oath and the Measure demanded the utmost.

He turned to Ferrin, who had remained nearby, clearly distrustful of their mad companion. "It is time to muster our forces." The commander did not even glance at Liam of Eldor, but he could sense him listening and hoping for another opportunity to plead his case. "Awaken Crandel. See if he is fit to travel. Survey the area and see what equipment might still be of use to us." Stoddard paused. "If you can do anything speedily for some of the bodies, go ahead. I will go and speak to the bronze. I have a plan in mind."

"Can you walk so far, my lord? I could lead you over—"

"I will do it on my own, thank you." His legs wobbled, but sheer willpower kept him going. After taking a deep breath, the Knight of the Rose started slowly in the direction Ferrin indicated.

He found the injured bronze leviathan lying on his side, with his wounded limb dangling. The dragon opened his eyes as the human approached.

"Lord Stoddard . . ."

The rumbling voice was a pleasure to hear. It was the first time since the disaster that the knight did not have to strain to make out another's words. "Razer. How do you fare?"

"Hmm? Fare? I live . . . that's more than can be said of the others, eh? What happened?"

"You do not recall the chaos dragon?"

The elderly bronze stared. "Oh, yesss. That thing." His eyes widened in sudden recollection. "That *thing*. It tore their throats out!" The dragon suddenly tried to rise but made the mistake of attempting to put weight on his injured limb. He nearly collapsed onto his visitor, who stumbled back. "I'll tear *it* apart!"

Strong arms caught Lord Stoddard. "I've got you, my lord."

Wrenching himself free, Stoddard eyed the peculiar young man. The ever-present Liam was beginning to unnerve him. He had not expected the boy to accompany him to the dragon. "Thank you, but I can make do without your aid."

Nodding sadly, the youth retreated. The senior knight turned to find the bronze dragon peering at the newcomer. Razer appeared to have forgotten his injuries as he studied Liam of Eldor. "I don't know you," the dragon rumbled. Reptilian eyes narrowed. "Or do I? I forget so much . . ."

"Lord Stoddard," Liam interrupted, his voice quivering slightly. For someone who claimed he was ready to do battle with a dragon, Liam did not seem prepared to be confronted by even a friendly one. The young man was shaking now. "The chaos dragon should be nearly recovered from its exhaustion. Aramus isn't far away! We must hurry! We might still have time to save the people!"

"True!" roared Razer, his inspection of the young human over and done with in light of these urgent words. "How many knights remain, my lord knight?"

"Only three of us. We are wounded but functional. I do not know, though, how much we can do against that monster—"

"If I have to use my hind legs to kick it all the way back to its master, I will try, Lord Stoddard, but it would greatly improve the odds if I had a knight with a lance on my back! I'm ancient, and I know that. I'll take whatever odds I can get."

The Knight of the Rose mulled over matters. They had some ordinary lances, but none of the legendary dragonlances. For the most part, those were in the hands of the Knights of Takhisis. Stoddard and his men would just have to make do with the weapons at hand. At least their lances were sharp and well-crafted; surely they would be enough to pierce the hide of the starlit abomination. It was the only course of action they could attempt. "I think we can find at least one serviceable lance. As for a knight to wield it, you need look no further than myself, Razer."

The bronze dragon actually chuckled. "That's the spirit! We'll rip the beast's throat out just as it did to my companions!"

Stoddard knew Razer would do whatever Paladine deemed possible. Leaving the bronze to recuperate a little longer, the senior knight returned to the scene of the carnage, still trailed by Liam.

"I should be the one to take your place, Lord Stoddard," the young man insisted loudly. "I admit I've not been trained in the knighthood and this is the first time I've really experienced combat, but I—"

"With each word you utter, you are making as good a case against yourself as I myself could, lad." Stoddard paused to look Liam in the eye. "Go back to wherever it is you come from—Eldor or the heavens, I do not care which— and remain there until it's all over." He turned away and continued on without waiting to see if Liam would try to follow him once more.

The senior knight found Ferrin and Crandel slowly going about the task of arranging some of the dead and their belongings. Crandel, a Knight of the Sword whose appetite had always gotten the best of him, noticed the commander first and slowly straightened to attention. The left side of his head was bound with cloth and one arm was wrapped against his torso. His round face was pale, drenched in sweat.

It was clear that Crandel would not be able to take the place of Stoddard on the dragon's back even if the senior knight preferred for him to do so. That left only Ferrin with which to deal. Ferrin would certainly think he was the most logical candidate to ride into battle against a creature they had little hopes of wounding, much less defeating. And Ferrin was probably correct.

"I need the best lance that you can find," Stoddard informed them. His eyes drifted to one of the already-salvaged weapons, its twisted form clearly disqualifying it from further use. "There has to be at least one in proper condition."

As expected, Ferrin raised objections to Stoddard's role in

the plan. "My lord, you should not risk yourself on the back of the dragon. I am the one least injured and—"

"—and the one in the prime of life, I suppose," Stoddard growled. "You have been given a command, Ferrin. Locate a lance for me. That is all."

"Why not simply use the one the boy brought with him?"

The other knight had spoken too quietly. "What was that?" asked Stoddard.

Ferrin repeated what he had said, then pointed off to the west. For the first time, Stoddard scrutinized Liam's massive steed and the equipment lying next to it. The horse, upon close inspection, was a marvel, a brown giant larger than any the knight had seen before, but what interested him most was the lance Ferrin indicated. Long and sleek, clearly fashioned by a skilled smith, Liam's lance may have been old and stained, but it was in far better condition than any of the weapons they were likely to find.

Belatedly he realized that beside the lance rested a dented, worn sword and armor that, while somewhat archaic and rusted, had to have once belonged to a Knight of Solamnia. So Liam was the son or descendent of a knight, unless he had stolen the armor from some grave.

He did not want to think about grave robbing. The important thing was, Ferrin was right; the lance Liam had brought along on his insane quest was perfect for their need. Stoddard nodded. Ferrin started toward the weapon.

"What are you doing?" asked Liam, who, though a respectful distance behind them, had heard their every word.

The Knight of the Rose blocked his way. "We need that lance, son. You yourself have reminded us how important it is we stop that beast before it seeks to destroy Aramus. Well, that lance and the bronze are our only hope! If you want to truly fight the menace, you will help us now by staying out of the way."

"But I've got the best chance . . . and the only chance of any of us! And I have to use that lance! You just don't understand!" Liam started after Ferrin, but Crandel stepped into his path and easily tripped the young man. Liam fell face first into the dirt. Before he could rise, Crandel planted a foot squarely on his back, pinning him to the earth.

"Let him up, man." Stoddard took the youth's arm and helped him to his feet, but Liam slipped from his grasp and darted toward Ferrin.

The other knight lowered the lance and put his hand on his sword. Liam paused.

"If I may, my lord," called Ferrin. "Perhaps I can convince this one of his foolishness by giving him his first taste of the skills needed to survive combat."

Stoddard nodded gravely. In one swift motion Ferrin reached down and seized the old blade next to the armor, gently tossing it toward the young man, who stared at it a moment before picking it up. Liam looked at the knights in some confusion.

Drawing his own blade, Ferrin faced the lad. "Show me how well you fight. Show us what the son of Huma of the Lance can do."

Liam started. Lord Stoddard once again gave Ferrin the nod. A grim expression spread across the youth's face. Holding the sword in both hands, he took a step toward Ferrin, tentatively swinging his blade.

The knight twisted slightly, so that his opponent's weapon cleaved the air. The weight of Liam's blade carried him forward, stumbling to the ground. Stepping back, Ferrin waited until Liam had regained his balance, then made his own attack.

To Stoddard, who knew the other knight's skill, it was clear that Ferrin was toying with him. Ferrin's blade flicked again and again, each time easily pushing through Liam's guard. Not once did he so much as graze the boy, but Liam had to know that he was being merciful.

Another wild swing left Liam wide open. This time, his adversary did not hold back. Ferrin brought his sword up, striking Liam's hands with the flat of his blade. Yelping, the boy released his hold, his own weapon landing harmlessly at the knight's feet.

"Yes, I would say you are ready to face the beast," Ferrin commented with a condescending smile. "Especially if you want to be its supper."

Anger overwhelmed Liam of Eldor. "It wasn't fair! I wasn't prepared!"

Stoddard and Crandel came up behind the boy. "That's the point, though, is it not, lad?" returned the senior knight. "Besides, even prepared, you would do little better than you did now."

"I could so." Still furious, Liam started after Ferrin again, but Stoddard seized one arm and held fast. Crandel gripped Liam on the other side. Finally the youth calmed down.

"I am sorry, son, but we have no more time for this. We need your weapon. We know how best to wield it. You should see that even with all your good intentions, you lack much of the necessary training. Even the son of Huma of the Lance needs experience in battle."

The boy did not answer him, his attention still focused on Ferrin and his lance.

"You do see my point, Liam?" The senior knight hoped that he did. If not, it might be necessary to use more forceful measures to keep the young man from interfering.

"Yes . . . yes, sir, I see," Liam said finally.

Nodding to Crandel, Stoddard released him.

While the youth looked on resentfully, the three knights began the arduous process of carrying the lance back to the dragon over the uneven ground.

The bronze stirred, his eyes gleaming when he saw what they had. "Found a worthy lance, did you, humans? Doesn't look like much, but I suppose it'll do!"

They lacked a proper saddle, but Ferrin managed to concoct a substitute. It did not have to be perfect; all of them knew that the rider would get one, maybe two strikes at the chaos dragon before the monstrosity struck back.

Throughout it all, they paid little attention to Liam, so little that when Stoddard finally looked around for him, he at first thought that the young man had fled. Liam was unstable enough to attempt something foolhardy with or without the lance.

You can do nothing more for him if he has gone off on some wild quest, Stoddard told himself. Worry about Aramus and its people.

However, Liam had not run away. The knight noticed him at last, standing and looking out over the devastation wrought by the chaos dragon. In one hand he held the rusted sword. As the Knight of the Rose observed him, Liam threw down the sword in disgust and sat himself down upon a rock, where he buried his face in his hands.

Leaving the young man to his own inner demons, the veteran warrior turned to his companions. His concentration now fully trained on saving Aramus, he addressed the old bronze. "Razer, is there any chance that you could carry all three of us?"

"I . . . could. For a very short time. Aramus isn't far. I don't know how much strength I would have with which to fight after the journey, though."

"So be it. Then only one of us will ride, the one who wields the lance. Ferrin, you and Crandel will take the remaining horse and keep up as best you can—"

"My lord," interrupted Ferrin, eyes calculatingly narrowed. "I wish you would reconsider! I am the lightest. I will be the least burden for the dragon. I say again, I should go in your place!"

"The decision has been made." Stoddard stared at the other knight until Ferrin finally assented. Moving closer, he added, "I have one more command for you. Do what you can for the lad. Bring him with you. He should not be out here alone in his condition."

Clearly it was not a duty that the other desired to perform, but Ferrin was a loyal soldier. "I will try to teach him some of the duties of a squire. If we survive perhaps he may yet become a knight."

"Very good." Stoddard believed no more than Ferrin that such a thing would actually happen. If the Knight of the Rose and Razer failed, it was likely that they would all be dead before the next day, or two at most, had passed.

"Are you ready, Razer?"

"I've been ready for quite some time, human. I look forward to the challenge!"

The leviathan's bloodlust encouraged the warrior. He needed Razer eager and sharp.

Ferrin and Crandel saluted. Stoddard returned their salute, then positioned himself. The lance rested comfortably in his grip despite the makeshift saddle.

"Lord Stoddard!"

A hand on his arm made him start. The knight glanced to the other side and found the stubborn Liam there. Recovering from his surprise, he snapped, "Stand aside, lad! We need to be off. You stick with Ferrin and Crandel. They will endeavor to teach you a thing or two."

"But you have to listen to me! There's a secret you ought to know!"

"I think you've told us enough secrets—"

"It's about the lance . . ." Liam leaned closer and muttered something of which Stoddard could catch only a fragment. When he realized that he had spoken too quietly, Liam tried again. "It's one of the original dragonlances, my lord."

"It's what?" Stoddard actually took a second look at the weapon before realizing how foolish it all sounded. The lance was a suitable tool, but hardly one of the magical weapons of lore. No dragonlance he ever heard of could possibly look so worn and dingy.

His eyes glowing, Liam continued. "It is! One of the very ones my father used." He noted Stoddard's skeptical expression. "I swear it's true!" Aware that he still had not convinced the knight, the youth reached to grip the lance. "Once you see it in all its glory, you'll believe."

Stoddard cocked his head, waiting. Liam clutched the lance, staring at it as if something would happen. However, the weapon did not suddenly gleam with the light of Paladine's blessing. It did not grow and stretch its point so sharp that not even the toughest dragon hide could withstand it. It remained an all-too-earthly weapon.

The Knight of the Rose gently removed Liam's hand. "I thank you for your concern, lad, but we cannot delay any longer. Stick with Ferrin and Crandel."

"But—" Liam seemed to deflate.

"I will meet with you in Aramus. Paladine watch over you." The senior knight nodded to his counterparts, who saluted him. To Razer he added, "I am ready."

"Hold tight, then! Stand away, humans!" The moment it was safe to do so, the bronze dragon spread his wings, rising swiftly into the air. Stoddard watched his companions down on the ground retreat, then clouds obscured his view. He prayed to Paladine for the safety of not only his men, but of Liam of Eldor and all the inhabitants of Aramus, then remembered belatedly to ask for some protection for himself.

Against the chaos dragon, he would accept all the aid the gods could grant him.

* * * * *

Stoddard must have nodded off despite the desperation of the situation, for the next thing he knew, Razer was shouting to him.

"I see the port city, but no sign of the beast!"

His partial deafness and the coursing winds made it nearly impossible to make out the bellowing words of the bronze leviathan. The knight leaned forward, shouting, "How does the city look? Is there much damage?"

This time, Razer's voice rang clearer. "I see no smoke or wreckage, but the sun is going down and we are still a little too far away for these old eyes of mine! Give me a moment or two more, then I can say for sure!"

It would be a miracle if the chaos dragon had not yet attacked Aramus, but Stoddard nurtured hope. He waited for what seemed an eternity before the dragon cried, "It looks intact! The towers, the roofs, and even the walls! I see ships sailing into the harbor!"

Praise Paladine! Stoddard shouted in his head. Apparently Liam had been correct in this one regard. Despite the seeming ease with which the chaos beast had decimated the knights, it evidently had exerted itself and did need time to recuperate.

Of course, that left unanswered the question of where it was at this precise moment.

Razer turned his head toward Stoddard. "Do we land at the city gates?"

RICHARD A. KNAAK

With no sign of the chaos dragon, Stoddard thought it best to do so promptly. At least they could warn the inhabitants about what was coming. Perhaps Aramus could start an evacuation. Certainly the people risked more by staying rather than fleeing. They could always return . . . provided the knight and his reptilian companion somehow seized victory.

"Yes, proceed to land!"

Razer turned his gaze away and started his descent. Stoddard found himself sighing in relief. Admittedly, he preferred to stall as long as possible before facing the chaos dragon. His hearing might never be the same again, but his other injuries needed time to heal.

Razer, too, needed rest. Sitting atop the dragon, Stoddard could feel the effort of each ragged breath of his massive companion. The ancient creature had pushed himself to the limit to reach Aramus so soon.

Despite there still being some sunlight, stars were already visible in one quarter of the heavens. The knight recalled that it had been daylight when the chaos dragon had attacked the Solamnic force. That fact did not necessarily rule out a night assault from their enemy, but it did raise his hopes that they had at least until morning.

"Bind yourself as best you can, human! I've only got three good limbs on which to land, so I can't promise perfection!"

Stoddard did as demanded, bracing himself. For the first time he recalled that he had not eaten all day, something that benefitted him now. Razer's landing did not promise to be a smooth one, and the thought of a full stomach—

The ground suddenly rippled and shook.

The bronze dragon barely rose up in time to avoid being swallowed by the shifting earth. It was all Stoddard could do to avoid falling off as Razer wheeled on his side and swooped back up into the air. The knight caught sight of the nearest city walls already beginning to crumble, but could think no longer of Aramus.

"Where is he? Where is he?" The bronze giant righted himself, peering around in the growing darkness. "I don't see him anywhere!"

Shaking his head, the knight could no longer see any stars. "To your left!" he suddenly shouted. "To your left and above!"

The chaos dragon made no further attempt to hide itself. A portion of the sky rippled and swirled, forming into the whirling star field that vaguely resembled a dragon. Its glittering, soulless eyes focused on its foes, who steeled themselves for a frontal assault.

"Ready yourself!" Stoddard and Razer both found fresh determination in the rush of adrenaline. The bronze pushed forward, swiftly narrowing the gap between himself and his adversary. All trace of weariness had vanished.

Stoddard prepared the lance. They only needed one good strike.

The chaos dragon opened its huge maw, but now, instead of the deafening roar, it spoke.

"You . . . will . . . die."

With that, it slammed into Razer. The bronze tried to grapple with it, but despite his immense size, he was dwarfed by the chaos dragon. Stoddard tried to steady the lance, but it was impossible to find the mark in the warped reality created by the monster.

They were all but dead now. The knight realized that. They were as good as dead and everyone below would follow. Despite the best efforts of the knight and the dragon, the creature had easily conquered them. It had laid in waiting for them: a classic trap and the pair had flown blithely into it.

The chaos dragon tried to sink its fangs into Razer's throat, but the crafty old bronze dodged it by keeping his head low. Unfortunately, he could not protect his wings as well, and these his monstrous foe rent as they fought. It became harder and harder for Razer to keep aloft and completely impossible for Stoddard to find any position in which to maneuver the lance.

"I . . . am losing my ability . . . to fly," gasped Razer. "I'm sorry, Lord Stoddard . . . I'm sorry."

It was all the knight could do simply to stay in the saddle. Roaring its triumph, the chaos dragon released its hold on

Razer. The bronze tried to swipe at the monster, but failed even that gesture. Both dragon and rider plummeted.

To his credit, Razer did his best to cushion both of them. The dragon used what was left of his ability to fly to slow their rapid descent. Nonetheless, when Razer at last struck the earth, the knight was thrown from his saddle.

Stoddard landed on his side, the pain from his earlier injuries magnified a hundredfold as he bounced and rolled over the ground. At last he came to a stop, hurting with such intensity that even to breathe brought him agony. Lying on his back, the veteran warrior stared up at the sky from which he had fallen, seeing nothing. There was only the pain.

Thankfully, he lost consciousness.

When he woke, evidently not more than a few seconds later, it was to find Razer an unmoving form and himself unable even to sit up. The old dragon was clearly dead, having twisted his neck upon impact. He had sacrificed himself to save his human rider. Stoddard almost wished for oblivion, but then he saw the vast form of the chaos dragon dart overhead. A part of him wondered why, with the beast so close by, the land around him was stable.

A hand gently slipped under his back. With the newcomer's aid, Stoddard managed a sitting position. He was astonished to discover no broken bones. Twice now he had survived disaster. The knight did not know whether to give thanks for his incredible luck or curse the fact that twice now he had suffered extreme defeat.

"I'm sorry, Lord Stoddard. I took longer than I thought. I guess the trap was meant for me. I think it knows I've been pursuing it."

"L-Liam?" Again? It was not possible. The boy should be far behind with Ferrin and Crandel. He could not have journeyed so far in so short a time. Stoddard had never known a horse to be so swift.

"Yes, sir. Here, drink this." A hand came around and placed a small water sack next to his lips.

Stoddard began to drink, then noticed the hand. It was clad in a gauntlet much like his own, emblazoned by the sign of the crown. The gauntlet was rusted and battered.

The senior knight forgot about both his injuries and his thirst. "Liam, how did you—"

"There's no time, sir." The hand released him and a figure stepped around in front of him, a figure whose every movement was accompanied by the clank of metal on metal.

Liam of Eldor stood before him clad in the full, if somewhat ragged, regalia of a Knight of the Crown, the same order to which his supposed father, Huma of the Lance, had belonged. The visor of the old helmet was up, revealing the earnest young man's pale features.

Looking at him, Stoddard felt almost like weeping. The foolish lad's obsession had such a hold on him that Liam could not see he was flirting with death. All the armor would do was attract the chaos beast's attention. It would certainly not stand up to assault.

The chaos dragon chose that moment to swoop overhead again. It was circling closer to the port city, obviously preparing for its killing spree. Around the beast, the sky roared with thunder. Lightning flashed repeatedly.

"I have to stop it . . ." The Knight of the Rose tried his best to stand, though his legs refused to obey him.

Liam said something, but Stoddard only heard unintelligible sounds. The would-be knight leaned closer. "I said that your right leg is bleeding profusely, my lord. Can't you feel it?"

He could not. The entire leg was numb.

"You shouldn't move." The young man drew back. "I thought I could make it here before you . . . but I failed again." Liam glanced upward. "I won't fail this time. By my father, that I swear, Lord Stoddard."

It was too much. Stoddard had had enough of the young man's delusions. "You are *not* the son of Huma of the Lance, lad! He lived . . . centuries ago! If you try to confront that creature you will only succeed in killing yourself!"

The young man continued to gaze at the monster. "My father was a knight. He dedicated his life to honor and the protection of others. Est Sularus oth Mithas. I've always wanted to emulate him. I was meant to follow in his footsteps."

"Listen to me, boy! You—"

Liam stiffened, his eyes widening at some sight beyond the senior knight's vision. "I have waited too long. It's heading toward Aramus. This is my last chance."

Liam made a move toward Razer's still form. Stoddard reached out, seizing hold of the boy's ankle. "There's nothing you can do by yourself! Help me to your horse! Together we can ride to Aramus and at least help guide a few of its people to safety!"

"No. I must save the city. I must save *everyone*."

Despite his best efforts, Stoddard could not maintain his grip. Liam pulled free and hurried off. The Knight of the Rose dragged himself around, trying to keep an eye on the brave but addled young man.

Liam retrieved the old lance from where it had fallen, hefting it with surprising ease. He whistled and his miraculous horse trotted into view. Despite the size of the lance, Liam bound it swiftly and securely in place, then mounted his huge steed. With one last regretful look at Stoddard, he rode off.

"By Paladine! No!" Drawing upon strength he did not even know he had left, the knight managed to rise to his feet and stumble after Liam for a few steps. He made it only as far as Razer before slumping to the ground. The figure receded in the distance, dwarfed by the horrific form circling high above the doomed port city. It would have made for a glorious episode in some heroic epic save that Stoddard understood the futility of it all. There would be nothing heroic about either the destruction of Aramus or the death of the young man.

Perhaps the beast will not even notice him, thought Stoddard.

No sooner had Stoddard voiced that thought, however, then the chaos dragon, seeming to overhear him, suddenly whirled around. Turning from Aramus, the dragon headed straight toward Liam of Eldor.

Whatever the truth of Liam's heritage, something about him had indeed caught the attention of the chaos dragon. Now it raced toward him like a starved wolf toward a staked lamb. Eagerness radiated from the beast. The destruction of Aramus had been relegated to a distant concern compared to destroying this foolish mortal who thought he was a knight.

Stoddard knew exactly what would happen next, though he prayed that he was wrong. The behemoth dived toward Liam, who raised the lance as high as he could while urging his brave steed on. The chaos beast roared . . . and suddenly the landscape surrounding the tiny figure on horseback shifted and twisted. Hills sank, new ones formed. Lightning struck with renewed fury and a mighty wind threatened to rip trees from the earth.

"Run, Liam," the knight whispered. "At least make a dash for it! He might get distracted . . . lose interest."

Liam did not budge, however. He continued on his collision course. His weathered lance seemed a pitifully small weapon against so great and terrible a leviathan.

A sudden swell before them tossed both rider and animal backward. The horse jerked around as it flew through the air, its death a certainty even before it smashed into the ground. Liam was tossed even higher, almost as if he were destined to meet the dragon in the sky.

Stumbling to his feet, Stoddard managed a dozen steps before exhaustion overtook him again. His head swam and he nearly blacked out. Unfortunately, he could do little but watch with horror as Liam tumbled to the ground.

Lightning struck, momentarily obscuring the final passing of Liam of Eldor. The dragon of chaos flew overhead, its huge maw unleashing yet another roar of triumph.

Tears rolled down the senior knight's cheeks, tears for a deluded quest. Mad Liam might have been, but his bravery would have done any warrior proud. It was one of the tragedies of war that such bravery of the common folk so often went unremembered.

The chaos dragon began to circle back, clearly once more intent on the destruction of Aramus. The wholesale slaughter to come sickened Stoddard even more than the sadly inevitable death of Liam.

Questions filled Stoddard's head. *Paladine! I know that you fight the struggle elsewhere, but cannot some of your* divine power be used to save Aramus? Is there nothing that can be done?

Lightning crackled again, illuminating the ruined landscape where one brave soul had delayed the coming tragedy for at least a few minutes.

The knight blinked.

A ragged figure stood there, trying with effort to raise the lance. Lightning struck once more, seeming to leave a glow around the man and the weapon. For some reason now, Stoddard thought, the lance looked longer, deadlier than before.

The chaos dragon was fixated on the feast of souls ahead and yet for some reason it happened to look back . . . and suddenly its fury was renewed. The huge beast roared and turned in an arc toward the insect that did not have the good manners to die. The star field that was its body swirled with an intensity that mirrored the monster's anger.

The fearsome sight turned Stoddard's stomach. How many times would he have to witness the lad's death?

Liam propped the back end of the lance on the ground, then gripped the weapon as if he meant to hurl it at the chaos dragon. Insane Liam most certainly was, but to Stoddard there was something in him that could have been worthy of a son of Huma of the Lance.

The chaos dragon dived toward Liam, its maw open in a piercing scream. Even as far away as he was, and despite his partial deafness, the noise made the knight wince. How Liam could maintain his stand under such an assault truly amazed him.

Stand the lad did, though, the lightning giving both his armor and the lance a strange shine. The leviathan continued its ear-splitting scream. Long talons stretched toward Liam. The land grew violently fluid.

This time he will not survive, thought Stoddard. Paladine, watch over him.

As if Stoddard's words had been taken to heart by the great god, a sudden change came over Liam. He glowed brighter than ever. He appeared to grow larger and, as the knight watched, larger yet, his shape somehow changing. His form grew longer, sleeker . . . and turned a shimmering silver. Wings burst from his back, ripping through his armor like tissue.

Now he was a gleaming silver dragon, as large as Razer, that stood poised on hind legs, gazing up at the charging monstrosity. Stoddard almost forgot his amazement as he admired his beautiful strength and shimmering form—in some ways manlike, in others clearly reptilian.

I am the product of their union. Their son.

Stoddard's mind reeled, filled with half-forgotten tales of Huma, tales which included Huma's love for an elven woman who turned out to be the silver dragon known as Heart.

It cannot be, Stoddard kept repeating to himself. Liam cannot be who he says he is.

The change that had come over the lance was just as remarkable. No longer did it seem aged. Now it, too, was smooth, gleaming, and its tip so sharply pointed that it promised to pierce even the toughest hide.

A dragonlance. Even if it weren't glowing, Stoddard would have recognized it for what it was . . . for what Liam had said it was.

If Stoddard had been startled by Liam's transformation, the chaos dragon was likewise stunned. The behemoth virtually halted in midair, its terrible cry cut off as it tried to make sense out of what had happened to its once-insignificant prey.

With paws that resembled hands, the silver dragon raised the magical lance and threw it toward his foe.

The dragonlance struck true, piercing the servant of Chaos in the chest while it was still trying to recover its momentum. What seemed fire and molten lava burst from the wound, showering the silver dragon below. The monster roared its agony. As it shook in pain, the air and earth around it also quivered. Lightning flared, torrential winds blew, and the earth shook.

The silver dragon suddenly dropped to all fours, clearly beset by some sort of agony, although Stoddard could not puzzle out what was happening. While he was occupied so, the chaos dragon recovered enough to try to pull the lance free. Seeing that, the silver dragon took to the sky.

The light of Order clashed with the madness of Chaos as the pair collided only a short distance above the ground. The chaos dragon roared as the silver's bulk shoved the magical lance in deeper. A new, furious storm burst from the monster's chest, a violent eruption that caught the silver in the face.

Blinded, he could not dodge the talons that slashed at his head and ripped through the side of his neck, sending a shower of blood to the ground below.

The wound was a serious one, but the silver did not soften his assault. He used his weight to press the dragonlance deeper and deeper. The chaos monster raised its head high and, as Stoddard watched helplessly, unleashed a great torrent of fire and black rain that washed over the silver dragon.

The force of the assault flung the silver back. On fire, he spiraled earthward, crashing hard against a hillside. Stoddard prayed he would rise again, but the courageous silver remained motionless.

The chaos dragon had little opportunity to savor its triumph. Flame and black rain continued to burst from its chest. It tried to remain aloft, but its flying grew wild and reckless. The deeply embedded lance tormented the beast. It roared, the lightning and thunder seeming to echo its pain.

Then a bolt of lightning struck the metallic lance. The chaos beast lurched. A second struck, then a third.

Four jagged bolts hit the dragonlance in unison, and the chaos dragon exploded.

Even from far away, the force with which the leviathan exploded was enough to send Lord Stoddard reeling to the ground. A shower of fire filled his view—the remnants of the monster falling earthward.

Stoddard struck the ground headfirst and his helmet could not save him from oblivion.

* * * * *

A brilliant light dragged him away from the comforting darkness. Stoddard opened his eyes to see what had to be torchlight illuminating Razer's battered form. A hand gingerly touched his shoulder, and someone shouted, "This one looks to be alive!"

Several figures moved into the veteran warrior's field of vision. There were at least six, two fairly old men and the rest young lads not quite into manhood. The apparent leader, a thin elder who likely had spent more days of his life as a fisherman than as a warrior, saluted Stoddard, then said something that the knight could not make out.

When the man finally realized what was wrong, he raised his voice. "I asked if there were any more of you around here."

Stoddard nodded. "The other . . . dragon . . . the boy."

The thin elder figure muttered something to one of his younger companions, who muttered something back. Frustrated with his inability to understand them, the injured knight tried to rise.

The leader put a hand on his arm. "Easy now. Forgot that you don't seem to be able to hear that well. It's a wonder we're not all hard of hearing after that beast. What the boy said was that we only found you and one other knight, the one from the Order of the Crown. We also found the bronze there and the starlit monster in pieces all over the place."

Stoddard shook his groggy head. "No. Not—" He paused. What about the silver dragon? "Please . . . I need to see the other knight."

"If you think you can move well enough . . ." The patrol leader snapped his fingers. Two of the young men helped Lord Stoddard to his feet. "By the way, I'm Acting Guard Commander Billus and this modest lot comprises the bulk of our city's defenses right now. You are—?"

"Lord Stoddard." But the knight paid his rescuer little mind; he was more concerned with the still form they were leading him toward. The riders from Aramus had laid the figure on a makeshift sled hooked up to one horse. Someone had partially covered the body with a blanket, but Stoddard could see the facial features.

Liam. Liam in human form.

"Found him on a hillside. His back was broken. So were

his arms and a leg. Must have taken a nasty tumble from the top of the hill. He was already dead when we arrived."

Liam had transformed into a dragon, but here he was now, human and once more clad in the ancient armor. How was that possible? The knight continued to stare at the still figure.

"I'm sorry about what happened to your friend here and to the bronze dragon, too," Billus commented, trying to soothe Stoddard's heartache. "We all saw the beginning of the battle and how the bronze and his rider tried their best. When the two of them fell out of the sky, we were certain we were next. Then we could just barely make out what happened next. The bronze dragon. Brave creature, that. Kept coming back. We shall honor both of them for their efforts." The acting commander sighed. "Still can't believe it! Everything seemed lost, then in the end the storm itself saves us. Lightning! Can you believe it? Lightning just comes out of the sky and strikes the monster again and again! Must've been the hand of Paladine himself!"

Stoddard finally tore his gaze from Liam as he realized what the other man was saying. "It was not Paladine. It was him. The true hero of this battle was Liam of Eldor. The son of Huma of the Lance."

Around him, the soldiers of Aramus paused in their activity. Billus blinked. "I must be a bit deaf after all. What did you say?" He looked at the body. "Who'd you say this one was?"

Before he realized what he was doing, the words spilled out of the veteran warrior. "Liam of Eldor. The son of Huma and the silver dragon . . ." The tale came easily now that he believed. Liam had spoken the truth. How else to explain all that he had witnessed? How else could the chaos dragon have been defeated?

They listened. He gave them credit for that. However, they clearly did not believe him, even though as a Knight of Solamnia his word should have been accepted as truth. He read doubt in their faces as the story culminated in the thrown lance, the struggle between titans, and the lightning drawn to the dragonlance even after the beast had slain the brave silver dragon. They listened, but they did not quite believe.

"The son of Huma?" Billus squinted at the body, then studied his companions. "Who took charge of the lance we salvaged?"

A youth built like a blacksmith stepped forward. "Got it over here, sir."

With the commander in the lead, the group walked over and inspected the weapon. Billus's tone became even more skeptical. "A dragonlance. It's sturdy, I'll give it that, but it looks mighty rusted for one of Paladine's blessed weapons."

Stoddard did not deny that. The lance looked as he had first seen it, a poor relic that appeared to have been left out in the elements for much too long. There were not even any scorch marks from where the lightning had repeatedly struck it.

He began to wonder if he had imagined the entire episode. Perhaps he had dreamed the curious events. Perhaps . . .

The commander led them away. "Well, son of Huma or not, what's clear is that he was a brave lad who gave his life for us riding the bronze into battle. We'll treat his memory right, believe me. In the meantime, I think we need to get you to a healer. Quickly."

There was no use trying to convince them; they would never believe. Ferrin and Crandel might, but even they would probably suspect that their commander had simply imagined the entire drama while reeling from his injuries. Even Stoddard had to wonder . . . but no, he couldn't have imagined everything!

"There'll probably be a celebration tomorrow and a funeral of honor for your friend," added Billus as the guards helped the wounded knight mount one of the horses. "Tomorrow we'll also do something for the bronze."

They thought that Liam and not Stoddard had ridden Razer into combat. It would have to suffice. Liam would at least get the honor due him as a member of the Solamnic Order. Whether or not he was the son of Huma, he would be remembered for his bravery, for his honor during a time of crisis. He would be remembered for his ultimate sacrifice.

"Est Sularus oth Mithas," the Knight of the Rose whispered, as one of the guards pulled the blanket over the young warrior's face. Many, many more brave souls, human and otherwise, would be sacrificed in the course of the war against Chaos, but for now, one city would celebrate a most extraordinary protector.

Liam of Eldor, Knight of the Crown . . . and to Stoddard, there was little doubt, the son of Huma.

Personal
Kevin T. Stein

"I will have the thief dead, and the girdle returned," Malefiche had said. "But the thief's death is more important. Remember that, Borac. Kill the thief. After this, I will not have need of you for some time."

Pressed against the shadows of a dark walkway, Borac peered around the corner into the narrow, crowded street, the words of his patron lingering in his thoughts. Malefiche was a cleric high in the ranks of Takhisis's chosen, and, as a black dragon, Borac was obligated to follow the man's orders. However, something in the way the cleric spoke, something in his insistence that the thief be killed, made Borac cautious. Malefiche was powerful and clever, but not more intelligent than a dragon. Not more intelligent than Borac himself.

Ultimately, humans could not be trusted. If only he could divine the cleric's ulterior plan. There were rumors of a deadly "secret guard," from which no one was safe—not even the Dark Queen's own dragons. And there were some dragons missing . . . The answer would come in time.

This part of town was filled with activity. It was that time of night when good people were going to sleep and the adventuresome were ready to have some fun. Or what they considered fun. The only thing Borac had in common with humans was a love of gambling.

The two men with him—and they were men, not dragons in human form like himself—waited in the alleyway behind, waited for their orders. Borac fingered the amulet around his neck that granted him a human's body, a stronger and better looking one than either of theirs, he thought. He was tall, dark, and yes, handsome, except for his left eye, which was milky white, dead. The two henchmen did not know Borac was a dragon, a fact which he would reveal to them only under dire circumstances.

The town reeked with the scent of humans, the smell of their fear and boredom. Fear was one of the many human weaknesses Borac despised. He hoped the two men behind him followed his example of "strength through decision," as he liked to call it.

He cared nothing about the two men, not even their names. He called them Gray and Black. Gray was of medium height, thin, with fine, quick hands. He was good with a knife. Black was stronger than Gray, wider in the shoulders, with strong arms. Both men had dark, close-cropped hair, dark brown eyes, and the same type of shabby clothes. There was little to distinguish them from anyone else in this border town. They could be mercenaries, or soldiers, or travelers. They could be anyone. And as Borac's . . . minions—no, his trainees—if a local saw them holding a bloody dagger while executing their duties, nobody would be able to pick them out of a crowd. Just two more anonymous faces. They were, in fact, dressed the same as Borac.

Gray and Black were Borac's . . . backup. He scorned to consider them bodyguards. As two seasoned soldiers, they could easily handle themselves in a fight. And Borac could easily sacrifice them to save himself if necessary. And the weapons they carried, weapons garnered from his own personal armory, were enchanted. Valuable, but not overly so, and not of much use to a dragon. Borac would willingly sacrifice these as well.

Borac continued to stroke the amulet, carefully watching the door to a particular tavern. Black dragons could not change their shape at will, as could other dragons. The amulet had been a gift from Malefiche, when the two had forged their first alliance. Black dragons were known for their independence, so the alliance was one of convenience. Malefiche bought Borac's service with the amulet, which the dragon had long coveted. It allowed Borac to change to human form, but unfortunately it carried a curse with it. If mortally wounded as a human, Borac would not return to dragon form, which might be the only means of saving himself. He detested the thought of dying in human form.

The tavern Borac watched bore no name on its hanging

sign, only the poorly engraved image of a boar run through with a broken spear. His "assignment"—the thief—was staying in the tavern's upstairs room. Borac did not know the man's name, but he was easily distinguished by a stocky frame, flaming red hair, and the girdle over whatever armor he chose to wear. Plain-looking, made of tooled leather, the girdle was actually magical.

Borac hissed a sigh. He would kill this nameless little thief, accomplish the mission without fail; he always succeeded. But it was all such a waste. He hated Malefiche for his willingness to trade the life of a dragon for that of a human, and for the completion of whatever else Malefiche had in mind. Borac hated all humans for their petty, ambitious, short-sighted behavior.

However, hatred had no influence on the mission. He did not hate this thief, nor anyone else he had killed for the Dark Queen. Hatred was not . . . professional, as the humans called it. Borac knew full well the folly of personal involvement with a kill. The moment an assassin struck out of anger, revenge, or pleasure, he was dead. There was a graveyard of humans who had listened to Borac's teachings, ignored them, and died. He glanced at Gray and Black, who were waiting patiently. They would be next. They were human. He stared back out into the street.

"Have we lost the man?" Gray asked quietly.

"No," Borac returned, suddenly annoyed. There was no need to ask the question, except human impatience. "Why do you ask?"

He heard the man shrug. The answer was toneless. "We have been waiting for some time."

Borac focused his attention on the people entering the tavern. He made a point to remember the faces of those who had battle experience, those who smelled of magic. They might prove dangerous, hinder his plans. There was still no sign of the man with the girdle. "Nothing has changed."

Malefiche had warned that the thief would not be easy to kill. The magical girdle bestowed a giant's strength to the wearer. The girdle's return was the secondary objective, according to Malefiche. The thief's death was primary.

Otherwise, the dark cleric would simply have hired another thief for the job. The fact that the thief was armored with magic ensured that Borac, with his own extraordinary strength, would have to take the job. He thought of ways he might use Gray and Black to save himself, by way of contingency. At the moment, their loss would not be significantly felt, especially after that last inane question.

The two men shifted from foot to foot. Borac could feel their gaze on his back, their glancing, silent words of impatience to each other.

"Why are you in such a hurry?" he demanded, memorizing the face of a thin woman whose ancestry was probably elven.

Neither man responded. Borac turned to face them. He could smell the reason; it hung on their bodies like a fog. "You're afraid."

Black frowned deeply, and Gray took a half step back.

Borac waved a hand dismissively. "I know your histories in the army of the Dark Queen, both of you. You're both distinguished enough." He stared hard into Black's eyes, then Gray's. "If you were not afraid, I should kill you myself. A man who is not afraid on his first mission is mad or a fool." Borac turned back to the street. "And I have time for neither."

The two men resumed their places in the shadows, no longer shuffling. Borac was satisfied his speech would shut them up and keep them still, at least for a short while. Humans were like dogs in this respect.

But after waiting another thirty minutes, even Borac was growing weary. "There's no sign of our mark. It's past the time when he was supposed to show. Go inside the tavern and see if he is in there."

Gray and Black nodded their understanding; Borac was pleased that they did not salute. He had told them to confirm orders in an unobtrusive manner to ensure that, if seen by a local, there would be nothing to connect them to the military that had scattered and splintered in the many years since the War of the Lance.

The two men walked into the street with a practiced gait that made them look casual, when in fact they were carefully inspecting every window and alley. With his superior hearing, Borac heard the men whispering to each other, mentioning things that should not be said. He would later reprimand them, emphasize the necessity of blending in, which did not include talk of a mission. It would take them several days to recover from his "instruction."

When Gray and Black were halfway up the street, the man they sought stepped out of the tavern. Borac did not recognize the thief as someone he knew, as he had thought he might. Anyone who could steal from a cleric of Takhisis would most likely be someone on the inside, someone connected with the Temple. A lieutenant or counselor, perhaps.

The thief glanced both ways before leaving the safety of the tavern. Such behavior was not unusual. Caution was often the better part of valor, especially in a border town. The man did not seem to notice Gray or Black.

Spotting the mark, Borac paused, leaned against the wall of an outbuilding. Cracking his hard knuckles, he left the comfort of the shadows, and quickly walked past his two men, though on the opposite side of the street. The red-haired thief was moving into the rougher part of town. Borac motioned with a tilt of his head for Gray and Black to follow. They fell in step behind him, a few easy paces back. Borac considered casting a spell to confirm the magic on the girdle the man wore. He decided against it. There might be a mage nearby who could feel the magic working, and that could jeopardize the assignment.

Borac wondered at the stupidity of the thief. Surely he must have known his life would be forfeit! Or was it all a sham, a ploy . . . a trap?

Borac smiled a bitter half-smile. He had made many enemies in his years of service. The Dark Queen's army, an army comprised mostly of capricious, untrustworthy humans, was rife with petty rivalries and conflicts.

There was talk of a new army forming, an army of knights dedicated to Her Dark Majesty. There was talk of honor and selfless loyalty. Borac didn't believe it.

Even the dark clerics were not above plotting. Malefiche had recently aligned himself with nobility from the north, nobility whose family Borac had murdered in the past. When alliances were forged, sacrifices were often agreed upon. Borac suspected he was the pawn about to be sacrificed to secure this new alliance. He was the assassin, but this mission might be an attempt on his own life.

Borac ground his sharp teeth through the half-smile. If the cleric was cheating him now, lying about this mission, Borac would have his revenge. But he had to complete this task first before he could know for certain.

He would allow nothing personal to interfere.

The thief continued walking, doing nothing out of the ordinary that Borac could see. There were no signals to hidden cutthroats in alleyways that would indicate the thief knew he was being followed. Walking behind Borac, Gray and Black were quiet, though their breathing was labored. Nervousness, excitement. Borac frowned, displeased.

The thief came to an intersection and stopped, looked to the right. Gray and Black caught up to Borac. Borac stepped onto a shop's wooden planked porch and turned his head toward the window as if looking inside, while actually maintaining his observation of the mark. His two men followed suit.

Two strangers walked up to the red-haired man, greeted him with handshakes. Borac saw a palm-sized black gem surreptitiously passed to each man. A red gem would have been for a red dragon; a black gem indicated a black.

"There is but one dragon to kill, the one dragon who murdered my brother in his sleep," the thief said in low tones, just loud enough for Borac's superior hearing. "He's in this town. He's been sent here on a job for Malefiche."

"What is the dragon's name?" one of the strangers asked. "Do we know him?"

"His name is Borac. The body is to be returned to the Temple as usual."

Borac looked carefully at the strangers' faces. He recognized them, had seen them long ago in Malefiche's retinue. His suspicions were confirmed. He was being sold out. The two put the gems in their pockets. One of them brushed aside his jacket, revealing a long, curving sword embossed with intricate runes.

The breath in Borac's throat caught, choking him. He grasped the windowsill to hold himself steady. His fingernails gouged marks into the hard wood. He could feel the power of the enchanted sword, even at this distance. He was not sure how long he stood before he was finally able to draw breath, but in that time, his blood turned thick and cold.

"What have you done, Malefiche?" Borac whispered. "What have you done?"

Neither Gray nor Black had moved, not wanting to give themselves away. They had no idea of what was going on, of course. They could not have heard the whispered words.

Borac put a hand over his good eye. He concentrated his thoughts on the mission. But he found it difficult to focus. The smell of iron mixed with blood—blood of dragons!—filled his human nose. Those men carried weapons of dragonbane magic, whose creation was revealed only in a single, ancient tome, the *Draconus Dictum*. A clerical work, it showed how to create weapons of dark magic designed to kill dark dragons. And the weapons were made from the vitals of the dragons themselves!

Borac knew of the *Draconus Dictum*, though not all of his kind did. It revealed many things about dragonkind to the reader. He had believed it to be destroyed. Why the Dark Queen had ever given such knowledge to humans, Borac could never understand. And now, it stood to reason Malefiche had discovered the tome. Borac wondered who amongst his kind had been the first murdered to create the bane weapons. He was next.

"After this, I will not have need of you for some time," Malefiche had said. Borac ground his teeth. The words of the flame-haired thief were confirmation. Borac was to be sacrificed for a new alliance, his body ground down to be forged into another dragon slayer's sword.

"Who are those two men?" Gray asked softly.

"The 'secret guard.' Assassins!" Borac replied. "They are hunting me!" He could see his reflection in the window, his dead eye staring back at him. As predicted by the prophets of damned Paladine, evil finally fed on itself. Clerics of the Queen of Darkness now trained, equipped, and employed men to slay their own allies. Why? To ensure loyalty and wholehearted support? To keep the difficult dragons like himself in line? Borac snorted.

The dragon hunters and the thief continued to confer. The thief was giving Borac's description as Borac had once given the thief's!

"Do we end the mission?" Black asked.

Borac considered fleeing, but that would mean they would follow him, track him. His hatred rose to his lips, heat and acid. He wanted to kill them. He wanted to kill Malefiche.

But killing them was not his mission. As much as he hated to admit it, he was in his own mind honor-bound to complete the mission. Borac turned his good eye to the man. "Of course not, idiot!" he hissed. Black stepped back. "Our assignment ends when that man is dead!"

Borac's men nodded, ashamed. He was satisfied they would not ask such a question again. He cleared his thoughts. "I did not tell Malefiche I was hiring help. They won't be looking for you."

Gray let his hand fall casually to his belt, inside of which he held a brace of throwing knives. "What shall we do?"

Borac nodded backward, toward the dragon hunters. He maintained outward calm, but inside he was filled with rare fear. "Kill them. Kill them both, and quickly! Bring me their weapons!"

If his men failed, he would have to face the dragon hunters, but they would be weakened, maybe wounded. The quicker he was done with this job, the quicker he could attend to the more crucial matter of the dragon hunters and the *Draconus Dictum*. And Malefiche.

"I will take care of the thief," said Borac.

The three stood a few moments longer, then parted. The dragon hunters headed off for another part of the town, followed closely by Gray and Black. The thief went his own way, followed by Borac.

The thief carried no dragon-bane weapons, and stalking him was easy. The man apparently believed the two dragon hunters would be more than a match for a single black dragon in human form. This amused Borac.

The red-haired thief entered another tavern near the outskirts of the border town. Business was brisk. Borac inserted himself into the flow of humanity and found to his displeasure that his stature was significantly different from that of the rest of the humans. He was far taller and stronger than anyone else in the tavern. He stood out in the crowd—never a good idea for an assassin.

The tavern was large and well-lit. Lanterns hung from the walls and support beams. A single bar extended along the wall at the back, tables and chairs crowded the floor. There was a good deal of gambling going on. Borac wondered if he might find time after the assignment to take the patrons' money.

Borac made his way to the bar, where he was afforded a clear view of the thief, whose red hair stood out in the shifting crowd as he took a place at one of the card tables. From the man's relaxed actions, it was obvious he still did not know he was being followed.

Perhaps he did not know he was being used as bait. He had told the dragon hunters that Borac was here on a job. He hadn't been told that he *was* the job! That would suit Malefiche's twisted humor. One of the many busy bartenders slammed a tankard at Borac's elbow. Borac tossed a steel piece to the man without turning back.

The thief was not a particularly good gambler, Borac saw, and hoped he could use this weakness when the time came to strike. Magical giant's strength or not, the human might try to bluff his way out of a desperate situation. But this red-haired human was not a particularly good bluffer. Borac watched as the man played hand after hand, losing some money, winning some money, drinking away his earnings.

An hour later, the thief rose from the table, his stack of coins depleted. Borac's good eye narrowed as the thief bent a steel piece between his fingers and tossed it to the dealer, who caught it in midair with a look of astonishment. Borac turned back to the bar, nodding to himself. No ordinary human could bend a steel coin. The girdle's magic must be real. He would be even more cautious.

The red-haired man pushed his way drunkenly toward the

tavern doors. Borac started to follow, then thought better of it. He turned back, grabbing the heavy tankard, and drained it quickly. He did not want the bartender to become suspicious. A man who ordered a drink but did not drink it was someone with more on his mind than a night out.

Borac casually made his way toward the tavern's twin doors. A fat man bounced up from his seat, blocking Borac's path. Borac attempted to push his way past, but the fat man was weaving drunkenly from side to side. Black acid, dragon's hate, touched the back of Borac's tongue. He stared hard into the fat man's eyes. The man gasped and collapsed into his chair. Borac looked toward the exit. The red-haired thief had turned at the sound of the commotion. He was staring directly at Borac. The thief's face was pale.

"Damn!" Borac cursed under his breath. He surged forward toward the door. When he finally stepped outside, he saw the thief running around a corner into darkened streets.

Borac tested the air. He could not smell the dragon-bane weapons. Hopefully, his men had dealt with the assassins. He let himself be guided by experience and the chase.

Borac turned a corner and found the thief attempting to force his way through a crowd of revelers, fear shading the man's features. Borac followed quickly, easily pushing people aside, no longer concerned about concealment. He wanted this mission over.

The thief found an opening in the crowd and dashed off. Borac followed close behind. The thief turned a corner, running fast. Then he rounded another corner, trying to lose himself in the darkest parts of the town. Borac ran faster—

He awoke, found himself lying on the ground, realizing from the pain in his jaw that he had been ambushed and knocked out. Movement caught his eye. The thief raising his fist for another blow. Borac rolled aside. The thief's fist smashed the cobblestones of the street to dust. Borac twisted to his feet.

"You're no match for me!" the thief snarled. "Not with the magic!"

Borac did not grapple with the man. His human form could not match a giant's strength. He let the thief charge, using the man's momentum against him and hurled him aside, off-balance. The thief's head impacted against the stone wall of a building. He fell hard and lay still.

"Apparently a giant's strength, but not a giant's thick skull," Borac said. He examined the girdle around the man's waist, attempted to find the clasp. It was hard to see in the darkness, but he managed to undo the clasp and remove the girdle. He felt it tingle in his hands. Definitely magical.

Tossing the girdle aside, Borac shook the thief awake. The dragon was now in complete control, and his mission was about to end. However, there was more information he needed.

"Who sent you?" he demanded of the human.

"You know who sent me!"

"Who?" Borac asked again. Reaching out, he grabbed the man's shirt, dragged the man close. "Who exactly?"

"Whoever it is," the thief replied, "you can bet he'll send more dragon hunters."

Borac's good eye narrowed, but he fought back the anger.

"Who?" he demanded for the third time.

The thief laughed and spit at Borac.

"Two can play that game," said Borac.

He let the tiniest drop of his dragon's hate bubble from his lips and fall on the man's chest.

The black acid ate through the long red beard, through the thin leather armor the thief wore under his clothes, and into the skin of his chest. Instead of screaming with pain or begging forgiveness as Borac expected, wanted, the thief gritted his teeth, glaring.

Borac forgot the instruction he had given to Gray, Black, and a score of other dead humans. More of his hate frothed black at his lips, and still the thief did nothing but snarl in return.

"Kill me, then!" the man cried, still held in Borac's inescapable grip. "Murder me! Murder me, as you did my kin!"

The thief's words reminded Borac of something, but he couldn't at the moment recall what. His hate rose fully from his stomach.

"Haven't you the guts?" the man taunted.

Borac opened his mouth to let the man see the black pool forming there.

"What are you waiting for? You want me dead! You hate me! Kill me!"

* * * * *

Black and Gray were waiting at the tavern marked with a spear and boar. Sitting at a table, they were playing at dice. When Borac appeared, they both waved their hands.

"Never do that again!" Borac hissed under his breath. "The mission is not over until we leave the town." The two men looked chagrined. Humans were such fools. "You have killed the dragon-bane . . . the assassins?"

"We did," Gray said.

"And their weapons?" Borac demanded. He started to pray to Takhisis that the humans had not lost them or sold them. Borac cut his prayer short. Why should he pray to a goddess who had given these humans the means to destroy his own kind? He would have to think about that.

At any rate, his prayer was answered. "We wrapped the swords up carefully and put them on the horses," Gray returned. "They looked special."

"If you only knew," Borac muttered. He rose from the table. It was time to leave.

"And your mission? Was it successful?" Black asked.

Borac was silent. His jaw ached from where he had received a blow of giant's strength, but the bone had not been broken. It made him wonder how much punishment his human form could withstand. Perhaps he had underrated this body.

"Is the man dead?" Gray asked. "Or need we go back after him?"

"You need not go back," Borac stated grimly. He had a great deal on his mind, not the least of which was his upcoming confrontation with Malefiche. And, most probably, more dragon hunters.

"Then the mission is finished," Black said.

Borac held up a traveling pack. "I have the girdle," he said.

"But the thief still lives."

Both Gray and Black blinked, startled. Borac turned and glared at them both. He could not hope that they would understand.

"I could have killed him. But he did the one thing that prevented me from taking his life."

The two men remained silent.

"He said, 'Murder me, as you did my kin.' " Borac ran his hands through his black hair. "I hated that little man, that petty human and his partners sent to kill me as the final price to forge an alliance. But he reminded me of something. He reminded me of all the things I had taught you," Borac said, gesturing to the two men. "I couldn't kill him as I did his brother, his brother whom I don't even remember. I hated him. I wanted him to die by my hands. I had lost my detachment, my 'professional distance.' "

Gray and Black continued to stare. Borac sighed, hoping this last explanation would be sufficient for them to understand. "He did the one thing that prevented me from taking his life. He made the matter personal."

The Dragon's Eye
Adam Lesh

"Bring the Dragon's Eye to my employer in the sewers of Palanthas by midnight tonight or your wife will die."

The weaselly little Theiwar dwarf looked up at me with a twisted smirk on his face as he delivered his message. He was pale and dirty, as are all of his kind, with bulging white orbs for eyes. He licked his lips too much. I longed to slam the door shut in his face, but I dared not. I had to find out more. I dragged the filthy creature inside my room.

"How do I know that you're telling the truth?" I demanded.

The dwarf gave a sickening giggle. He reached into his pouch, removed a dirty rag, and handed it to me. Unfolding it, I didn't know at first what I was looking at, then I recognized it as her earring. Snarling, I grabbed the front of the dwarf's jerkin in one hand, lifted him off the ground and slammed him into the wall of the inn. He didn't look so smug anymore.

"What have you done to her, you bastard?"

"N-n-nothing more than this. I swear on my honor!"

"Your honor," I sneered. "Worth less than the dirt on the floor."

I started to kick him, then reflected that whatever punishment I inflicted on him might be passed along. I contained myself . . . barely.

"I think your employer's made a big mistake. The Dragon's Eye is reputed to be a fabulous diamond. Do I look like I own a fabulous diamond?"

"He knows you don't own it." The dwarf grinned evilly. "He wants you to obtain it for him. You'll find the Dragon's Eye in Ashton Manor."

"Why me? Why not find a thief to do the job?"

"Thieves won't go near the place. We thought that a warrior—especially an elf warrior of such renown as yourself—

might have a better chance of snatching the Eye and escaping alive."

"You could have just hired me to do the job," I stated.

"Why go to all that expense when this way we get your services for free?" the dwarf giggled again.

I glared at him and he shrank away from me, flinging his arms in front of his face.

"Don't hurt me anymore," he wailed.

"Get out! And remember, if you harm a hair on her head, I'll rip out every single hair on your body using red-hot tongs!"

I sounded bold to cover my fear.

He laughed, slid a note out of his pouch, hurled it in my face, and fled.

The note contained directions to my wife's prison, located in the maze of mysterious passageways that made up the Palanthas sewers. I stowed the map in my pouch.

Ashton Manor. I'd heard stories about that dreaded place. All manner of deadly creatures were said to prowl its grounds, guarding its secrets. There was precious little solid information about the house itself. As the dwarf had said, the thieves of Palanthas gave it a wide berth. They claimed that at least a dozen of their comrades had gone in, but not come out. I had less than three hours to find the diamond and return with it to Palanthas. I started to say a prayer to Paladine, then remembered that he wasn't around anymore. I was on my own. It was going to be a long night.

An hour later I stood outside the tall iron fence that surrounded the perimeter of the gloomy estate. Now I understood why only the bravest—or stupidest—thieves had dared enter it. Most magic had vanished from Krynn, but whatever fearful curse had been laid on Ashton Manor still remained. I have traveled many dark and perilous places, but none were more daunting than this. Death waited on the other side. Only the thought of what would happen if I failed impelled me forward.

The fence was no challenge. Boughs from a tree stretched over the fence rails. I climbed the tree and carefully inspected the grounds. That proved to be a waste of time. It was like a jungle—with twisted trees, bramble bushes, choking vines, hideous flowers, and tall grass. I could hear low growls and snarls—the sound of a large beast moving through the thick foliage.

Saber in hand, I crawled along the sturdiest bough of the tree and dropped silently to the ground. It was like a swamp—slimy and muddy. Outside the wall, the night air was cool and dry. Inside, the heat and humidity wrapped around me like a wet blanket and soon I was soaked in my own sweat. It was as if I had entered a rain forest. The stench of rot and decay and the sickening smell of death lily made me gag.

It was eerily quiet, too quiet. No sound, not even from insects or birds, penetrated the deathly silence. The soft wet squish my boots made in the muck sounded as loud as drums. The growling noises had ceased. Perhaps whatever had been making them was stalking me now. I kept waiting to feel savage claws rip open my back. I kept walking.

Suddenly, I halted. I could see dark shapes up ahead.

Guards, I thought. I waited, tensely, for them to leave their posts. They never moved.

After a while, I crept forward and saw that they would never be likely to move again. They were stone statues. There were seven of them: three humans, two dwarves, and two kender. All except the kender had expressions of horror frozen on their faces. These had once been alive. They'd been attacked by . . .

Basilisk!

A terrible roar sounded from the tall grass to my right. Betrayed by my instincts, I looked in its direction, right into its eyes. My arms and legs grew stiff, my breath caught in my throat and my thoughts grew sluggish. Like the others, I was beginning to succumb to its terrible gaze. It took every ounce of strength in my body, but I managed to close my eyelids. The spell was broken, but now I was effectively blind. I stumbled to my left, hoping to hide in the undergrowth. A swat from its massive claw sent me sprawling and opened three bloody wounds in my side. The pain roused my flagging energy. The basilisk tried to sink its teeth into my flesh, but I rolled away. Unfortunately, I caught a lungful of its poisonous breath. My stomach roiled as I struggled to my feet. In the past, when faced with a basilisk, I would have used my magic, caused its deadly gaze to reflect back into its own eyes. But magic was gone, gone when Solinari set, never to rise again. I had no choice but to fight.

My limbs were stiff, my reactions slowed. I was half sick from the poisonous breath and I dared not look the beast in the eye. I held my sword in limp hands, feigning exhaustion. The basilisk sought to end the duel quickly. It charged straight at me. Swiftly I grasped my sword in both hands, lifted it, and drove it into the basilisk's skull, right between its lethal eyes.

It twitched once and died.

You can almost always fool a basilisk like that.

* * * * *

Ashton Manor was the most bizarre dwelling I had ever seen. Turrets, minarets, and gables sprouted from a pentagon-shaped frame. No one knew who had originally built the place; it had appeared a few decades ago, during the time of the War of the Lance. Lord Ashton—as he had called himself—had been a red-robed human mage rumored to have great magical powers but lacking in common sense. He should have known the original owner of the Dragon's Eye would track him down, no matter how many times he moved his house.

It took me a long minute of searching just to find a door in that crazy quilt of corners, flying buttresses, and leering gargoyles. When I did find the door, I couldn't open it. Although it seemed none too sturdy and I could not sense any magical locks, no amount of kicking or pounding budged it an inch. There were no windows on the ground level.

I had bound my wounds from the basilisk's claw, but my side ached. I was weak from loss of blood. This is one I owe the Theiwar's boss, I thought, as I removed a coil of rope from around my waist. I attached a grappling hook, whirled it around my head, and let it fly up and over the top of the house. It landed on a chimney, striking the roof with a slight clink, barely audible even to me. I pulled on the rope to secure the hook. The chimney crumbled and the hook slid back down. My second attempt met with success. I wrapped the hook around a gargoyle's neck.

I climbed the wall of the mansion to a balcony about twenty feet off the ground. I crawled across the balcony and found another door. It opened easily, far too easily. Now I was being invited to come inside. I heartily wished I could have refused that invitation.

Sweat dripped off my forehead and I was panting from my exertions as I slipped through the door. I had no time to rest. Once inside, I found a torch on the floor, as if it had been placed there on purpose for me. I lit it. I stood at the end of a long corridor. Moldering tapestries hung on the walls. I missed my magic. A light spell would have provided a soft, continuous glow, in contrast to the torch's flickering, smoky fire.

Doors stood just off the corridor. Opening several, I peered inside. This floor was empty, except for some broken pieces of furniture and mildewed artwork. I had entered the house with no idea of the diamond's location. I had expected to search the house from top to bottom, but once inside, I began to receive a mental impression of where the Dragon's Eye was located. In the center of the corridor was a long staircase leading to the ground level. I headed down.

The ground floor was like a cave. At first I thought the walls were of rough-hewn stone. Then I realized that the wooden walls had petrified! The floor was deep in oozing muck that sucked at my boots, making it impossible to move quietly. The nearly unbearable heat and humidity produced fog that swirled around me. I could barely see my own feet.

Like all elves, I despise caves. Give me the cool green of a forest, or even the dirty streets of a city, but you can keep musty, smelly, wet caverns.

I had no idea where I was going, the Dragon's Eye led me—to no good end, I had to assume. I slogged through the muck. A sudden shifting beneath my foot and a barely audible click alerted me. This time my instincts served me well. I dived forward, feeling something whiz over my body. I landed—splat—in the foul mud. I rolled to my feet, none too gracefully, causing pain to shoot up my wounded side. Cautiously, I walked back to check the trap I had narrowly avoided. I might have to return this way and I wanted to make sure the traps were sprung. Shoving away muck, I found that applying pressure to either of two stepping stones triggered two blades that shot out from slots in the walls. An ugly way to die.

The corridor opened into a large dining room. A huge, ornate, oak table stood in the center, but there were no chairs. I guess it cuts down on the amount of food your guests eat if they have to stand up during dinner. Wine racks lined the walls around the room, some with bottles still in them. I wouldn't have tasted that wine for all the steel in Flotsam. Cobwebs—enormous cobwebs—filled the room. I found something wrapped in the silken threads. Moving closer, I could see feet sticking out the bottom. The feet weren't moving. Drawing my sword, I backed out of the room slowly, and torched the cobwebs.

A gigantic, blazing whisper spider launched itself out of the fiery room, knocking me over in its haste to escape the flames. The spider towered over me, its legs as long as I was tall.

A spell came to mind and I spoke the arcane words, simultaneously making a complicated pass with my left hand.

Nothing.

No magic. Right. Damn.

I dodged a web strand the spider fired at me. I rolled to the side and struggled to regain my feet without dropping either sword or torch. The effort sent waves of pain through my body, but I had to keep the torch from going out. I waved the flaming torch at the spider, holding it at bay for a few moments. The spider fired another web strand—not at me, at the torch. Snagging it, the spider yanked the torch out of my hand. The torch flickered feebly on the muddy floor. I had to reach it before it went out.

The spider attacked me again, running toward me, snapping at me with its long fangs. I jumped back and sliced off part of a leg. Furious, the spider lunged to finish me off. It sailed past me and crashed into a wine rack, smashing some of the bottles. Drenched with wine, the spider continued its attack, fangs dripping poison. I dived for the torch, snatched it up, and flung it at the spider. The flames ignited the alcohol on its body. The spider burst into flames. I tried to get out of its way, but I slipped on the slimy floor and ended up rolling underneath the blazing creature. Its dead weight crushed me. Two ribs snapped, sending waves of agony through me. Worse, the dying spider bit me in the chest, sending burning poison into my veins.

I thrust up with my still-free sword arm, driving the saber into the creature's body. It curled up, withered, and died.

Dragging myself to my feet, reeling from the pain and sick from the poison, I sheathed my sword and limped back to the kitchen. The flames had burned out, leaving the whole area covered with black soot. A large wooden door was set into a stone wall. The door was locked.

I kicked the damn thing down.

As I stepped into a small antechamber, a voice rang in my aching head:

Get out now or meet your doom!

There was no sound; the voice was embedded in my brain. I didn't respond.

Inside the room were wooden stairs leading up, but no other entrances or exits. I searched for concealed doors, but found none. The stairs led to a small landing, with more stairs going up. As I climbed to the landing, the voice spoke again:

I warn you to leave or you will most certainly die!

I ignored it.

I reached the landing. Looking down at my feet, I saw the trapdoor—too late. The door fell open and dropped me into a chute. I slid down the chute to some unknown but presumably horrible fate. I tried to stop my fall, but the sides of the chute were slick and my hands slipped off. Desperate, I grabbed iron spikes from my belt, one in each hand. Twisting, I managed to slow my descent by driving the spikes into the sides of the chute. I stopped. I hung from the spikes, my feet dangling. It was pitch dark, but I could feel cool air blowing on my legs. My wounds had torn open, pain shot through my chest and side, but I held on. Looking down, I could see nothing. I couldn't hold on much longer. Minutes later I heard some dirt clods that I had dislodged hit the bottom. Blood dripping from my wounds followed them.

Kicking out with my legs, I felt what I hoped was a ledge or perhaps the lip of the pit. I pulled myself up onto the ledge. Light flickered ahead of me. Limping around the edge of the pit, I entered a long corridor.

I heard a scraping and whistling sound above me. I dived forward. A huge stone slab crashed down behind me, cutting off my way out.

I leapt to my feet, running, leaving a trail of blood behind me.

No, no! I mean it! You're going to die.

As I neared the end of the corridor, a portcullis came crashing down from the ceiling. I dived for it, just slipping under it. Jumping to my feet, I drew my sword.

I stood in a large, torchlit chamber. The walls were rough-hewn and uneven, obviously of poor craftsmanship. A dwarf who examined this place would be hard pressed to hold down his gorge. Water dripped down the walls, leaving lines of mineral deposits in its path. The torches on the walls sputtered feebly, leaving parts of the chamber in deep shadow. Crates had been stacked neatly on one side of the room, and a table and chairs stood in another. Tapestries hung on the wall, away from the dripping water.

"That's the trouble with you elves," came a voice from the darkness. "You never listen."

A light flared. The ugliest human I had ever seen sat on a throne in the center of the room. A strange staff with a wickedly curved hook at one end leaned against the right side of the chair. On a pedestal, glittering in the torchlight, was the Dragon's Eye.

The Eye was a fist-sized diamond with very unusual coloration. The center was flawed in such a way that when light struck it, the diamond glittered like a prism, making it look like an eye winking. Legend had it that this was the actual eye of an ancient red dragon. Mages had cut out the eye and changed it into a diamond. Prior to the Chaos War, the Eye had been a very powerful magical artifact, capable of producing blasts that imitated the breath weapons of all the true Dragons of Krynn. Now, of course, who knows? Maybe it was just another fabulously large, immensely valuable diamond.

"So, you did come for the Eye," said the human, who was shrouded head to toe in white robes. "Well, there it is. It's worthless, you know. All its magic's gone."

"Then you won't mind if I take it," I said, stepping forward.

The human glared at me. "Good poker player, are you? Very well. I am the Guardian of the Eye. It still retains its magic, though I am not sure how. I have been assigned to guard it until the mages could study it."

"I do not want to hurt you, sir," I said, "but I need the Eye. Lives are at stake."

The human shook his head. "I am sorry. Whether you want it for evil or good, I cannot allow you to take the Eye. You would upset the Balance."

"If you won't give it to me, I guess I'll have to take it."

From my belt, I drew a short metal rod—a gift from a grateful gnome. Pressing one stud caused it to telescope out and lock into place. I now held a light but sturdy quarterstaff. While the Guardian might have no compunction about killing me, I had no desire to kill him.

My opponent rose and shucked off his robes. He was a thin, hirsute human about six feet tall, wearing only a loincloth. His small flat nose, wide jaw and mouth, and protruding lower teeth gave him a simian appearance, but his amber eyes spoke of great intelligence.

He picked up the hooked staff and swung it around his head a few times, causing the muscles to ripple along his slim but powerful torso. Under normal conditions I might have considered us evenly matched. Not now.

We faced off: a wounded elf against a rested human warrior. I was in for the fight of my life.

With an overhead swing, he attacked in a flash, attempting to impale me on the sharp metal hook of his staff. I barely parried his first assault, twisting my staff and lunging for his midsection. He deftly dodged my thrust.

He came at me with a series of vicious attacks, using his superior condition to his advantage, trying to wear me down. Still feeling the effects of the basilisk's gaze and the spider's poison, I assumed a defensive posture, concentrating on keeping that wicked hook away from me. While I did not get cut by the hook, I was taking a great deal of punishment from the blunt end of his staff.

Within a few moments, he realized that his tactic was not working. He was rapidly tiring while I was conserving my strength.

He backed off, panting from exertion.

"Is this necessary?" I demanded. "As I said, sir, I do not want to hurt you, but I must have the Eye."

"I will fight to the death. I must," he insisted.

He attacked, trying to hook my staff out of my hands. I resisted for a moment, then let go of my staff with one hand. His hook slid harmlessly off the end. The sudden lack of tension threw him off-balance.

I launched my attack. Planting one end of my staff on the ground, I swung up and struck him in the chest with my feet. I bowled him over, knocking the wind out of him. As he struggled to rise, I touched the stud on the staff, converting it once again into a short metal bar, and drove it into the base of his skull.

He was out cold.

I collapsed next to him, panting. The last of my strength was gone; the blackness claimed me.

* * * * *

I awoke to find him still unconscious next to me. Removing some pieces of rope from my pack, I bound him tightly. His sharp nails would free him in time, but not before I was long gone.

I removed the Dragon's Eye from the pedestal. Once, I would have been able to sense its magic with my own. Now it was just another lump of rock to me. I dusted it all over with the special powder I had brought, powder that vanished a moment after being applied. I pulled on a pair of leather gloves, picked up the diamond, and put it in my pack.

A quick search revealed the exit the Guardian used to get in and out of the chamber. Once outside, I could tell from the position of the new moon that had only recently come to Krynn that I had less than an hour to return to Palanthas and make my rendezvous.

I found my horse where I had left him, outside the mansion wall. I galloped south, back to Palanthas.

As I drew near the city, I was forced to slow my horse's pace. In the few years since the Chaos War, a number of petty lords had gained and then lost control of Palanthas. The latest, and so far most powerful, was Lord Bryn Mawr, commander of a force of nearly five hundred thugs and brigands that he called the City Guard.

He maintained a strict curfew and kept his troops reasonably well disciplined, which made it tricky to sneak into the city at night. But there were still ways into town after dark—for a price.

I tied up the horse about a mile from the city. I would need him later, but it was too risky to try to enter the town on horseback.

As I neared the city walls, I turned northwest, circling around the town to the sea. I stripped off my boots, stowed them in my pack, and dived into the cold water. The half-mile swim to Palanthas's harbor invigorated me and rinsed away some of the blood and filth from my clothes.

Cutting noiselessly through the water, I swam toward the docks, one pier in particular. When I reached the pier, I started to climb a makeshift ladder. Hands reached down, grabbed my wrists, and dragged me onto the dock. A knife pressed into my throat.

"The password—or your head and neck will be parting company, elf!"

" 'The Thieves Guild still rules.' Does that satisfy you, Tarl One-Eye?"

"Ah, 'tis you. Pass on quickly. A patrol approaches."

The big man with a patch over one eye released me. I scurried from the pier, entering a secret tunnel near the docks. By the time the patrol arrived, they would find drunken

Tarl, asleep in his boat. I was inside the city.

I emerged from the tunnel. Turning a corner, I actually bumped into one of Bryn Mawr's bodyguards on an otherwise deserted street. I recognized him and, unfortunately, he recognized me. He reached out and grasped my arm.

"By the Lost Gods, I've got you at last, elf assassin—"

I slid my dagger beneath his breastplate and into his gut. He dropped away from me, dead weight.

As he fell, another guard stepped from the tavern onto the street. He saw me standing over the body of his comrade and immediately let out a shout. He drew his sword and ran at me. The tavern door burst open and more guards spilled into the street.

The guards chased me down the street and continued on my heels as I twisted and turned down Palanthas's streets and alleyways. They soon fell back, their beer bellies weighing them down. But their shouting attracted another patrol. On the run, I removed the rope from my waist again and attached the grappling hook. I let fly. The hook grabbed the first time and I climbed as quickly as my wounded body would allow. My pursuers arrived just as I hauled myself over the top. I fled across the rooftops.

The guards did not give up, not with one of their own dead.

Within seconds, scores of guardsmen were searching rooftops throughout the city. They were relentless. My only hope of escape was to get into the sewers. I had only minutes until my rendezvous.

I stood on the roof of a large inn—the Fist and Glove. I dropped down, grabbed onto a windowsill and used my momentum to swing myself directly into the window. I smashed through the shutters and landed on a bed—an occupied bed. A fat little man sat up and let out a shriek that could have been heard in Flotsam. "Sorry, wrong room," I said, jumping from the bed to the floor.

Everyone in the inn was awake, tumbling out into the halls to see what was going on. Two guardsmen were entering the front door—my only way out. I raced down the stairs and darted right between.

They struck out with their fists, missed me, and hit each other.

I kept running.

I headed down an alley, to one of the many openings leading down into the sewers. Just my luck. One of the guards was standing on it! I was running out of time. I cartwheeled forward into a handspring, landed on my feet, vaulted up and at him, somersaulting in midair to come down on him feet first. The bone-jarring impact knocked him flat.

I moved the heavy grate to the side, and climbed down the ladder, stopping just long enough to pull the grate back in place over my head. The guards would soon find their unconscious comrade and realize that I had escaped into the sewers, but even then it was unlikely they would chase me down here. The Thieves Guild still ruled this part of Palanthas, at least.

Once down the ladder, I lit another torch. The ceiling of this section of the sewer was taller than most, so I could walk upright. I checked the markings on the wall—markings made by those who find it safer to travel underground than above—pulled out the map, and headed off toward my meeting. I saw no sign of life, except the ever-present rats. Then, an eerie giggle sounded down the tunnel behind me. I looked back, saw nothing.

A few minutes later, I heard that giggle again, but this time I also heard the scuffing of cloth on stone as well.

I walked faster.

Suddenly, I was surrounded by small, filthy creatures with matted hair and dirty faces. The stench nearly knocked me down. They grabbed hold of me from all directions at once, clinging to me and yelling.

"Oh boy! Dinner guest! You like some nice juicy rats?"

Gully dwarves!

They had me surrounded. I didn't want to kill any of the wretched creatures, but I certainly did not have time to dine! I struck at them with the flat of my sword, hoping to frighten them away.

I frightened them, but not away. At the sight of naked steel, they all screamed in unison and, throwing themselves at me, wrapped their arms around my legs and waist and cried out for mercy.

I waved my sword, but it was a feeble gesture. I didn't have the strength to peel two dozen gully dwarves off me. My feet left the floor. They were carting me off, an unwilling guest.

Suddenly, they shrieked in panic and dropped me into the muck. I looked up to see a huge ogre wading through fleeing gully dwarves.

"You are late, elf," the ogre said with a sneer.

He led me through the sewer to a heavily fortified door. He pounded his fist against it. A small shutter slid to one side and a pair of eyes looked through. The door opened.

I entered a bleak, cold, stone room. The air tasted stale, like that of a tomb. Inside were another ogre, the Theiwar from before, and a female elf clad in black leather. The female glared at me defiantly, her dark eyes smoldering. No sign of the captive or the kidnapper. I looked around, searching the shadows.

"So, elf, you have it? The Dragon's Eye?"

The voice was both beautiful and ghastly. A Silvanesti tenor with a goblin chorus. A gold dragon swimming in a sea of blood. Light swallowed by darkness.

It pained my soul to listen to it.

"I have it," I cried, searching for the monster I had come to confront. "Is my wife safe?"

The creature emerged from the shadows. Cold dread filled my heart.

The elves called them "chaos-spawn" because they had apparently been borne of the Chaos War. This particular spawn looked to be some terrible cross between reptile and bird. It stood nine feet tall, with bright red, scaly skin that was streaked black, like molten lava. Its head was long and thin, its eyes protruding from either side of its noseless face. It opened its small thin mouth to speak, revealing rows of razorlike teeth that could cut through flesh and bone in an instant. It had two bony arms, with clawed, three-fingered hands. Above and below each arm were two tentacles that waved incessantly. It had two legs, back-bent like a bird's, each with three claws. For all its bizarre and terrifying appearance, it moved gracefully, fluidly.

And then I saw Mara.

One of the spawn's tentacles was wrapped around her body and one hand was closed around Mara's throat. A dirty, bloody scarf covered the side of Mara's head. She looked more angry than afraid.

The chaos-spawn reached out a clawed hand.

"Give me the Dragon's Eye!"

"Release my wife first."

"You are in no position to bargain. Hand me the stone or I will rip her throat out!"

To emphasize the point, it pressed its claws into Mara's flesh. Mara gasped in pain. I could see blood.

"Stop! You win!" I cried.

I removed the Dragon's Eye from the pouch and held it out to the creature in my gloved hand. The chaos-spawn snatched the diamond and held it up to the light.

"The stone's worthless," I said, hoping to distract it. "Its magic is gone."

It laughed horribly.

"That's what you think! Fool . . ."

The chaos-spawn clutched at its throat. The diamond fell from its limp hand. With a low moan, it toppled to the floor and lay there, helpless.

Mara sprang away from it, crying, "Look out for her!"

The female elf drew her long sword and attacked me. Drawing my sword, I met her charge. The ogre who had rescued me from the gully dwarves jumped to help me, landing a hammer blow to the neck of the other ogre. Mara attacked the Theiwar, using bare hands.

The dark elf and I circled each other, each trying to gauge the other's skill. She could detect my weariness, my slowed reactions, and she pressed her advantage. She hammered at me with constant attacks, numbing my arm as I deflected her powerful blows. The two ogres struggled together; there would be no help from that quarter. The Theiwar fought viciously, keeping Mara occupied.

A cut slipped though my defenses, re-opening the bloody

wound on my chest. The elf, her dark eyes blazing, howled in triumph and attacked again, with increasingly less finesse and more brute force. My head swam and my vision blurred. One last blow and my sword dropped from my nerveless fingers. I fell to my knees. The elf raised her sword for the killing stroke. Suddenly, she screamed and pitched forward. My "wife" stood above the fallen elf. Mara jerked the Theiwar's dagger out of the dark elf's back.

Mara unwound the scarf from his head.

"Where have you been?" he demanded.

I saw the Theiwar slumped unconscious on the other side of the room.

I was covered in blood—most of it my own. My ribs were broken. I was still sick from the poison. I grinned at my partner. "I stopped in a tavern, had a few drinks. Why? Were you in a hurry, wifey dear?"

Mara looked down at the dress he was wearing and grimaced. "You won't tell anyone about this! You promised!"

The ogre—actually a member of the Dragonsbane team assigned to deal with the chaos-spawn—laughed and shook his head. "But *I* did not promise!"

We gathered around the comatose chaos-spawn.

"What did you give it?" Mara asked me.

"I coated the Eye with the most powerful paralysis poison I could find. It could knock out a whole troop of draconians. I hope I didn't kill it."

"Not much chance of that," responded the ogre. "Is the rest of the team in place?"

"Slight change of plans. There was a little excitement above before I got here. The streets are crawling with guards. We have to get to the docks. Tarl's waiting for us in the boat. Do you know the way through the sewers?"

"Think you can carry that thing that far?" Mara asked.

Org nodded and bent over the chaos-spawn. I carefully retrieved the Eye from the creature's hand. The ogre hoisted the spawn over his shoulders. We went back through the sewers. When Org deemed we were close to our destination, we climbed up and out. The docks were empty. Tarl was watching for us, motioned that all was safe.

Org carried the creature to the pier. After making sure it was still unconscious, he wrapped the beast in a large leather bag, gave it a potion to make sure it would sleep during transport, then dropped the bag into a huge crate. We loaded the crate onto a waiting ship.

I reached into my pouch and retrieved Mara's earring. I pointed to the one Mara had forgotten to remove. "You look lopsided."

He snatched off the earring, tossed them both into the sea.

"What next?" he asked.

"They'll take the chaos-spawn back to the tower. The sages will examine it, then we'll know what to expect the next time we encounter one."

"No. I meant what's next for you?"

I looked down at the Dragon's Eye still in my gloved hand and sighed. "We Dragonsbane are not thieves. Now I have to put this back."

Dragonfear
Teri McLaren

"Here, put this key back around your neck! Quit lolling around and fetch me a clean cloth, Carlana," Frenzill grumbled in a barely audible voice as he closed his recipe book, locked the door, and ascended from his ale cellar. "And look happy, girl. How many times today have you tripped over that face, hmm?"

"But, Father," Carlana protested, hurrying to thread her way through barrels and glasses to reach for the cloth that was only inches away from Frenzill's own hand. She wearily put down her crowded tray and blew a strand of copper hair away from her pale face. "I've been working all day without a moment's rest."

"Look happy, I said," Frenzill whispered harshly. "Now serve that tray and get back to the floor."

Carlana stared long and hard at her father and wiped away the unshed tears of frustration that brimmed at her wide blue eyes. She dropped the heavy ale cellar key and its even heavier chain around her neck and wearily took up her tray, but she refused to smile.

Frenzill frowned at her back, then began to polish the same mug for the fifth time since lunch, this time energetically pursuing a speck of dust that had smeared into a greasy streak when he wiped it. Another cinder? More soot? He sighed as he stared at the black smudge that had transferred to his white bar cloth.

"Yer gonna wear 'em both out," smiled Gisrib from his well-shined barstool. "Someday that girl is gonna leave you so fast that all you'll hear is the sound of a slamming door."

"Not my Carlana. She wouldn't dare. Some day all this will be hers," mumbled Frenzill, snapping the cloth at a drowsy fly over Gisrib's head. His aim was better than he had expected, and the doomed insect buzzed straight into the foamy head of the lanky farmer's ale. Gisrib shook his head, cast a bleary, soot-rimmed eye on his preoccupied host, and motioned for another. Frenzill pushed the nearly full tankard aside and grudgingly drew Gisrib a fresh one. His last ale barrel was nearly empty and the Midyear Festival began tomorrow. Plenty of ale was always needed for the festival, but this year the brew had taken longer to age properly. Frenzill knew it would be ready by tomorrow. He held out his hand for Gisrib's payment.

"Didn't come to eat, too, Frenzill. This 'un is free, by my reckon," Gisrib protested, eyeing Frenzill's soft palm. "Say, will the new summer ale be ready by tomorrow? Tradition—"

"By tomorrow, Gis. For the celebration, of course, and tradition," replied Frenzill, annoyed at the question.

Gisrib shook his head, knowing Frenzill too well to believe him. "When I lived in Doriett, our brewers always brought 'er in early for the tasting."

"Yes, so you tell me every year," replied Frenzill coolly. Gisrib was continually harping about his birthplace. But then, old Gisrib, even after seventeen years, was still considered a newcomer in Hiddenhaven. "Gotta go now. Enjoy your ale." Frenzill restored the over-polished mug to its place on the mantle and signaled to Carlana to take his place behind the bar.

"Well, set me up again before you go off to watch the wars," said Gisrib, this time offering payment. "And don't let any dragons in," he added drily.

Frenzill sighed heavily again, his watery blue eyes suddenly hard. When Gisrib turned up his mug, Frenzill deftly plucked the thrashing fly from the first mug of ale, topped off its contents, and served it up, his face never changing expression. Watching him in horrified silence, Carlana threw down her tray and flew through the doors to her private quarters, the muted sound of retching following her. Gisrib lifted an eyebrow, shook his head when he could not identify the reason for Carlana's sudden retreat, and took a long, satisfying swallow of his "new" mug of ale.

Frenzill smiled quirkily, tossed Gisrib's coin into his pocket, and pulled on a light cloak against the afternoon chill.

The air outside the inn usually had a fresh tang to it, making this a pleasant time of day for Frenzill to perform his most onerous and boring duty, a turn at the town watch. But today, like yesterday, the breeze was sour with smoke. Where is this infernal soot coming from? The fighting can't have moved that close, he pondered.

As he strolled to the edge of town, Frenzill noticed that the streets of Hiddenhaven were abnormally deserted. Only a few women hunched over the community gardens, pulling weeds and laughing—had they laughed just a little louder when they saw Frenzill? He stared them into a properly respectful silence, then covertly checked his trousers when a wagon full of hay rolled past. He glanced over his shoulder to see if his coat was smudged with any of the ubiquitous soot and shook his head in irritation.

Where *is* everyone? he wondered, but the empty lanes didn't bother him, since, by the shadow of the town square's sundial, he knew he was a good half hour late for his turn at watch. And after all, it was wartime, the sounds of the distant battles often carrying across the vast valley on the evening breeze.

He huffed to the top of Hiddenhaven's huge, ancient wooden gate and stared out at the dark clouds that hung draped like a shroud across the eastern skyline. There has been no storm, no lightning in weeks, he thought, his narrow, pasty face crinkling into a grimace as he licked one crooked, wet finger and held it to the air, confirming the rusted weather vane's direction in the acrid breeze.

Below him, a couple of young boys ran up, their faces flushed and grinning, their hands full of miniature wooden knights and horses.

"Is there any fighting out there, Mr. Frenzill?" called one, a ten-year-old terror whom Frenzill vaguely recognized as the baker's son. "Can we come up and see too? Everyone's talking about the wars today. About a dragon! It's coming here, you know."

Frenzill only glowered at the eager faces below and moved on down the wall. There is far more smoke than yesterday, he mused. Or the day before or the day before that. And now the wind is picking up and blowing it all our way. What a bother. Just in time to cast a pall over the Midyear Festival. Frenzill looked at the swirling dark clouds, making shapes of them in his imagination. A mug, a barrel, a bag of coins. He shook his head slowly as he turned from the bleak sky to survey his tidy little town. Twenty or thirty bright banners already hung from freshly washed windows for tomorrow's celebration. Pity how dirty they were getting.

Fronted by rose gardens and cobblestone streets, well-kept shops lined the wide, shady town square. From his high perch on the gate, so long unopened that its hinges and locks had rusted shut, Frenzill could clearly see his own pride and joy, the House of Fine Spirits. He had hung a big red banner from his uppermost window. "Welcome," the flag proclaimed. "The Best Brew in the World." Fancy scrolled letters danced over a frothy mug of ale. It *was* the best brew in the world, he thought smugly, and he was the only one making it.

The current season's batch, fifty huge barrels, all clearing toward a bright, perfect amber, filled Frenzill's specially made cellar. With such an abundant new supply, he would be well on his way to becoming the richest man in this very rich little town. Someday, he might even be mayor.

But here I am, thinking too much about the color of the sky instead of the color of my ale, he frowned. A stronger draft of smoke wafted into his sensitive nose, making him snort in disgust. He started down the ladder. A turn or two around the square—which needed a good scything, he noticed critically, making a mental note to upbraid the lad responsible—and he would go back to the inn again, watch duty or not. Despite the smoky skies, Frenzill had seen nothing going on in the valley and, after all, Hiddenhaven was far too isolated to find itself in the path of the fighting.

For seventeen years, the town had suffered no intrusions from the valley's other far-flung communities. In fact, except for Gisrib, the three shepherds, the two miner families, and the few cotters who farmed the apron of land surrounding the western side of the town walls, hardly any of Hiddenhaven's populace had ever travelled anywhere else. Frenzill took a last long look toward the east and muttered a particularly colorful curse at the soot-filled sky as he shimmied down the rickety old ladder.

"Hallo the gates!" cried a weak, muffled voice from somewhere to Frenzill's left.

Startled, Frenzill missed the last two rungs of the ladder, skinning both knobby knees clean through his fine worsted leggings. Cursing even louder, he whirled, searching for the inconsiderate oaf who had hailed him. But the women had moved far out of earshot, the wagon driver had gone into the inn for a drink, and Frenzill was faced with the alternatives of a talking donkey or someone calling to him from outside the gates.

He brushed off his knees and craned over toward the low, narrow shepherd's gate, which everyone who had any business outside the walls used. It, too, was locked tightly.

Frenzill snorted again and began to walk away.

"Good sir, if you are still there, please . . ."

Frenzill halted, listened again, turned around and warily strode up to a large knothole in the main gate and peered out, one bloodshot blue eye pressed firmly to the wood.

"Down here," rasped the voice.

Frenzill lowered his sight line. He could not believe what he saw.

There in the thorny hedgerow shivered a haggard, half-dead stranger.

"Please, sir, I would not trouble you, but I've had naught to eat or drink in the two days since I had to leave the river behind," said the man. "I am unarmed, as well, sir. Please . . ."

Frenzill removed his eye from the knothole and cast a worried glance over his shoulder. This he would have to deal with, and very quickly. He'd probably have to go outside to do it, too. He sighed, returned to the peephole, and addressed the man in his frostiest tones.

"You, there—state your business and remove yourself from the hedgerow. Can't have you dying in the thorns, especially on my watch." Be the devil to shift you out of there, thought Frenzill. He drew a small, jewelled dagger from his sleeve just in case he had to remove the stranger a little more forcefully.

The stranger stumbled from his thorny cover, receiving several new gashes in the process. Frenzill had little sympathy, since his own knees were still stinging. The innkeeper unbarred the main gates and pushed them back to reveal the stranger.

"Thank you, sir. I thought I was done for. You're the first person I've seen since I've been on the run. I tried your gates, but, funny thing, they were locked," said the bedraggled man. "But then, I figured it must be because of the wars, and maybe you already know about the coming danger." The man looked up, searching the sky nervously.

Danger? Frenzill could see no danger. The stranger was covered from head to toe in soot, and his clothing was singed at the hems and sleeves. His hair was all but burned away. Great waxy, white blisters mottled one side of his face, and he limped badly. His lanky frame towered over Frenzill's by at least a foot and a half. He smiled gratefully at Frenzill as the innkeeper refastened the gate, then held out one very dirty, well-calloused hand in greeting. Its middle fingers were wrapped in a darkly stained shred of his cloak. Frenzill merely shifted his dagger behind his back and ignored the outstretched hand.

"What is your name, stranger, and again, I ask, what is your business here? And what of this danger?" queried Frenzill. The back of his neck began to crawl a bit, as it always did when the gate was open.

"Harald, sir, and I'll trouble you for nothing but a bit of drink, just enough to give me courage and take my feet a few leagues farther where I can be safe," said the stranger, looking fearfully up at the smoky skies. He stumbled and collapsed into Frenzill's unwelcoming arms. The smell of smoke nearly knocked over the slightly built innkeeper.

* * * * *

"Well, finally you're awake. Now, what was it that you said about danger and being safe, and how did you get burned?" Frenzill removed the crushed garlic clove he had been holding directly under the stranger's swollen, battered nose. His eyes red and watering, Harald sat up slowly and stared at the cozy room around him.

"Where am I?" he began, a note of trepidation in his scratchy voice.

"You are in my inn. I dragged you here myself, completely against my better judgment, and you have been unconscious for too long a time. And you have gotten both me and my chair filthy, so would you please answer my questions?" Frenzill could hardly contain his impatience.

Upon realizing he was indoors, Harald bolted from his chair, only to sink back into it, apparently weakened by the sudden movement. He grabbed his head and shut his eyes tightly. Offering no assistance, Frenzill sighed and drummed his fingers on the wooden table top.

"Sir, of course I will tell you," Harald began, his voice a mere whisper. "But I am so thirsty. Please . . ."

Frenzill looked darkly at him, then muttered, "Surely, surely. My daughter will get you something to make the story come quicker; a pint of our finest brew will help loosen your tongue and make you feel safer. Always does me," he added under his breath, a troubled frown etching itself ever deeper into his long, thin face. A thirsty stranger, thought Frenzill. This can only be trouble. He shouted to Carlana.

Frenzill fretted, wiping his brow, as Carlana drew Harald a mug of ale. Frenzill gave her the sign to add a generous splash of water, and then bade her to bring him a pint too, his eyes never leaving Harald's hunched form. Seventeen years since last a stranger entered Hiddenhaven, he thought. Seventeen years of peace and quiet down the waterspout. What would everyone think if they found out I dragged this beggar into town? Still, Harald had mentioned danger, and from the looks of him, he might know something about all that smoke. Better listen, then send the man on his way as soon as possible. Preferably in the dark of night. The rooms would be filling up with regulars soon. Frenzill had to act fast.

"Did you notice anyone about before you hailed me?" Frenzill gently prodded as the weary man blew the froth from his glass and downed the ale in what seemed to be one long swallow. The man looked up, his eyes dark and distant.

"Oh, sir, no, no, no one at all, only yourself. I had been hiding in the good thick cover of your hedge for a short rest. And a fortunate thing you came. I mean, just look at me. My appearance would have frightened the goodwives or the children who might have happened upon me, probably most of the men as well. I know I look a sight—like something from the Abyss itself." He shuddered, careful to keep his voice low. Frenzill, staring at the man's blistered and blackened face, nodded in agreement.

"So tell me, uh . . ." began Frenzill, his nose burning with the smell of singed hair.

"Harald, as I said before. Sir, please, if you wouldn't mind, could I have another glass? That ale was wondrous good. Mind if I smoke my pipe? My hands . . ." Harald held them forth, their tremors noticeable.

"Yes. I mean, no, please, light your pipe. I'll get you another draught," replied Frenzill, thinking the pipe's aroma, no matter how foul, would mask the stifling odor of the stranger's burned clothing. But the man had better start talking soon. Free ale, even if it was liberally watered, was not the house specialty.

The stranger tossed down the second glass as quickly as he had the first, then wiped his mouth on his sleeve, or what was left of it. "Well, sir, I came from Jasper Ridge. Up in the hills. I'm a tree cutter by trade. Never bothered nobody or nothing; I just cut my logs and float 'em down the river to the town just below the ridge. Maybe you know it?"

"Doriett. Yes. Know it's there is all, though. We keep to ourselves here in Hiddenhaven. Please *do* go on," said Frenzill, his eyes darting once more toward the door. "What is this danger you mentioned?"

"Well, I was coming to Doriett to collect my pay from the mill when I saw it," said Harald slowly, biting his pipe stem and seemingly unfazed by Frenzill's impatience. "And never in all my days has there been anything that frightened me so much as . . ."

"As . . ." Frenzill's blue eyes were locked on Harald's fearful black ones.

"As the *dragon*," Harald whispered.

He tapped off a bit of ash trailing from his hat. Frenzill watched the ash fall softly, lazily, upon his newly swept floor, and then his face seemed to drain of its scant color as rapidly as the stranger had drained his cups. "Wait. Did I hear you say—are you talking about an actual . . . *dragon*?"

"Dragon, sir. Big red one, renegade from the wars, no doubt. Flew right over me, breathing fire and flame like a forge." Harald puffed his pipe into life with a couple of quick breaths. "Smelled like the end of the world. I couldn't move once I looked up at it, and it's a miracle that I was left alive. Wouldn't have been, except I just chanced to take a longer road to town than usual, one that had a lot of tree cover. The dragon had bigger things on its mind than me."

Dragon? A real one? Frenzill swallowed hard, trying to think. All that came to mind was that Doriett was an ugly, noisy, muddy river port. No appreciation for the finer things, especially good ale. They'd drink puddle water there and think it was nectar, thought Frenzill. But perhaps there was good news after all in this. "The town, what did you say happened?"

"It was awful, sir. Nothing left but cinders. I went down to see for myself when I got my senses back, then ran as fast as I could in the other direction once I saw what the thing could do up close. Lucky I saw you at the gate. Almost didn't, with that big hedge all the way around the place. I swear I hate to have bothered you, but I wouldn't have made it without your help. I'd have died for sure if you hadn't found me. I thought you already knew about the dragon and the fires, and maybe everyone was already gone, but I'm sure glad you weren't. The least I can do for you in return is to warn you."

"Warn us? What about the fires?"

"Sir, I can't stay here any longer, good as you have been to me, and sweet as the ale tastes. The dragon is headed this way for sure, and if he don't come himself, the fires he already set will be at your gates inside of another day, maybe sooner even, depending on the changes of the wind, of course. I feel much better now, and I'll just be going, if you don't mind. Say, you're welcome to come with me if you like." He glanced at Frenzill and then at Carlana, who looked longingly back at him but kept her silence. "There's plenty of room in the high country caves," he continued, "and I think we could make them before full dark. But we should leave now."

Harald tipped the shreds of his floppy hat, took a long, appreciative look at the tidy little room, smiled his thanks to Carlana, and made slowly for the doorway.

Frenzill stared at him, horrified. "Leave? Leave Hidden-haven? You can't be serious—and the Midyear Festival is tomorrow. My ale . . . my money," he murmured, almost to himself.

Harald stopped in mid-stride, a look of concern and pity in his dark eyes. "Well, then, sir, may your gods keep you safe. I'll not be back this way again. No timber left to cut in Jasper Ridge. None here pretty soon, either. Thank you kindly for entertaining a stranger. May the blessings of your generosity return to you."

"No, Harald, please, wait. Um, tell me more about this dragon, if you will."

"Well, sir, I'm sure you already know about how the beasts hate towns and such. I really think I need to go now, before the dragon or his fires catch wind of your fine village. I surely don't want to see that sight again." Harald limped toward the door.

"You can't leave now, Harald—you must tell me how you managed to survive, and what exactly happened to Doriett. I mean, is everyone . . ." Frenzill pleaded. Harald patiently turned and faced Frenzill, but it was clear he'd rather be five steps out the door.

"Dead? Without a doubt, all of them. I saw it myself. I survived by pure chance, sir, and by the protection the gods give to the honest pilgrim. The creature just didn't see me amid the wreckage of the burning forest is all I can figure. And it seemed to take out its fury on the town itself, for whatever reason. No, sir, I can't stay, much as I'd love to. You've been kind. Oh, I'm so sorry—almost forgot to pay you. I found this on the street in Doriett. It's a little melted on the edges, but it's still full weight in silver." Harald fished around his scrip and brought up a misshapen coin. "Full weight for full measure," he said smiling, and tipped his hat yet again. "I think I can find my own way out."

"I'll be happy to show you, sir," murmured Carlana, offering her trembling hand to him. Harald's ruined face broke into a surprised smile. He took the girl's hand gently, being careful not to smudge it with soot.

"Um, could you tell me exactly what you saw, Harald? I mean, about just how the dragon attacked the town?" Frenzill cut in, determined to shake every last bit of information he could out of Harald. "Did they make any defense? Why didn't it work?"

"I suppose they just had no fair warning, sir. That's all it could have been." And with that, Harald disappeared through the tavern's back entrance, limping away into the cool, smoke-riddled dusk, Carlana at his side.

Frenzill slammed his fist down hard on the polished table and fumed for a long minute, trying to think of what to do.

"Frenzill! Why the dour face, my good fellow? Set them up and we'll have a game," a resonant voice boomed from the opposite doorway. "And what is that smell? You need to clean your chimneys," added the mayor. "Ha, perhaps we all do, eh? Air's been foul for days now, don't you think?"

Frenzill nodded, his thoughts on the impending destruction of everything he had worked for. He would have to tell the mayor about Harald and his story. "Sir, the oddest thing has just happened—"

"Oh, you mean the stranger Henrich brought in? I could hardly get through the crowd to take him to the gaol," chortled the mayor. "Too bad about his family, if you can credit his story in the least. I think he's just a little touched, don't you know? Tried to sneak in with the sheep! Touched, he is." He tapped his white-haired temple and rolled his dark, heavy-lidded eyes.

Frenzill placed one hand upon his empty glass, as if to steady himself. "Sir, you mean to say there is anoth— I mean, a stranger in town? Where is this fellow?"

"Oh, in my protective custody, of course. Put him in the gaol. Nobody uses it anyway. Can't have him free and talking to the villagers. But say, it was your turn at watch, eh? I thought you'd seen him, or at least the crowd he drew as Henrich brought him to me." The mayor peered narrowly over his frothy mug at Frenzill."

"Well, yes, yes, it was my watch, sir. And I was there, nowhere else to be sure, but I believe I must have stepped aside, ah, for a moment, distracted by the overgrown square. That gardener!" Frenzill lied nervously, understanding now where the rest of Hiddenhaven had been when he'd found Harald.

The mayor gulped down a generous swallow of ale and shook his head, more interested in his news than Frenzill's excuse. "Fine stuff, Frenzill, despite what old Gisrib says. Hope this year's batch is as good. Oh, but to regress, Henrich brought the man straight to me. He's working on breaking up the crowd now. Lot of strong talk out there. Lot of folks excited and ready to leave town. A few of the flighty ones have already gone over the back wall. Threatens to spoil the Midyear Festival. Well, I'll have to make certain he is put out tonight after dark, with food to take him far enough down the road, and then a good knock on the head to make him forget where he's been. But he told the strangest tale. About a red dragon, if you can imagine that! Of course, as I said, who could credit it but the faint of heart, eh? Man's wild with fear, and quite mad, I'm sure," muttered the mayor.

Frenzill could only swallow drily. "I'll see to his meal," he said hastily, and darted off to the kitchen, leaving the bewildered mayor holding forth to an empty chair.

Snatching up a withered turnip and a crust of bread, Frenzill threw on his cloak and ran for the gaol. When he arrived at the tiny stone building at the end of the village's most obscure street, a small crowd still lingered outside, speaking in muted, argumentative tones, their faces grim and concerned. Henrich had not done a very good job, it seemed. In fact, he himself had run for the hills.

". . . can't stay here! Clearly, he has seen it!" a voice from the crowd rose toward panic.

"I'm taking my family away right now. Meet us at the sheep gate in five minutes if you're coming along. I'm not waiting for the dragon to show—too late then," said another.

"But where will we go?"

"The hill caves! Under cover of the forest. Hurry!" The crowd scattered, some of the villagers bumping into Frenzill as they ran to their homes to gather a few provisions.

Dodging them, Frenzill slipped inside the gaol's back entrance and fumbled the cresset from the wall. Stirring it to life, he held the glowing lamp high as he walked down the dark corridor.

The man crouched in the dirty straw of the cellar, rocking back and forth on his heels, mumbling something over and over. When he saw Frenzill, he turned his head away from the light and moaned softly.

"There, there, my good fellow. It's only me, old Frenzill, and I've brought you some dinner. Lift up your voice and tell me what has made you so afraid." The innkeeper tossed the turnip and crust of bread to the young man through the bars, but the stranger only stared out from under his hood at him, his eyes wild with terror and his face abnormally pale and covered in soot.

"It's after me, isn't it? The dragon is coming, and we are all going to die! Please, you've got to let me go, I have to get out of here," he wailed, his voice rising to a pitch.

"Ah, quiet now, fellow, just tell me about this dragon, and we'll make sure he doesn't get you, all right? You are perfectly safe down here, you know. Safest place in the village, actually," Frenzill chuckled, tapping the filthy wall with the toe of his boot. "Good thick stone above and around you. Virtually dragonproof."

The young man seemed to take a little comfort in those words and settled into sense. "Sire, my name is Simon Bell, and I have come from Wellshimmer. My family was burned alive in the attack, and only I have fled. When the dragon—" He caught his breath at the memory, but went on, Frenzill's rapt attention coaxing him. "When the dragon appeared, I became so afraid I could not put one foot rightly before the other. I fell as I ran, and hit my head." He touched an ugly purple bruise at his temple. "When I came to, everyone was dead, my poor parents' bodies sprawled over me, and the fire had eaten up the remains of the only home I have ever known. . . ." He trailed off, his eyes distant and filled with renewed terror. "I must be away from here! It was just that I was so tired and hungry." He edged toward the bread, a slight, crooked smile on his face as he bit gratefully into the hard crust. "Thank you, good sir. May the gods bless you in kind."

Frenzill considered young Bell's story for a long moment as he watched him chew. Then he turned and left the man mumbling again quietly in the dark cell. Frenzill climbed the stone stairs out into the cool evening, hung the cresset back upon its hook next to the keys, and slowly walked back to the House of Fine Spirits.

Wellshimmer was only a couple of days to the east, he thought. Doriett was two days beyond it. A dragon, and the beast is routing civilization from the valley for certain and moving westward steadily. I must tell the mayor it's for real; I must warn everyone, and what about my ale? Frenzill wrung his bony hands, his heart filled with foreboding.

The Midyear Festival was tomorrow.

But the dragon could be here any minute. And people were leaving!

Frenzill blotted his brow with his sleeve and composed himself, feeling it best to try to deal with the crisis in a way that would avert as much panic as possible.

But then, Frenzill didn't know about the third stranger yet.

The green-clad archer was standing outside the inn, with the mayor and a wary group of townspeople gathered around him, listening.

"But what will we do?" cried one of the merchants, a man who had just invested all of his life's earnings in his newly expanded shop.

"How big did you say it was?" a woman's worried voice piped up from the back of the crowd.

"But you have been running—is it that close?" shouted Gisrib, his empty glass still in his hand.

The archer, a man of about fifty, his face flushed red beneath his thick, graying beard and his tunic drenched in sweat, begged their silence with raised hands. "Good folk, I have no time to explain, only enough to give you this warning. As I said, you had best run for the hills with me. I am the sole survivor of my scouting party. Any moment, you will see the dreaded creature in your own skies, but that moment will be too late. If you look upon it, you will surely be struck with a terrible fear, for did not all of my fellows die where they stood? I was washing my face in a pool of rainwater when I saw the thing reflected up at me, over my shoulder, its flame spouting from enormous nostrils and its scales so bright red that they looked like fire upon diamonds. Its rage bore down upon our camp and my poor companions with no mercy, and now they all lie where they fell, no more than a heap of burned bones amid the ashes of our gear. I tell you, we must away, or join them! The beast may be on the wing even now!" As the archer ended, half of the panic-stricken townspeople immediately rushed out of the sheep gate, leaving house and home, intent on saving their lives.

Then Frenzill shouted, his voice rising above all the others, a note of command in it he had never found before. Besides, he had just had an idea.

"Stop, all of you!" he bellowed to the remaining villagers, his small frame shaking. "I have an idea. Let us go down into our sturdy cellars, where it is surely safe, and let the beast pass us over. When it finds no one out and about to incite its wrath, it will think Hiddenhaven is abandoned, and leave us and our fair town alone."

And then I can go back and get my ale when everyone returns, he thought to himself. I'll sell it to you for double the price. You will be so grateful to me for saving your lives that you'll pay even more, if I ask it.

The archer turned, his sharp eyes finding Frenzill in the space of a single heartbeat.

"Oh, sir, that is a brilliant thought, worthy of action. And none too soon, for the skies appear exactly as they did just before the creature bore down upon us. Lead us then and we will be safe."

"Yes, let us follow Frenzill's suggestion," added the mayor, and the rest of the crowd instantly charged toward their cellars, everyone bumping into their suddenly snarling neighbors in the hurry. Frenzill was almost crushed before he could turn himself amid the stampede, the archer catching him up just before the blacksmithing twins ran him over with their hobnail boots.

"Easy, good sir! Careful, lads! This is the man who has surely saved us all," called the archer indignantly. Frenzill gulped and touched earth again, brushing the dark hobnail prints from his shoulder. But as the street had suddenly emptied, another thought struck Frenzill.

His own cellar was locked, and Carlana—and the key—were nowhere to be seen. The sky boiled above him with dark clouds, and a fine rain of soot had begun to fall, its tiny particles dancing down on Frenzill's head. There was no time to find his daughter. He would have to go to the safest place in town. The gaol.

He eyed the archer roundly and gently disengaged his collar from the man's burly, soot-covered hand.

"Thank you, soldier, for your help. I should be making sure my townspeople are comfortable. I am the innkeeper, after all. Have a good journey, and may the gods favor you with all due speed." He smiled toothily, still trying to yank his cloak away from the archer's other dirty hand.

The archer did not let go. "Sir," he said, "I had hoped to shelter with you, especially since I came to warn you, and now there is no time at all to be safe. I have come out of my way to help spare your town from this grave danger, and now, one of its most prominent and wisest citizens would turn me out to fend for myself before a *dragon?*" The man's eyes were wide with disbelief.

"Let go, stranger," said Frenzill, his voice suddenly full of daggers. "You have no place here. We have to protect ourselves."

The archer shook his head in amazement and let go of Frenzill's cloak just as a rolling cloud of smoke poured over the walls. The archer ran behind Frenzill anyway, finally catching up with him at the doorway of the gaol.

"Sir, you are an innkeeper—are you quite sure you have no room for me? The others seem to have found shelter elsewhere," he pleaded, coughing in the swirling black smoke.

Frenzill shoved the forlorn Simon Bell out the door, slamming the portal shut.

"He's put me out, too, sir," Simon Bell cried. "What will we do now?"

The archer grinned widely and lifted the cell keys from their nail, placed the correct one in the lock and turned it until it clicked.

"Why, have a fine Midyear Festival, of course. I think I know of some famous ale that needs drinking," he crowed from outside the heavy iron door as Frenzill stared at him in utter shock and amazement through its small window.

"Then shall I get Guyler, Rouben?" said the other one as he straightened his back and began wiping the soot from his face.

"Yes, Kevo, tell him to load the ale and open those rusty gates," said the archer. "We'll have to take the wagon through them."

"My ale? A *wagon*? Who are you?" shouted Frenzill from the safest place in town.

"We are the Cobbin brothers from Doriett," said the archer, pulling off his cap and removing the false beard from his face. "That same Doriett, which, by the way, is still standing and quite prosperous. So prosperous that we have run out of ale for our celebration." Rouben smiled in more than fair imitation of Frenzill's best publican grin.

"But what about the dragon?" Frenzill sputtered.

"Dragon? Did someone mention a dragon?" said another voice from behind Rouben. Guyler Cobbin, his tree-cutter's disguise shed, joined his brothers. "The brewers of Doriett have a certain talent for blowing smoke, too, Frenzill," he smiled.

"But you can't leave me here!" said Frenzill. "There is nothing to eat!"

"I believe I left you the turnip and some bread, good sir," called Kevo as he jangled the keys. "A man's generosity always catches up to him."

"You'll never get to my ale!" called Frenzill angrily. "You don't have the key to the cellar."

"Yes, he does, Father, and now he has this, too," said a sweet, tired voice from somewhere beyond the iron door. Carlana held up a dusty volume of neatly written pages in front of the little window.

"My recipe! Carlana, how could you?" cried Frenzill, pounding on the unyielding door.

"You always told me it was my dowry. Well, seems I'm getting married, Father. Gisrib here will let you out in a day or so, *if* he forgives you for what you did to his drink today," she called back to him, her other hand in Guyler's.

"Carlana!" Frenzill shouted after her as the gaol door slammed hard behind them.

"Ah, Frenzill," smiled Gisrib as he jangled the keys in Frenzill's face. "Why are you so distraught? After all, we'll leave you the dregs. Oh . . . and happy Midyear Day!"

Tavern Tales
Jean Rabe

"WhatareyoudoingMaquestaKar-Thon?" The gnome talked so quickly his words ran together, sounding like an insect buzzing around his white-haired head. He balled his tiny nut-brown fists, set them on his hips, and stared up at his companion. "Irepeatwhatareyoudoing?" The gnome was clearly upset, but it wasn't his distraught state that hurried his tongue. He normally talked very fast.

"What I am doing doesn't concern you," came the satin-cool reply.

"ButMaquestaKar-Thon. . . ."

"Lendle, I'm watching them load cargo onto the *Perechon*." The smooth voice had an edge to it this time. "They'd be able to load it much faster if your machine wasn't right under the cargo hatch. They have to work around it."

"ThatisnotwhatImean!" The tip of the gnome's head barely came up to Maquesta's hip. The captain of the *Perechon*, Maq was a tall and lithe half sea-barbarian with ebony skin, midnight eyes, and curly raven hair that fluttered in the strong early-morning breeze. She was also half elf, though her ears—trimmed by her father years ago when elves were hunted along the Blood Sea Isles—were as smooth as the sea on a windless night.

She inhaled the salt-tinged air, stretched, and glanced down at the gnome. Her expression was cool, and her eyes unblinking. "I haven't the time to trade banter with you today. I've a few errands in town before we leave and—"

"Irepeatthat'snotexactlywhatImean." The gnome rocked back and forth on the balls of his small feet, idly fidgeting with a pearly button on his red shirt. "Whatareyoudoingby-takingonahaulingcontractnow?" He paused for a brief moment to catch his breath. "DangerousbusinessItellyou. Dangerous. Thisismostcertainlynotthetime to—"

"Lendle, slow down. I can barely understand you," she said, drawing her lips into a thin line and putting her hands on her hips. Her dark eyes locked onto the beady ones of her diminutive friend. Lendle was the *Perechon's* cook, engineer, and resident tinkerer.

"I said, what do you think you're doing taking on this hauling contract, Maquesta Kar-Thon?" He addressed her formally, as he always did. And now he talked deliberately at what was an agonizingly slow pace for him in order to accommodate her. "This is a very bad time to be sailing the Blood Sea—to be sailing anywhere for that matter. Better to stay in port, wait out the war, then take on a contract or two when everything's settled and nice and peaceful. You don't see any other ships in this port loading their cargo holds, do you?"

"The only other ships in this port are fishing vessels, and they're getting ready to go out in the harbor—fishing."

The gnome pursed his lips. "But the war."

"The war." Maquesta narrowed her eyes.

"In the Abyss," he said, continuing to carefully enunciate each word so his sentences didn't run together. "Last night. Over dinner. We heard about it."

"In the tavern," Maq said, as she let her breath out slowly. She waved her arm in the direction of the shore. "*Late* last night."

"The men were talking about a battle brewing in the Abyss—gods and knights warring over the fate of Krynn. Dragons and wizards and everything."

"We heard it *in the tavern*, Lendle. It was a *tavern tale*, the product of a few too many ales and too many wagging tongues. We need money, and taking these crates of Mithas Brandy south to Cuda will get us money."

"We could take the brandy in a few weeks or months. We could—"

"I'm the captain. The contract is signed."

"Who will pay?" the gnome grumbled. "We won't get any steel until we make the delivery. And if there really is a war in the Abyss, gods and knights warring . . ."

"Then Krynn will be destroyed."

"My point exactly," the gnome said.

"If Krynn is destroyed, you won't have much to worry about," Maq replied evenly.

"Some consolation."

"Then put ashore—your machine and all. We'll have an easier time loading cargo in the next port without your contraption in the hold." She was serious, her icy tone told the gnome as much. The ship came first with Maquesta. It always had and always would. And when she made a decision, she stuck by it. "We'll leave in an hour—with or without you."

"Idon'thavetolikeit," the gnome said after she walked away.

The *Perechon* punctually pulled away from the docks under full sail. Lendle's dark eyes fixed on the choppy water off the port bow, and his stubby fingers gripped the railing so tightly that his skin turned pale around his knuckles. "If the war wasn't enough to worry about, Maquesta Kar-Thon, there's the Maelstrom," he grumbled to himself. The Blood Sea's whirlpool lay to the west, and the gnome imagined he could see the edge of its vast rim. "The war. The whirlpool. We should have delayed."

"Kof is being careful," Maq said. Quiet like a cat, she had padded up behind him. "I don't intend for us to get anywhere near the Maelstrom. The *Perechon* is much too valuable to risk in those waters. We'll stick to the coast of Mithas, pass by the Eye of the Bull, reach Cuda on the southern part of Kothas, and deliver our cargo. Simple. Then I'll treat the crew to a day in the largest Kothas port."

The gnome looked past her to the ship's wheel. Kof's thick hand was wrapped around the king's spoke, his eyes staring at a point over the *Perechon's* dragon-headed prow. Kof—or Bas Ohn-Koraf, as the gnome usually formally addressed him—was a minotaur with a horned, bull-like head, massive shoulders, and muscular legs that ended in polished black hooves. His body was covered with coarse red-brown hair, and the scant clothes he wore always complimented the color. The minotaur was Maquesta's first mate and trusted friend. He superbly handled the swift two-masted ship.

"He just better keep us on course—and the *Perechon* in one piece," Lendle softly huffed as he reluctantly released his handhold on the railing. He went over toward the minotaur. "I'm too old to be looking elsewhere for work. And I'm too young to be sucked down to the bottom of the sea in a big whirlpool." The gnome stared up at the first mate.

"Stop worrying so much," Kof softly scolded.

"Worried? Me?"

"I'll admit, I'm worried," the minotaur said, his massive bull face suddenly solemn, his large, round eyes intense. "I'm worried about what's for supper. My belly's rumbling."

"Swordfish stew," the gnome quickly returned. "I'll put it on now."

While the crew ate, Lendle busied himself in the cargo hold working on his oar machine. It was a hollow brass sphere, looking vaguely like an overturned soup kettle that gleamed warmly in the dim light of the gnome's lantern. The top was coated with a copper sheath broken by twin pipes that rose at odd angles for about two feet before they joined a hammered steel cylinder that pointed to a large trapdoor. The door led from the cargo hold to above deck and the gnome had constructed his machine directly below it. This meant Lendle had to also construct a pulley system that would enable the *Perechon's* crew to load cargo around the machine.

Stacks of crates, all safely deposited via the gnome's pulley system, ringed the machine and extended into the shadowy recesses of the hold. Each was plainly labeled Mithas Spiced Brandy or Mithas Mulled Brandy. The gnome had noted that there were twelve bottles to a crate when he pried one open, and he had counted one hundred and twenty-four crates in all. The bottles were carefully packed with straw, their corks waxed into place. Lendle had expropriated one mulled bottle, and had set about using the viscous brandy as a lubricant along the base of the brass sphere, where at evenly spaced intervals stiff, coiled wires extended outward, giving the invention a bit of an arachnid appearance. The coils ran between the crates and across the width of the hold, where they were wrapped around oar handles.

A small brick fireplace, not much bigger than one of

the crates, sat next to the brass sphere. Lendle used an old bellows to coax the flames, which produced steam from an apparatus resembling a giant teakettle. The steam ran through a tube from the kettle to the sphere. And in principle, the steam powered a series of gears inside the machine—which in turn caused the coiled wires to rotate and the oars to move.

The last time everything functioned properly (he had actually gotten the machine to work twice) was a little more than seven months ago—and at that time the machine had worked tirelessly for nearly three days before it finally belched and wheezed, spit free a few gears, and stopped. Lendle wasn't quite sure what he had done to make it work—or what had happened to make it quit.

So each day he continued to tinker with his machine, fine-tuning the gear alignment, twisting the coils, polishing the sphere. Sooner or later he would get it to work again so the *Perechon* would have the capability to continue on its appointed course in the event of calm seas and no wind.

Lendle yawned and took a swig of brandy—the bottle was still about half full after the machine had been coated to his satisfaction. No use wasting what little was left. The thick liquid warmed his mouth, and he felt it race down his throat and into his belly. He sat down between the coiled wires, leaned back against a crate, and listened to the gently groaning timbers of the ship and the incessant soft patter of rain against the deck. He took another long swallow.

The gnome suspected it was near midnight. He closed his eyes and took his time finishing the brandy. It was exceptionally good, he had to concede. It made his fingers tingle and his toes sweat. No wonder the merchant in Cuda was paying so much for this stuff. Lendle drained the last drop and thrust the cork back on the bottle. He used the heat from the small fireplace to remelt the wax around the top, then put the empty bottle back in the crate. He was careful to reseal the crate so no one would be the wiser. The merchant in Cuda would simply think one of the bottles—or maybe two or three before the voyage was up—somehow leaked.

The gnome stretched, concentrating on the patter of the

rain. A couple of hours' rest would do him good before he'd have to get up at dawn and start on breakfast. Swordfish stew and eggs, he decided. He put out the fire, patted his machine good night, then grabbed his lantern. His stubby legs carried him through a gap between the crates and toward a ladder that led to a small hatch that would take him up near the bow of the ship.

"Toomuchtodrink," he scolded himself as he swayed back and forth, trying to grab onto the ladder for support. But his fingers missed their intended mark, and he felt himself falling. His nose struck the hold floor, and the lantern fell. The gnome sighed with relief that neither had been broken. "NomoreMithasBrandyforme," he said as he rose to his knees and righted the lantern. He'd sit up top for a little while, clear his head, and let the rain wash away some of the effects of the brandy before he crawled under the covers. He gripped the lowest rung tightly as he felt himself pitching to the left. "Wait!I'mnotdrunk." He swallowed hard, then added more slowly, "At least I'm not *that* drunk. The ship's rocking."

* * * * *

What had begun as a soft, warm rain had quickly turned chill and driving. Maquesta strained to peer through it as she fought to keep the wheel steady. Above her, the sails alternately snapped and filled, teased by the fickle, gusting wind. The masts creaked in protest, and all around her came the sound of feet slapping against the slick deck. Her crew was doing its best to keep the rigging tight and to tie everything down.

"Kof! Catch that line!" she shouted. A rope from the mizzenmast had frayed loose and was whipping madly about, threatening to pull free part of the lowermost sail.

Through a crack in the trapdoor, the gnome looked out and spotted Bas Ohn-Koraf hurrying toward midships to comply, his large hands catching the offending rope. Everything was so dark on deck, the minotaur looked like a shadow among shadows. Despite Kof's great strength, he seemed to have trouble with the line.

The gnome felt the bow of the ship rise as it crested a breaker, then felt it dip and lean to port. He heard the crash of a wave hitting the side of the ship, and he grimaced as water washed over the deck and through the crack in the trapdoor, drenching him. The gnome muttered a string of curses, threw the door open all the way, and climbed up just as the *Pere-chon's* bow rose again. He balanced himself, no mean feat given how much brandy he'd consumed, then stepped carefully and deliberately, not wanting to lose his footing and fall. "WhatishappeningMaquestaKar-Thon?" the gnome asked as he quickly headed toward her.

"A storm!" she shouted to him. "Coming out of nowhere!"

The ship pitched toward starboard this time and Maquesta braced herself. Lendle wrapped his arms around her leg to keep from falling. "Canhardlyseeanything!" he called. The gnome gazed up through the rain. The sky was a murky gray-black, so cloud-covered that it effectively hid Krynn's three moons. The gnome knew it was easy to get turned around in a gale-force storm, especially when you couldn't see even one star to steer by. He scowled. "I don't like this one bit, Maquesta Kar-Thon," the gnome grumbled. "Not one bit."

"Neither do I," she said sternly. "Neither does anyone on deck. But I don't need you to tell me—"

Kof's approach cut off the rest of her words. "The line's tied down, for all the good it will do us. The lower mizzen sail's ripped. No way to patch it in this tempest. I called Rogan down from the crow's nest."

"I'll hold her steady," Maquesta said. "Take Rogan and make one more pass to be sure that everything's tied down, and then—" This time an odd sound interrupted her, a loud whistling, a keening howl followed by a roar that seemed to grow in intensity in the space of a few heartbeats. She glanced toward the starboard side, Lendle and Kof's gazes following hers.

The wave was difficult to see at first, the sea being so dark, like ink, and the sky being not much lighter. But Maquesta's vision was as keen as an elf's, and she strained to separate the sky from the water. "Come on," she whispered, "where are you?"

"Ican'tseeanything!Toodark!" the gnome shouted. "What-isit?"

Maquesta saw it then, a hundred yards or so from her ship. Taller than the *Perechon* and extending to the edge of her vision, it was a wall of pounding water bearing toward them. "Squall!" she shouted, as she turned the wheel hard to port. "Get all the men on deck now! Watch the rigging! Now!" There was an unaccustomed urgency in her voice, and it spurred Kof and Lendle to action. Kof spun on his hooves and headed toward the aft section. The minotaur issued orders as he went. "Away from the rails! Squall! Brace yourselves! Grab that line!"

"Squall? Oh no!" Lendle released his grip on Maquesta's leg and headed toward the hatch at the back of the ship that led to the crew's quarters. He'd try to help roust any men who might be sleeping through this commotion. The gnome spotted two sailors tying themselves to the mainmast, and another holding onto the mast's rigging.

Lendle had been at sea for decades and thought he'd encountered just about every weather condition imaginable. A squall was something he'd blessedly missed out on—until now. Squalls were rare and dangerous, caused by shifts in the temperature and changing wind directions. The winds could pass sixty knots and were every bit as dangerous as a cyclone, though not as long-lived. And they could kick up monstrous waves.

"Steer into the wave, Captain!" the helmsman called to Maquesta. To the gnome, the man's words sounded like a whisper over the wind and the roar of the water.

"Not *that* wave!" Maq answered. She turned the wheel farther to port, in the direction the wave was traveling.

Despite her best efforts, Maquesta couldn't put enough distance between the huge wave and the *Perechon*. Lendle's small mouth fell open and he found himself at an uncustomary loss for words as he watched the wall of water bear down on the ship. The rain was coming sideways now, driven by the wind, and it pelted the gnome, stinging his face and hands. Water was everywhere, and all he could hear was the noise of the wave.

"We can do it," Maquesta spoke as if coaxing herself. "Come on, come on. No!"

The wall of water struck the *Perechon*, the sound deafening and the wave dark like pitch and filling their senses as it swallowed them. It lifted the ship while at the same time acting as a great hammer, pounding against the masts and the deck with all the men struggling to find purchase.

The air rushed from Lendle's lungs. He felt himself flying, and his mouth and lungs filled with salt water. The gnome's small body was slammed into the railing, and his arms flailed out, trying to grab onto something, churning through the water for what seemed like an eternity before wrapping around a rail.

Maquesta had locked her arms around the wheel. Her head struck the king's spoke and her chest was driven against the wheel, pressed in a watery vise. She fought to stay conscious and in control as the fierce water continued to batter her.

Kof had only a heartbeat's warning. He shouted to the men, his words lost in the caterwauling of the wave. He hit the deck and grabbed onto the base of the capstan as the water rushed over him. Something harder than the wave struck the minotaur's back, and his fingers lost their hold. Whatever hit him pinned him to the deck, keeping his face below the water. His eyes flew open wide, and his muscles strained as he struggled to push himself up above the water where he could breathe.

The *Perechon* fell with the wave, then rode high with the next swell. It pitched madly, listing far to port, then to starboard, threatening to capsize when another sizable wave washed over the deck. But then the ship bobbed upright again, giving everyone left on deck a chance to grab lungfuls of air.

"Kof!" Maq cried over the still-keening wind. "Someone help him!"

Lendle pried himself loose from the rail as the torrent of rain continued. He coughed to clear his lungs and glanced toward the aft section, where part of the mainmast had broken and landed on the minotaur. The gnome scrambled toward Kof. Already a few hands were struggling to free the first mate. Lendle listened to them bark orders at each other, even as he heard another roaring sound growing and drowning out the men's words. Another massive wave was headed their way.

He futilely added his small fingers to the task, huffing and grunting, then grabbing onto the broken mast for dear life as the second wall of water struck. The sailor next to him was washed away, and the gnome felt the man's clutching hands brush briefly against his short legs. When the wave receded this time, the sailors finally managed to lift the mast section off the minotaur. As Kof struggled to his hoofed feet, the deck rose beneath them again as the *Perechon* topped a massive breaker. In that instant, the wind caught the mizzenmast's twisting sails, and with the wave's help toppled the ship over on its side. Several sailors slid from the deck and over the rail, swiftly disappearing from sight.

After several long moments, the *Perechon* partially righted itself. However, it still listed so badly to port that all those left on deck had to hang onto something to keep from tumbling into the sea.

"She's taking on water!" cried a sailor who had managed to climb up from the crew's quarters below as he held onto the rigging.

"We're capsizing!" bellowed another. It was a cry that was quickly passed along the deck until it reached Maquesta's ears. "The *Perechon's* sinking!"

The waves receded for a moment, and the minotaur took a quick glance about to take stock of the men. He kept a grip on the capstan with a big hand and waited for the next breaker to strike. His breathing was labored, his broad chest rose and fell quickly. "We've no way to save the *Perechon* in this storm, Maq!" His big voice carried just enough for her keen ears to make out his words.

She nodded to him, motioning to midships.

"The longboats," Kof called to Rogan. "Get them in the water. Be fast about it. And make sure Maq gets in one of them. I'll see to these men."

"Thelongboats?" Lendle sputtered. The gnome was

balancing on the broken section of the mainmast. "Thelongboats. Capsizing. Sinking. We're—"

"Abandon ship!" Maquesta shouted. Her heart hammered in her chest as she said the words. With no one watching her, she allowed a lone tear to spill over her cheek and mix with the rain. "All hands—abandon ship!"

The gnome's small face, reddened from all the exertion, suddenly blanched. He sucked in his breath, felt his fingers tremble. "Thisismyhome!Yourhome!Iwillnotabandonship!"

"Abandon ship!" Kof echoed as his great arms directed men toward the longboats. He turned toward an approaching sailor. "Anyone left below?" The sailor shrugged and hastened to get a seat on one of the boats. The minotaur headed toward the hatch to the crew's quarters. "Lendle, get on a boat," he called over his hairy shoulder. "Now!"

The gnome stared slack-jawed as he watched the first longboat ease away from the side of the dangerously listing *Perechon*. "Kofwecan'tabandonship!" he called. But the minotaur had already disappeared below deck. Lendle whirled to see Maquesta directing a few sailors toward the bow. She looked defeated, a sagging shadow among the broken rigging and fleeing crewmen. The gnome heard her order Rogan twice to leave the *Perechon*. He was the second mate and was arguing that if Maquesta was staying with the ship, he was staying. But he finally gave in. Maquesta looked up, spotted the gnome, and pointed toward a longboat.

Lendle shook his head. "Mymachine!" the gnome called back, doing his best to make his small voice heard above the wind. "Gottosaveatleastpartofit!" He didn't wait for her reply, but hurried toward the cargo hold, pushing aside a corner of the fallen mainsail to find the large trapdoor. From the ship's odd angle, and his precarious perch, opening the door was difficult, but the ship tottered farther to port, the door flew open, and the gnome and the sail were pitched into the hold.

Kof clambered back onto the deck a moment later, three sailors in tow. "That's all of them!" he called to Maquesta. "Get yourself on a longboat!" The minotaur's eyes were rimmed with red as he took a last look around the *Perechon's* littered deck. He let out a frustrated sigh as he saw Maq stubbornly refusing to budge.

"You first!" she ordered the minotaur. "I'll follow you—with Lendle!" She ran her fingers along the *Perechon's* wheel, as if bidding it farewell, then hurried toward the cargo hatch.

* * * * *

Lendle's fall had been stopped by an unyielding crate filled with Mithas Spiced Brandy. He groaned and climbed off it, carefully inching his way between crates both broken and intact. The hold was as black as midnight, and he couldn't even see his fingers in front of his face. But he knew every inch of the place by heart. His head brushed against the sail, which must have caught on something above, most likely the cylinder part of his precious oar machine. Water sloshed around his ankles as he took a few steps and felt the sphere in front of him. Though the gnome considered the *Perechon* a loss, his oar machine was another matter. It seemed undamaged to his questing and probing hands. As his fingers continued to dance over the surface of the sphere, his feet tangled in a few coils at its base.

"Notdented," he observed. "Goodgoodgood." The brass sphere was what he most wanted to save, as it was a costly piece of equipment because of all the gears inside he'd so carefully purchased and put in place through the years. The coils could be replaced relatively easily and inexpensively.

He felt his way to the small stove. He worked quickly to light a fire and to right the teakettle contraption. He made sure the tube that carried steam to the sphere was still affixed, then he used the faint glow of light from the stove to see where the sail dangled. He tugged the cloth free, pausing for a moment when he thought he heard someone calling his name. "Thewind," he decided as he tore a large piece of the sail free and began hooking it about the base of the sphere. He used a cutter he'd snared from his pocket to snap the coils, fastened the wire at the sphere's base through the sailcloth, then glanced about at the crates of brandy.

"Mulledwouldbebest," he mused. "ShouldworkIthink. Shouldworkfine."

"Lendle!" Maquesta leaned over the cargo hold opening and repeated the gnome's name. She saw the faint glow of his stove's fire and a mass of sail, and she heard him sloshing about. "Get up here—now! That's an order!"

She whirled toward what was left of the mainmast, planning to grab a section of line and throw it to him. But at that moment another wave washed over the deck, carrying Maquesta with it. The *Perechon's* captain was tossed over the side.

Kof had been holding his longboat to the side of the ship, waiting for Maquesta and Lendle. When she went sailing past him, he pushed off, stretching out his long arms in a desperate attempt to catch her. But his hands closed around water only, and he was lucky a sailor grabbed his thick waist to keep him from falling over, too. "Get the boat closer!" the minotaur bellowed. The water was dark, and she was difficult to spot. "Maq!"

Maquesta fought to keep her head above the water, even as she felt herself wash away. As she rose with a small swell, she spotted Kof and several of the sailors paddling toward her.

"Hang on, Maq!" the minotaur shouted.

He was yelling something else to her, but she couldn't hear him. His deep voice was drowned out by the great clamor of wind and water. Another wave was bearing down on the *Perechon*, a mountain of water as forbidding as the others, but coming from the other direction. Maq kicked furiously to stay above the water, to keep air in her lungs. As strong a swimmer as she was, her efforts were futile. She saw Kof leaning over the bow, his muscular arms outstretched, then felt herself being dragged under by the current, drawn down into an inky blackness that even her elven eyes couldn't penetrate. Water rushed down her throat. She kicked furiously in order to break the surface, sucking air deep into her lungs, then holding her breath as another wave sent her below.

The sea was whipped into a frenzy. A great rumble cut above the wind and the roar of the waves, sounding like an earthquake. The rumble came again, and as it died the wind picked up even more. The waves washed over the sides of the longboat, threatening to capsize it, too.

"Bail!" Kof ordered. "Faster, or we'll go under like an anchor, mates!" The sailors used their hats and hands to scoop the water out, though they could barely keep up with it. Kof saw Maquesta go under—twice. Now there was a gap in the cloud cover overhead, the first respite from the utter darkness of the storm. It was just enough to let a few stars wink through and shed some light on the captain clinging to what looked like a rocky outcropping of coral.

"Maq's alive!" he shouted to his fellows. "Closer! That's it, that's it. Got her!"

Maquesta was exhausted and bruised, barely conscious. But summoning the last of her strength, she grabbed Kof's arms and pushed off from the ridge, slicing her legs on the sharp coral.

His muscular arms lifted her over the edge of the boat, then she felt herself slammed against its bottom planks as another wave struck, pushing the small craft back toward the *Perechon*. The water folded over the boat, pummeling her already-aching body. Then the wave receded as quickly as it had come, and the minotaur pulled her up as the men resumed bailing. She brushed the sodden curls away from her face and glanced about.

"Kof!" she sputtered. "There's the *Perechon*! Somehow the wave righted it!"

"Praise Habbakuk," one of the sailors breathed.

The minotaur's round eyes, peering through the darkness, spotted the battered craft. The ship looked crippled, its mainmast twisted and splintered, its sail laying across the deck like a shroud. But its mizzenmast was intact, it was no longer listing, and hope filled his massive chest. "Unsinkable," he whispered, remembering that years ago the ship was sucked down into the Maelstrom and then miraculously spat out along a far shore. "Praise Habbakuk, indeed."

"Hold tight!" Maq shouted. She gripped the sides of the longboat tightly as the small craft rose on a wave and smacked into the side of the *Perechon*. She noted with relief that the other longboats were also returning, either under their own power or nudged by the wind.

Within several minutes, the men had scampered back onto the deck. Though exhausted, they scurried about, tugging the mainsail free from midships.

"Trim the mizzensail!" she shouted, trying to be heard above the thunder that filled the air. "What's left of it, anyway," she said to herself as she and Kof made their way to the wheel.

The minotaur cocked his head. "That noise—there's got to be another wave coming. We should head east. We can't be far from Kothas now."

Maquesta nodded. "If we can find a shoal, slip inside and get some cover, we can get out of this peculiar weather and then . . . Gods! Is there no end to this? Kof, get the men below, on the oars!"

The minotaur paused only a heartbeat when he followed Maq's gaze and spotted the new source of her concern. A few hundred yards off the *Perechon's* bow, the ocean dropped away into a great roaring waterfall. There was a cleft in the sea that looked like the maw of a great beast, black and empty and so big across that in the storm's darkness he could barely take it all in. The cleft was ringed by water that plunged who knew how far toward the bottom. And the *Perechon* was heading straight toward it.

"I've sailed this sea lane for years," Maq said, though not loud enough for anyone to hear. "*That* was never here before."

"The oars, mates!" Kof roared. He stomped his hooves, and firmly shook the shoulders of the sailors who were staring mutely. "Move! Get below and man the oars!"

"By the mighty loins of Habbakuk!" Rogan cried. "We're doomed!"

"We're certainly doomed if we do nothing!" the minotaur curtly returned. "The oars!"

They hurried to oblige, shouting prayers to the gods as they went. Then a wheezing, groaning, clanking, ringing, belching, and banging started that grew in intensity until it was accompanied by the snap of timbers as a section of the deck shattered. Slivers of wood spewed in all directions.

"In the n-n-n-name of all the gods!" a sailor shouted. "What is it?"

"It's Lendle!" Rogan hollered.

The minotaur looked toward the gaping hole in the deck. At first it appeared as if a bulbous ghost were rising through the opening. But the thing kept going, revealing itself to be a balloon made of sailcloth. Beneath it dangled a sphere with rods and cylinders poking out at odd angles, and below that—suspended in a crate labeled Mithas Mulled Brandy— sat the gnome. In one hand he held an opened bottle of brandy. The other hand fidgeted with the teakettle-like contraption that was barely visible over the top of the crate. He was pouring brandy into the pot, and it in turn was belching steam into the sphere. A line ran from the balloon-sail to the gnome's mouth, and as he tugged on the line, the oar machine soared higher.

"Thought you abandoned ship!" he called to the men. "Thought you said the *Perechon* was sinking!"

"The ship righted itself!" Rogan called.

"But we'll be sinking soon enough!" the second mate added, as he gestured toward the pounding waterfall and the massive opening in the sea.

"Amazing!" The gnome's eyes grew wide. "Wonder how it got there? Never seen it before. Sailed these parts before, too. Amazing!"

"Get down here, Lendle!" the minotaur shouted, as he joined the men retreating below deck.

Lendle shook his head. "Definitely never seen anything like it! A waterfall in the middle of the ocean! Amazing!"

The flying oar machine skimmed across the deck. So distracted by the incredible ocean cleft was the gnome that he was paying no attention to how he was steering the machine. It lurched to a stop and became snagged in the mizzenmast's sail. "Ohdearohdear!" he tittered, as he poured more brandy into the teakettle. "Notagooddevelopment!"

He emptied the bottle, tossed it aside, and reached for another. "Morepower!Gottobreakfree!" The teakettle whistled shrilly, and other noises erupted from Lendle's machine. "Gottogetmorepower!" The flying machine strained against the rigging. "More!" He emptied the second bottle, reached for the third. Slick with rain, the glass neck slipped through his stubby fingers, shattered atop the cook-stove. "More . . . oops. Fire!"

* * * * *

In the dark hold, the sailors had to feel their way toward the oars, wending between crates, broken bottles, and the discarded pieces of Lendle's machine.

"Find an oar and then put your backs into it!" Kof bellowed. "If you want to live, give it everything you've got, then give it more!" He groped around until he found an empty bench, snatched up an oar handle, and set to work. "One, two, three!" he called, repeating the cadence as more men joined him.

"The gods brought this storm!" the minotaur heard a sailor call. "The gods will kill us all."

"The gods? Some dark god," another replied. "Takhisis, no doubt. The Dark Queen."

Maquesta was alone on deck, fighting against the wind, pulling hard to starboard in an effort to turn the ship around, and concentrating on trying to shut out the noise of the storm. The rain pelted down and the wind howled, pushing the *Perechon* closer to the edge.

She barely felt the ship surge beneath her as more men took up oars. Their efforts would not be enough, she knew. There weren't enough men, enough oars, enough time. Maquesta closed her eyes and thought about Kof, Lendle, and her father who so many years ago taught her to sail and to love the sea more than life. She had loved this hard life, had hardened herself to gain her crew's respect. No soft words for anyone. No regrets.

"Fire!" Lendle continued to call. But his small voice was lost in the howling wind, the pounding falls, and the incessant rattle of his machine. Despite the rain, the fire grew, engulfing the cookstove, burning the gnome's pants, reaching up and consuming the balloon-sail. Flames licked about the other bottles of brandy Lendle had stored on board. The glass cracked, Lendle screamed in fear, and an explosion rocked the air.

Maq's eyes flew open as she was flung away from the wheel, landing hard and sliding toward the far rail. Her head struck the posts, momentarily stunning her. She shook her head and blinked, then gritted her teeth as the air whooshed across her face.

The ship flew, propelled by the force of the explosion of Lendle's machine. Like a stone hurled from a well-aimed sling, it shot across the chasm and churned through the waves on the other side.

Maquesta crawled toward the wheel, pulled herself to her feet, then gripped the spokes as the ship lurched to an abrupt stop. "What in the name of—"

"Maq!" Kof dragged himself up from below. The minotaur stumbled toward her and glanced about. "Lendle!" Bits of copper and brass, broken brandy bottles, and a shattered teakettle were strewn across the deck. A badly charred lump, vaguely resembling a gnome, lay in the center of it.

The lump slowly raised its head. Lendle's face was blackened and clean-shaven now, for his beard and hair had been burned away. "Mypoormachine," he mumbled. Then he lost consciousness.

The rain was coming softer now, almost a gentle drizzle. The clouds overhead thinned and drifted, and the wind died down to a soft breeze. Rogan gingerly carried Lendle below, as Maquesta, her face impassive, offered a silent prayer to the gods that her small, brave friend might live.

Kof stood at the rail at midships, watching as the cleft mysteriously sealed itself. It was as if the strange waterfall had been nothing more than a bad dream. The sea smoothed around the *Perechon*, and the sky became clearer.

"We were lucky," Rogan said, as he joined Maquesta and the first mate. "The gods were smiling on us. We were very lucky."

"Were we?" Maq wondered aloud. She continued to stare at the calm sea.

The water was as flat now as a sheet of glass. The stars were mirrored on the sea's surface, as was a single pale moon, large and full, that hung just above the horizon.

* * * * *

Two weeks later the *Perechon* limped into Cuda's port on the southwestern coast of Kothas. A third of the brandy crates had survived and were being off-loaded under the watchful eyes of Maquesta and a still obviously singed Lendle.

The gnome sagged against a piling and shook his head. "My machine," he grumbled. "I'll have to start all over again."

"Your machine worked well enough," Maq said flatly. "It saved the *Perechon*."

"I don't have enough steel to buy all the parts I'll need for a new one. We lost two-thirds of our shipment, two-thirds of our pay."

"I've a remedy." Her dark eyes met the gnome's beady ones. "I've just secured us a new contract—hauling wool north to Karthay. They'll start bringing it on board within the hour. And since there's no machine in the hold, we can take on a full load. The pay is good—half up front."

"Why don't we take the wool in a few weeks, a month? Maquesta Kar-Thon, with there being one moon now, the tides are different, the sea is *different*. We should wait in port for a while until everything settles—until we know what we're dealing with, until we know the repercussions of the war. Why, last night in the tavern they were talking about—"

"The contract is signed."

"Maybe a brief delay, Maquesta Kar-Thon."

"The pay for this contract is too tempting to turn down."

"Tempting, maybe. But—"

"Then put ashore—now." Her tone was sharp, her eyes flashed. "Build your machine on someone else's ship. Fill up their cargo hold with your foolish inventions." She drew her lips into a thin line. "I'll not turn down an attractive job just to satisfy you."

"Good pay, huh? A new cookstove would be nice," the gnome admitted. "I could use at least a dozen copper rods for my oar machine. Thick wire, a funnel, and . . . What about the tavern tale?"

Maq looked at him sharply.

"I know," said Lendle with a sigh. "Then Krynn will be destroyed, and I won't have anything to worry about." With a scowl, he disappeared below deck.

"Within the hour," Maq called after him, her eyes sparkling. Out of his sight, she allowed herself a rare smile.

The Dragon's Well

Janet Pack

"Old man! What do your visions tell you? Are you going to find water today?"

Laughter and catcalls followed the tall, bent, gray-haired old man as he made his way through Gurnn. Nodding pleasantly, smiling and waving his free hand—the one not gripping his precious stick and the battered old shovel—Tarris Canrilan walked on through the withering heat with his peculiar, loose-kneed gait.

The old man, formerly the town weaver, usually began shuffling around the community at daybreak, and continued until he plopped down, exhausted, for his meager noon meal. He was inevitably pleasant, but full of nonsensical phrases he presented as precious jewels of wisdom to those willing to engage him in talk.

Today Tarris appeared different—there was a firmness and a hurry to his step, an abnormal brightness to his dim green eyes, an impatience to get somewhere. Not many of the heat-tortured town denizens, sweating and growling at one another from tiny patches of precious shade, noticed the difference. Reldonas Fittering, the former town crier, did.

Being curious and an inveterate gossip, a gawky bird who poked her bill into everything she found interesting, Reldonas lived for juicy rumors and fresh information. Her sharp ears often allowed her to put two distantly related facts together and come up with a synthesis bordering on fact. She raised a hand above her eyes in order to shade them, and watched Tarris until the old man finally passed between two buildings and away from her sight.

The cause of his behavior didn't occur to her until the sun had nearly blistered her hand. She edged close to a shadowed wall that offered some relief from the unremitting rays. The mundane movement of her shoulders touching the partition that enclosed Gurnn's spring (dried up this last year and a half because of changes wrought by the Chaos Years) seemed to stir an idea in the back of her mind.

Could this be the beginning of the excitement she'd been craving these many months?

Moving away from the spring's gritty grave, Fittering scuttled to the office of Elothur, the Town Leader of Gurnn. She knocked on the ill-fitting door, which rattled beneath her bony knuckles.

"Enter."

In the town leader's voice sounded layers of frustration, sadness, and hopelessness brought on by a third year of unrelieved drought. He was one of the last who still tried to uphold a semblance of normalcy in his life by going to work every morning and attending to the business piled on his desk.

He barely glanced at her. "What do you want?" flew from his mouth before his usual pleasant mask slipped over his face.

"Town Leader," Reldonas gasped, her homely visage reddened by heat and exertion. "I have news. Tarris Canrilan has seen his fourth vision!"

"So?" Elothur leaned back, looking at the odd woman through bloodshot brown eyes surrounded by wrinkles of sun-baked skin. "What is that to me?"

"He's on his way to that copse south of town to dig again today," she said. Dust wafted from her short dark hair turned pasty brown from the powdered loam of once-fertile fields three days' ride from Palanthas.

The town leader took a long moment to think, browned hands folded upon the cracked wooden table before him. The table had once been very valuable, but heat and dryness had ruined it, like everything else precious in the town. And like everything and everyone else, it was on the verge of collapse.

"I believe you're correct, Reldonas," Elothur said in a disinterested voice. "Thank you for the news." He bent again to his work.

"Aren't you going to do something?" Fittering sputtered.

He spoke to her as to a recalcitrant child. "What would you have me do? I've let the last of the guards go so they can scrounge scraps for their own families." He sighed. "Everyone I know has pressing responsibilities. I'd like to do something, but—"

"I'm the one who can watch him, Town Leader. I'm on my own now."

"I thought you were caring for Gwillar's mother Delphas . . . Ah, I had forgotten she died during the last bout of sickness."

He glanced out the slits between the shutters sheltering his window, and sighed again. The sky glowed its usual bright blue, made harsh by the sun's glare. There hadn't been more than a wisp of cloud across its candescent countenance in several months. Three tenacious years of this horrible drought had brought everyone he knew to the verge of despair. Crops had withered in the fields and fallen to dust. After that, meat animals had begun dying, their ribs and spines poking through their thin hides. Most of the bodies rotted where they fell. The land was covered for weeks with a stench that adhered to Gurnn despite consistent dry winds, gusts that brought illnesses healers could not diagnose. Half the town had sickened, and fourteen had died, including Reldonas's adoptive mother—Delphas—and Tarris's beloved wife Renyalen. Some townspeople claimed she had been the old man's last link to sanity.

"Very well." The town leader turned back to his visitor. "Since Tarris claims to be having visions, and appears to be searching for water with that divining stick of his, he does bear watching. A little more water would benefit us all since the reservoir is almost dry. I figure two weeks' worth is left, at the most. You have the assignment, Reldonas."

"I'll report back to you several times every day," she offered.

"That's not necessary. Only the important developments. In those cases, come swiftly."

"I will! Thank you, Town Leader."

"And Reldonas?"

"Yes?"

"Do try to get the old man to fill in those holes he keeps digging. Someone's going to get hurt."

"Yes, sir!"

The town crier turned spy stumped out of the office into the baking sunlight. Moving quickly despite her limp, she stopped at Gwillar's house to borrow a skin of water and a bag of dried food. She'd repay it as soon as she could, she promised, intending to do just that. Hordes of promises she hadn't kept in the past never bothered her. Without wasting any more time she headed south, aiming for the same copse of dying trees as did Tarris Canrilan.

She saw dust hanging in the air from his digging before she spotted the old fool himself. He was waist-deep in a hole, shoveling at an even pace and muttering to himself. Each time he brought a full spade to the surface, a plume of brown arose to taint the wind that blew its furnace-breath across the land. Above him, the bare bones of dying trees rattled fitfully against each other.

"Dragons tell me to dig here, water down below. Dragons tell me . . ."

Reldonas limped closer. Tarris paid no attention.

"Good day, Master Weaver," she said. "I have a message for you from Town Leader Elothur."

Green eyes, more canny than they'd appeared for months, regarded her as the old man leaned on his implement.

"I know what it is," he said, his quickness surprising her. "He wants me to fill in the holes." Tarris began to dig again. "Tell him I'm sorry, but there's no time, no time to waste."

"Why?" she asked.

"Because liquid will bubble from the ground. That's what my dragons promised. And it's going to be very soon. I must be ready."

"What must you be ready for?"

"The next vision, of course." Tarris, stopping for a moment, regarded her curiously. He climbed out of the hole and propped his shovel against a tree trunk.

Odd, Reldonas thought, how he tries to behave as if perfectly normal. He was probably the craziest of them all. Everybody in the town had changed a great deal as their

work, their lives, their very minds evaporated in the unfalter-
ing heat. But she had not changed, not that much. There was
just this little nagging in her mind that craved excitement. She
wiped sweat from her forehead, leaving streaks of mud.

"When will your next vision come?"

The old man chuckled, a sound as dry as the wind. "When
the dragons tell it to, it will be time." He picked up his
"finder" stick of hazel, and, holding the forked end gently in
his gnarled fingers, began carefully stepping through the
copse.

About the size of the thickest part of the old man's thumb,
the stick had been stripped of its bark and smoothed. It was
gaining a patina from Tarris's hands. Its single end pointed
straight ahead. Reldonas Fittering could not figure out how a
lowly tree branch could ever indicate the presence of water.
Nonetheless, she watched, fascinated.

The hazel wand trembled. Tarris stopped, backed up three
steps, and paced over the same area again. Nothing.

Suddenly the straight end of the stick plunged downward.
The old man marked the dust with his finger, carefully laid
the "finder" beyond harm, retrieved his shovel, and began
digging. Dirt again fountained into the sweltering air.

Intrigued, Reldonas stumbled to the far end of the copse
and sat down in the shade to think. Could the old fool's
visions be correct? Was there indeed water beneath the layers
of dust, water that could save Gurnn?

Reldonas's peculiar knack for figuring things out worked
again. She realized suddenly that not all the trees around her
were dying, only the ones farthest from where Tarris was digging. That meant there must be water somewhere nearby that
was keeping some of the trees alive. Perhaps Gurnn's only
hope did rest on the visions of this crazy old man.

Creeping now, trying not to divert the old man's attention,
she slunk to the edge of his first hole and peeked within.

She did not know what she expected to see. At first the
shadows confused her sun-dazzled eyes. Willing patience,
she allowed a few moments for them to adjust. Was it just
darkness at the bottom of the hole, or was that actual seep-
age? With a sigh, Reldonas lowered herself in.

"Mud." She tested it again with a finger. "Real mud." Moisture and coolness felt foreign against her skin. She rolled a little ball of proof of the old man's claims into her palm, then knotted it in the frayed hem of her robe. Only then did she survey her options for climbing out.

Her first two attempts were unsuccessful; she fell to the bottom with painful results. Determined, Reldonas finally heaved herself out of the hole, got to her feet and limped back to town at her best speed. She found Elothur sitting glumly in his office, head in hands. He looked up slowly, as if reluctant to face another small crisis.

"News? Already?"

She plunged into her story, her voice betraying pride. "I've seen Tarris's stick indicate water!" she finished. "What he says is true. Look at this!" She untied the mud from her robe and offered it to the town leader. "Not all the trees in that copse are dying. If there is water in one place, certainly there will be in others."

"That's possible, I suppose." He poked the mud, found it real, and fingered it in wonder. "I have other news, however." Elothur's face was an overburdened mask. "Thienborg Skopas fell down one of Tarris's holes today. He's bruised, and demands satisfaction."

"Call a town meeting for mid-afternoon." The time when it's hottest, and tempers will be too, Reldonas said to herself, tingling with anticipation. "When people hear my report, they will look upon Tarris with new eyes!"

"Very well," replied the town leader. "Can you guide the weaver, get him here close to the right time?" Tarris had not been famous for punctuality since his wife had died.

"I'll try. He's so focused on his mission it will be difficult to interrupt him. You realize, don't you, that Thienborg could have caused the accident himself, wanting nothing more than a scapegoat on whom to blame all his troubles?"

"I suspect that." A ghost of a smile twitched the dry corners of his cracked lips. "Your work has proved useful as always, Reldonas. Thank you."

"It is good to be appreciated, Town Leader."

But as she limped from the dusty office, the former town

crier felt her work was not yet done. She headed directly for the bit of shade sheltering Thienborg Skopas, Tarris Canrilan's accuser.

* * * * *

"Come, my dragons, come. It's time, past time!" Tarris muttered the chant to himself aloud while he dug, trying to persuade the noble beasts to appear. He hated the thought that the final vision would take the dragons away from him.

He knew he couldn't keep his dragons, they'd told him that several times. At least he'd have memories of his beautiful metallic-hued companions for the rest of his life.

They appeared whether he waked or slept. Time of day or night meant nothing to his dragons. The trio—gold, bronze, and silver—always appeared in the distance where he could see their huge wings furl and strong tails lash. They always turned one by one to regard Tarris, coming closer until their magnificent heads filled his mind's eye. Their mouths never opened when they spoke to him, but their dark, richly cavernous voices resounded in his head and they seemed to know everything about him.

During the first dream the dragons had spoken of Krynn's aridness and of Tarris's hidden ability to save people by finding liquid with a stick. At first he worried that he really was going crazy until he went hunting for the simple implement that, the dragons claimed, would allow him to bring about the salvation of Gurnn.

A forked stick had not been difficult to find. The correct forked stick eluded him for months. His hands had searched for a certain "feel" of wood, discarding one after another until he found an old hazelwood stick, debarked and bleached nearly white. His fingers clamped around it and he took it home. That evening the second dream occurred. He'd waited little more than seven days for the third, all the while walking through daylight's blaze and ascertaining the hazel stick's feel.

He learned to hold the "finder" in a loose grip, long end pointed ahead of him like the feeler of some ungainly insect. Any time it dived toward the earth, Tarris marked the spot with a stone or a twig. The old man didn't mind that he forgot about his holes almost as soon as he found them. They represented his practicing with the "finder." He smiled and went on about his business. The dragons had told him that he would find liquid, if he showed faith and was conscientious.

After the dragons visited him the fourth time, he began carrying an old metal shovel along with the forked hazel twig, his small hide waterskin, and a bag of preserved meat and fruit. Wherever his stick pointed, Tarris dug with an energy and dedication that, at first, many townspeople envied. But when he didn't find any water, and the holes began appearing all over town, they began to dismiss him—and worse.

Stopping to rest, absently rubbing the smoothed surface of the wooden handle with blistered fingers, Tarris remembered the old Gurnn. The place used to be pretty, he thought. Now bleached like the bones in the surrounding pastures, it was all one dun color beneath the castigating sky. The people looked exhausted from labors they continued to perform only because of a thread of hope it might rain soon. Those who didn't do anything all day preferred to wallow in the shade, full of self-pity.

"Many people are avoiding me these days. A few are openly hostile. But I can't let that interfere with my work. Oh, no, I can't let a little thing like that interrupt me."

People who hadn't minded being friends with Tarris before, when he was the town weaver, no longer wanted anything to do with him. Tarris sorely missed the neighborliness he used to maintain with nearly everyone in the community, but he was dedicated to his visions.

As the humans of Gurnn ostracized him, the dragons became Tarris's only friends. He often talked to them whether he saw them or not. This habit set him even more apart from the townspeople.

"If I find water, it will be worth all the difficulties, all the labor. 'Liquid will bubble from the ground,' they said. I *must* find it, and soon. Come, my dragons."

"Master Weaver, Town Leader Elothur requires your presence."

"Who's that?" Tarris peered suspiciously up and through the trees.

"Reldonas Fittering. I was here earlier today."

"Can't go. Have to dig." He did, and most energetically.

"I saw your dragons," Fittering fibbed.

"What?" Canrilan stopped throwing dirt to look around. "Where?"

"In the square. Will you come?"

"They wouldn't all fit in that square. Too small for three dragons."

"They wanted me to find you."

"My dragons," he said slowly, "talked to you?"

"They said to come to the square. Please, it won't take long."

"Well . . . I suppose it's possible." He climbed from his shallow hole, slung the shovel over his shoulder, and picked up his precious "finder." "I can't leave work for very long. It's almost time for the fifth vision, you know."

Chattering inanities, Reldonas led the way back to Gurnn. The old man kept silent, even when he saw the crowd filling the town square. He stopped a moment, sucked in a deep breath as if taking in courage with the searing air, and then stepped forward.

Derisive murmuring followed Tarris as he shouldered toward Elothur, who was standing near a group of towns-people clustered in a sultry patch of shade. The town leader's sweat-streaked face was impassive. Reldonas joined him, standing at his shoulder, her birdlike eyes bright. Elothur drew a breath but Tarris spoke first.

"My dragons are not here. I must get back to work."

"You and your stupid . . . work!" spat a stocky man behind Elothur. "All you're doing is making life harder for the rest of us. I could have been killed falling down one of your holes! I'm badly bruised as it is, and you're to blame."

Cries of "Exile him!" and other imprecations against the visionary rose from the crowd.

Tarris, a slight frown of puzzlement between his brows, looked steadily at the complainer. "Who are you?"

"Thienborg Skopas," said Elothur, voice edged with heat and tension. "He's a fellow citizen. Thienborg wants you to stop digging because your holes are a public danger." The town leader turned toward the people, raising his voice. "Tarris is only trying to do something constructive. Look what he discovered earlier today." The townspeople pressed forward to see the pathetic little mudball Reldonas had brought to him. "This proves the possibility of water. Water means life. Do you truly want him, the only one of us who seeks water, to stop?"

"If he's our only hope, we're doomed!" shouted a widow who'd lost her sons and husband during the last wave of sickness.

"Digging up mud isn't going to help us!" another cried.

"What about those damned holes?" snarled Thienborg. "I deserve some compensation in return for getting hurt!"

The town leader leaned toward the man, opening his mouth as if to make a speech. It then seemed as if the sun abruptly leached all the energy from him, and his shoulders slumped. The town leader waved a hand in dismissal, turned, and walked away.

Grumbles sounded from the audience, backed by the sibilance of unceasing dry wind. Thienborg's smoking gaze never left the old man, but Tarris didn't notice. His green eyes were fixed on something far beyond the edge of the crowd.

"I deserve consideration!" exploded Thienborg. He displayed bruises on his arms, his chin, his legs. Several of his friends shouted their support.

Tarris had heard, and his eyes focused. "I'm sorry." His apology got lost among the clamor. "But my dragons are not here. I must go and look for them."

"We've got to make him stop this crazy talk of dragons!" howled Thienborg. "And stop the digging. Throw him out of town, I say. Let him dig elsewhere and bother other people!"

The crowd cried out against the former weaver, but Tarris had vanished.

* * * * *

All the rest of the day Tarris walked and dug wherever his "finder" stick pointed. By sundown he'd dug eight new holes. Satisfied with a good day's work, he sat down to his meager meal of dried fruit and meat, and three sips of water.

He didn't want to return to his stuffy, cluttered dwelling for the night. He didn't want to return to the fear-choked atmosphere of the town. He wanted to stay out here where the houses were few, where the gleam of stars seemed friendly, and where he, by the light of the moons that would rise later, could continue his digging.

He felt more peaceful than he had in a long time. This place was refreshing after the tensions of Gurnn. His spirit sang, the hope he nurtured in his heart swelled and filled his being. He would find water, he *knew* it!

With a suddenness that amazed him, the vision came to him. In the near distance he could see the three of them approaching, his dragons of gold, silver, and bronze. They stretched their wings in languorous movements, flexing each muscle of their magnificent leathery pennons. Their tails lashed, stilled, and lashed again, sweeping through the air like scythes.

The old man sighed in pleasure at the wondrous nature of the scene. Slowly, very slowly, they noticed him. The bronze was first, snaking his head out and then advancing. The silver peered, nodded, and followed the bronze. The first two were trailed, somewhat reluctantly it seemed, by the gold.

The dragons fastened their knowing eyes on the old man, silently looking past his human shell deep into his soul.

Tarris didn't wait for their words to fill his head. "I dug a lot of holes yesterday and today. And there was a town meeting called about my work."

We know, the silver dragon said, nodding. *You acted correctly.*

"But someone hurt himself falling into one of the holes. He blames me, says that my visions are foolish." His face and eyes glowed. "I know they—you—are real."

It is that sort of conviction that makes you ideal for this mission, stated the bronze, moving even closer to Tarris. *You are the type that carries through no matter what if you think the goal is important.*

The silver one's huge eyes fastened on the former weaver.

JANET PACK

Don't you think the others are jealous?

Tarris ducked his head, nodded acceptance. "I shouldn't be worried. You've guided me well this far." He straightened and threw his shoulders back like a soldier standing at inspection. "I've been practicing every day with the hazel stick, doing exactly what you told me to." His voice hurried with excitement. "I think I might have spotted just a bit of moisture in the bottom of one of the holes I dug today."

The bronze dragon nodded. *That's how it begins. Sometimes it takes a long time to find the right spot.*

Just remember to be patient, the silver added. *Patience is the key.*

"Yes, yes," the old man said eagerly. "I am patient, you know I am. But the rest of the townspeople aren't."

We know that, the bronze added.

The gold dragon finally spoke. *We have final instructions for you.*

"At last!" Tarris exclaimed, his heart racing. "I'm ready."

East of town you'll find a small valley, began the bronze.

The old man frowned. "The one with the pyramid of rocks at the lip, or the one with the whitebark trees?"

The one with the pyramid of rocks.

The silver dragon took over. *Go into that valley and continue until you come to the base of an outcropping of stone. The outcropping is substantial, and it is the primary feature of this valley. You will know you are there when you reach the end of the defile. Pace sixteen steps to your left from the stunted tree growing at the right-hand side of the wall.*

Rest now. Try to be there by mid-morning. It is in that valley you will find the precious liquid. This is the last time we will communicate with you.

Suddenly the dragons weren't in his mind any longer. A bubble burst, returning the stars and the night. Tarris leapt to his feet.

"I now know where to find the water!" he sang, almost dancing with excitement. "I know, I know! Thank you, dragons! Thank you, Paladine, and all the gods of good!"

Content and tired, Tarris curled up on the ground to sleep. His shovel rested upright in the dirt nearby, his precious hazel wood stick lay beneath his hand. A beatific smile curled his lips and smoothed the age wrinkles on his forehead.

He dropped immediately into dreams of his dragons. Behind the three dragons, water cascaded into a lovely pool surrounded by green grasses and ferns. Its sound almost covered the delighted shouts of the people of Gurnn, frolicking in their liquid treasure.

* * * * *

The next morning, Tarris awoke just as dawn colored the sky. His excitement almost kept him from eating the last of his dried fruit. He persisted, knowing he'd need energy for the morning's exertions. The old man washed the morsels down with sips of water from his nearly empty waterskin. For once he didn't notice its bad taste. Being so close to the end of his mission made the mud-tainted water seem like the fine wine he'd had once long ago, the leathery fruit more like the sweet viands that used to be available.

Hitching his shovel over his shoulder, he picked up his "finder" stick and headed toward the valley with the pyramid of rocks that marked the entrance. It was a fair walk. Tarris didn't mind. His heart sang silent duets with the few birds that still warbled morning greetings. His loose-kneed steps covered the ground at a good pace, delivering the old man to the rocky valley a little before mid-morning.

Shuffling and slipping sounded behind him. Tarris knew without looking over his shoulder that Reldonas Fittering was following as best she could with her clumsy gait. The old man smiled. She'd missed the vision, but she'd be close enough to witness water breaking through the parched ground.

He entered the valley slowly, the hazel stick held before him, eyes and hands alert for its slightest quiver. Walls of soft limestone surrounded him, but the wand led him straight ahead, toward the deep end of the valley.

"It is as my dragons said," he murmured.

The stone walls narrowed; Reldonas still followed. The old man put her out of his mind. After some time the valley floor widened again. Tarris concentrated with all his being, thinking only of the water he was destined to find.

The hazel stick led him to the rock outcropping at the end of the valley. Grinning in delight, he lowered the "finder" and spoke loudly so Reldonas could overhear. "Sixteen steps to the left of the stunted tree, they said." He looked around. "Where is the tree?"

No tree, stunted or not, grew where the dragons had indicated. A desicated stump had long ago cracked away and rolled to the valley floor. The same hue as the pale rock, it seemed just another decayed stone lying with the rest at the foot of the outcropping.

Tarris paused, rummaging through his brain for inspiration, searching with eyes that squinted at the glare of sun dappling on stone.

"It must be here. It must!" His voice echoed loudly from above and behind him. Reldonas's close footsteps also sounded in his ears, the noise compounding until it seemed as if his single follower became a crowd. "The dragons said so. They would not lie to me."

He backed away, one step, then two. The heel of his sandal caught against a large stone, and he fell backward.

Sun-blazed rock seared him through his clothing; his shovel bruised his shoulder. Dust caught in his nose and mouth. He coughed. Tarris swept a hand across his tearing eyes as he grabbed for his precious hazel stick, hope sagging, and forced himself to peer one more time at the rock wall.

"There! That must be it!" The vague outline of a tree was incised in the stone. It could be detected only from a certain vantage point. The old man scrambled up to run his fingers over the miraculous sight.

"Thank you, dragons," he muttered with heartfelt gratitude, turning left. "Sixteen paces from here." Carefully he counted each step, the "finder" held before him. The hazel stick remained uncommunicative until the sixteenth step.

Then the stick bowed with a suddenness that awed the old man, practically yanking his hands down level with the talus at the base of the outcropping. Excitement surging through his blood, Tarris set aside his precious stick, unslung his shovel, and began to dig.

"Sure as rain, what that stick did was amazing." The former town crier was perched over his shoulder on top of a huge stone. Tarris didn't waste any energy by replying.

It was hard going for someone more used to the weight of dust and caked ground. On his knees, he moved aside the rocks as best he could; his old muscles couldn't hope to lift a shovel full of them. Sweat sluiced down Tarris's face. His throat burned from thirst, but he refused to drink—he promised himself he wouldn't touch any more liquid until he discovered his new well.

Tarris first noticed the other noises when his hole was knee-deep. He dismissed the strange murmurs and shuffling, thinking they were echoes or the movements of Reldonas above. When they kept growing in volume, he finally looked up.

"Good day," he said pleasantly, stopping for a moment and nodding to the crowd of townspeople gathering around and above him. "Look, here is where the dragons said to dig a well. The water will save us all. I call it the Dragon's Well."

Odd, but no one returned his friendly greeting, particularly Thienborg Skopas, who stood near the edge of the hole with arms wrapped across his chest and eyes as hard as the stone beneath his feet.

"Please excuse me," Tarris said, his hands bloodied from broken blisters. "I have much work to do."

"Your work means nothing, crazy old man," Thienborg spat. "You didn't have visions, and there's no water here. Never has been, never will be."

Tarris stopped again. "The dragons told me—"

"The dragons," sneered Thienborg. "There's no water here, I tell you!"

"My dragons don't lie!" protested Tarris. He turned to the others. "You all know me, have known me for many years. Have I ever lied to you?" He held pleading hands out to them. "Have I?"

Tarris gasped as something struck him from behind. A stone hit him, then another and another—a rain of rocks that was hard and painful at first then soft and gentle. Soon he no longer felt them. The old man tried one last time to speak. His lips moved, but words did not come. He had dropped the shovel somewhere. He tried to look for it as more stones hit him in the head. Knees buckling, he crumpled into a heap and rolled to the bottom of the hole he had dug, face turned toward the blinding sun.

Reldonas's weird cackle sounded against the wind.

"Dug his own grave," croaked Thienborg. "Got what he deserved."

"Hold!"

The crowd turned toward the shout. Town Leader Elothur and two of his former guards ran toward them, pounding down the valley floor. The trio stopped at the horrifying sight.

"No," whispered Elothur, shocked. "Oh, no. Has it come to this?"

Shaking, the town leader climbed into the hole. He knelt, bruising his knees on the stones. Gently he cradled Tarris's gray head against his dusty robe. The dying old man opened dazed eyes.

"My friend," he whispered as Elothur bent to hear. "Do you see them? My dragons! They rejoice with me. I did find liquid for the town, I found . . ."

His voice faltered. The old man's eyes fixed on something far away as the light in them died. His smile remained.

Feeling as old as Ansalon itself, Elothur laid down the old man's head and rose slowly.

"Dug his own grave," one of the crowd echoed caustically.

The town leader whirled. "Yesterday morning he said that his dragons promised he'd find liquid. And he did."

"His own blood!" Thienborg sneered.

"More than that." Elothur pointed. They all looked. A bit of dark moisture bubbled up from beneath the old man's body.

The group gasped, watching as precious water seeped from under Tarris's dusty robe. The town leader touched his finger to it and straightened.

"Liquid bubbling up from the ground, just as he promised," he announced in a grim voice.

"Let's have a taste!" exclaimed Reldonas, skittering down from her rock and peering from behind him.

"No." Elothur sounded tired, defeated. "This water is tainted. We decried him, shunned him, murdered one of our own. Now we dare not drink."

"Why not?" Reldonas Fittering asked.

Elothur showed his wet finger to the crowd. They leaned forward, shoving each other to get closer to see.

In the drop of crystal water curled dark, whiplike tendrils of the old man's blood.

The Magnificent Two
Nick O'Donohoe

The wind whispered all around, dry and insidious, reminding the valley that no one was a farmer any more. Harri pulled his cloak tight despite the heat, trying in vain to shut out the dust.

He nearly missed the inn; only a trick of the wind told him there was a building outside his field of vision. He raised his hood to look at it.

The shingles were cracked and dry; the first rain would leak through them. The sign was a simple ale stein, battered enough to suggest rough treatment inside. Below it, prominently, was a rack with pegs for swords, axes, maces, and other less identifiable weapons. A skull mounted on the rack for emphasis had an axhead still embedded in it.

But the inn was clearly full, and the rack was empty. Harri looked at the empty rack thoughtfully and tucked his cloak carefully over his sword. Just before opening the door, he tucked a scroll in his belt, taking care to let it show over the top of the belt.

Heads turned toward him, then quickly away, hiding faces. Hard times breed caution.

He smiled at the barkeep (it was clearly too late to call her a barmaid), a voluminous but still pretty redhead with her hair up but falling down. With no welcome at all in her voice she said, "Welcome to Peacedale."

"Nice name," he said, glancing about and trying to guess where the patrons were hiding their weapons. He brushed the gray dust out of his graying hair. "Something to cut the dust?"

She held out her palm. "Something to cut costs?"

He grinned and set his pack on a chair so he wouldn't have to bend over. He nodded to all the occupied tables, focusing momentarily on a slender blond lad who sat with his chair

leaned against the wall and watched Harri with interest. He
looked away and his eyes came to rest on a table where four
men in battered cloaks were slouching on the wood benches
and pretending not to watch him. He reached into his pack
with one hand, automatically keeping his sword arm free.

A few of the people in the bar looked like they might be the
man he had come to meet. Harri tossed the barkeep a coin,
watching without surprise as she tested it with a knife. He
took the offered ale and drained half of it. When he lowered
his tankard, the barkeep was still watching him.

He smiled at her. "I can tell you like new faces."

She shook her head without smiling or frowning. "You're
not a trader." She hadn't spoken loudly, but others turned
their heads fractionally. "You're not a cleric, and Paladine
knows you're not a farmer. What brings you here?"

"Change of scenery," he said amiably. "I thought a trip to
the mountains would be good for me."

She shook her head slowly again.

Harri sighed. "The truth?"

She nodded.

"All right. Some months ago," he said to her, loudly enough
to be overheard, "the valley of Rockhaven, just beyond the
pass to the north, was raided by a red dragon."

Out of the corner of his eye he saw heads bob slightly.

"The town," he went on, "was nearly destroyed, and all
of its heirlooms taken. Presumably the dragon was acting
for the Dark Knights and planned to give their wealth to
Takhisis.

"Then the Solamnic Knights, accompanied by dragons,
came, and several Dark Knights arrived to engage them."
He shrugged. "Nothing but a skirmish in a larger war. The
dragon hid his loot in the mountains, made two marks in
certain rocks to find it again, and joined the battle."

He watched the customers for a reaction. No one stirred in
the slightest; this much was well-known.

"The combat was fierce. It was also loud, and these hills are
prone to rock slides." He ran a finger across the table, leaving
a clean swath in the fine powder. "Especially when it's dry
and grasses and shrubs are dead. There was an avalanche,

and the dragon's treasure was buried," he finished lightly, as though the final statement didn't matter.

The barkeep said tiredly, "I've heard that story all summer. I've heard it from dreamers, thieves, miners, and even a few dwarves with no sense and a taste for spirits. What makes your version different?"

"The dragon is coming back."

The slender blond lad sat up straight. A ripple of unease went through the room.

"His name's Auris. He's left the service of the Dark Lady, and that means he'll come back here. He's going to find his gold again if he has to tear Rockhaven apart."

The customers looked at each other covertly. "Dragons," the barkeep said flatly, "are bad for business."

"If I could find that treasure ahead of him, then I could wait there for him. Then when he showed . . ." He looked around expectantly, then sighed. "Ah, well."

"And you would do this of your own good heart?"

Harri smiled modestly.

"Are you a knight?"

"I've trained as one."

The barkeep looked dubious. "A cow can claim to be a horse—"

"Till you saddle her, yes." He rummaged in his pack. "But if I were only claiming to be a knight, would I have this broken piece of breastplate?"

He held up the piece of metal so that the innkeeper could see the engraving. "Est Sularus oth Mithas," he said solemnly, impressively. "My honor is my life."

He leaned forward. "I'll sell it for a fair price."

The barkeep gaped. "Your honor?"

"No, no," Harri said irritably. "The breastplate. I'll even buff it first." He saw the slender blond lad staring at him and added smoothly, "Ventures like these require cash. No sacrifice is too great."

"You're sure you got this while in the Knights of Solamnia?"

Harri said righteously, "It was a gift from a brother knight who no longer needed it."

"He left the knights as well?"

Harri glanced automatically at the scar on his forearm, looking away quickly. "He became a permanent pacifist."

"Quite a life change, that."

"The biggest."

The slender blond man spoke up. "So it wasn't your breastplate?" His voice was surprisingly high.

"Not at first, no." Harri went on hastily, "The knight who gave it to me said Auris had marked his cache with two lines in rock, set at right angles. If you sighted down the two lines, they would meet at the cache."

The barkeep sighed. "And after the battle, because of the avalanche both marks were lost." She said "lost" like she might say "spilled" or "unprofitable."

"Are you sure?" he asked. "What about the stories that one of them has been sighted?" He glanced around, one finger touching the scroll at his belt.

"Tell me."

He waved a hand dismissively. "Just stories, I guess." He drank up.

Another voice broke in, "We'll all be telling stories about you, too, when you're dead and gone, Harri Gundervall."

Harri turned toward the back of the inn. The four men at the table had all turned around. One of them, a bulky man with stringy brown hair, said in a hoarse voice, "You can't be planning to fight a dragon alone." He glanced toward the door. "Unless you've got a force of men waiting outside."

Harri, one hand hidden, answered easily. "I usually work alone." He regretted his response immediately. He tried to cover by smiling amiably. "Have we met?" They looked at him stonily. He said with more edge, touching the scroll again, "Corresponded recently?"

The brown-haired man shook his head slowly and grinned, showing remarkably bad teeth. "Your name has come up in our line of work."

Harri winced. "Favorably, I hope," he said, but it was unlikely.

The man stood slowly. "You're also called Harri the Human Kender."

"An old nickname."

The man said levelly, "Harri Gundervall—swordsman, sword instructor, mercenary, thief."

"Not necessarily in that order."

The man's grin spread. "There's a reward for you."

The other three men at the table stood as well, each with a hand hidden from sight.

Harri gestured to show his empty hands. One was near a slit in his cloak. "I'm a peaceful man."

They all chuckled, and the brown-haired man said, "Not half so peaceable as you're about to become."

The slender blond lad stood hastily and moved back as all four men rose from the benches, throwing aside their cloaks. One drew a sword, one a mace, the other two battered and stained fist-axes.

"No killing," the barkeep said anxiously. She dragged a small child over to her and hugged him, all but burying him in her bosom and apron.

What happened next was very fast. Without hesitating, Harri threw his cloak over the first man's head and tugged down, smashing his face into the table. He kicked at the bench, which flew up into the air and smacked one of the men edging forward. As the man collapsed, groaning, Harri grabbed the first man by the armpits and, grunting, heaved him into the arms of a third antagonist, who dropped his sword in order to catch his friend. The third man was helmeted; Harri slammed his sword hilt into the helmet, ringing it like a gong.

All three men lay still. Wine from a spilled goblet had not finished running off the table.

He heard an inarticulate cry and a thud behind him. He spun, suddenly hard-eyed, and for the first time held his sword blade forward in his hand.

The slender blond lad had strung a rope between the legs of two tables, tripping the fourth attacker. The end of the rope had a weight on it. It must have been a neat throw.

The tangled-up man on the floor looked up in horror and let go of his axe. "Mercy!"

Harri raised his sword, then an eyebrow as he saw the rest

of the inn staring at him. He turned to the barkeep. "No killing, you said."

She nodded, still clutching the small child tightly.

"A true knight," Harri said grandly, "is generous in victory."

As he bowed to the prone man, he bumped into the table seemingly by accident. It tipped, the corner smacking the fallen man on the forehead. "Oops. That must have hurt." He lifted the man's eyelid, noting with satisfaction the glazed look. "Well, he'll wake up soon enough. Let me check him for injuries." He snapped his fingers. "Towels, please."

He bent over the bodies, feeling them tenderly for wounds. The onlookers, impressed, never noticed three purses disappearing. He bundled towels under the heads of the unconscious men and stepped back, rubbing his hands.

Harri turned to his young ally. "I would have gotten him," he began, and stopped. The slender blond lad was actually a young woman, wiry and muscled.

She said calmly, "I couldn't be sure. Are you really going to hunt down Auris?"

He nodded. "However long it takes." He added casually, "He's sure to come back for his gold; if I can find it first and wait . . ." He let the sentence trail off.

"I'll go with you." She recoiled her rope and added, "I'm solely interested in the money, of course, but I'll help with the dragon."

He shook his head. "I work alone." But he was intrigued. After all, she had known enough to sit with her back to the wall, where she could watch front and rear doors easily. And not even he had realized that she had a weapon.

She looked stubborn. "You need help."

"You'd be risking your life," he said to her. She nodded vigorously. "And you'd have to take orders."

She nodded, more slowly. "I'll earn my share."

He reached out with his right arm. "Your hands on it."

Impulsively she clasped his hand with both of hers. "My name's Gem."

Less impulsively, Harri swung his left fist into her chin,

catching her as she dropped.

He propped her up in a chair, casually palming her purse. "She'll be safer here, poor thing. . . . Barkeep? How much for water when she wakes up?"

The barkeep shook her head. "My treat."

"Good woman." Harri saluted her and strode out, trying not to let any coins jingle. In spite of missing his appointment at the inn, it had been quite a profitable stop.

* * * * *

The road to Rockhaven took Harri through a narrow pass marked with ruts left by cart tracks. He walked briskly, seeing gold ahead in every rock and rut. Harri, whistling as he walked, had the road to himself.

Or nearly to himself. After a few hours he glanced over his shoulder and saw someone in a worn cloak slip quickly out of sight behind a boulder. He peered nearsightedly as though he had seen nothing, then turned and continued to the next bend.

Harri paused there, in sight, pretending to reread the scroll he had displayed at the inn:

> You know of one mark left by Auris the dragon. I know of one as well. Meet me in the inn at Peacedale.

He put the scroll away, disappeared around a corner, scrambled up the rock face, and leapt down onto his follower, knocking him flat and pinning his (no, her, he realized with annoyance) arms to her side. "You're easy to surprise, Gem."

"I'm not surprised. I planned for you to see me."

"Plan better."

She smiled innocently, then brought her knees up so fast that Harri had the wind knocked out of him. The next thing he knew, their roles were reversed. She was on top, straddling him with her knees.

"You can never do it alone," she said.

"I never intended to. Someone sent a message for me—" He stopped, struck by an awful suspicion.

Gem looked back at him. "Who was it?" She got up and backed away.

He sat up, staring at her long and hard before turning away, shaking his head. "It was signed—"

"Anyone can sign a name."

"—and sealed—"

"Ah. That's different."

"—by the sheriff of Rockhaven."

"The sheriff!" She nearly spat it out. "Half a fool, like you. I'm solely interested in the money." She leaned forward. "But you must know something about the two marks or you wouldn't have bothered to come here."

Harri only said irritably, "I've come to slay the dragon."

"He may be hard to kill. He must be a huge dragon, or he couldn't have piled up all that gold."

Harri winced. "Did you emphasize 'all that gold' to anyone before you left the inn?"

She peered downhill, back from where he had come. A large cloud of dust filled the roadway from side to side. "I might have."

Harri was running before she finished, heading for cover on higher ground. Beside him, Gem panted. The approaching dust cloud had separated into a line of sprinting, armed men.

He was above her on the slope, searching out a crack in the rock ledge. He stamped on it once, peered down the slope, then carefully pulled a leather pouch from his pack. With exaggerated caution he poured a stream of blood-red grains into the crack. He pulled out some charred cloth and tucked it gently into the crack, waving Gem away.

Gem tiptoed close, fascinated. "What's that do?"

Harri struck a flint against his sword on the cloth. "It explodes, if I can get it lit."

"Did you get that from magicians?"

"From gnomes."

Gem backed up as though the flint had started a brushfire. She looked astonished and pitying. "You bought an explosive sight unseen from gnomes?"

"Not bought it, exactly. And not sight unseen. It exploded when they tested it."

"You mean *something* exploded. Something always explodes when a gnome runs a test."

He grinned. "They were testing this at the same time." He showed her a second pouch, this one with purple powder. "Supposed to lengthen memories, but after testing it they all wandered off. Forgot what they were doing." He bent back down over the cloth.

He was blowing furiously on the charred cloth where a spark had taken hold. The cloth turned red, then flamed.

Gem watched him, then peered interestedly at the dust rising in the distance. "We fought only four men at Peacedale. They seem to have found friends."

Harri, fumbling with a braid of cloth, grunted. "It says a lot about the shape the world is in today that men like that can find friends."

There wasn't time for any more banter. Harri pointed to the oncoming band, now clearly defined even in the dust. They were jogging easily, spread out to keep out of each other's dust. "When they get close, light a small twist of the rag." He scrambled back down the slope and dashed across the road.

Harri was concealed on the opposite slope when the band of men arrived. The man whose helmet Harri had struck led them. He was, Harri noticed, completely bald, missing a tooth, and in a foul humor. Harri felt in his pockets absently, remembering that he had robbed three of these men.

Suddenly Gem tossed the weighted end of her rope over a tree branch and swung, high and wide, across the hillside above them.

They spun to look at her. Harri, also watching, was distracted as he noticed what he wanted too badly to see: a tiny wisp of smoke, rising from the place Gem had left.

As he watched, the smoke ended in a brief fountain of sparks. Harri dropped flat, covering his ears.

Nothing happened.

Harri stood up as Gem, swinging back on the rope, kicked a boulder loose. It knocked free two more rocks, then eight, then twenty.

The falling rocks thundered and echoed in the pass. The

band of men turned, startled, as an entire section of hillside detached and slid down toward them, quickly obscured by a rising dust cloud. They backed away from the rock slide quickly but were engulfed in the dust.

Harri half-skipped down the slope, sword drawn, and waited just beyond the billowing dust. The first man, half-choking, stumbled out of the cloud and onto Harri's blade before he had time to swing.

The second man followed, unready, and the third tripped over him. The rest followed, more prepared, but still coming out one by one.

After killing over a dozen armed men, Harri paused, mainly because no one else was emerging. He waited, panting, his guard still up.

Two more figures emerged, swords ready, kerchiefs wrapped around their noses and mouths. They came forward in a tight bunch; they had been guarding each other's backs until they could see.

Harri braced himself as the men spread out on either side of him. A hoot echoed seemingly from the sky, and the oncoming men froze.

Gem swung down in a fast arc, feet pulled tight into her body. As she connected with the nearest man, she straightened out, her boots smashing into the man's ribs.

He grunted, toppling onto the ground. Gem's swing carried her forward into the other man. He took a swing at her, but she easily kicked the sword out of his hand and then followed through with a second kick that connected with his head. He fell sideways.

Gem dropped off the rope and spun around anxiously. Harri, standing alone, was wiping his blade. He nodded to her. "Thanks."

She stared, dazed at the bodies surrounding him. Finally she said softly, to herself, "You killed everybody."

"Sometimes you have to." He looked over at her. "It's not as much fun as farming, is it?"

They stood panting. The dust slowly settled around them. Gem tensed. "What do you mean?"

He tapped the rope with his sword. "You pull it taut like

it's a gate and you swing on it like it's a hay rope. Whatever else you are, you were a farmer once."

She looked down at the corpses. "Not anymore."

* * * * *

Harri and Gem emerged from the narrow pass into the valley of Rockhaven. Small parched fields dotted the valley. At the upper end, quite near the pass, was a dry well and a knot of homes. At least half the homes were piles of rubble. The sere yellow leaves of the half-dead trees were a match for Gem's hair, and Harri was intrigued by the depth of feeling she showed as she stared at Rockhaven.

Harri scuffed at the dust, shaking his head. "How can anyone live here?"

"Most farmers take second jobs," she said.

Harri grinned up at the mountains opposite them. "Then they should be treasure hunters. Can't you just smell the gold?" He turned to Gem and said reprovingly, "This time, don't tell everyone about—"

But Gem had disappeared, running on ahead. Harri frowned and hurried after her, thinking—not for the first time—that she was more trouble than she was worth.

He caught up with Gem, who was trailed by an old man leaning on her arm and a mob of respectful townspeople. The old man bowed slightly to Harri. "I am Caranis. Rockhaven thanks you."

"It was nothing," Harri said modestly. "Thanks for what?"

"Not only will you rid us of Auris, you will retrieve our treasure." He gestured back at the narrow pass. "And you've already defeated half of Robled's band of raiders."

Harri's eyes narrowed. "I'll do *what*?"

Caranis the Elder's smile was tempered with sorrow. "The others have spent these months ripping our homes apart, burning our crops from their fields, searching for the missing marks of the treasure. Today, as most days, they are searching in the mountains with Robled himself."

Harri said, "I've never heard of Robled." In his travels, Harri had met a great many thieves and raiders.

Caranis frowned. "He's large and muscled like a dwarf, and has bright red hair, and he's always angry." He stared up at the mountain. "Mostly we see his men. Robled only leaves the mountain to ask questions, attack our homes, and take food."

Harri looked from one gaunt face to the next in the mob behind Caranis. "Where can he find food here?"

The old man shrugged.

Harri shrugged back. "Speaking of the dragon's lair"—he avoided saying "treasure"—"can you tell me where the marks left by the dragon are?" He said carelessly, "Both of them, if possible."

"Like all who live here, I know of none." Caranis pointed up the mountain. "There to the west is the mountain range where Auris the dragon hid his gold. Walk along it, if you wish, and see if you find the dragon's marks or his gold. What you are sure to find is the rest of Robled's men, and Robled himself. They still seek the treasure."

"That explains why they wanted me dead," Harri muttered.

Caranis laughed out loud. "Though of course they couldn't defeat you." He rested an arm on Gem's shoulder. "The sheriff here has told me of your courage and skill—"

"The *sheriff*?"

Gem smiled calmly at him. "Remember how I said all farmers worked second jobs?" Her eyes still looked innocent.

Harri's looked angry and hard. "Why didn't you say so back at the inn?"

"I wanted to be sure you were the right man. Also, I wanted to see how you handled yourself in a fight."

"Which is also why you goaded the men at the inn into following me."

"They didn't take much goading."

Caranis's amusement faded, and he shook his head. "I'm sorry, lady sheriff. I myself can take only so much goading."

They looked at each other. Gem said to Harri, "Give it a try?"

He looked from her to Caranis and finally said dubiously, "Maybe."

She gripped Harri's arm with surprising strength. "May Huma watch over us."

Harri said easily, "We'll be fine," but he looked thoughtful.

* * * * *

As they walked out of the village, Harri said bitterly, "Do you really know where one of the lines is, or was that a lie too?"

"I haven't really lied to you, have I? I do want the money." She smiled. "There's no more reason why I should trust you."

"I told the truth. I came here after a man wrote me—"

"A sheriff," she corrected. "And not a man."

"How did you know to write me, anyway?"

She shrugged. "Robbers aren't the only ones who know about the price on your head. You've been asking too many people about the treasure hidden in Rockhaven."

He scratched his head. "My mother always said my big mouth would get me into trouble. Well, she said something more complicated, about gully dwarves trying to oil kender, but it amounts to the same thing."

She frowned, staring at him. "There's one thing you didn't lie about to me, or you'd never have come here—you do know where one of the lines is."

"Yes, and so do you." Harri wondered for a moment if they both knew the same line. "You told me you were a mercenary."

"You hinted that you were a knight."

"I have taught a few how to fight."

"It's not the same thing. Knights have honor."

"You want to know about honor and knights?" Harri, pretending exasperation, handed her the breastplate he had displayed in the bar. He turned to show her the back, where someone had scratched a rough map with a blade. "The knight who wore this drew a map on the inside." He pointed. "Rockhaven, the mountains, and one mark."

She stared at it, and her face lit up as though it were reflecting the gold. He pulled the breastplate away quickly. "So is it the mark you know?"

She frowned, looking suddenly mystified. "Weren't you going to sell this?"

"To the barkeep? Of course. I could simply memorize the map, and a little cash is always a good thing." He stared shrewdly at her. "What else is bothering you?"

Gem, troubled, could barely find words. "But if it were real, wouldn't the knight have turned this over—"

"To his commander?" Harri grinned and said again, "Of course." He leaned over as though sharing a joke. "He wasn't wearing his armor any more when he sketched it. You figure it out."

She said in a small voice, "Where did you meet him?"

"On the road, months ago. I was his teacher once. He was trying to raise money for a raid on Rockhaven . . . by robbing me. Foolish of him and ungrateful, considering all I'd taught him. If he hadn't mentioned Auris's treasure, I never would have searched him for a map after we . . . talked."

For a long time she said nothing. Finally, she said, "We'll do your mark first."

"No, yours."

"Maybe I should kill you right here and now, and just take the breastplate."

"Be my guest." He added, "You might want me to help thin out your robbers for you."

He half-expected her to pull her sword. Instead, she chuckled. "I'll show you my mark first, just so that I'll be sure of where it is you're heading." She added firmly, "And if you don't kill me, I'll be right behind you."

* * * * *

She took him down below the village toward the farm fields. They were surrounded by low stone walls and inhospitable land. On the way down she commented, "You've never done as much good as you're about to do because of me."

Harri had no reply. He felt certain that Gem was overestimating his potential goodness.

The farm fields were close in front of them now, as was a

narrow, nearly dry stream. Gem bounded down with a reck-
lessness that would make even a kender whistle admiringly.
Stumbling and swearing, Harri followed her.

Gem ran toward a south wall. She pushed on the stones,
grunting and straining fiercely.

The mortarless rock resisted, then toppled slowly. She
shoved frantically at the bottom rocks, pushing them to one
side.

"Are you sure this is the place?" Harri asked dubiously.
Suddenly he had a revelation. "You hid it yourself, during
the dragon battle."

She nodded, grinning. Harri knelt immediately, grabbing
at rocks and tugging them aside as though he were wrestling
them.

They stood and stared at the neat, carefully etched line in
the stone. They followed the rest of the wall with their eyes,
slowly turning toward the slope, and almost mechanically
walking uphill following the line.

Halfway up the slope he asked, "Who hid the other mark?"

"A rock slide. Unless your student, the knight, hid it.
Before I could sneak up the mountain, the other mark was
gone."

Following the marks on the shield, they drifted to the left
as they climbed. They walked quickly, fired by the closeness
of the gold and the fact that Robled's men might be watching.

Eventually Harri, turning the breastplate this way and
that, stopped and announced, "This is it."

They quickly shifted enough rock to reveal the other line,
then set up two cairns so they could align themselves with it
as they walked. They edged across the mountain sideways,
hundreds of feet above the valley floor. Harri spent most of
his time watching his feet, trying to avoid loose scree.

"Look up once in a while," Gem warned. "Remember, the
old man said the rest of Robled's band are waiting."

Harri rolled his eyes, but he rested one hand on his sword.

The first body they came across, one that had been killed
by a blow to the head, surprised them.

The second, nearly decapitated, disturbed them.

At the fifth body lying there, in two neat halves, Gem said,

"Wait a minute." Harri was about to ask her if she felt faint when she climbed up on a rock, standing tall, balancing by resting her hand on his shoulder. "There are at least ten more bodies ahead."

"I guess we're not the only ones to have gotten this far."

"Maybe all the treasure hunters are dead."

Harri gazed back along the line of corpses, none of which had red hair. "All but one," he said thoughtfully.

"How tough can he be?"

Harri pointed to the bodies ahead. "Ask them."

Many corpses later they paused to rest. The walking was hard work, and finding corpses was discouraging.

He sat on a boulder above Rockhaven. The fields below, a series of barren squares bounded by carefully piled dry-stone walls, spread beneath him. "This is terrible farmland."

"You can't imagine how beautiful these hills are after spring rains when they're full of flowers."

"I'll be long gone by then."

Gem smiled. Harri, thinking of her previous smiles, didn't like that.

After hiking for much of the afternoon, Gem said suddenly, "Here." She pointed to a stone wall below, then back the way they had come; they were in the right spot, plainly in the scar of a recent rock slide.

Harri blinked and stepped out of line. The landslide vanished. He stepped back in line and found it again. Unless you knew where it was, it was almost invisible.

Harri rolled away one rock after another. The rocks above shifted dangerously.

For a while they strained at the boulders. As the sun sank lower, Gem said, "Do you have any more of that exploding powder? Let's try it again. If it doesn't work, we may as well try the memory powder."

He pulled both bags out, weighing them thoughtfully. "It might work."

Hundreds of sparks, two small piles of red and purple powder, and many banged knuckles later, they had exhausted their resources and patience. "And it might not work," said Harri.

Suddenly Gem leapt out of the way as a boulder dropped past her, loosening others above and below. A tunnel the height of a man was revealed.

Gem looked at it dubiously. "I'd love to be sure that won't seal right up again in another landslide."

Harri grinned at her. "One of us could stay outside."
He cocked an ear, listening to a rumble growing behind them. "I guess we don't need these after all."

The rumble had been more rock falling. The slide had opened the cave still further; the opening was huge.

"Right." Harri grabbed Gem by the shoulders, pushing her back down the trail. "Go to Rockhaven. Get me a cart and something to draw it. Two horses would be ideal." He looked up at the sun; this had taken too long already. "Two cows will do."

"Why should I trust you?"

"How will you get the treasure to town if you don't?"

She barely hesitated before turning and dashing down the trail. Harri watched with satisfaction, turning around in time to see a large red-haired man drop from above and slip into the cave.

Harri frowned. The red-haired man—Robled, he remembered—was the last of the treasure hunters to be dealt with. He checked the edge of his sword absently, then wrapped his cloak around his other arm in lieu of a shield. He strode into the cave, his mouth set and grim.

He stepped aside quickly, avoiding being silhouetted in the entry. He ducked, feeling the floor and half-crawling to one side, giving his eyes time to adjust. He looked away from the light—

—and dropped his jaw, nearly dropping his sword as well.

The light was shining on a pile of gold coins surmounted by three tooled bracelets. Other items were strewn about the cave floor.

With his free hand, Harri picked up a heavy gold candlestick. He looked at it and smiled in a way he hadn't since he was a small child and his Uncle Benbow had given him, after his promise to always be good, a genuine double-bladed knife.

A shadow fell across the gold; a muscular human figure tiptoed toward the entrance, turning his head from side to side.

Harri drew back against a stalactite. "Robled?"

He heard a low chuckle. "That's one name."

"You killed all your gang," Harri said, looking around for a second weapon. There was nothing but gold. "Now that's greedy, killing the help."

"They weren't much help. Besides, I didn't need them once I had you to lead me to this place. If you found it first, that only made my job easier, Harri Gundervall."

Harri moved quickly behind a pillar. "How do you know my name? And even if I were this person, and I'm not saying I am, why should I be afraid of you?"

The man seemed to swell in the cave entrance. "No special reason." The man gave a chuckle, the tone of which changed in the middle.

No. The *throat* changed.

Harri's own throat went suddenly dry, his legs twin posts of water. He felt as much as smelled the change in his own sweat: dragonfear.

The silhouette in the entrance shifted and grew until it blocked nearly all incoming light. Its eyes glowed, peering into the darkness. "No special reason, except that I intend to kill you." The shape moved forward, its claws scratching on the cave floor. It was a dragon, *the* dragon. Auris, in all his malevolent splendor, stood before Harri.

Trembling uncontrollably, Harri looked helplessly at the candlestick in his left hand, the sword in his right. He could think of nothing but the sunlit opening the dragon had left behind.

So he hurled the candlestick at Auris's shining right eye.

The dragon roared, ducking his head. Sword in hand, Harri charged.

Auris howled deafeningly, as the blade sliced into his chest, glancing off his breastbone. The sword twisted in Harri's hand, but he held on to it. A single swipe from the dragon's claws sent him flying against the wall.

"Now, thief," Auris roared triumphantly, "for once in your

whole miserable life, you may be said to have a glowing career!" His nostrils flared and his chest expanded as he inhaled before breathing destruction on Harri. The mercenary, winded and bruised, lay flat against the cave wall and waited.

And heard a muffled choking. He looked up and saw Auris, astonished, clawing at his throat. Gem burst into the cave and heaved something back at the opening. Then she swung the weighted end of her rope around in the air, and loosed it to wind around Auris's jaws and clamp them shut.

Gem gave a quick, frightened look toward Harri, who shouted, "No!" But Gem had already hopped onto and off of a low stalagmite and tossed another rope around Auris's neck. The dragon was pinned in place.

Auris, his uninjured eye bright with fury, lashed his entire body from side to side. Gem whirled in the air like a hoopak, smashing against the cave walls.

Harri leapt forward and ducked as Gem flew over, cutting the rope as she passed. Gem dropped to the floor and lay still. Auris, turning around, opened his jaws to breathe fire over them both.

In the cave, the noise was deafening. A noxious blue-green flame shot forward out of the dragon's mouth before the dragon exploded backward, leaving a blinding afterimage and a terrible sulfurous stench.

Harri threw his sword aside and dashed over to Gem's body, snatching her up.

With her first conscious breath she stared up dazedly and rasped, "It's a wonderful thing to fight side by side with a hero."

"I'll say."

"He blew out of here?" she asked.

"You knew he would."

With more honesty than he liked, she said, "I really hoped he would. I figured I could count on him using his dragon-breath, and that would be enough to ignite the powder. I couldn't count on the powder exploding, though."

She tried to stand unaided and collapsed, spitting out a sharp, pithy phrase about female half-elves and their unlikely use of an even more unlikely gnome engine. He helped her to the mouth of the cave and they stared in wonder at the white, smoking trail across the sky, curved like a bow. Beyond it a dragon flew calmly south.

Gem said in awe, "What does it take to kill one of them?"

"I hope I never truly need to know." He watched as Auris, disoriented, drifted from side to side. "He's forgotten about us. The memory powder?"

"And the explosive. Neither of them works by itself, apparently."

Harri scuffed at the ash-gray residue left by the powder. "I'm glad they work at all. Too bad you couldn't have staged a trial run."

"You were the trial run," Gem said.

Harri blinked. "Before, when we were trying to move the rocks?"

"That's right." She frowned. "If I'd gotten the dosage right you'd have wandered off and it would have simplified things. Except maybe for the dragon."

Harri watched the trail of smoke dissipate. He looked at the gold, then, speculatively, back at Gem. "You're not just going to let me take it, are you?"

"No," she said. "I'm not. Not without a fight."

He chewed his lip. "It's a lot of gold. Could be quite a fight."

"I'll die before you get it all."

"I'll die before leaving it behind." He amended practically, "Or, preferably, someone else will."

Gem, he noticed, had recoiled what was left of her rope and tied a rock to the cut end. She was starting to swing the end of it.

He laid a hand on his sword, not really wanting to do what he had to do.

A commotion from outside stopped them both. Harri cocked an ear. Gem's lip curled. The babble of happy voices grew closer.

"You had a prearranged signal, didn't you?"

"I was sure that you'd win."

Caranis stepped inside the cave. "And I knew you would

prevail—a man like you." He spread his hands. "What can we give you in thanks?"

Harri looked behind himself at the shining loot and forced a thin smile. "No payment. The deed is all."

There was a murmur of approval outside the cave. Harri went to the entrance and squinted as he looked out into the sunlight. All of them had empty bags, open caskets, small, well-worn purses with the draw strings loose.

Harri said resignedly, "I wouldn't mind filling my pockets . . . at least."

Caranis looked surprised. "You didn't tell him?"

It took Harri a moment to realize that Caranis was addressing Gem.

The old man turned to him, arms spread wide and pleading. "These are dangerous times. We have a saying: Bad harvests make bad men. Just look at what has happened to Peacedale. Then there are rumors of wars all over Krynn. Such times breed thieves."

Harri folded his arms, ready to take offense. "But—"

"So we need a swordsman of skill and courage. And we are willing to pay."

Harri, his mouth hanging open, said nothing.

"Plus," Gem pointed out, "with a price on your head, you'll be safer here."

Caranis finished, "You'll be working for the sheriff."

Finally Harri found his voice as he turned to Gem. "That would be quite a life change."

" 'Be generous in victory,' you said," she said. "You hand up the treasure; I'll watch." Gem, clutching her ribs on her left side, tottered into position.

The villagers filed past slowly, wide smiles on their faces. Harri ducked and rose, carrying double handfuls of gold piled so high that some pieces inevitably spilled on the floor. Gem beamed, helping dole it out to the villagers with her good arm.

Harri nodded curtly to the men and women. "Don't thank me." With his left foot he quietly shoved the dropped pieces into a crevice for later. "It's just my job."

As the last of the villagers filed past, Gem bent down and

picked up some of the pieces. She didn't spot them all, Harri noted. His eyes widened as she filled her pockets. "Hey, what about me?"

Gem smiled. "I ought to save for my dowry, don't you think?"

Harri opened his mouth to reply, then suddenly thought better of it and snapped his mouth shut. He glared at Gem, his jaw set and firm. "I work alone."

All the same, knowing Gem, he was already getting used to the idea.

There Is Another Shore,
You Know, Upon the Other Side

Roger E. Moore

On a hot and miserable night, I woke up to the sound of Captain
Hayrn's snoring and muttered a particularly ugly curse. It
had taken me an hour to fall asleep in the smothering heat,
even with the ocean as flat as sand, and suddenly I was
wide awake again and knew I would stay that way for
hours more. I groaned and opened my eyes, my thoughts
red.

It felt like midnight. I lay on my back, bare as a baby, on
the *Flying Lobster*'s warm, smooth foredeck. Above me the
black mainmast pointed into an infinite sea of twinkling
stars. On some other night it would be beautiful. At the
moment, it stunk. I was not very fond of the old captain just
then, either, even if he was a really nice guy who had given
me a job four years ago when no once else would, had
taught me how to sail, and had loaned me money in tight
times. It was too hot to care about anything. I pushed myself
up on my elbows and looked down at my body in the star-
light.

My skin is brown as bread crust from long hours working
in the sun, and my long hair is bleached white as a gull's
wing—which by chance is also my name, Gullwing. I'm
both elven and human and proud of it. (I never say "half-
elf"—there's nothing wrong with not being "all human.")
Most days I can pass as either an elf or a young adult
human depending on how I dress and act. I'm thin-limbed
and wiry, and I know some Kenderspeak, so I can even pass
for a tall kender if I put my hair into a topknot or back
braid. Changing my looks hasn't hurt my social life, that's
for sure. I like women, they like me, and Captain Hayrn
gets a good laugh on mornings when I stumble back to the

boat from a bedroom in a new part of town.

Sweat ran down my face in the night, and I tasted salt. My eyes stung. I blinked and looked up again. The night was empty; the three moons were down and the weather was mostly clear. No breeze stirred the water. We were two days north of Palanthas, our home city, fishing for giant moon-fins but having no luck. They'd gone deep to escape the day-time heat, but they weren't coming up at night, either.

No fish meant we'd get no money from the market back in Palanthas. It was typical of our luck over the last year. Captain Hayrn had almost no steel left to pay me, but I didn't care about that. I was broke but it didn't matter as long as I had the sea and something to read. As for food, I knew people who would feed me and places to steal more if I needed it.

Old Hayrn knew how to get by, too. He was a fine com-panion, really—a quiet old North Ergothian who was patient to a fault. His boat, the *Flying Lobster*, was all he had left in the world, and he cared for it like a son, when he was sober. Once he had lots of steel coins and a family, he said, but when I asked where they had gone, he hesitated and said, "That was in the old days, Gull," and nothing more. I guessed either the War of the Lance or Hayrn's drinking had something to do with that. I never asked again.

A bright light flashed across the night to my left and interrupted my murky thoughts. I turned in surprise, look-ing under the rail to port, but saw nothing but dark, flat water. Was that lightning? I couldn't imagine how it could be—no rain clouds were out. It would have been nice to have had the white moon, Solinari, up and full this evening so I could have pulled out some papers from my cabin and read a bit. History and fables were what I collected and loved best.

I had a prickling sensation. I drew back from the railing. Something enormous and invisible was coming over the waters, and it was right upon me. I sensed it only by instinct. I had to escape or else—

A flaming-hot wind scorched every inch of my bare skin as it swept over the boat. I thought my face had been burned off. I don't remember exactly what happened until I found myself clutching the starboard railing on my knees, screaming for the captain. I felt I was either on fire or had the worst body burns in history. The pain was beyond all belief. The old boat groaned, thrown half over on its side by the searing blast. I must have hit the railing and grabbed it by reflex when I fell back. It was a miracle that I hadn't gone straight into the water.

For a few minutes I was blind, convinced that my eyeballs were baked. Hayrn shouted incoherently at me from below deck. Tools and nets and chains and barrels crashed around together in the hold as the *Flying Lobster* righted itself. I thought the old man would be crushed flat by falling cargo and gear.

The boat righted itself as the wind died again. My vision came back, though everything was blurry and my eyes ached. Another flash of light burst over ship and sea. I tried to shield my face, thinking I would be burned again, but nothing happened this time.

More flashes came, very fast. It was like lightning without thunder, lightning without shape or form. I raised my face, sobbing a bit from the pain and shock, and saw that the flashes were reflections on the bottoms of scattered clouds on the horizon. All was silent.

I sat up on my knees, gripping the rail with one hand and getting control of my shattered nerves. The flashes of light ended as a flickering yellow glow washed over the low clouds. Long, curling tongues of orange and red flame then leaped up like bright water in a distant fountain. The great flames were not far away. Fiery colors rippled on the dancing waves as they slapped the side of the boat.

I remembered there was a little island about five or six miles off in the direction of the great fire. We'd sighted it late in the evening and had been fishing off its reefs in hopes of finding a school of giant moonfins. My eyes focused, and I saw the island at the bottom of that vast rolling jet of flame. Great trees on the isle burst into balls of fire as I watched.

"Zeboim's teeth!"

I jumped, but it was Captain Hayrn. He'd come topside

without my knowing it. "Gods have mercy!" he shouted. "That's a volcano!"

If a volcano had erupted on that island, we'd be dead in only a few seconds more. I half believed him, even as I thought it didn't make sense. There had been no mountains on that island, nothing at all like the volcanoes I'd seen along the coastline of mountainous Sancrist Isle.

Captain Hayrn's feet thumped the deck as he headed aft for the sea anchor crank. "Hoist and away, boy!" he shouted back, his voice ragged with fear. "Hoist and away, or we'll die!"

Hayrn's command shook me from my stupor. I staggered to my feet and scrambled for the mainsail hoist, head spinning. I did not seem to be as badly burned as I'd feared. I shivered and stole a glance at the titanic flames. The sight stopped me cold for a moment.

Now their rippling, rolling form was that of a huge, fiery man, a burning giant that grew even as I watched it in dull astonishment. The giant had long hair and a beard of fire. Armor that glittered like a great, bright mirror appeared over its chest. The burning giant raised its arms up into the clouds themselves, which faded away when it touched them.

It was a god or a monster from the Abyss. Either one was far more dangerous than a mere volcano. I abruptly threw myself into my work. My aching arms turned the crank, hauling up the sail. My sore eyes strayed back to the burning giant on the island. It seemed to me that it was turning around—in our direction.

Rumbling thunder rolled over us from the burning island. After a moment I realized it was the fiery titan's voice. I thought it laughed, and there were words in the thunder, garbled by distance but still triumphant.

Our boat groaned as Hayrn hurriedly hauled in the sea anchor's rope. The burning giant faced us fully. It saw us. There was no mistaking it. I stared into the giant's night-black eyes, and my mind went blank with terror. The mainsail crank fell from my hands; I sank back, limbs paralyzed. It was a dreadful sensation. I could neither look away, nor flee, nor cry out.

A blazing arm lifted, stretching out from the giant's body right in our direction. Its fingers made a tossing gesture. From its fingertips flew a tumbling ring of flames that rapidly grew larger as it fell through the air toward us. It was terrifying and unearthly. Just seeing it robbed me of willpower.

Hayrn grabbed me by my shoulders then and shook me violently. He shouted at me. In my condition, his wrinkled black face and short white beard looked strangely unfamiliar, as if I'd just bumped into him in a Palanthas market. Hayrn looked back, saw the whirling, flaming ring was upon us, and threw me down on the deck under the boom and half-furled sail, near a heavy crate.

A deafening roar grew all around, like a wind in the throat of a typhoon into which our boat fell like a feather. The ring passed over us; our fishing boat went right through its center. The boat lurched sharply. The crate near me slid and struck me hard in the forehead. With that, I was cast into a deeper night than I had ever imagined possible.

* * * * *

"Hayrn," I whispered.

"Gull, wake up." A cool, wet cloth touched my forehead. Blessed water ran over my burning face.

I opened my eyes.

The sky was blue, with white clouds and a yellow sun.

"Thank the gods!" Hayrn shouted. He leaned forward and grabbed me, holding me in his arms. "I thought you were going to die! Thank all the gods above and below!"

Confusion reigned for a few minutes. Old Hayrn wept and praised the gods and finally told me that it was the morning after we had seen the fiery giant. I'd been unconscious from the blow to my head. I managed to sit up after an hour more of rest.

My skin was raw and inflamed, already peeling a bit but not quite as red as a bad sunburn. Still, the slightest touch was unbearable. I got up and tugged on a pair of loose breeches, gritting my teeth against the pain.

Old Hayrn had looked after me while I was unconscious. When I was up, he showed me the sea anchor rope. It had been cut through as cleanly as if sliced by a razor. The anchor was gone. We hauled up the mainsail together and caught the wind, heading south to Palanthas and home.

Not long after, I found myself at the tiller staring aft at the horizon. Nothing seemed real to me yet, even in the daytime; the events of the night before were murky, like a bad dream.

"It was a god, maybe," said Hayrn. He sat on a water cask, a trailing net limp in his hands. He had made no progress in fixing the net's broken strands.

I frowned and looked back at him. "Which god?" I thought the being did not fit the description of any god of our world of Krynn that I had ever read about or heard of.

Hayrn curled his lips in to chew them. He looked down at the net in his hands as if he'd forgotten what he'd meant to do with it. He made no reply.

The sail snapped. The wind was picking up. The day was fiery hot, but the wind made it almost intolerable.

I shook myself and scanned the horizon. The white moon, Solinari, was rising due east as always. I turned away to check the tiller's mount.

Something felt very wrong. What was it? I looked up at the moon again for a good, long time.

"Captain Hayrn," I said. I rarely called him that.

He grunted, then got up and made his way over to me at the railing. He saw the moon. After a moment, he gasped and whispered, "By the names of all the gods!"

After a moonless night, the red moon almost always rises before the white one. The red moon, Lunitari, should have been up first this day. Any sailor of Krynn would know this. But a white moon was up instead.

That white moon was not Solinari.

The new moon was huge, far larger than Solinari. It rose like another world above the sea, almost frightening in size. I feared it might be rushing down to crush us beneath it, but it did not move. On closer inspection it seemed that the moon was also not truly white, but had a faint blue cast to it.

It was a monstrosity, a thing as alien as a two-headed fish or a purple sun.

As I stared at it, I also noted this huge blue moon's other peculiarity. In the middle of this moon was a small dark spot, from which pale lines radiated out almost to the sphere's edges. It took a while for me to identify what it reminded me of.

It looked exactly like the pupil and iris of an eye.

* * * * *

We sighted the Gates of Paladine on the afternoon of the second day after. The heat was tolerable now. The new moon rose and set and rose again over the days, always staring down on us. Conversation was spare in our boat. We mended the nets and lines, ate our meals, drank our water, stared at the lone moon, and avoided comments about it. We passed schools of giant moonfins and never dropped a net or line. We needed to be home.

I kept watch as we neared the Gates, the mountainous entrance to the great Bay of Branchala. The western Gate of Paladine is far higher than the eastern one; the former is actually the northernmost peak of the Vingaard Mountains. The forested cliffs of the eastern Gate are still two hundred feet high at their lowest, though.

Something seemed different to me about the eastern Gate. More trees seemed to be visible there. The lowlands down to the shore were also broader than I remembered. I brushed this realization off uneasily and looked for other vessels instead. Coastal traders and fishing boats would be out in abundance on a bright day like this.

I quickly spotted two small boats like ours, several miles off, and squinted to pick out their identities. Oddly, I didn't recognize either one, though one had the looks of a Hylo boat. Most of my kender friends in Palanthas were originally from Hylo, and a few were sailors. I squinted as I tried to make out the faded brown design worked into the sail of the other small craft. As we drew nearer, I could tell it was a pair of crossed swords over which was painted an open eye.

I had never seen that design before.

I looked south toward the bay and spotted a larger ship. It was a merchant galley under full sail, heading for the Gates and the open sea. It would have left Palanthas about three hours ago. I signaled the captain, who came over to stand beside me and frowned. His eyes were not as good as mine, but he knew every ship in the world, every sail and insignia. He said nothing as the galley drew nearer.

On the galley's main foresail was painted a huge, pale-blue eye over a jewel-like sun. Silently we watched the great ship as it passed to port by a hundred yards. The *Flying Lobster* rocked and bobbed in the broad wake. The galley's crewmen stared at us in curiosity as they passed, going about their labors.

"Must be a new ship," murmured Old Hayrn, clearly confused. "Maybe from Kalaman, a new trading company. Funny about the sail, though. . . ." He paused and looked around, scanning the shores of the Bay of Branchala with growing distrust. His gaze fixed on something behind me, and his lips parted in shock. I quickly turned to look.

Split Rock was gone. During the Cataclysm almost four hundred years ago, the True Gods punished the Kingpriest of Istar for attempting to dictate to them and corrupting their worship. They had flung a vast, fiery mountain down on the city of Istar and destroyed it, sending it and the kingdom of Istar to the bottom of the Blood Sea, many hundreds of miles to the east. In the Bay of Branchala, as all the world shook from the gods' attack, an overhanging rock broke free from a mountainside and fell into the bay. The huge rock split in half when it hit the bottom of the bay, and there it stood, sporting a wide crack from top to bottom that you could see from miles away. It was a great place for finding crabs.

Split Rock was gone—but there was a huge cliff projecting from the mountainside above the spot where it used to be. I looked at the cliff and the water below it a dozen times before the enormity of it hit me. What was wrong with the world? Had we missed something? Had we been gone too long?

"Gull, pinch me and see if I'm asleep." Hayrn's black face was almost gray. He was unsteady and held on to the railing. I was just as deep in shock and no steadier on my feet.

"This can't be right," he continued in a low voice. "I . . . maybe it's an illusion, something one of those wizards cast as a joke. That would do it. And the new ship, it must be from Kalaman or the south." He drew a hand over his face and sighed. "That must be it. Caught me off my guard there, that's all."

His words made sense. My nerves calmed a bit.

Then I remembered the blue eye on the galley's sail. And the moon.

I looked up into the huge new moon's placid gaze. The eye of the moon looked back. No spell that I knew of would turn three moons into one. I wondered if the new moon saw me. It did not seem such a fanciful thought. I shivered, looked down and away.

We sailed on. Within the hour we passed a coastal city to starboard, a city of gray walls, round white domes, and short, broad towers that rested below a broad, high cliff. The last time I had shaded my eyes and looked at that spot, only days ago, a little fishing village rested there among a jumble of overgrown rocks. No trace of that village remained where the gray walls arose.

Hayrn murmured the names of Paladine, Zeboim, and a dozen other gods as he stared at the city, his weathered hands gripping the rail until his knuckles cracked.

* * * * *

Three hours later, we saw Palanthas.

Palanthas was huge, much bigger than when we'd last left it. A great tower rose out of the sea before it, a lighthouse with a huge blue sphere at its lofty top. I thought it was two hundred feet high, at least. The harbor was filled with ships, hundreds of them, many more than I'd ever seen or dreamed of. Bells and horns sounded over the water, fragments of curses and shouts mixing with them. Gulls screamed overhead, waves slapped at our bow, and flags of every color of the rainbow snapped in the wind over the docks and walls of the mighty city.

We lifted our astonished eyes and saw wide, stone-paved roads rising into the Vingaard Mountains, the highways thick with caravan traffic. Homes and gardens covered the lower slopes. Towers of every sort, some higher than three stories, stood out over the city itself. Everywhere we looked there was color, activity, noise, and life, far more of each than we had ever known in the bustling Palanthas we'd last seen days ago, the Palanthas we knew as home.

"No minotaur ships," said the captain. I had not thought to look for them, but I did then and saw that he was right. "No Ergothians, no gnome steamers. Those are elven, I think."

"That one," I said, pointing. "What's that emblem with the broken chains on the sail?" The broken chains surrounded an eye, but I did not mention that.

Hayrn was tight-lipped. He shook his head, eyes hard and narrow.

A small craft without sails approached us with surprising speed. It was painted yellow and had a yellow pennant that flapped from a short mast atop a cramped cabin. Atop the mast was a small blue ball. A bald man in yellow pantaloons and a white shirt waved at us, then raised a horn to his lips and shouted at us. I was able to understand that we were being directed to a dock to unload our catch, but the harbormaster's words, clear as they were, were not quite the words I had once heard spoken in Palanthas. His Solamnic accent was measured, precise, and thick with command, but the vowels were clipped and his pronunciation was off, as if he were a foreigner who had learned our tongue from another foreigner.

Hayrn swallowed, then raised his hands and shouted a brief acknowledgement. The harbormaster stared at us, then turned and called to someone in the cabin. After a pause, a thin-limbed human in a white tunic—I guessed her to be twenty years at most—came out of the cabin and shaded her eyes in our direction. After a glance, she turned to the harbormaster and shrugged, returning to the cabin when the bald man dismissed her with a wave of his hand. The harbormaster waved us on, looking around for other ships to direct, and the yellow boat started away, moving swiftly and soundlessly on a high wake by some surely magical means.

But it was not the boat's magical movement that caused my stomach to knot up and my mouth to go dry.

"She had a collar," said Hayrn in disbelief. "She had an iron collar around her neck, like she was a slave."

There were no slaves in the Palanthas we'd known. Slavery was outlawed everywhere in Solamnia, as it had been for hundreds of years, long before the time of the Cataclysm.

Like lost sheep guided to an unfamiliar pen, we sailed into the harbor.

* * * * *

There was a bad moment when we docked. A stone-faced woman gripping a sheaf of papers told us to hand over our berthing fee. Hayrn gave me a puzzled glance, then cleared his throat and went into his cabin, returning after a moment with a couple of steel coins. I grimaced; it was almost all the money we had between us. He handed these to the woman, who took them and eyed them in disgust.

And threw them back at Hayrn's feet.

"*Real* money," she hissed.

Hayrn and I looked at each other. He slowly picked up his coins and went back to his cabin below deck, returning with something in his right fist. He held it out to the woman, who took it when he opened his hand. It was a thin gold chain, something he wore as a good-luck charm in town.

The rock-faced woman dropped the chain in her pocket and spoke rapidly and angrily to Hayrn. I made out part of what she said. She was furious with him. She was fed up with taking baubles from ignorant fishermen from dirty coastal towns who couldn't civilize themselves enough to use real currency. She called Hayrn a disgrace to the dominion of Greater Ergoth and said he could stay three days, no more. Then he could sell his catches in the Abyss for all she cared. She turned on her heel and left without a look back.

The dominion of Greater Ergoth? I glanced at Hayrn, who looked at me dumbfoundedly before nervously scanning the dock. Dockworkers around us continued unloading fish from other boats with barely a glance in our direction. All of them wore iron collars around their necks. Most were human males, but some were dwarves or half-elves, a few of them were human women, and one was a little male gnome. They kept their eyes down, never meeting my gaze.

Slaves—they had to be slaves. I almost said something to Hayrn then, but decided against it out of caution. I looked around the docks as Hayrn was doing. Seen close-up, the city was as alien as it had been at a distance. Clothing styles had changed—baggy pants for human and elven men, that was weird. Women had long skirts that brushed the ground. Colors were subdued but plentiful. Humans and elves, a broad dwarf here and there . . . but no kender. That was strange. You never got to the docks in Palanthas without running into a dozen of them trying to get on everyone's boats and explore them. A lot of the kender were my friends, though they drove Hayrn crazy. No kender at all.

It suddenly dawned on me that the fishing boat I had seen at the Gates, the one with the Hylo-like colors, had been crewed by humans. I was sure of it. Hylo, though, was a kender nation on the big island of Northern Ergoth, west of Palanthas. I'd assumed the humans were just Solamnic helpers working for a Hylo fishing family over the summer. But kender should have been on deck, too. And minotaurs— there weren't many, usually, but you always noticed them from their size and animal body odor. Now there were none.

My gaze fell on the little gnome with the huge iron collar around his neck who struggled silently with a large basket of fish. I looked around and saw in the center of a small open plaza by the docks a toothless old man chained by his neck collar to a thick wooden post. Children threw stones at him as he covered his white-bearded face with bony hands.

A whip cracked somewhere, and a woman screamed briefly. No one acted as if anything unusual was happening at all.

"May as well take a look around," said the captain. I nodded. We left the *Flying Lobster* moored behind us and set off with uncertain feet into this strange new city.

It was definitely Palanthas, and it was definitely not. I recognized a building here and there, frowned at many others. The streets were almost but not entirely the same. People's clothing had changed. I picked up a couple of leather pouches on the way—a skill a kender friend taught me years ago. Coins clinked inside them, and I hid them inside my waistband until later. Best not to let Hayrn see them and get stirred up, much less let a constable see them and jail me for a thief.

Still, we had to eat. I pulled two coins out, silver ones, and told Hayrn I'd found them on the ground. He took them gratefully, then pointed to a small tavern, a place called the Joyous Sirine, which had an overly endowed naked green lady on its door sign. The place had a flattened-straw floor and smelled of stale sweat, wood shavings, and cheap ale, with a whiff of vomit and a touch of used latrine. Inside were humans, half-elves, and elves, most of whom looked at us with fading interest when we entered. The patrons were dirty but their clothing seemed well made, better than I usually saw in Palanthas—our old Palanthas, that is. We took seats at a corner table in back, near an open window looking out at a wood-plank alley wall three feet away.

"I don't understand," Hayrn said, hiding his mouth behind a dark, calloused hand. He nervously pulled on his chin whiskers as we waited to be served.

"What's a dominion?" I whispered.

Hayrn glanced out the window at the wooden wall, hesitating before he spoke. "It's a country that's part of an empire, one that has its own government but still follows the emperor's lead."

"Ergoth never was a dominion in someone else's empire," I said. I read a lot of history in my spare time. "Have you noticed that there are no kender around here?"

Hayrn looked at me in surprise. "I . . . huh," he said, looking around again. "I'll be. Well, maybe this place was too boring for them this week." His voice drifted off as a dwarf in filthy clothing approached our table.

The dwarf seemed intoxicated, his step unsteady and his face red and swollen. He looked old, his ratty black beard streaked with gray. An iron collar, an unusually thick one, was visible beneath the beard. He had small cloths draped over his hands, which he offered to us when he reached our table. He did not look up. We took the cloths to wipe our hands before eating—and froze.

The dwarf's hands had been cut off at the wrists years before. Each stump was wrapped in rags held by leather bands laced tightly to his forearms. The right band had a narrow, copper hook on it that projected from the stump.

Lowering his arms, the dwarf mumbled something that neither Hayrn nor I understood. I leaned closer; the dwarf took a wheezing breath and repeated himself in the strange Solamnic. His breath smelled worse than a rotting horse.

"He asked us what we wanted to have," I told Hayrn. The old man swallowed and asked for ale for us both. The dwarf departed, and we were left alone with our thoughts until he returned. Two mugs of ale were clutched to his chest, held there by his forearms. He wove his way unsteadily around the other patrons, who ignored him, and finally bumped into our table. Some of the ale spilled over his sleeves. The dwarf bit his lower lip in frustration or embarrassment.

"Thank you," I said in a low voice when the mugs were down and the dwarf was turning to leave. He took a step away, stopped, then turned and nodded to me without looking up. For a moment he had an abnormal touch of dignity. He took Hayrn's offered coin, muttered something into his beard to us, then left.

"What did he say?" asked Hayrn, frowning.

I watched the dwarf go. Something bothered me about him. "He said his name was Duggin and we were welcome to stay." What was it that had—

It hit me. The dwarf hadn't actually said we were welcome; he'd used a different phrase: "May you find whatever you need, and more." It was a common kender phrase, and he'd said it in Kenderspeak, the language spoken in Hylo and all other places where kender gather. It was the first time I had heard it spoken anywhere in this new Palanthas.

I got to my feet, trying to look calm and casual. The dwarf passed through a door, probably into a kitchen. "Nature calls. Be back in a moment," I said to the captain. Old Hayrn didn't respond. He'd taken out the other coin I'd given him and was staring at it.

I walked away, thoughts whirling around ways to get the dwarf alone somewhere and ask him some important questions. The latrine would likely be in the alley over a sewer, if this Palanthas was like the old one. The alley door was open . . .

The old dwarf slave came out of the kitchen again, carrying another mug. He brought it to a nearby table and was on his way to the kitchen again when I said, in Solamnic, "I'll have another myself." The dwarf glanced up at me and our eyes locked for a second. Then he lowered his gaze and went into the kitchen, returning after a minute with my mug.

I reached for it, turning my body so that no one could see my face. "The alley," I whispered in Kenderspeak.

The old dwarf looked up and stared at me with dark, red-rimmed eyes. I tilted my head toward the alley door, then wandered off in that direction, carrying my mug and hoping nobody would notice.

The smell outside told me that I'd found the latrine—a narrow hole in the ground that probably led to the sewer through clay pipes. I leaned against the wall and waited.

The dwarf did not appear for several minutes. I was about to give up when he stepped out, then slowly wandered over. He raised a handless arm, indicating my drink.

"I haven't seen any kender here, Duggin," I said quietly in Kenderspeak, handing the dwarf my empty mug. He said nothing in return, merely taking the mug and holding it to his chest with one arm as he stared at me without expression.

Maybe a different tack would work. "I'm not from here," I said, still using Kenderspeak. "My captain and I want to know a little about this city. We don't know many of the customs, and I thought you might be—"

"Stop it," said the dwarf. His words were slurred, but otherwise it was perfect Kenderspeak. "You are mad and a fool to use this language so freely. Someone will overhear."

I stared down at the dwarf, speechless. Even drunk, he spoke with such authority that I felt indeed that I was every bit the fool he said I was.

The dwarf looked me over. It seemed to me that he stood a little straighter. "Where are you from?" he asked, pronouncing the words with more care.

It took a moment to get the word out. "Palanthas," I said at last—in Solamnic. "We're from Palanthas. You said something to me that only kend—"

The dwarf raised a hand to stop me. His eyes narrowed, and he shook his head slightly as if he clearly thought I was lying to him. "I was a fool, too. Now go home and forget that you know that tongue, if you would save yourself," he whispered in Solamnic. He turned to go back into the tavern.

"Duggin!" I reached out and caught his shoulder. "Duggin, where are we? What's going on?"

The dwarf turned, dark eyes coldly fixed on my hand. I let go of him. He considered his reply without looking up at me.

"You cannot be so ignorant," he said without anger, "but you deserve an answer anyway. You are in Palanthas, capital of the dominion of Solamnia, in the World Empire of Istar. Go home." He went back into the tavern and slowly shut the door on me.

Dominion of Solamnia? World Empire of . . . *Istar?* Istar had been dead for almost four centuries, destroyed when the gods took revenge on its Kingpriest for his blasphemies and his attempt to control them. What kind of joke was this?

I went back in the tavern, hunting for the dwarf. Old Hayrn met me as I came in. He grabbed my arm and held up a silver coin in front of my eyes. I looked, then took it and studied it closely.

One side of the silver coin showed a map of an island that I did not immediately recognize. The words "Istar Triumphant" were stamped along the edge in formal Solamnic. I held up the coin with the words at the top. Thus oriented, the "island" suddenly looked familiar. It was actually Ansalon, our home continent—but Ansalon as it was ages ago, before the horror of the Cataclysm shattered the landscape. I remembered well the shape of old Ansalon from maps a historian-sage once showed me. The Blood Sea of Istar, the eastern islands, the western islands—all were absent from the engraved coin's map. Northern and Southern Ergoth and most of the western islands were replaced by the ancient kingdom of Ergoth. In the east were the lands of Istar itself, with a many-pointed star showing the location of the capital.

I silently flipped the coin over.

An open eye looked up at me.

* * * * *

We left the tavern and headed down the paved street, followed by the calls of fruit and pottery vendors. I had no idea where to go.

"Istar," said Hayrn in disbelief. His gaze flitted around us at the street scene, taking in a million unfamiliar sights. "Istar. We're back in Istar."

I said nothing. I couldn't believe it was true. It had to be a spell, an illusion of some kind. There were details that did not add up—the moon, the image of the eye, the size of Palanthas. Palanthas had never been as large as it was now, even before the Cataclysm washed away its seafront and flooded the city. And dominions—Solamnia and Ergoth had never been a part of Istar, at least not in the legends and histories that I had read or heard.

"We're in the past," said Hayrn, talking to himself now. "Over four hundred years in the past." He was quiet for a minute, then said, "It was the monster, the flame-giant. It must have cast a spell on us and thrown us back in time."

That part made sense, even as wild as it was. The fiery giant had certainly been the cause of our trouble. But . . . back in time? The Cataclysm had been in the year 1 A.C., and it was 383 A.C. now, so we were at least 382 years in the past if Hayrn was right.

"Xak Tsaroth." Hayrn stopped dead in his tracks.

"What?" I looked around. Hayrn was staring at a passing horse-drawn wagon loaded with wooden crates packed in straw. On each crate was a large, round symbol, showing a city with a black obelisk at its center. Around the edge of the symbol were the neatly stenciled words that read "Xak Tsaroth Red—Bottled 375 I.T."

We watched the wagon rumble on. "Xak Tsaroth wine," I said, starting to feel a little hysterical. "Sure, why not? If we've gone back in time, then the city of Xak Tsaroth hasn't been destroyed by the Cataclysm yet, so it's still selling wine to every—"

"The year," whispered Hayrn. Something in his voice made me shut up; there was a strange new look on his face. The old man suddenly walked over to a man that was looking in a bakery window. I started after him.

"Forgive me," Hayrn said, pronouncing his words carefully as the man looked him over. "Forgive me, but I am not good with adding figures. I saw a wagon go by with wine bottled in 375 I.T. Could you please tell me how old that wine is now?"

The man, whom I judged a farmer by his clothing and calloused hands, scratched his shaven chin. He then looked down at his fingers and counted off, mouthing the years to himself. "Eight years," he said, looking up. "It's the year of Istar Triumphant 383, praise the Godking, so the wine is eight years old. Should be about ready for the likes of us, eh?" He winked and raised a hand in farewell, then went into the shop.

"Three eighty-three." Hayrn was staggered. His weathered black face went slack. "It's . . ."

"Did he say the Godking?" I said softly. " 'Praise the Godking'? Who is that—Paladine?"

Then a new possibility came to me, the same thought that had struck Hayrn. "Oh," I said. I looked up at Hayrn, then looked around again at the bustling, enormous, wondrous city of Palanthas, untouched by Cataclysm or war. I saw it with brand-new eyes.

We hadn't gone back in time at all, I realized. It was still the same year as it had been when Hayrn and I had last left Palanthas: 383.

But Ansalon was whole. No Cataclysm had occurred. Istar was triumphant, a world empire, with Solamnia and Ergoth as its dominions.

Time had not changed. But history had.

"Paladine and Takhisis damn me," said Hayrn, his words rolling out like his last breath. Several passersby overheard his oath. They frowned and looked back in annoyance as they walked off. "Pagan blasphemers," one of them muttered.

We set off again at a slower pace, heading nowhere in particular. The street curved off to the left. I recognized the name of a side street and knew we were walking right through the spot where the great Temple of Paladine was supposed to be. Of course, no temple was here since it had been built after the War of the Lance, and there had probably never been a War of the Lance on this world. I did not even know if there was a Paladine here.

But I had an idea about who the Godking was. I could not bring myself to put the thought into words.

An onionlike spire appeared above the rooftops. It was white in color, like some of the marble buildings around us, but with thick streaks of red in it. Hayrn and I both saw it, and knew what it was, yet walked toward it anyway. The full tower, with both of its side minarets and the grove of tall trees at its base, appeared around the bend in the street. We walked until we came right up to the edge of the grove, where we stopped and stared.

Before us, humans and elves walked without fear in Shoikan Grove, at the very foot of the Tower of High Sorcery of Palanthas. The green oak trees of the grove rustled in a summer breeze, their branches welcoming clouds and sky. I remembered that the grove had been cursed before the Cataclysm, cursed so horribly that no rational being or creature would dare set foot there. The tower's white stone had even turned black. The curse had been laid by an angry wizard when the last Kingpriest of Istar had tried to take it away from the wizards' conclave, just before the Cataclysm.

Everyone in Palanthas knew that much of the tower's history.

But there was no trace of the curse. I could almost believe that we had come back in time to a point before the tower was cursed, except that I looked up and saw part of a curved symbol carved on the uppermost minaret. I had not noticed it until we had circled part way around the tower. It took just a moment to realize that the whole symbol was an eye, painted blue. It was the same eye I had been seeing all along, on sails and signs and wagons and everywhere. It was probably the same eye looking down from Krynn's only moon.

The Kingpriest of Istar, said some legends of the Cataclysm, had eyes of watery blue.

"I guess you finally got that tower back," I said at last, to no one in particular.

* * * * *

When I was small, my parents played a game with me called What If. What if, my father would ask, the sun was green? How would the world look in green light? What if wool grew on trees? What if birds swam and fish flew? What if bugs could talk? What if there had been no Cataclysm?

My mother had asked that last question. What if the Kingpriest had been a nice man and had not tried to conquer or dictate to the gods of Krynn? What would the world have been like if the Kingpriest had not tried to enslave or kill everyone who wasn't a human or elf? What if he had not tried to destroy evil by destroying everyone's freewill? Such hard questions only confused me as a child, and eventually my mother and I went back to picturing a world in which bugs could talk.

But we had never thought to ask what the world would be like if the Kingpriest had somehow conquered all the gods and perhaps even become a god himself, and then gone on to conquer the entire world under the banner of Istar.

We had never thought to ask, but Captain Hayrn and I knew the answer now.

* * * * *

I thought I would faint. I staggered about after that until the captain gripped my shoulder to steady me, but his fingers trembled and betrayed him. It took two hours to find the Joyous Sirine again in the confusion of the streets. The sun was setting behind the high western peaks around the bay, but the sky was still bright and the shops were busy.

"We should get back to the boat," the captain muttered. "We don't want to get into any trouble here. We should shove off and look elsewhere, find some other place."

"But where would we go?" I asked evenly. "Istar's a world empire now. Where would . . . There it is, the tavern."

"Western islands," he said, dropping his voice as we approached. "Northern Ergoth . . . oh." Ergoth was still part of the continent of Ansalon, not broken into islands as it was—would be? would have been?—after the Cataclysm. "Sancrist, then. It was still an island, I think. Still *is* an island."

We entered the tavern, faces blank and muscles tight. The place was just as smelly as before but more crowded. Tallow candles burned everywhere, adding a burnt stink to the air. Two elves at a table quietly got up and left as we entered. We took their seats and waited.

"This dwarf, Duggin—" Hayrn began.

"Shh." I didn't see him around yet.

Old Hayrn curled his lips inward, chewing on them and eyeing the crowd. People glanced at us occasionally, but mostly ignored us.

The dwarf with the iron collar appeared shortly, carrying mugs to patrons. I thought he caught a look at us, but he did not react and instead went back into the kitchen for more mugs. We waited tensely, studying the walls and table in silence. Finally, Duggin came back and stopped at our table, again offering hand cloths and waiting for our order.

"Praise the Godking," I said, trying to make it sound

normal so we'd fit in. I realized in a heartbeat that it was a
serious error. Several nearby patrons stared at me with surprised and suspicious expressions. The dwarf did nothing. I
hurried on to cover up the mistake. "We'll have . . . um, ale,
and a bit of meat and bread."

The other patrons frowned but went back to their business. Duggin looked me over briefly. He seemed very sad
all of a sudden. His pale lips moved. "You should have left,"
he whispered.

The captain leaned close, ignoring the foulness of the
dwarf's breath and body odor. "We don't know where to
go," he said softly, his words almost buried in the back-
ground chatter of the tavern. "We are not from this world.
This is not—" He broke off, looking frustrated.

"If you are from Palanthas," said Duggin evenly, "this *is*
your world."

"No!" said Hayrn. "No, this is not—oh, what's the use?"
He covered his face with his hands and groaned. "Gull, we
should get back to the boat. Maybe we should find that
flaming giant again and see if he throws us back into the
right world."

The dwarf's eyes flicked from Hayrn to me and back.
"Flaming giant?" he said in Solamnic with an edge to his
voice. "What flaming giant?"

"Duggin!" Startled, we turned to see a bald, burly man in
a stained kitchen apron making his way through the evening
crowd. "Duggin, damn you, we have people waiting! Get
your short stinking butt on the move!" He caught sight of
us, then focused on me. His face changed. It was as if I could
read his mind.

"You!" he shouted. "You two were in here spending that
stolen money earlier! Thieves! Thieves!"

I had no clue as to how they knew the money was stolen,
but it hardly mattered.

I was closest to the burly man. I slid out of my seat,
caught hold of the back of my chair with both hands, and
flipped it straight at the oncoming man's face. The old chair
burst into pieces but knocked the man back into a table,
upsetting it and knocking several patrons onto their backs

as well. I jerked our square table out from under Hayrn's elbows and turned it over to block pursuit. As one, Hayrn and I bolted for the tavern door and dodged past the dwarf. We'd been in bar fights before and knew when it was time to run.

But someone was already in the doorway when we got there. The two elves who had given us their table were back with some friends: men wearing white robes over some kind of light metallic armor. On the front of their white robes was a sun, over which was a blue eye.

The Godking's men.

We fought like rabid dogs. They got us anyway.

* * * * *

There wasn't much to do in the magistrate's dungeon cell. Old Hayrn had gotten the worst of the beating, but he never uttered a word of complaint. He sported a black eye, many bruises and scrapes, and a long cut on his forehead that had bled through the crude bandage he'd wound over it. He'd stayed on his feet through the fight far longer than I had. My head ached, and I threw up until my stomach was empty. It didn't make the cell smell any better or worse.

Duggin shared our small abode. He was locked up with us under suspicion of aiding thieves and monsters, and perhaps for being a disobedient slave. The magistrate meant me when he'd added the part about aiding monsters, thinking I was a kender. They finally figured out I wasn't a kender, merely "thieving, filthy, unholy garbage," as the jailers put it when they shoved me into our cell. One of the elves who'd given us their table had identified me as a kender by mistake. It was my back braid. I heard from a jailer that the elf had collected a bounty for me. I understood at last why there were no kender around.

I finally stopped throwing up and lay on my back on filthy straw, staring up at the dark timber ceiling of the cell. If my head would stop pounding, I thought, there was a chance I would live. Until I was executed.

"You said something about a flaming giant," said Duggin.

ROGER E. MOORE

He sat near me, waiting to see if I needed help throwing up again.

Hayrn grunted. "Forget it," he muttered. He sat on the other side of me, staring at the locked cell door.

"Old man," said Duggin in irritation, "I am less stupid than you think. Do you think I am a fool because of these?" I couldn't see what Duggin was doing, but I knew anyway that he was holding out his arms, displaying his stumps. "Do these make me stupid? Am I a fool because I am a slave? Tell me about the flaming giant."

"You wouldn't believe it," said Old Hayrn. "I don't even believe it."

Duggin snorted in disgust. "Try me."

"We were fishing for moonfins," I said. It hurt my head awfully to say anything, but I suddenly wanted to tell the whole story, everything. After a while, Hayrn added his own embellishments. We must have talked for an hour or two. My headache eased and my stomach settled as we did.

"This is not our world," I finished. "The flame-giant threw us here. Istar was destroyed and the Kingpriest was killed by the gods, Ansalon is broken up, and the True Gods rule." I turned to Duggin. "Are the True Gods here, too?"

Duggin's lips pressed together. He looked down at his wrist stumps. "They are alive," he said slowly, "but they are not gods now. The Kingpriest threw them down. He is the only god. All others are broken and enslaved."

My throat went dry. I turned my head to look at Duggin. "Enslaved? The True Gods are slaves?"

"They are no longer gods," said the dwarf in a dull monotone, "but they are immortal and in physical form, and all are slaves. Most are in Istar, I believe. I do not know what has become of them all." He swallowed. "Zeboim, she never became a very good slave. I hear she is dragged through the sea by galleys, half-drowning for weeks at a time. Gilean . . . Gilean was blinded and his libraries were burned. He is in Istar, in a stable. Takhisis has been . . . ill-used, and I don't know where she is now. She was in Kalaman, but she . . . she is made to travel a lot, for performances." His voice faded into silence.

"Paladine," said Hayrn in the silence. It was a question.

Duggin's face changed. His jaws clenched tight, and his dark eyes glittered. He said nothing, only lowering his head.

"How did it happen?" I asked. "The Kingpriest was just a man. He was a priest, I know, but he was just a man. He couldn't conquer the gods just by himself."

Duggin glanced up at the heavy cell door and the narrow window through which lantern light came. "He was just a man, but he had help."

"Did the flame-giant have something to do with this?" I asked. It seemed silly but it was as good a guess as any.

The dwarf stirred suddenly, getting to his feet. He'd asked many questions about the giant we'd seen and the island near which we'd been fishing. "We have to get out of here," said Duggin, walking to the door. "We have to get out of here and go to that place where you saw the flame-giant. We haven't much time."

"Knock out the guards when they serve us our dinner, maybe?" said Hayrn sarcastically. "Maybe they'll throw us into the sea and let us swim for—"

"Shut up," said Duggin. He brought one of his wrist stumps up to his face. I couldn't see what he was doing at first. Then he tugged his head to one side, as if pulling on something he was biting. He was straightening the copper hook on his right wrist sheath.

"What are you doing?" said Hayrn.

Duggin ignored him. I sat up on my elbows to watch. The dwarf stood in front of the door, his back to us, and began to work on something with great concentration.

Maybe a minute went by. There was a click, then another click.

The door creaked. It was open slightly.

"Come with me," said Duggin. "The guards are not around."

Hayrn and I got to our feet, too astonished to ask questions or to do anything else. Duggin looked back at us with a glare. "Get moving," he said flatly. It was an order. We followed him.

I looked at the door as we left. The huge padlock on the outside had popped open. How? I looked back at the handless dwarf, but he was nearly out of sight down the lantern-lit hall. Hayrn and I hurried to catch up with him.

I didn't believe it was happening, but only a few minutes later, we were on the street in the darkness. Almost no one else was out except stray cats and dogs. I looked back at the magistrate's marble building. There was no sign that anyone was aware that we had escaped.

"Our boat is at the second pier, left side, third or fourth down," whispered Hayrn nervously. "Single-masted fishing boat, the *Flying Lobster*."

Duggin made no reply. He led us down alleys I'd never seen before, moving as swiftly as if he'd been born and raised here. I had trouble believing this was the same ragged dwarf who had served ale to us earlier in the day. He must have been an amazing thief in his younger days. It was little wonder that, as he'd informed us, he had been crippled and enslaved when they'd caught him.

"Stay out of the moonlight," the dwarf said at one point.

"So nobody sees us?" Hayrn asked.

Duggin angrily turned to look up at Hayrn. "The *moon*," he shot back. "The *moon* will see you. Don't be a fool."

"The *moon*?" Hayrn was incredulous.

"Captain," I said, tugging his sleeve, "he means the God-king can see through the moon. It has his eye on it. He probably got rid of the other moons when he got rid of the gods."

"But . . . but," Haryn protested, then fell silent. Duggin didn't correct me. We hurried on in the darkness.

We reached the docks, where the dwarf made us stop for a moment in the shadow of a plank warehouse. He looked across the stone-paved plaza that led to the great docks themselves. I smelled the sea in the wind, heard waves slap the wooden piers. Sailors and dock guards called to each other several hundred feet away under the moonlight.

Duggin looked across the plaza for a long moment, apparently listening for anyone approaching. Then he turned to us again and began to poke at our clothing with his wrist stumps. "Pull something over your heads," he said. "No, that

won't work. Wait." He moved away from us and hooked his
stumps into a bunch of coarsely woven sacks and shipping
blankets, flipping them at our feet. "Put these over your
heads. Tear holes in the sacks for your arms. They're not that
strong—they were being thrown out. That's better. There."
The dwarf arranged a torn blanket over his own head with
my help.

"The guards won't recognize us anyway," said Hayrn in
sulking protest.

"The Godking will," said Duggin. "He's probably been
watching you since before you got to the docks here."

Hayrn started to reply, then sighed heavily and finished
covering himself. At Duggin's signal, we walked calmly
into the moonlight and headed for our boat.

Our path took us close to the place where I'd earlier seen
the old, bearded man chained to the post. My vision was
good enough to tell that the old man was still there, lying on
the ground as if asleep. Small rocks, dead fish, and rotting
fruit surrounded him; my nose was very clear about the
latter two as we approached.

"When I tell you to run," whispered Duggin, "you had
better run like you were on fire." He suddenly veered to the
right, walking straight for the old man chained to the post.

I sensed at once that Duggin was doing something forbid-
den. The old slave was apparently being punished for some
awful crime, and no one was supposed to get near him or do
favors for him. I glanced about quickly, looking for guards or
others who would report us, but none could be seen in the pale
light. A cool breeze washed around us from the quiet bay.

Duggin dropped to his knees beside the fallen figure. He
reached down and carefully lifted the old man's head by
slipping an arm stump under his neck. Duggin touched the
old man's cheek with his other stump and whispered something. I didn't catch what he said and leaned closer to hear
better.

"Hey," said Duggin softly, "I need the stone."

The old man's lips moved. He still seemed to be asleep.

"Wake up," said Duggin, more urgently. "The stone. I
need the stone now."

The old man's eyes opened, looked about in confusion, then focused on the dwarf. "Dugg'n Reh-ammer," the old man wheezed, his words badly slurred. "Bezzy day atha forge?"

"Busy day," said Duggin tenderly. "Very busy day at the forge. I need the stone, Fiz."

The withered old man grinned. He looked ghastly. "Doorknob," he said. "Yeh gave it t'Lunin . . . Lunitari. S'gone."

Duggin shook his head patiently. His face was only inches from the old man's. "Long ago," the dwarf murmured. "That was very long ago. I need the stone now, Fizzie. Hurry. Change it back. I've got to have it."

"But I don' *have*—" said the old man, more loudly.

Duggin shushed him. "*Now*, Fizban," he said. "I've got to have it *now*. Do it."

"Stupid Dougan," said the old man, pronouncing the dwarf's name differently than I'd heard: doo-gan. "Stupid Dougan Redhammer. Won' lemme sleep. Doorknob. Loss li'l gray stone." He struggled up on one elbow, out of Duggin's arms, rocking uncertainly as if he were about to fall over at any moment. "Here." He looked down at the pavement, then with excessive care he put one bone-thin hand flat against a round pavement stone before him. "Here," he repeated. "Stupid Ist'rans never found it. Put one right pass'em. Stupid Kin'pressed never saw it either. Big doorknob."

The round, flat stone changed as he spoke. It swiftly became a huge, many-faceted, gray crystal, a gem the size of a market melon. It sat in a dirty little pit in the street where the paving stone had been. Hayrn and I stared, oblivious to everything else. The old man sank back down to the pavement again with a ragged sigh, exhausted. His neck chain clinked, then was still.

"Is that the Graygem?" Hayrn asked in a strangled voice. "Is that the Graygem of—"

"Shut up!" Duggin snapped. He quickly seized the faceted stone between his stumps and managed to stuff it under one arm, under his blanket. "Thank you, old friend," he murmured to the old man. He leaned down and kissed the man on the forehead. "Sleep in peace."

The dwarf got to his feet. Tears ran down into his dark beard.

"Fizban," I said. I thought I was immune to further shocks, but I was wrong. "He's Fizban? The crazy wizard?"

The dwarf stared at me angrily, clearly taken aback. "How in the Abyss would you know anything about Fizban?"

"The War of the Lance!" I snapped back. "Fizban was the old wizard who helped the Heroes of the Lance! You remem—oh, *damn*!" I myself remembered too late that no one here knew anything about that war. Not even the God-king or the fallen gods would know. It had never happened on this Krynn.

I stared down at the old, toothless, bearded man sleeping on the stones. I felt such horror and sorrow in that moment that I was sure it would kill me.

"Fizban," I said. "Cut him free and let's take him with us!"

Duggin caught my arm with a wrist stump and steered me toward the docks. "You can do nothing for him, boy," he said swiftly, his voice hard. "The Kingpriest fed him poison. He has no mind left. He had just a little magic left. Leave him alone and let's—"

"Duggin," said Old Hayrn. "Guards."

"Hey!" someone shouted. I shot a look where Hayrn indicated. We'd been spotted. A group of three guards broke into a run toward us. Two of them were trying to draw short swords as they ran. "Halt!" roared the leader, only two hundred feet away. "Stay where you are!"

"Run!" Duggin said, and he bolted in the direction we'd told him our ship was docked. He was the fastest dwarf I'd ever seen in my life. With no armor or weapons, we had no hope of fighting the guards. We jumped aboard our fishing boat as fast as we could. The three guards were right behind us, swords drawn and swearing at us in the name of the Godking. In the hurly-burly of the moment, as I flung away the dock ropes and grabbed for a pole to shove us out to sea, I heard Duggin shout, "Halt, yourselves!"

There was a flash of a peculiar light. Startled, I dropped

the pole and had to grab for it to keep it from rolling off the boat and into the bay. When I was ready to push us off, I saw that the three guards were still on the dock, standing in strange, frozen positions as if caught in the act of running. A halo of magical light danced around them.

I looked around and saw Duggin holding the faceted gray stone between his wrist stumps, aiming it at the guards. He then sat down on the deck, grumbling to himself as he tried to get the stone under his cloak again. His arms slipped, and he dropped the huge gem on the deck. Disgusted, he got to his feet. "The Abyss with it," he said angrily as I shoved the boat out into the open water. Hayrn had the mainsail up, but a breeze was pushing us back toward shore.

Duggin looked around, saw our predicament, and bent down carefully to pick up the stone again. "Winds blow!" he shouted, holding the stone in the direction of the sail. As more stomping feet sounded from the dock, a sudden wind burst upon us and filled the sail. The boat lurched; I fell over, losing the pole for good in the bay. The wind picked up steadily, blowing us away from the docks until we were far out in the Bay of Branchala, heading north for the Gates of Paladine.

Duggin sat down on the deck, dropping the huge gem beside him. I could barely see the iron collar around his neck in the moonlight. He sighed loudly as he stared up at the white moon above and its wide eye, watching our flight.

The dwarf with no hands slowly grinned. "I got it back, Kingpriest," he said. "I got it back, you traitorous selfish toad. You miserable dirt ball of a deranged demigod! You . . ." His curses became more pithy, savage, and shocking by the minute. My ears actually burned. No one in the world ever swore with such feeling as Duggin did then.

The dwarf finally ran out of breath and lay back, panting. The Graygem glittered dully beside him.

"Great Reorx!" I exclaimed.

At my words, the dwarf turned his head to me. His face was pale in the moonlight. He looked as if he'd aged a hundred years in the last few hours.

"I'm sure glad someone remembers me," he said. His

eyes closed, and he drifted off into sleep as the wind carried us away from Palanthas and into the reaches of the sea and the night.

* * * * *

We sailed north for a day and a half. Several ships tried to catch us, but we outran them with wind summoned from Duggin's gem. The moon stopped moving in the heavens on the night we escaped. Instead it hovered above us, watching us through day and night thereafter. It was largely because of that that I stopped thinking of Duggin as Duggin.

"Thanks," he said when I got a cup of fresh water for him. He noticed I was staring at him, and he lowered his cup to stare back, black eyebrows raised.

"What should I call you?" I asked.

The dwarf grunted and sipped his drink. "Dougan Redhammer would be fine." He drank again, then set the cup down. "Yes, I used to be Reorx, but I'm not a god now, thanks to the Kingpriest, so there's no point in treating me like I'm awfully special. I liked being Dougan Redhammer. It was the avatar I was using when everything changed. Dougan will do."

"Dougan," I repeated. I nodded and went on with my chores, catching more fish to tide us over until we reached the island.

"Please tell us about the flame-giant," said Hayrn. Like me, he had become very quiet and respectful of our guest— and partner in crime, perhaps. I listened as I worked.

Duggin—Dougan gave a short laugh that had nothing funny about it. "Had to be Himself, lads," said Dougan somberly. "Himself and no other. That island on your world and ours, that's where the Irda live. Not many of them live there on this Krynn, my Krynn—assuming that you and I are from different Krynns. Damn crazy idea. The Irda island, now, it's a big secret, but you know how people get around and word gets out. Anyway, my guess is that your Irda, they must've gotten their hands on your world's version of this." He patted the gray stone beside him—the

Graygem or Graystone of Gargath, the artifact that long ago transformed all Krynn and brought chaos and change into it. The Graygem had altered the nature of magic, transformed the lands, and given birth to monsters, minotaurs, dwarves, and kender.

The god Reorx had forged the Graygem, I recalled reading once. It had been quite special.

Dougan took a deep breath. "Idiot Irda must have figured out how to break this thing open. Had to have been what happened on your world." He grimaced at the thought. "Can't have done them any good. I wouldn't like to have been there when it broke."

"Why?" I asked. I had entirely forgotten about catching fish.

Dougan hesitated. "Well . . ." He scratched at a whiskered cheek with a wrist stump. "Well, see, when the Graygem was made, it had this . . . it had, um, this . . . other god inside it, and it wouldn't have been a good idea to let this other god out." He looked at me with genuine pity. "If that is what happened on your Krynn, if the Graygem was broken open, I doubt very much that you have a home left to return to."

Old Hayrn and I absorbed the news, or tried to. "Oh," I said. "The flame-giant, that's the god inside of the Graygem, the one you call 'Himself.' "

Dougan nodded, looking away to the north.

"If this god came out," said Hayrn carefully, "what would he be likely to do?"

Dougan swallowed and rubbed his face. "Nothing good, I fear," he said quietly. "Nothing good. He . . . well . . . he was angry at being trapped in the Graygem, to begin with, and he, um, wasn't very fond of us—the other gods, that is. He'd have . . . revenge on his mind, I'm sure, and—"

"Was he more powerful than you, then?" asked Hayrn abruptly. It was the very thought that was floating around in my head, too.

The black-bearded dwarf was silent. He stared at the horizon, then looked down at his stumps before putting them under his armpits as if warming them.

We didn't talk again for several hours. We were eating

dinner—fish, of course—when I put my wicker plate down
and said, "So, our world is destroyed. Was destroyed.
Blown up or something."

No one spoke. I got up and walked to the other end of the
boat and sat down and began to cry. It felt like I cried for
hours. After a long while, Dougan came over and sat with
me.

"I have no idea what happened on your Krynn," said
Dougan gently, embarrassed. "I have no idea. There's no
way we can know."

"What are we doing now, Dougan?" I asked, coughing
and wiping my eyes. "What are we going to do when we get
to the island?"

The dwarf looked down at the deck as he spoke. I realized
he was making this up as he went along. He had no idea
what to do.

"Well," said Dougan, clearing his throat, "the Irda have
powerful magic. I can use some of the energy from the
Graygem to work a few spells, but with the Irda's help, I
think I can regain some of my old power. Not all of it, but
enough. Maybe enough. This new god . . . this Godking is
killing Krynn, Gullwing. Whole races have been destroyed,
wiped out to the last, over the past three hundred and
eighty-odd years." He took a deep breath. "There are no
kender left these days. Minotaurs and goblins went long
ago. The gnomes are probably next. Gully dwarves'll go last,
maybe, but they'll go. Every nation on every continent is
enslaved. Folks look free at first glance, but even those who
are most free—the humans and elves—are prisoners to the
Godking's whims. We live under the most awful tyranny in
the history of the world, of *any* world, and we have to do
something to bring it down. Even if it kills us, we have to
try, or else this Krynn will die."

He sat with me and talked and talked. Hayrn and I asked
about this Krynn and its history, and he told us everything.
He told of the horrors of the Years of Hunting, what the
races marked for death called it when the genocidal armies
pursued and slew them. He told how the Knights of Solamnia rebelled but were driven down and broken by the magic

of the Godking's priests. He told how the wizards were stripped of their powers in a single night, all of the rebellious mages at once, when the Godking brought all the moons together and unified them, seizing the sources of wizard magic. And he told how the former gods, thrown down on that day long ago, were enslaved and tormented, abused and injured. Dougan knew the fate of most of the old gods, his face bleak with rage as he recalled their tales. Even the fate of the evil gods upset him, as if they were bad apples but still a part of his own family.

Old Hayrn and I agreed to help any way we could. We wanted to repair the world, do anything to set things right again. I did not say that I had nothing else to do after my own world was lost, but that was true enough, too.

* * * * *

We sighted the island of the Irda at dawn on the second day. I felt a sense of dread when it appeared, but made myself get over it. We had no choice. Hayrn tied the old sea anchor rope to a rock in a shallow lagoon, and we left the *Flying Lobster* behind when we set off to look for the inhabitants. Dougan shoved the Graygem into a bag and had me tie it to his waist and pull his shirt down over it. He looked like he had an ale belly, but it would do.

"The key to the Irda," said Dougan, scratching with a wrist stump at his cheek whiskers as we walked through the brush, "is that they don't look like what you think they look like. I mean, they're supposed to be beautiful, as the legends say, but they could appear ugly as sin and you'd never know they were Irda. Darned annoying, but clever. Could be people, could be animals, could be anything. Keep an eye out."

"Footprints," said Hayrn, not a minute later. He pointed to a patch of dirt ahead of us. Indeed, an assortment of footprints was there—bare feet, fairly small. The tracks looked rough and old.

"Irda," said Dougan with visible relief. "By my beard. Well, they should be—"

His words ended in a gasp. We saw the Irda village at the same moment, as we came over a ridge. We stopped dead.

It was difficult to tell what their homes had looked like, as they had been so thoroughly destroyed. It was hard to tell what the Irda had looked like too, since only white bones remained of them. I looked down and drew back, having almost walked into the rib cage of one. They seemed to have been like large humans. Whatever more they had been like in life, there was nothing beautiful about their fallen, bare skeletons.

Dougan spread his arms, his wrists pushing Hayrn and I back a step. "Lads," said the black-bearded dwarf, "we need to get out of here *now*."

I knew instinctively that he was right. I turned to head back to the boat.

"But where would you go, Reorx?" asked a voice out of the still air.

We jumped as if a cold hand had touched each of us at the same time. We looked in every direction but saw no one.

"Where would you go, Reorx?" asked the voice again. It was a man's voice, an older man, I thought. The voice was gentle and calm. It disturbed me greatly.

"Don't run, lads!" shouted Dougan. "Stand by me, close to me. We can't outrun him. Stand by me and talk. It's all we can do."

"Good advice, if late," said the voice. Something bright appeared to my right. I turned and saw an old, balding, clean-shaven man standing among the bones of the Irda. He seemed to shine like a mirror reflecting the sun. I put up my hand to cover my eyes, but soon lowered it again. The man was standing barely fifty feet away. He wore pale yellow robes with the emblem of a rose or sun on his chest. Rays streamed out from the emblem in all directions.

The man's face was lined with years of strain and weariness. I had the idea that godhood had not been as kind to the man as he'd once hoped it would be. Still, his watery blue eyes bore the gleam of triumph. Something had worked out well for him after all.

"Did you bring it, Reorx?" asked the man in the robes.

"Haven't got anything for you," said the dwarf. He hunched down, handless arms crossed over his belly. "Nothing."

"You are lying, Reorx," said the man, "and I am angry that you are lying to me. Are these the accomplices in your theft?" The watery blue eyes flicked from me to Hayrn, then back to the dwarf. "Where did you get them? Two fishermen I have never seen before, who appeared on my world out of nowhere on the open sea. I know every being on the face of my world, Reorx, every being but these two. Where did you get them?"

"I didn't get them, but if I did, it would be none of your damned business, you flabby-faced old dung-eater!" growled the dwarf. "Jump in the Abyss if you want to know."

The robed man shook his head slowly in disapproval. "Your manners did not improve during your captivity. I was obviously too lenient in assigning your punishment when you stole the Graygem from me."

The robed man—the Godking, I knew—noticed my wide-eyed reaction to his statement. He gave me a thin smile. "Oh, so these fellows were not aware of your earlier crime? You didn't tell them that you took the Graygem from me after I used its powers to destroy evil, to bring down the false gods and elevate myself to my rightful place in the heavens? Without the Graygem, I would have never managed all that I have accomplished. I can admit to that. Strange that it would turn up in my possession right before I called on the old gods from Istar and demanded they set the world aright. It came to me as if the stone had a mind of its own, wouldn't you say? The old gods tried to break me and ruin my kingdom, my righteous nation and all my followers as well, but the gods fell before me instead. The Graygem brought me to power, but it has obviously done little for you, O Handy One, O Worker of the Tools of the Forge."

The only sound for a few moments was the dwarf's labored breathing.

"I hate you," said Dougan in a low voice. He sounded as

if he were going to cry. "Oh, how I hate you, you evil bastard dog."

The robed man sniffed. "Evil, indeed," he said. He walked toward us, his feet invisible under his pale yellow robes. "Give the Graygem back to me, Reorx."

"How did you know we were coming here?" I asked. I had to think of something, anything, to stall what was coming.

The robed man halted and looked at me in surprise, as if I had spoken out of turn.

"I see everything," he said. "I look down over day and night and see everything. Have you not noticed my moon with the great eye upon it? I think you will try to go home from here, wherever your home is. Is it underground? In wildspace? On another dimension or plane or world or time? No matter. I got here before you and . . . cleaned up. I also blocked all exits from this place. You'll stay here from now on."

"Stay here and be killed," I said.

The man looked at me and sighed as if I were a child who had said a simple and obvious thing.

"What about a bargain?" I asked, my throat dry.

The robed man's eyes widened. He raised a hand to stroke his bare cheek. "A bargain?" he asked. "You *are* joking."

I looked at Dougan, who was turning toward me. I had not time to regret what I was going to do next.

I lifted my right foot, spun on my left one, and kicked Dougan in the small of his back. The blow knocked all the wind from his lungs and threw him flat on the ground. I was on him in an instant, a startled shout from Old Hayrn ringing in my ears. It took only a moment to tear the bag loose from under Dougan's shirt, the bag he could not grasp since he had no fingers.

I danced back with the bag, clutching it to my chest. "I will give you this bag and its secret if you allow the three of us to live," I told the Godking. "You cannot harm us in any way or set us up to be harmed. Do this or you'll not get the bag."

Dougan's hoarse coughing and gasps for air were the only sounds that passed between us for a bit. However, a peculiar thing began to happen as I clutched the Graygem in its bag. I began to want it for myself. I began to think I was merely bluffing when I offered to give the bag to the God-king. I began to think that with the Graygem, I could *beat* the Godking.

"I think I will just take the bag from you and punish you for your presumption," said the Godking. There was no trace of humor in his voice or expression.

"If you could, you would have by now," I said quickly. "You wouldn't be toying with us like this. You're the only god left on this world, but you cannot get the Graygem from me. You don't know all of its powers and neither do I, but I sure will try to use them if you hurt us!"

Suddenly I wanted him to try it. I wanted to blast him. He was just some human who had become a god. I had the Graygem. He would look like burnt chicken parts when I was done with him.

The Godking and I stared at each other for what seemed like ages. I had never gambled in my life as I was gambling at that moment—but I kept thinking it was a gamble I couldn't lose. It was the Graygem doing that to me, and I knew it, but I had it and couldn't stop thinking I was invincible.

With all my effort, I shook off the Graygem's whispers in my mind. I knew what I had to do.

"Your word," I said, forcing the words out. "Your word that we will not be h-harmed, and you can . . . h-h-have th-this."

"No!" screamed Dougan, pushing Hayrn away from him and lunging toward me. I moved back, and the dwarf collapsed on the ground, gasping in pain from the kick I'd planted on him. "You don't know what you are d—" His voice broke up into a racking cough.

"I cannot let you loose upon the world, you know," said the Godking, ignoring the dwarf completely. "I cannot have everyone know that I made a bargain with a mortal. It wouldn't do. But you can sail north and find a haven among the islands there. There used to be dragons on them, but I

244

cleaned them up a few years ago, much as I had to clean up this little island last night. You can take your fishing boat and go north, but if I ever see you leave the next island you find, I will simply kill you and your . . . associates and be done with it."

I thought about that. I didn't look at Hayrn or Dougan. I fought the Graygem's strengthening whispers inside my head.

"Ag-greed," I said. I couldn't stop stuttering. "When I g-give you this b-b-bag, l-leave us here. We will leave on our own. Th-the secret is . . ." I steeled myself, then walked forward, making a wide circle around Dougan and Hayrn, and held the bag out to the Godking. As he bent down to take it from me, I came within a hair of commanding the Graygem to blast the silly old man into a cloud of blood particles. I shut my eyes, clenched my teeth, then forced myself to say the words I had in mind, so the Godking along would hear them.

I felt a huge weight lift from me. I let go of the bag as the Godking took it. He smiled at us one last time—and vanished.

Dougan's screams echoed across the dead little island for an hour.

* * * * *

Dougan wouldn't talk to me after that. He wouldn't talk to Hayrn either. If we tried to get near him, he struck at us with his useless stumps and screamed until he could make no more sounds. We left him rolled in a lump by a small fir tree.

"Frankly," said Hayrn, his fist balled up as he talked to me later, "I may just beat the crap out of you for him."

"Get in the boat," I told him, exhausted and angry and not in the mood for any back talk. I was furious that I'd given up the Graygem, and at the same time relieved beyond measure. "If we can't get Dougan, we may have to leave him here, though I don't want to. We may not be safe here, and we'd best—"

"The Abyss with you!" Old Hayrn roared at me. "You betrayed us! You betrayed the world!"

"I saved your butt!" I screamed back, all self-control gone. "I saved your stupid butt and his too and the whole world's! The Godking *couldn't hear what we said*, don't you see? He can see everything we do from his eye on the moon, but he can't hear anything we say! He doesn't know about the Graygem! He doesn't know what it is! He doesn't know anything! Nothing!"

Hayrn huffed, face glowering. "Doesn't know what?" he asked.

The Light struck.

It came from the east. We whirled and shielded our eyes from its radiance even under the noon sun. Moments later, a sudden prickling warmth brushed over my face and arms. It must have come all the way from Istar, from the Godking's main temple there, but I could still feel the heat. I was glad we were not closer; I already knew what that would have felt like.

Hayrn and I watched the eastern horizon. More flashes came in rapid succession, less bright that the first. Then a red glow began to stain the air.

"Get Dougan!" I shouted. "I'll untie the boat!"

Hayrn looked back at me in confusion. "What's happening? What did he do?" he asked. Then he got it. "You!" he exclaimed, swinging around to look at me with huge eyes. "You told him to *break* it!"

"Get Dougan, you idiot!" I screamed. "Get Dougan before we roast here!"

He got Dougan. Dougan was curiously silent, responding to nothing. I had the boat ready when they returned, and we poled off and were away in minutes, oaring hard. Not that it would help us if the Godking came back, but running away was all we could think of.

The eastern horizon grew redder and brighter. Enormous streaks of lightning snaked across the heavens there. Clouds, torn to pieces by tremendous winds, raced from the horizon toward the zenith in great waves. Dougan sat on the deck and watched the increasingly violent display, saying nothing except once when I threw down a blanket near him. He leaned close to me before I could back away from him.

"That's Himself and the Kingpriest, going at it," he whispered, as if sharing a private secret. "Wanna bet on who wins?" He smiled, then went back to watching the sky, face going blank.

It began to get hot. Extremely hot. Hayrn and I covered the ship with blankets and bailed water over everything topside. We then dragged Dougan below deck. I threw overboard all flammable materials that I could find—lamp oil, cooking oil, papers, scraps of string and wood.

I was the last to go below with the others. The island of the Irda was already smoking in places. Steam was rising from the sea, cloaking the world around us. And I had caused it. Dougan had been certain that the god inside the Graygem was more than a match for himself and probably all the other gods as well. The Graygem god would likely be a match for the Godking, then, too. I hunkered down with the old man and the crippled dwarf in the little cabin, and I prayed to anyone who would listen that the heat would not last too long or grow too great.

I believe I understood then, too, why all of this had happened, why Captain Hayrn and I had been sent here. The Graygem god wanted nothing more than to take revenge on those who had captured it, the True Gods. What better revenge than to break all other Graygems everywhere, on every Krynn across every line of history, and set their prisoners free? The fiery titan of our world surely chose us to carry out that mission. But how had he known we would accomplish that? Would others be chosen from this new Krynn and sent across time to other Krynns, so that more Graygems would be broken, more gods released, more Krynns destroyed, one after the other like children's blocks falling down in an infinite row?

It was too much to think about, and too hot to bother.

We heard a rumbling pass over the sea, growing louder like an avalanche. The wood floor itself began to smoke in the fiery heat. We tore off our clothes and sat on them to protect our legs from the hot floor. I flung water from our boat's casks freely over us. I soon smelled real smoke and knew the *Flying Lobster*'s upper deck had caught fire. The end was upon us.

Then the light outside faded rapidly, turning a dark, colorless gray. The rumbling ended. The temperature began to fall and grow chilly in mere heartbeats. It was silent for the time it takes to draw and hold a long breath.

Dougan sat up and looked at me. I could barely see him, but something in his face frightened me. I drew back.

"Gull," he said. He lifted an arm. His wrist stump glowed as if it were a flame. "I have a little magic in me now," said the dwarf. "It came from the Graygem. Take it and go home."

The howling father of all hurricanes hurled down upon us and struck in the next second. The boat went completely over on its side in the screaming wind. I fell back against a wall. Something heavy fell on top of me. I heard water roaring into the hold.

"Gull," said the dwarf who had been a god, speaking as if nothing had happened. "Wake up, and go home." Something touched my forehead in the mad darkness of the end of the world. A moment later, the madness and the world were gone.

* * * * *

"Hayrn," I whispered.

"Gull, wake up." A cool, wet cloth touched my forehead. Blessed water ran over my burning face.

I opened my eyes.

The sky was blue, with white clouds and a yellow sun.

"Thank the gods!" Old Hayrn shouted. He leaned forward and grabbed me, holding me in his arms. "I thought you were going to die! Thank all the gods above and below!"

Confusion reigned for a few minutes while I tried to make sense of the world. Hayrn wept and praised the gods and finally told me it was the morning after we had seen the fiery giant. I'd been unconscious from the blow to my head. I was feverish and sweating. And I had been raving.

"You said the most incredible things," said Hayrn, beaming with relief as he gave me a drink. "It is of no consequence now, though. Rest and sleep. Rest and sleep."

I tried to sit up, but my head spun. I lay back and closed my eyes. I wanted to sleep very much, but I had to find out.

"The moons," I said. "Where are the moons?"

"Sleep," ordered Hayrn. "The moons are not up yet."

"Wake me when they are up," I whispered, feeling myself fade. "Wake me."

"I will," he said.

Home. I prayed it was home. My home.

Then I surrendered to the peace and darkness and dreamed long of nothing at all.

The First
Gully Dwarf Resistance
Chris Pierson

The scant regulars who still patronized the Broken Spar looked up from their drinks in a pickled haze, the silent misery on their faces yielding to fear as Gell MarBoreth, Knight of the Lily, swaggered in. They hurried to move aside, not daring to meet his haughty gaze, as he marched across the tavern toward his customary table. The barkeep poured and served Gell's usual flagon of ale with remarkable speed, then withdrew without asking for so much as a copper in payment. Such were the benefits of being part of a conquering army.

Gell had said as much to Rancis Lavien, his comrade-in-arms and drinking companion, a few nights ago. Rancis, typically, had grinned and chuckled softly. "I know that's why I joined the Knights of Takhisis—for the free drinks," he'd said.

Gell had laughed, then shaken his head as his friend sipped his Lemish white wine. "Not that," he'd said. "It's the respect. These people know who we are, what we could do—*would* do—if they crossed us. They don't want that, so they let us do what we will."

"That's not respect," Rancis had noted solemnly. "That's terror."

Shrugging, Gell had drained his ale. "Does it really matter which it is? Do you really want these peasants to like us so much?"

Rancis had raised his eyebrows, regarding Gell with the bland expression that always heralded some deeply pithy remark. "Not really," he'd answered. "Do you really want them to hate us?"

Gell had considered that for a while, then had thrust the thought aside.

Today, Rancis stood and saluted as Gell pulled back his chair. Despite the formality of the gesture, there was an air of mockery about his friend that would have infuriated Gell, had it come from anyone else. He'd known Rancis Lavien for years, though—since Lord Ariakan had drafted them both into the Dark Queen's service—and he knew his friend meant no real disrespect. It was just his way; the only thing quicker and sharper than Rancis's sword was his wit.

"May I have the honor of being the first to offer my sincere congratulations on the auspicious event of your promotion, sir," Rancis proclaimed in a deep, almost reverent voice. His eyes twinkled.

Gell felt himself beginning to flush—Rancis's behavior was drawing stares—and hurriedly returned the salute. "Don't do that again," he said quietly as the two sat down.

"You're the one who's so keen on respect," Rancis shot back. He toyed with his wine glass—today he was savoring an Ergothian red—and fixed his eyes on Gell. "Besides, I really am glad for you. Knight-Warrior MarBoreth. Has a ring to it, wouldn't you say?"

Gell shrugged. Inside, of course, he was beaming with pride, but there was no way he'd give Rancis the satisfaction of knowing it.

As it happened, Gell was one of the heroes of the Battle of Caergoth. When his talon had been outmaneuvered and all but slaughtered by the foul Knights of Solamnia, he had fought on, holding the line until Subcommander Athgar had been able to send in reinforcements. He'd killed twelve knights single-handedly during the battle. Afterward, Sub-commander Athgar himself had lauded Gell's bravery. The promotion was his reward.

Rancis had held the line too, fighting at Gell's side, but hadn't received any of the same honors. He hadn't even allowed Gell to speak on his behalf. "Why in the Dark Warrior's name would I want a promotion?" he had asked. "I'm happy where I am."

That was Rancis. Gell, on the other hand, had been over-joyed at the prospect of moving up in the ranks. He desperately wanted to lead troops of his own, and now his chance had come. It wasn't much—he had a dozen of the towering brutes the knights used as foot soldiers at his disposal. But it was a start.

"So, young warlord," Rancis remarked, "received your first mission yet?"

Gell nodded. "Subcommander Athgar gave me my orders this afternoon. He's gotten word of a pocket of rebels down by the wharf. He wants me to flush them out."

Rancis whistled, genuinely impressed. "That's quite an honor," he said. "There's plenty of men who'd give their shield arms to go after rebels. Athgar must think you're going places."

"Let's hope so," Gell replied, flushing.

"Well, when you get to be Emperor of Krynn, promise me you won't forget all of us peons back here in the rank-and-file, sir."

Chuckling, Gell shook his head and quaffed his ale.

* * * * *

Gell raised his hand, signaling a halt to the brutes who walked behind him. Obediently they stopped, fingering their swords and glancing about warily. Even after weeks of campaigning in Solamnia, they were still leery of the sights, sounds, and smells of large cities. Still, Gell didn't doubt that once they found the rebels they would fight with their customary viciousness. He glanced behind him and waved one of the brutes forward.

Typak, the largest and smartest of the brutes, stalked up to stand beside his commander. "My people are nervous," he said, his words marked by guttural accent. "This is a strange place."

Gell was inclined to agree; he'd never been comfortable around the wharf. "It's because you grew up in Tarsis," Rancis had observed one night. "You just can't get used to the idea of a harbor with actual water."

But that wasn't it, at least not entirely. Though he'd never be so foolish as to reveal it in front of his troops, Gell was also worried about the rebels. Resistance was a problem in any city the Knights of Takhisis conquered—there would always be heretics who didn't share the Dark Queen's Vision—but in most places insurrection had been quelled fairly quickly once the public executions had begun.

The rebels in Caergoth, however, were infuriatingly tenacious; it didn't seem to matter how many of them the knights hanged or beheaded—they just kept on fighting. The dastards had raided supplies, waylaid messengers, sabotaged the knights' attempts to repair the city's sundered walls. Word had it that they were even behind the disappearance of one of the feared Gray Knights. Time and again, they'd eluded Subcommander Athgar's best efforts to weed them out.

That had changed three nights ago, though, shortly before Gell's promotion. On that day, the rebels had made two costly mistakes. First, after pilfering the knights' food stocks, they'd left behind a trail that led straight back to the wharf. Second, in their panicked haste they'd dropped a note of instruction that revealed the identity of their leader.

"His name's Hewick," Gell told Typak. "He's a Wizard of the Red Robes. Whatever happens, Subcommander Athgar wants him alive. If we can take other prisoners, that's just as well. The more of these caitiffs we can draw and quarter in the town square, the better."

Typak nodded and grunted. He would have preferred to wet his blade with the rebels' blood and be done with it, but Gell was his commander, after all.

Gell led his troops onward, toward the docks where fishing boats bobbed listlessly in the water. He wiped sweat from his forehead, inwardly cursing the inhospitable heat. It was late afternoon, and still there was no hint of the cool, pleasant breezes he'd heard most port towns enjoyed. There was also no sign of anyone in the streets, which was unusual for a wharf at any time of the day. But that was to be expected; the knights had imposed martial law, forbidding the locals to leave their homes without escort for as long as the rebels evaded capture.

Gell thought he might have preferred it if there were people around. The growing darkness, the silence, the sheer barrenness of the wharf—they all made his scalp prickle. He couldn't even hear a dog barking or a child squalling. Out of the corner of his eye, it seemed the shadows in the harbor's many alleyways were moving, but whenever he looked straight at them, they fell still. He found that his hand, clasped tightly around the hilt of his sheathed sword, was sweating in its gauntlet. It wasn't entirely because of the heat.

It was a long walk along the wharf, toward the row of old, run-down storehouses. In the stillness, the soft rattle of his armor sounded to him like the clamor of a thousand temple bells. Behind him, he could sense the brutes' edginess as they glanced around, searching for signs of ambush. Gell did the same but was more circumspect about it, calmly noting rooftops and corners where an archer—or a wizard—might lie in wait. Despite the danger of such an attack, though, Gell had refused Typak's advice that they move stealthily, through the shadows. "That's how elves and goblins fight," he'd admonished, "not Knights of Takhisis."

So they walked on, down the middle of the broadest street of Caergoth's harbor, the brutes jumping whenever a wharf rat skittered from one shadow to the next. Finally, after a few minutes that felt like hours, he signaled once more for his troops to halt.

Typak hurried forward, his face questioning. Gell held up a hand before the brute could speak, then nodded toward a dark, narrow laneway. "That's it," he said. "Our scouts tracked the rebels to that alley." He looked around, feigning aloofness so Typak wouldn't realize how tense he was, and eased his sword out of its scabbard. "Let's go. And stay close."

They started down the laneway, the brutes clustering so close together that Gell wondered how they'd have room to fight if the rebels confronted them. He surveyed his surroundings with a practiced eye. Above, the buildings leaned inward, over the alley; even at midday, the lane would be swathed in darkness. What few windows existed had been boarded up, which was good. Refuse was piled high all around—rancid filth left to rot in the ungodly heat—and they had to pick their way through it as they went. The stench was awful and made the brutes—used to the fresh, open air of their distant homeland—all the more wary.

Undaunted by the nauseating reek, Gell walked on. He could see signs that someone—a fair number of someones, in fact—had passed this way recently. This is it, he thought. We'll find what we're looking for this way. A quick fight, a few prisoners, then back to the garrison, victorious. There might even be another promotion in store for me.

He was smiling at this thought when, with a suddenness Gell could scarcely believe, the alleyway came alive.

Later, when Gell had time to reflect, he managed to sort out the order in which events had occurred. At the time, though, it all seemed to happen at once. First, a torrent of fish guts fell on them from above. Gell leapt aside, avoiding the worst of it, but the brutes got drenched. They gagged and staggered, wiping slime from their eyes, noses, and mouths. Second, a furious shriek rose from all around them. Third, the ambushers who had been lying in wait beneath the heaps of garbage sprang at them from every direction.

"Trap!" Gell shouted as dark shapes surged around him. His warrior's training taking over, he lashed out with his sword, aiming a blow at his attacker's throat. His blade whistled through air and struck the wall to his left, sending chips of plaster flying. Gell felt something strike his legs, just above the knees, and stumbled back with a shout. Behind him, he could hear the brutes yelling in alarm, but that wasn't his concern right now. Instead, he thrust his sword, trying to skewer his opponent. Again, he hit nothing at all.

A second later, it occurred to him to look down. When he did, he saw the reason neither attack had found its mark: he had been swinging above his assailant's head. The vicious rebel who had attacked him was barely four feet tall, its pale skin crusted with dirt, its hair and beard matted and tangled. Its scabrous arms and legs were flung about Gell's right shin, and it seemed to be trying to gnaw through his armor with broken, yellow teeth.

Takhisis smite me, Gell swore inwardly. We've been ambushed by gully dwarves.

The thing on his leg began to make low, growling sounds that it apparently believed sounded fierce. Scowling in irritation, Gell tried to shake it loose, but its grip was fast. Behind him, the brutes were yelping in pain; plainly, their vaunted protective war paint wasn't much good against gully dwarf nails and teeth. A furtive glance over his shoulder confirmed his suspicions—his troops had bunched themselves so closely together that they didn't have room to fight. He cursed himself for not telling them to spread out sooner.

"Why you no fall down?" the gully dwarf on his leg demanded indignantly. "I hit you real hard. You s'posed to fall down."

Glowering, Gell raised his sword to kill the wretched creature. At the last moment, though, he changed his mind and smacked the gully dwarf on the forehead with the flat of the blade. The creature's expression of irritation gave way to an odd sort of perplexity, then it dropped to the ground, senseless.

The effect was instantaneous. "They got Glert!" cried one of the other gully dwarves. "Run!" yelled another. Shrieking in panic, they scattered in every direction, shoving past Gell and the stunned brutes as they fled in abject terror. Within seconds, they were gone.

The brutes sagged against the walls, moaning as they clutched at bleeding arms and legs. To Gell's eye, their wounds didn't look all that serious, but the filth and slime were quickly making things worse. Typak, who had somehow gotten badly scratched across the right cheek, staggered toward the knight. "What in the name of the ancestors was *that*?" he gasped.

Gell scowled. "Gully dwarves," he said. Apparently, there were no such things where Typak came from. Lucky devil, he thought. "They're like rats, only bigger and not as bright."

"I never fought a rat before," Typak wheezed. "But I think maybe these were worse."

"They're just a nuisance," Gell snapped. "It's your fault you got hit so hard. You were too close together. How do you expect to fight if you don't have room to swing a sword?"

Typak began to answer, but just then one of the brutes doubled over with an agonized groan and sank to his knees. Gell's first reaction was to look around for a second ambush, but he quickly realized that wasn't it: the other brutes were looking ill, too.

Their wounds are fouled, he realized. All that muck's gotten into their blood, and they're getting sick already. He knew the brutes were no longer in any shape to fight, and began to wonder how long they had before their illness worsened to the point where they wouldn't even be able to walk. It was over, just like that; they couldn't go on.

He'd been beaten on his first mission. By gully dwarves.

"What do we do now?" Typak asked.

Gell yanked off his helmet in disgust. "We go back," he snarled. He glanced down at his feet, where the gully dwarf that had attacked him now sprawled, snoring softly. "And we take *that* with us."

* * * * *

The crowd parted a bit more speedily than usual when Gell strode into the Broken Spar that evening. Some of the locals glanced at him and muttered under their breaths. He felt his temper beginning to flare at this, but fought to keep control. It had been a difficult and disappointing day, and it wouldn't do to lose his composure. He calmly headed for his table.

Rancis looked up as Gell approached, and wrinkled his nose. "Is that fish I smell?" he asked, puzzled.

Gell counted slowly to ten, as he'd learned to do when rage got hold of him. "Barkeep!" he shouted, thrusting aside the flagon of ale already waiting for him. "Bring me some brandy!"

Obediently, the barkeep hurried over with a snifter. Rancis watched as his friend drained the glass in one long draught. "I trust," he said, "that things went not quite as well as you'd hoped."

"That should be obvious," Gell snapped. "If things had gone as well as I'd hoped, I'd have brought the rebels back in chains, and I'd be drinking *real* brandy with Subcommander Athgar, not slop in this hole."

"I see," said Rancis sagely. He sucked his lower lip pensively for a moment. "Would you care to tell me what happened?"

"We were ambushed."

"By the rebels?"

"Not exactly."

Rancis's brow furrowed. He took a careful sip of the straw-colored Kalaman vintage he'd chosen for this night's indulgence. "Well, I hope you gave as good as you got."

Gell shrugged. "I doubt it. Half my men are too sick to move, and the rest I wouldn't trust to lift a sword. My second-in-command nearly lost an eye, too. But we *did* take a prisoner."

"Well, there you go," Rancis said, trying to sound cheery. "Who did you get? A wizard? A cleric of Paladine? A Knight of Solamnia?"

The second snifter of brandy slid down Gell's throat. He muttered something incoherent.

"What was that?" Rancis asked. "I didn't quite catch—"

"I said, 'A gully dwarf'!" Gell snapped. Some of the locals glanced at him, but he glared balefully back, and they quickly found something more interesting to look at.

Rancis blinked. "I'm sorry," he said. "My ears must be playing me up. I could swear you said, 'a gully dwarf.' "

Gell set down his snifter in a not-at-all-gentle way, leaving a jagged crack down its bowl. "I *did* say that."

"Ah."

"That's what attacked us. That's what made my men sick."

"Ah." Rancis took a deep breath. "Not rebels, then?"

Gell shook his head angrily.

"I see," said Rancis. He stroked his thin moustache for a moment. "You *do* realize we can't execute gully dwarves, don't you? It wouldn't do anything to get you that respect you crave—you'd look more fearsome if you went around stepping on slugs."

"We're not going to execute it," snarled Gell. "I brought it back here to ask it a few questions."

Rancis's jaw dropped wide. "You're going to *interrogate* a gully dwarf?" he exclaimed, aghast. "The bloody things are too stupid even to count to three. How do you expect it to tell you anything useful?"

Gell shrugged. "We found it near the end of the rebels'

trail," he said. "It must have seen something. I'll find out what I can."

"Whatever you say." Rancis took a sip of his wine, then looked up at his friend, his eyes narrowing. "You sure you're not trying to put one over on me?"

—seveneightnineten, thought Gell, gritting his teeth. "Yes," he growled.

Rancis made a holy sign in the air. "May the Dark Queen walk with you, my friend," he said solemnly. "You'll need her."

* * * * *

To Gell's surprise, Typak was waiting at the tent where the gully dwarf was being held. The brute, his face bandaged where he'd been injured the day before, bowed at the Dark Knight's approach. There was still a palpable aroma of fish about him. Gell decided not to mention it.

"What word of the others?" Gell asked.

Typak looked grave. "Not good. They'll live, but they're all in agony. It will be some time before they're well enough to fight."

A particularly violent and sacrilegious curse occurred to Gell, but his knightly decorum kept him from speaking it aloud. "I suppose there's no way that can be helped," he said. He glanced at the tent, steeling himself. "If there's nothing else, we have work to do."

Typak stood aside, bowing again. Gell took a long, deep breath, then threw back the flap of the tent. Ducking his head, he stepped inside.

Though bound and gagged, the gully dwarf found some way to moan pathetically as Gell and Typak entered. Gell bent down and tried to remove the gag, but the terrified creature flopped away from him, its eyes bulging in fear. Even when the knight seized it by the front of its grimy tunic, it twisted its head this way and that, keeping him at bay. In the end, Typak had to hold the dwarf down while Gell loosened the muzzle. Once the gag was off, the creature tried to bite off the knight's fingers.

"Damn it!" Gell swore, jerking his hand back. Typak pushed the gully dwarf down in the dirt. It began to whine, a high-pitched, reedy sound that made Gell's spine hurt. "Don't do that again," the knight growled, "or my friend here might have to step on you."

The gully dwarf started, then glanced up at Typak. The brute answered with a suitably vicious smile. "Sure, sure," the dwarf agreed hurriedly, growing deathly pale. "I do like you say." He stared at Gell for a moment, his eyes narrowing. "But I *still* think you s'posed to be dead. I hit you *real* hard."

"Well, I'm not," Gell shot back. "Now, you little gutter-licker, what's your name?"

The gully dwarf thought about this for some time, stroking his greasy beard. "Glert! My name Glert!" he cried at last, then grinned up at the knight, his face aglow with jubilant pride. "Did I get it right? What me win?"

Gell frowned, perplexed. "Win?"

Glert nodded enthusiastically, his teeth bared in an immense and rather grotesque smile. "Other man ask Glert questions. Play game: I answer right, he give Glert treats. Pretty rock, dead frog . . . that sort of thing. He promise to give me great treasure one day. Me know lots."

"I'm sure you do, but . . ." Gell's voice trailed off, his brows knitting. "Wait a minute. What do you mean, 'other man'?"

"Oh, him real nice. Pretty red robes, not like that ugly thing." The gully dwarf pointed a stubby finger at Gell's intricately engraved breastplate. "Him visit Glert's clan many times. Him treat Glert real good, not like you. You mean. Hit Glert on head."

Part of Gell wanted to do that again, but he checked himself. It looked like he was actually getting somewhere, despite Rancis's misgivings. "This nice man," he said. "The one in the red robes. What's his name?"

Glert furrowed his brow in intense concentration, and Gell worried that it might be hours before he thought of the answer. Fortunately, understanding soon dawned on the gully dwarf's face. "It real funny name," he said. "Hyook. Sound like he swallow something yucky."

Gell gasped. Hewick! So this little cretin knew the most

wanted man in all of Caergoth! "What else do you know about this . . . er . . . Hyook?" he asked. "Where does he live?"

"Oh!" Glert beamed. "Me know that. He live here, in city."

The beginning of a headache, a dull pain behind his eyes, began to make itself known to Gell. He put a hand to his forehead. "Can you be more specific?" he asked.

"Oh! Sure! Sure!" Glert answered. "Me can do that. Only—what 'specific' mean?"

Gell could sense that Typak was debating the virtues of just smashing in the gully dwarf's head and being done with it. He quickly cut in. "It means where in the city does Hyook live?"

"Oh!" Glert said, nodding enthusiastically. "Glert understand! You want to know if me know what *part* of city Hyook live in! Glert can answer that!"

His excitement growing, Gell found himself nodding right along with the delighted dwarf. "Good!" he said. "Very good! What's the answer?"

"No!" Glert replied, his grin amazingly wide. "Glert have *no idea* where he live!"

Gell stopped nodding. For a moment, he couldn't think of a thing to say. "All right," he snarled at last, recognizing a blind alley when he saw one. "You said you were part of a clan."

"Yes! Murf clan!" Glert answered. "Real big clan. Me just join. Lots of us down by big water. You meet others yesterday." He looked up at Typak. "Glert's friend Gorp try to poke out your eye. Gorp not have very good aim."

Slowly, Typak balled his hands into fists. Gell stopped him with a glance, wondering how much longer he could keep the brute in check. "Tell me more about this Murf clan," he urged.

"Oh, Murf clan many large," Glert answered.

"How many of you are—" Gell stopped, gasping in horror, but it was too late. Glert had begun to count.

"One, and one, and one, and one . . ." Glert recited, numbering fingers and toes and hairs in his beard. Gell counted along with him, but lost track around forty—not that he'd take a gully dwarf's word when it came to such brain-intensive work. "And one, and one, and one!" Glert finished finally. Smiling like a maniac, he held up ten fingers. "Two!"

This, Gell had been expecting. Typak, however, knew little of gully dwarves. The brute made a queer squeaking noise, his mouth hanging open. Gell might have laughed, were it not for the almost overwhelming impulse to take Glert by the throat and shake his teeth loose. "Thank you, Glert," he said tersely.

"No mention it."

"What else can you tell me about this—this Murf clan?"

"Hmm," remarked Glert, scratching his head. "Well, Hyook give us funny name. Call us 'First Gully Dwarf Resistance.' Me not know what that means, but me like Hyook anyway. He real nice, give me treats if I tell him things. I already tell you that."

"True," said Gell. "All right. Who's in charge of the clan?"

Glert blinked. "That not very smart question. Our leader in charge."

The pain behind Gell's eyes worsened. "I figured that," he said through tight lips. "But who's your leader? And," he added, holding up a hand before Glert could blurt out an answer, "if you say the one in charge is your leader, I'm going to let my friend here hurt you very badly."

Typak tensed hopefully.

Crestfallen, Glert shrugged. "Leader called Blim. Highmurf Blim. Him real smart. *Him* know where Hyook live."

"Good! Perfect!" Gell rejoiced. "Now, where can I find this Highmurf Blim?"

"Oh, me not allowed to tell you that," Glert avowed sternly. "Highmurf say, if anyone tell bad men where Murf clan live, he put us in stew."

"That's all right," Gell said, trying not to think of how repulsive that thought was. "You don't have to tell me where the Murf clan lives. Why not just tell me where *you* live then?"

Understanding dawned on Glert's face. He smiled. Gell smiled. Even Typak smiled. "I know that! And Highmurf not say not to tell," the gully dwarf rejoiced. "Glert live . . . with Murf clan!"

The smile froze on Gell's face. He let out a long, slow breath and began to massage his temples.

* * * * *

"Dwarf spirits," growled Gell, slumping into his chair at the Broken Spar. "Bring the bottle!" he called. The barkeep scurried to comply.

Rancis Lavien sat in silence, holding his Qualinesti wine up to the hearthlight to admire its deep ruby hue. He brought the glass to his lips, took a brief sip, and set it down. He did not meet Gell's furious gaze.

The barkeep set down a reasonably clean brass mug, and with it an old, grimy bottle of dwarf spirits. Gell poured himself a hefty dose and downed it, wincing at the pungent smell and fiery taste. Then he did it again. Wiping his mouth, he regarded Rancis with growing impatience.

"Well?" he snapped.

Rancis looked at him blandly. "Well, what?"

"Don't give me that," snarled Gell. "You've got something to ask me. Out with it."

For a moment, Rancis looked hurt, then he smiled. "Never let it be said I don't try to be discreet," he remarked. "Who won—you or the gully dwarf?"

Gell downed a third shot, thinking violent thoughts. "I thought it would be *easy* to outwit the little bastard," he muttered bitterly.

"Sometimes the unarmed opponent is the most dangerous," Rancis replied, quoting an old sell-sword's saying. "Maybe he just can't tell you what you want to know, Gell."

"No, that's not it," Gell answered. "I wanted to find out where he lives—even a gully dwarf should be able to remember that." He closed his eyes and pinched the bridge of his nose, praying to every god in the dark pantheon for relief from the pounding in his brain. "Do you have any idea how hard it is to trick someone who's too stupid to follow what you're saying?"

"Obviously, you've never met my brother," Rancis said mildly.

Gell let out a harsh, barking laugh, drawing furtive glances from the tavern's other patrons. He threw back another mouthful of spirits.

"Maybe you've had enough," Rancis said, touching his friend's arm.

"Lemme alone," Gell slurred, smacking his hand away. "I know when I've had 'nuff."

Rancis shrugged. "Suit yourself," he said. "You know what Subcommander Athgar does to drunkards."

That caught Gell's attention. Even after four shots of dwarf spirits, he could remember the last man in Athgar's comp-group who'd had too much to drink. His name had been Vimor Crenn, and he'd been much higher in the ranks than Gell was. Athgar had personally stripped Vimor of his knighthood, then he'd cut the man's throat with his own sword.

Gell jammed the cork back in the bottle and pushed it as far away as he could.

"That's better," Rancis declared. Respectfully, he signaled for the barkeep to take away his wine, as well as the spirits. "Now, let's see what we can do about your little friend," he said. "Sometimes, when you can't solve a problem, you need to step back and look at it from a different angle."

Gell nodded absently. "Fine," he muttered. "Do you have any suggestions?"

"As a matter of fact, I do."

Gell looked up. After a moment, he realized his friend was done talking. He counted to ten. "Well?" he demanded. "What is it?"

"You said you wanted to know where the gully dwarf lives, right?" Rancis asked.

Gell was stricken by a vivid image of his hands closing about Rancis's throat. "Would you quit playing games," he growled, "and tell me your damned idea?"

Rancis inclined his head indulgently. "All right, so be it," he said. "Let him go."

Blinking blearily, Gell regarded Rancis in bafflement. "Let—" he began. Then understanding hit him so hard, it nearly knocked him out of his seat. It was so *obvious*.

"Of course," he said, his lips curling into a sly grin that Rancis quickly mirrored. "Let him go!"

* * * * *

"I can't believe this is working," Typak muttered.

Gell grinned at the brute. "Never underestimate a gully dwarf's stupidity. That was our mistake yesterday—assuming the little squeak was smart enough to play mind games with. It should have occurred to me then: why have him *tell* us where his clan lives when he can *show* us?"

Typak shook his head ruefully. "If you had told me such creatures existed, I never would have believed you."

The two men looked ahead. Not two blocks in front of them was Glert, trotting happily down the street. They followed the stubby-legged creature at a leisurely walk, taking no pains to conceal themselves. Behind them walked another twenty knights and brutes, marching in formation. Subcommander Athgar had, upon hearing of Gell's plan, granted him temporary command of this company—out of amusement, Gell imagined.

They'd released Glert, left the garrison, and now they were at the wharf, drawing ever nearer to the Murf clan's lair. It was so stunningly simple that Gell couldn't help but laugh.

"Doesn't he realize we're following him?" Typak asked incredulously.

"Of course he does," Gell answered. "He just doesn't realize that might not be a good thing."

Suddenly, Gell stopped in his tracks. He grabbed Typak's arm, and the two men came to a halt, the troops behind them doing the same. They watched, silent and unmoving, as the gully dwarf peered around him. For a moment, Gell had the terrible feeling the little wretch was lost, but soon Glert nodded, mumbling to himself. Then he turned around, looked straight at the mass of vicious, heavily armed warriors, and waved.

"Hi!" he called, grinning.

Typak stared in disbelief. Some of the younger knights behind him snickered. For want of anything better to do, and feeling a bit giddy, Gell waved back. Then Glert was off again, trotting around a corner and down a narrow alley.

Shaking his head and chuckling to himself, Gell led his troops onward.

* * * * *

The sign on the door was enough to elicit a paroxysm of stifled laughter from several of the knights under Gell's command. He silenced them with a glare, thankful that his skull-shaped helm hid the fact that the corners of his mouth were doing a strange little dance of their own.

He glanced up and down the alley, where the brutes in his squad were busy jabbing piles of trash with their swords. There didn't seem to be another ambush waiting for them, which was good. On the other hand, of course, he was about to enter the lair of what he guessed were at least two-score gully dwarves. The creatures were cowards, yes, but they had been known to fight with unfettered viciousness when cornered. What he meant to do was akin to deliberately reaching into a wasp's nest.

"Leave the Highmurf alone," he told his men. "I don't care about the others. Just remember—we're not here to exterminate them. Don't kill anything you don't have to."

The knights nodded respectfully and readied their weapons. His breast swelling with pride, Gell turned back to the door they'd just watched Glert pass through, and his eyes fell on the sign. It read: "Secrut dor—Need paswerd for entur." Beneath these words, someone had crudely—but helpfully—scrawled "paswerd: stew."

For a moment, Gell thought he was going to lose control. Biting his tongue, he reached out and rapped on the door.

"What you want?" asked a voice on the other side.

This took Gell aback. What in the Abyss did they *think* he wanted? "Let me in," he answered.

"Can't," said the voice. "You no say password."

"Stew," Gell declared.

There was a moment of silence, then Gell heard the gully dwarf on the door's other side muttering to himself. After a while, the doorman raised his voice again. "You sure?" he asked suspiciously. "Me no remember. What it say on sign out there?"

Gell could sense the other knights' suppressed mirth crackling in the air. That was the last thing he needed: his men being unable to fight for laughter. He gestured sharply at them over his shoulder, and they fell still, their ingrained sense of discipline overriding all else. "It says 'stew,' " he growled. "Now open up before I beat the door down."

"Okay," the doorman grumbled. A moment later the door swung inward. Gell realized it hadn't even been locked; he could have just barged in at any time. A small chorus of snorts behind him made it clear the other knights had reached the same conclusion. He wasn't sure who would try his patience more today, the gully dwarves or his own troops.

As the door opened, it revealed an immensely fat gully dwarf wearing what looked like an old burlap sack. The creature blinked up at Gell in confusion, then its eyes went astonishingly wide as it noticed the other knights. Its mouth went slack with bewildered horror.

"Awk," the gully dwarf declared, and fainted dead away.

The knights looked down at the unconscious doorman for a moment, then began to chuckle openly. This time Gell couldn't help but join them. "Well," he noted, "that's one down."

* * * * *

Later, when he described it to Rancis Lavien, Gell compared storming the headquarters of the First Gully Dwarf Resistance to stepping into a hairy, foul-smelling tornado. The creatures ran everywhere, howling in panic and crashing into walls and each other in their desperation to get away from the advancing knights. As a result, there was very little actual fighting—Gell and his men just shoved their way through the gully dwarves' cramped, filth-strewn warren, kicking aside any of the wretches too stricken by blind terror to realize they were in the way.

That wasn't to say there weren't casualties, though. One young Knight of the Lily wrenched his knee badly when he slipped in one of the many puddles of unidentifiable slime that covered the floor of the den. And the unfortunate brutes who accidentally strayed into the warren's mess hall were so badly overcome by the stench that their fellows had to carry them back out immediately. On the whole, however, Gell's company made its way through the headquarters with ease.

They found Highmurf Blim huddled behind his throne, his hands covering his face, his entire body quivering in fear. The knights surrounded him, swords ready, but he continued to cower, refusing to look up. "Go 'way," he whined petulantly. "Me hiding. You no see."

At a nod from Gell, Typak stepped forward, seized the Highmurf by his grimy robes, and lifted him off the floor. Blim flailed around furiously for a few moments, but neither fists nor feet connected with the blue-stained brute, so he gave up.

"All right," he declared, his voice taking on a ridiculously lofty tone. "Me be merciful. We spare you."

Struggling to keep his composure, Gell signaled for Typak to set Blim down on his dilapidated throne. The brute did so a bit more forcibly than necessary.

"What you want?" the Highmurf groaned, wincing and rubbing his backside in pain.

"Just to talk," answered Gell. "I'll ask you a few questions, and—"

He was cut off as a wailing gully dwarf barreled into the throne room and straight through the knot of knights that had gathered around Gell and Blim. The creature was gone again, out the far end of the chamber, before anyone could overcome their astonishment enough to react.

"That my war chief," said Blim proudly.

Gell blinked, momentarily at a loss. "Of—of course it was," he stammered. Then he collected his thoughts and scowled in irritation. "Now," he began again, "I'm going to ask you a few questions. If you answer them for me, we'll leave."

Blim thought this over for what seemed a minor eternity. "That seem fair," he proclaimed at last. Eagerness sparked in his eyes. "Me like guessing games. What you want to know?"

Despite his best efforts, Gell couldn't fight the sinking feeling in his stomach.

* * * * *

Highmurf Blim looked down at the Knights of Takhisis from his throne, his piggy eyes squinting cannily. "Lemme get this straight," he said. "You want me to tell Hyook where you live?"

"No!" shouted Gell for what seemed like the hundredth time. He could feel his grip on his temper beginning to slip, and forced himself to remember that murdering the gully dwarf king in cold blood wouldn't be in accordance with the knightly ideal of honor. He counted to ten, found that it wasn't enough, and went on. By the time he reached fifty, he was calm enough to continue without raving. Still, there was a strange tremor in his voice when he spoke again. "One more time," he said. "*I* want *you* to tell *me* where *Hyook* lives. Got that?"

"Yup," said Blim nodding happily. "You want Hyook to tell me where you live." He peered around, a bit confused. "Only—Hyook no here. Why not you tell me yourself? That seem easier."

The headache was back with a vengeance, a great iron spike sliding down into Gell's brain. He rubbed his temples, praying to Takhisis for patience and some relief from the horrendous stench that permeated the gully dwarves' lair.

"Somethin' wrong with your head?" asked Blim. "I get medicine man. He fix."

Alarmed, Gell began to object, but it was too late. "Poog!" shrieked the Highmurf, driving the agonizing spike even farther into Gell's head.

A bent, scrawny old gully dwarf entered the room, his gray beard so long that he tripped over it twice as he shuffled toward them. "What happening?" he croaked, squinting myopically at the knights.

"Nothing," said Gell hastily. "It's all—"

"This guy got headache, Poog," Blim interrupted, jerking a thumb at Gell. "You got cure?"

"Course I do," Poog replied indignantly. He reached into one of his stained jerkin's many pockets and produced several scraps of something Gell didn't immediately recognize. He held the scraps out, and Gell realized he was being offered—of all things—willow bark. "Here," Poog said. "You chew. Help fix head."

Angrily, Gell smacked the medicine man's hand away, sending the willow bark flying. "Get that away from me," he snarled. Poog pouted for a moment, then sat down on the floor and began to sniffle.

Something inside Gell snapped. "Enough!" he roared. He drew his dagger from his belt, lunged at the Highmurf, and pushed the blade's tip against Blim's bulbous nose, causing the skin to dimple but not quite drawing blood. "Now," he hissed, his face livid, "I'm going to give you one last chance to answer me, and then I'm going to cut you a third nostril. Am I making myself clear?"

Blim stared cross-eyed at the blade at the end of his nose, tears streaming down his face. After a few failed attempts to find his voice, he nodded slightly.

"Good," said Gell. "No more games. Where does Hyook live?"

"Oh!" the Highmurf cried triumphantly. "You want to know where *Hyook* live! Highmurf can tell you that. Why you no say so in the first place?"

Gell found that the only sound he could make was a thin, high-pitched squeal.

Blim gave him an oddly sympathetic look. "That okay," he said. "Everyone make stupid mistake sometimes. Hyook live in big house on hill. He take Blim there once. Him have secret door, too. Not as good as Murf clan's secret door, though. Too hard to find."

Hesitantly, Gell lowered the dagger. It left behind a prominent red mark on the gully dwarf's nose. "Very good," he said slowly. "Where is the secret door?" he asked, then cringed, expecting it would take another hour to make Blim understand the question.

"Oh, that easy," the Highmurf answered. "There big room in house, many books. Secret door behind shelves by fireplace—Hyook pull big blue book on third shelf to open."

A straight answer! Gell wanted to dance. "All right," he said. "Thank you, Your Highness. That's what I wanted to know."

"Highmurf glad to help," Blim answered, beaming as he rubbed his nose. He held out his hand. "Now, what you give me?"

Gell's eyebrows shot up. It should have occurred to him before: If Hewick gave the gully dwarves trinkets in exchange for their aid, of course they'd want him to do the same. He cast about vainly, then fumbled for his purse. He produced a single copper coin, and put it in the Highmurf's hand. "There you go, Your Highness," he said.

"Ooh!" crowed Blim, holding the coin up in the dim light. "Shiny! You make Highmurf much happy. You go now."

Ordinarily, Gell might have been incensed at being dismissed so flippantly, but he was more than happy to comply. He rose and hurried from the room, and his men followed, leaving the gully dwarf king and his blubbering medicine man behind. Gell didn't stop, didn't look back, as he made his way back through the chaos of the creatures' hideout and out into the welcoming, comparably fresh air of the garbage-strewn alley.

At last, he knew! He knew exactly where they could find Hewick. There was only one hill within Caergoth's walls, and it wouldn't be very hard to figure out which house belonged to the wizard. As he led his company along the wharf back toward the garrison, he pieced together his plans. He'd report to Subcommander Athgar, request permission to lead the squadron that would storm the house—a request Athgar would be more than willing to grant, in light of Gell's success with the Highmurf. After that, when the Knights of Takhisis had finally captured the rebels, he'd be a hero again. There'd be more promotions, glory, and fame.

Before any of that, though, he needed a long bath. He stank of gully dwarf.

* * * * *

The door of the house flew open with a splintering crash. Swords drawn, three dozen Knights of Takhisis charged through. Behind them came a swarm of brutes, then, proudly, Gell MarBoreth, who had won the right to lead this assault. Beside him walked Rancis Lavien, his own blade gleaming in the dying glow of twilight. The two men exchanged grim, satisfied smiles as they strode down the darkened entry hall.

"The library!" Gell barked, his voice ringing within his helmet. "Look for the library!"

"I found it, sir!" called a young knight, from a door halfway down the hall. "Over here!"

Rancis clapped Gell on the shoulder, and the two friends hurried toward the man who had called out. They found him at the entrance to a large room whose walls were lined with shelf upon shelf of ancient books. Gell nodded in approval as he surveyed the chamber; the Gray Knights, he knew, would be interested in such a large collection. But the books weren't foremost in his mind.

He scanned the room, and spotted the fireplace. His armor rattling, he hurried over and searched the shelves on either side. As the Highmurf had promised, there on the third shelf was a fat tome bound in deep blue eelskin, the gold-leaf words on its spine long since worn to flecks. It was just as Gell had pictured it: anonymous, no different from any of the hundreds of volumes that adorned this room—or so it seemed. He brushed his fingers against it, then turned to Rancis. "Get the others in here. I want as many swords as possible. They may put up a fight."

Nodding, Rancis obeyed. Within moments, the library was crowded with knights and brutes, all tensely waiting for furious rebels to come boiling through the secret door. "Remember this," Gell told them proudly. "Today we finally got the best of Hewick of Caergoth." With that, he seized the book and yanked it from the shelf.

Nothing happened.

The only sound that penetrated the stunned silence that followed was the smack of Rancis Lavien smiting himself on the forehead. Gell MarBoreth's face turned blood-red, then darkened to purple as he stared uncomprehendingly at the book in his hands. He opened it, began to flip the pages. "What—" he sputtered.

"Uh, Gell?" asked Rancis, his voice low. "What shelf did this Blim fellow say the book was on?"

"I already told you," Gell snapped impatiently. "He said to look on the thir—"

His voice broke off with a strangled, choking noise as

realization dawned on him. "The *third* shelf," he said. He looked at his friend in horror. "Temptress take me, Rancis. What have I done?"

At that moment, on the other side of the city, the alarm bells at the Knights of Takhisis' garrison began to ring.

*   *   *   *   *

As night stole across Caergoth, the stubborn glow of sunset was met by a brighter light from the fortifications in the city's eastern quarter. Highmurf Blim watched with satisfaction as fire swept across the knights' garrison. To a passerby, he would have looked comical, standing at the prow of an old fishing boat manned by a crew of gully dwarves. There weren't passersby, though; the Dark Knights' curfew kept the citizens inside, and the knights themselves had more important things to do than patrol the harbor just now.

Poog, Blim's medicine man, hobbled up beside him, his expression thoughtful as he regarded the raging flames. "You know, Hew," he said, "I thought it was over when you mentioned the third shelf. You *know* we're not supposed to be able to count higher than two."

"It was daft of me, wasn't it, Caren?" Blim agreed. "It's a good thing that foolish young knight was too keen on finding our hideout to notice. And what was with giving him willow bark for his headache? Who ever heard of a gully dwarf cure that actually worked?"

"Just a little joke," Poog answered, his eyes twinkling. Willow bark had been a traditional headache remedy since the dawn of Krynn—but the medicine man had assumed, correctly, that Gell MarBoreth didn't know the first thing about herbalism.

The Highmurf eyed him curiously. "You have a sick sense of humor for one of your order, Caren." His bristly beard split in a grin. "But I must say you make a damn fine gully dwarf."

"Thanks," said the medicine man, with a pleased half-smile of his own. "You weren't so bad yourself."

Blim gave him a wink. "I suppose we should get going," he

said. "When they finally get those fires extinguished, they'll be out for our blood in the worst way." He looked over his shoulder, surveying his crew. His gaze fixed on one in particular. "Glert! Come here!"

The little gully dwarf who had led Gell to Blim's hideout hurried up, his eyes wide and bright. "We done?" he asked. "Do I get to ride on the boat?"

Blim smiled kindly and patted Glert on the head. "I'm afraid not, my little friend," he said. "We have a long and dangerous journey ahead of us, and you're better off staying where you know the hiding places. But I wanted to thank you, Glert. We never would have been able to do this without your help."

Despite being utterly confused, Glert beamed unabashedly. "Me glad to help. You play real fun game, Highmurf."

"Here," said Blim, reaching into one of the pockets of his ragged robes. He produced a copper coin, the same one the Dark Knight had given him, and put it in Glert's hand. "I promised you a treasure one day. This is yours—you've earned it."

Glert stared at the coin in amazement. "You mean it, Highmurf? This mine?"

Blim nodded. "Yes, little gully dwarf. It's yours—but we owe you so much more."

Glert stared up at him, blinking in bafflement. "I not understand," he said.

"I know," the Highmurf replied, heaving a small sigh, "but I'm afraid I don't have time to explain." He raised his hands, chanting in a strange, spidery language, and his body began to grow and change. Within seconds, the Highmurf was gone. In his place stood a stout, kind-faced man in a wizard's red robes. He turned back to his crew and repeated the incantation. One by one, the gully dwarves began to change into humans—a golden-haired woman, a dusky-skinned youth, a grizzled mercenary, and still others. Poog became a tall, gray-haired Revered Son of Paladine as Glert watched Hewick lift the shapechanging spell.

Glert's jaw dropped down to his chest as Hewick picked him up and lifted him onto the dock. "Farewell, Glert," the mage said as the cleric untied the bowline and the rest of the crew began to row toward open water.

Glert stood on the dock for a while, clutching his treasured copper coin in wonder as he watched the First Gully Dwarf Resistance row out past the breakwater into the dark. Then he went to find something to eat.

The Star-Shard
Jeff Grubb

This is a gnome story, which makes sense since I am a gnome. I am
not the gnome of this gnome story, however, and though I am
in the story, it is not my story, but rather the story of another
gnome, who is not me. But then again, perhaps it is my story
as well as the other gnome's. Understand me so far? Good.

The other gnome in this story is named Wun, or Wunderkin if you want to be more accurate, or Wunderkintheflash-
ofinspiration, if you want to be more accurate still. There is
even a longer, most-accurate name, which most humans
would not have the patience to hear.

As gnomes go, Wun is fairly typical to look at, small of
stature (smaller than I), bright of eye and brown of hair with
a closely cropped beard only slightly tidier than my own. He
is a friend of mine, and this is the story about how we nearly
stopped being friends. And all for a hunk of stone.

Wun and I live in Gnomespile, a sprawling village several
miles outside the human/dwarven town of Thugglesdown.
Our settlement is separated from the town by a tall, broad hill
called Thuggle's Tor. In general, humans and dwarves leave
the gnomes of Gnomespile alone (as do kender, after a brief
summer of explosions). There are about two hundred gnomes
in all Gnomespile, and most of us pursue our various inventions. All the roads out of Thugglesdown, I should note, lead
away from Gnomespile.

Wun is a wizard at mathematics, while I am a humble
researcher of the heavens who charts the movement of the
stars. The latter responsibility is a bit of a bother, since histor-
ical records show the stars moving about fairly randomly
over Krynn's night sky, forming into new patterns and constellations for no apparent rhyme or reason. I like to think
that if I study the stars long enough, I will be able to figure
out when and where they will next move. Wun often accom-

panied me on my trips into the open fields beyond Gnomes-pile to watch the stars and the moons. He always claimed the night air helped him think.

I suppose it started out there in those fields, on the flanks of Thuggle's Tor, in late summer, one evening after the moons had set. We were watching the stars. I was standing, craning upward with my lenses. Wun sprawled on his back, taking in the heavens. I know he was taking in the heavens, for he was not snoring.

There was a meteor shower that evening, one that appeared regularly with the second red moon of summer. As we stood (and sprawled on our backs) in the darkness, red-dish flares streaking against the night above us, our conversation went something like this:

Wun: What are they made of, really? The meteors, I mean.

I: I think they are pieces of the stars, which is why they glow as they streak across the sky.

Wun: I always thought they were the remains of great space-going vessels, or at least the garbage the captains of such vessels have thrown overboard.

I: Wouldn't we see the vessels themselves, moving against the sky? We only ever see the stars.

Wun (after being silent for a moment): What about the moons?

I (musing): If the pieces were breaking off the moons, we would see the moon with a chunk taken out, like a pie with one slice missing. We don't see any missing parts in the moons. Ergo, it must be the stars.

Wun (pressing the point): The humans say the stars represent the gods themselves. Why would parts break off a god? More likely it is trash tossed overboard from some stellar schooner manned by a civilization more advanced than our own.

I started to formulate aloud a theory about stellar fragmentation, that when the stars shifted against the heavenly vault, pieces of them would break off, like furniture being moved from one room to another.

One meteor came in low. Very low. So low that if I had been a human or elf, I doubt I would ever have had to worry about getting my hair trimmed again. There was an explosion as the star-stone smashed into the soft earth not a hundred feet from us. I was knocked off my feet by the force of the blow (Wun was already on the ground, and he later described the force of the stone striking the earth as giving him great empathy with a large flapjack in a skillet).

As we both pulled ourselves up, Wun turned to me and said, "Did you see that one coming?"

I had to admit that I had not.

We saw the jagged rip in the earth that the star-shard had torn through a nearby field, a single plow line ending in a smoking, glowing hole. Wun was already making for the crater. I was not far behind. Indeed, it was very important that we reach the landing zone before the area became polluted by humans, kender, or—worst of all—other gnomes.

The crater was about man-deep and shallow, a bowl with a great glowing stone at the center. The stone issued an aura of dappled green and shadow, which reminded me of a sphere of sea granite that had somehow been lit from within. It was cracked and fissured in many places, and steam was still issuing from these cracks as we descended into the pit. The meteor (or star-shard or star-schooner garbage) was already cooling as we approached.

Wun, already ahead of me, started hefting the remains of the meteor, breaking off pieces of the brittle, cooling shell. I thought briefly that the meteor might be another thing entirely, a cosmic egg of some star-dwelling bird. I quickly checked the sky to see if there were any other huge rocks (or rocs) descending on us. By the time I turned back, Wun had already pulled the statuette from the wreckage.

Statuette is perhaps too strong a word, for it implies a clear manufacturer or intelligent creator. What Wun had found seemed like a melted lump of glowing, greenish clay formed into a cone-shaped glob. Not really an accurate representation of anything, but at the same time it looked like a snake that had coiled into a striking position, then melted, with serpentine eyes near the top of a neckless body. I describe them as eyes, as opposed to, say, nostrils, only because they were glowing with the same radiance as the rapidly cooling stone. If pressed, I would say that melted statuette looked like a cheese-carving of a dragon that had been left in the sun too long and had gone all runny.

The green glow in the "statue's" eyes was matched by the enthusiasm in Wun's own orbs.

"Look! Proof of life among the stars!" he crowed.

I pointed out that if this were the case, it was proof that life among the stars was plagued with bad taste.

We were still arguing when the other gnomes arrived at the scene. Most pulled apart pieces of the now dimly lambent meteor and hauled them back to their own studies. No one else produced an artifact of the shape, size, or sheer ugliness of Wun's bauble.

I myself claimed a few of the smaller pieces, and the crater itself, and spent the next few days and evenings measuring all the particulars of the landing area. I also redoubled my efforts to determine the motions of the various planetary bodies. As a result I did not have much time for Wun, and a week passed before he sent for me from his combination house/lab/burrow.

Now, the gnomish quarters of Gnomespile are, by their nature, widely spaced and built into the rolling hillocks surrounding Thuggle's Tor. Basements and lab areas are set along the first floor against those hillocks; the older quarters are built deeper and deeper into the hills, as regular explosions tend to destroy the previous incarnations. Even though Wun mostly worried about mathematics, his quarters had been rebuilt at least a dozen times, and he had burrowed back farther and farther into the hillside, so his house now seemed to reside at the end of a wide, artificial canyon.

Wun's front room was typical of a gnomish household— comfortable chairs, stout tables, overstuffed ottomans, and every available flat surface covered with papers, notes, rough sketches, half-built prototypes, and forgotten lunches. Being wise in the ways of our people, I stood in the front room and called—no telling what experiments were going on deeper in the place. After a moment, the smiling, wild-eyed form of Wunderkin ambled out. He was holding a steel coin in his hand.

"Flip this," he said. "I'll call it in the air."

Puzzled, I flipped the coin, a ponderous old piece of currency from Tarsis, marked with some forgotten human on one side and a dragonlike giant bird on the other. As the coin spun through the air, Wun pointed at it and said, "Heads!"

I caught the coin and slapped it against the back of my arm. When I moved my hand the portrait side was face up.

Wun was delighted and asked for the coin back. Then, chuckling, he spun on his heel and retreated to his lab. "Thanks!" he shouted over his shoulder. "Come back tomorrow, if you please."

I was puzzled, of course, but not overly so. Gnomes by their nature do things that others might consider odd, and I went about my business (which on that day included helping another friend, Toomuchfire, extinguish his latest experiment). I didn't think about it again until the next day, when I presented myself in Wun's living room.

"Tails!" he shouted as the coin flipped, and indeed the bird-dragon came up. Again Wun took back the coin and retreated to his lair.

So it went for the better part of a week. I arrived at his house, flipped a coin, and Wun called it. He would only allow one flip, and he would not tell me why. At last, after he'd been correct five out of five times, I could contain my curiosity no longer. I confronted him on the matter.

"You've made an obedient coin," I said simply, holding the Tarsis steel piece tightly, threatening neither to return it nor to flip it until I got the truth.

Wun laughed. "Close, very close," he said gently. "Rather, I made a way of determining the coin's flip before it happens. In effect, a way of predicting the future."

Now it was my turn to laugh, and I fear it was not a polite laugh. Not even the sympathetic chuckle of one inventor for another's pet theories. It was raucous, loud, and extremely offensive. No gnome should ever laugh at one of his brethren like that, but I did. Perhaps it was a nervous reaction, since Wun announcing a breakthrough meant he had bested me on an important discovery. It was a horrible laugh, and I blame myself for what followed.

Wun's face clouded like a storm-filled sky, and there was a sharp tone in his voice as he explained. "Each day I have asked you to flip the coin. I have a calculating machine that determines the result of that coin flip before you flip it. Would you care to see it?"

I managed a nod, still sniggering, and followed Wun into the back rooms. I thought the earlier explosion in the field had rattled my companion's mind loose from its casing. And for a gnome, that was saying much.

The back rooms of a gnome's household are similar to the front, but less tidy. Here is where the real work is done (and the real explosions occur). Wun led me down a hall filled with charts and other bric-a-brac, and into a large chamber that extended into the shale strata of the hillside itself.

Mounted against the far wall was a curious device, curious even by gnomish standards. It looked like an armoire, gutted of its doors and drawers to leave only the frame, a hollow cabinet that was tipped slightly back against the far wall. Through the back of the cabinet, Wun had driven hundreds of ten-penny nails in a rough pattern. The heads of the nails were wrapped with thin copper wires that streamed upward to the armoire's crown. At the top of the cabinet, squatting like a dark king overseeing its kingdom, was the greenish lump of rock, resting on a copper metal plate. All the copper threads were connected to this plate.

At the base of the cabinet, beneath the maze of wire, was a pair of troughs. One was labeled "Heads," the other "Tails." The trough labeled "Heads" was filled with a number of small metallic balls, each the size of my thumb.

"I have calibrated the device for that coin you hold. I have found the device predicts accurately about a day in advance, but that might be a product of the size of the nail bed," said Wun, his irritation at my laughter fading. "Now, will you flip the coin?"

I pulled the steel disk from my pocket, rested it on the curve of my index finger, and gave it a solid flip with my thumb. It spun effortlessly upward and came to rest on a dusty pile of papers.

"Heads," said Wun, pointing at the ball-filled bucket.

Heads it was.

I looked at the trough filled with metal balls, then at the coin again. I reached out for the disk and flipped it again.

Heads a second time.

I frowned and reached for the coin, but this time Wun was too fast for me, snatching up the coin with a pudgy hand. "Best not to tear at the fabric of reality too much," he said, pocketing the disk.

I shook my head. "So does your machine predict the flip of the coin, or does it dictate the result?"

"That's one reason I had you do the flipping," said Wun brightly, pulling the metal balls from their trough and placing them into a small hopper. "I might influence the results. I think it merely predicts. The flipping of a single coin should be a random, isolated event with an equal chance of heads or tails. As such, it should be unpredictable over a long time. Yet the machine has predicted the results unfailingly each day."

I eyed the lump of star-shard atop the cabinet. "And this piece of rock?"

"Has something to do with it, enhancing the powers of the machine," finished my friend. "Indeed, in many ways it inspired my prediction engine. It does make sense, because of the laws of similarity. If, as humans have said, the stars are truly part of the gods, and the gods do have an effect on our lives, then a piece of the stars is a piece of the gods and should have an effect in a more localized environment. Care to watch the device in operation?"

I nodded and Wun climbed a short ladder, pouring the metal balls into another trough at the top of the machine. The small spheres clattered through a hole in that trough into the cabinet. The balls bounced through the metal pins, rebounding as they fell. Where they struck the pins, sparks danced, and the air smelled of a lightning storm.

When the balls had fallen all the way down, they were in the "Tails" box. All of them.

"Come back tomorrow," said Wun, smiling. "We'll see how we do."

I tried to spend the evening and the next day on my own work, but the draw of Wun's cabinet proved to be strong. I found myself back at my friend's home well before the appointed time.

I arrived to find Wun in the process of adding additional troughs beneath the cabinet of pins. These were color-coded bins with tags of black, blue, green, orange, purple, red, white, and yellow (alphabetical order, of course). Wun was hammering away at the bins, and I had to call to him to get his attention.

Wun looked more distracted than ever, and I wondered if he had remembered to eat that day. He shuffled up, handed me the steel coin, and returned to his hammering. I flipped the coin, and of course it came up tails. I flipped it twice more, and it came up tails both times.

I had an uneasy feeling that if I continued to flip it, it would continue to come up tails. I picked up the coin, and it felt warm to the touch, as if it had been left by the hearth.

Wun finished the bins with one last massive thwack of his wooden mallet and stepped back to admire his handiwork.

I handed the coin out to him. "Tails," I said simply.

Wun nodded and absentmindedly pocketed the warm coin. "I think I finally know what this can do."

"Beyond winning barroom bets?" I suggested.

"Weather prediction," he said. "I want to borrow some of your telescope lenses and mirrors to vent the light onto this machine. That way, we can figure out what the weather will be the next day, by the color the balls fall into."

He smiled. It seemed to me to be a tired smile.

I was Wun's friend and could not refuse him, particularly since I still felt guilty about laughing at him. My collection of mirrors and lenses had remained unused since the great planetarium disaster of the previous spring, and one gnome does not refuse another unused resources. I did feel a little put out by the fact that Wun was tromping all over an area I thought of as my own: the heavens. But at the time, I pushed those feelings deep down inside me and agreed. He was my friend, you see.

I returned in less than an hour, with a wooden box filled with prisms, glass panes, mirrors, and other sundries. In addition, I brought a jar of lenses sent from the elven kingdoms of the south, floating in a thick yellowish oil for their protection. By that time Wun was punching additional holes in his house, letting the light bathe his back room creation.

We spent the rest of the afternoon rigging mirrors and prisms. We set the lenses, still smeared with protective oils, in their holders, so the light of the sun would beam onto the spot where the test coin would normally rest. At last, toward late afternoon, all was in readiness, and Wunderkin let loose his torrent of metal balls.

The balls chinked and chanked as they ratcheted downward to the newly created troughs, sparking as they struck the metal pins. All of them took a slant to the left as they cascaded downward. Once it was done, the vast majority were in the blue category, with a few balls in white.

Wun gave a tired, happy nod. "Clear tomorrow," he interpreted, "with a few patches of cloud."

It was as his machine predicted. The next day the sky was clear with a few strings of high clouds. It was more than that. It was a blue sky, as solid blue as a kingfisher's wing, an almost brilliant blue. And the clouds were as wispy as a wizard's beard, and so white they hurt the eyes.

It looked unnatural to me, but I ascribed it to my own preoccupation. Normally, I would focus more on the weather at night, not during the day. Wun was delighted, but it was a worn delight. He looked thinner now, as if his work were devouring his life. His round cheeks were becoming shallow divots in his face, and his flesh was turning an old, jaundiced color.

I asked him about his health, and at first he shrugged. "Just dreams," he said in a distracted voice, his eyes never leaving the machine, topped by its melted rock. "Did you ever have dreams that took on a life of their own, that seemed to goad you, push you, encourage you to a greater goal? That's the way it has been since I . . . since we, I mean, discovered the statue."

I did not respond immediately, since such introspection was an oddity in my comrade. By the time I had recovered, the moment had passed. Wun dismissed his remark with an offhanded wave, and we proceeded with the experiment.

The prediction color for the next day was pure white, and indeed in the middle of the afternoon a fog bank rolled into the village, reducing the entire area to a blanket of cotton. Gnomes stumbled around blindly, and even the doors and windows did little to hold at bay the creeping tendrils of the surprisingly warm fog.

There was no keeping the predicting engine a secret now. Wun had told a few other friends, who in turn passed it on to others. A huge crowd gathered in mid-afternoon, as Wun continued to test his marvelous machine. As I walked through the chattering gnomes, I felt a little mystified by the amount of attention Wun had generated. And not a little jealous.

This time the result came up purple and green.

Wun was puzzled by the result, and I was a bit relieved. The predictive ability of the machine was making me nervous, and an impossible result might dissuade Wun from continuing his experiments. I kept a brave face for Wun, and said all the correct and encouraging words, but I felt that this would mark an end to this nonsense. But as I spoke, I kept my eyes on the cabinet. The star-shard glowered at me from the top of the armoire, like some malign cat.

I slept badly that evening. The slab of rock haunted my dreams. I saw it for what it was. It was a living chunk of the sky, a piece of the gods. But it had fallen from one of the dark constellations and was maliciously influencing the world around it. It was not predicting; rather it was dictating the future. A foul malevolence lurked behind those roughly hewn greenish eyes, and I felt that malevolence searching for me.

I finally drifted off in the early morning hours, calmed by the sounds of rain on the roof. Indeed, shortly before dawn, a storm passed overhead, becoming a heavy downpour. I slept until noon, and when I awoke saw the results of Wun's machine's prediction.

The rain had been heavy and surprisingly fertile. Every lawn and bush had seemed to grow in the passing storm, and even once-bare paths were covered with the vibrant greens of fresh grass. In addition, small purplish flowers, ones we had never seen before, had blossomed everywhere, their small splayed petals looking like violet asterisks.

I left the house to find most of the rest of the citizenry outside as well, investigating the new foliage. The flower petals had an oily texture, unpleasant to the touch. The village air seemed warmer after the rain, almost muggy. The other gnomes noticed it as well and, being gnomes, produced a number of bicycle-powered fans and sun-powered air-pushers. I felt there was more to it than simply a change in the weather, however, and thought of the uncommonly warm coin of the earlier experiments.

I walked into Wun's lab unannounced and found the cabinet of metal balls and pins unattended in the back of his lab, surrounded by its jury-rigged mass of mirrors and lenses. At the top of the cabinet, looking like a petty idol bedecked in its copper garments, was the rock. It looked larger and greener than ever, if such a thing were possible. The evil surrounding it seemed almost palpable.

I picked up a particularly large and effective-looking mallet.

My guts churned as I approached Wun's device. Was my reaction to all this pure jealousy? Wun had done what I had failed to do: predict the movements of the heavens. Was that what was urging me forward to smash this thing? Could I truly consider myself to be Wun's friend if I destroyed his great achievement, a machine that did exactly what it was designed to do? Just because of some strange weather?

I hesitated too long. I heard the creak of stairs behind me and the small voice of Wun calling my name.

I turned and saw him descend from the upper floor. He looked positively cadaverous, his white shirt stained with sweat and his smock dangling off his neck as if it were hanging on a hook. His eyes were sunken and deep lines chasmed across his face. He looked as if he had not slept in days, and, to be frank, smelled as if he had not changed clothes in twice as long.

"I thought I heard you," he said with a weak smile. "Thought of some adjustment to my prediction engine?"

"Adjustment," I repeated, then, suddenly aware I was

holding a large mallet, set it down quickly. "A small one. I don't even know if it is needed. I had a . . . a feeling."

"Feeling," hiccoughed the smaller gnome. "I've been getting those too. Feelings and dreams. A dream told me to build the cabinet, and a feeling made me use copper wire where cotton twine would probably have worked as well. And in the dream the star-shard is always waiting for me, predicting the future, saying what is going to happen next."

"How do you think it works?" I asked, regarding the cabinet. "I mean, *really* works?"

The smaller gnome shrugged distractedly. "I think time is a river, and what this device allows us to do is to go upstream, as it were, to sample the waters before they reach us. With time, we could predict great things, spell out warnings and oracles, tell of imminent problems and how we can best avoid them." His eyes grew misty. "It is a great invention. *My* invention."

"A river," I nodded. "But what if in sampling the time that is yet to come, the machine affects that outcome? What if, when the coin says heads, it is forcing the coin to *be* heads? What if by predicting a blue day, or a green day, it causes the surrounding weather itself to buckle or change?"

Wun frowned deeply, turning my words over in his mind. "As I said before, it really doesn't matter, does it? The future is the future, whether determined by random chance or predicted by a machine. A difference that makes no difference is not truly a difference, eh?"

"This just feels wrong," I said. "The weather, the flowers, the fog." I shrugged my shoulders, searching for the words. "Just wrong."

"Are you sure you're not just envious of my success?" asked Wun sharply, pulling himself up to his full height. "That you have not accomplished anything as important as this? That it is I, not you, who has unlocked the secrets of the heavens? Is that what seems *wrong* to you?"

I tried to form a response, but none came. I was too afraid that Wun was correct.

The anger seemed to suck more energy from Wun than he could spare. He waved a thin arm at me. "I am tired, old friend. Forgive me my mood, and please leave me to my dreams. I was surprised when you didn't show up to hear the prediction for tomorrow. Everyone else was here."

"Tomorrow?" I asked. "What is the weather for tomorrow?"

"Black and red," he said with a weak smile. "The balls say black and red. I am predicting a beautiful sunset."

I don't remember what I said, but I made my excuses and retreated to my own abode. All I could think of was the fact that Wun was right. He had succeeded beyond his wildest expectations. I was jealous, and I hated him and his success.

I wrestled with my sheets through another fitful night in which the nightmare images stalked my slumbers. The dragon-scaled rock loomed mountain-large in my dreams. A longitudinal crack erupted along one side, and from it blossomed a serpent's head. Then another appeared, then three more, all weaving and crying in strange tongues. The heads were different colors—red, black, white, green, and blue. And when the dragon heads saw me, they roared.

I awoke in a sweat. No, all Gnomespile awoke in a sweat as a humid layer of air began to settle on the city. The entire town was rendered colorless by the increased humidity, and the walls wept with dampness. Our own sweat felt oily, like the purple flowers.

Most of my comrades looked forward to nightfall, when the brilliant sunset that Wun had predicted would drive away the moisture and lift our heavy spirits. By mid-afternoon, half of them were already gathered on Thuggle's Tor, the better to watch the setting sun. Some brought basket dinners and many brought wine to keep the oily air at bay. I wandered among them and found them relaxed, there among the strange purple flowers, now heavy with star-shaped seeds.

I looked up at the pale, unimpressive sky and thought of the nights Wun and I had spent watching the stars. If Wun was right again, he would be able to come up with other uses for his machine, and he would be the one to determine the movements of the heavens themselves. He would become famous. He would no longer be my friend. Among the rest of the sweating gnomes, I felt alone.

Then I noticed that Wun was not among the others on the tor. At first, I thought he was dramatically prolonging his appearance, but as the shadows lengthened, Wun still did not materialize. The sun was barreling toward the horizon. It would be a nice sunset, but not an extraordinary one, with no hint of the promised brilliant red or black.

That's when I smelled the smoke, and realized that those colors could suggest another interpretation.

In retrospect, it was fortunate that most of the natives of Gnomespile were gathered on the tor, in that they were away from their labs in the vale. Looking behind me, I was the first to see the black smoke rising from the village, and the magenta tongues of flame visible from the tops of several buildings.

I shouted and my fellow gnomes reacted as one, rushing back down the hill to help put out the spreading fire. It looked as if five buildings, including Wun's, were already engulfed in flames, oily smoke billowing out their windows and doors.

The lush purplish flowers that covered the lawns seemed particularly susceptible to the flame. They swelled from the heat and burst like pods, scattering burning embers. As I and the others watched, two other buildings, doused in oily air, ignited from the flaming seeds.

As one the gnomes of Gnomespile rushed down the hill. As one we were slammed to the ground by the first great explosion of many that evening. Some half-finished invention succumbed disastrously to the heat, blowing the walls and roof off of its inventor's home. The ball of fire rose like an angry efreet, the shards of burning timbers spreading the fires to more buildings.

The explosion convinced most of my fellow gnomes that the best place to fight the fire was from the far side of the tor, far away from the flames. They set off in that direction at once, abandoning their wine and basket dinners in the process.

I, on the other hand, was determined to find Wun. It did not surprise me that his domicile was located at the center of the disaster. I choked on the ash that swirled around me and the winds that buffeted me, striving to keep me from Wun's house. The hissing of the flames sounded like serpentine laughter.

The forward half of Wun's house was thick with black billowing clouds of smoke, the tongues of flame as red as dragon's scales. I took a deep breath of the hot oily air and plunged into the back half.

I found Wun sprawled on the floor, unconscious before his altar of wood and metal pins. The cabinet was surrounded by blackened wood, but was otherwise surprisingly untouched by the fire. Atop the cabinet the star-shard pulsed and glowed of its own accord, as it had on the night of its arrival.

I would not have been able to lift Wun, had he not lost so much weight in the past few weeks. As it was, he was featherlight, and I could easily sling him over my shoulder. He spat ashes and in a weak voice said, "Black. It's all black."

Indeed, I saw that Wun had used the machine one more time, and all of the balls had landed in the black color category. I cursed, half-stumbling, half-dragging Wun out. As I pulled him through the front door, there was a groan, and the forward portion of the house collapsed behind us.

The fires in Gnomespile had worsened while I was inside, and small twisters of superheated air spiraled through the village, spreading ash and burning embers. I climbed the tor and felt the air sweeten as I climbed. Still, stars were dancing in my eyes when I finally felt the hands of the other gnomes take Wun from me. I only heard their voices, though they sounded as if they were at a distance. I had to take several deep breaths, clearing my lungs of the smoke before the stars faded from my vision.

The village was now wrapped in a black fog. Flames, red as the promised sunset, burst through the blackness, occasionally coalescing in fireballs. And there, where the rubble of Wun's house lay, was a flash of unearthly green, like a beacon. A beacon that called out to me.

I stood unsteadily and strode back down the hill into the burning village. I found the smoking wreckage of a large table leg, and, carrying it like a club, I headed for Wun's house. The collapsed part of the house had burned to little more than ashes, but there was a clear path to the machine. I stood before it for a long moment, regarding the melted statuette with its draconian eyes. I could feel it tug at me. Then I hefted the table leg and set to work.

The next morning Wun awoke in time for tea. My own home had been gutted by the fire but had not collapsed. As such, it was practically unique. The beams had held and the scorch marks added a bit of character to the stonework. The rest of the village had been devastated. Already there was the sound of hammering and sawing, however, as the survivors started to rebuild their homes and lives.

Wun was weak but the normal spark of curiosity had returned to his eyes. He would not be refused but demanded that I take him to the wreckage of his dwelling as soon as he was strong enough.

Wun made immediately for the back of the house, where his prediction engine had been. He found the armoire smashed beyond all recognition but not burnt. I suggested that a falling timber probably did the job, turning his invention into a tangle of splinters, broken wire, pins, shattered lenses, and scattered balls.

Of the star-shard there was no sign. Wun paced around for a good two hours searching for it, but at last his own physical state forced him to abandon the search. Wearily he agreed to let me put him to bed. It was three full days before he was capable of starting to rebuild his home. If he had dreams while he slept, he did not mention them to me.

Wun offered the theory that the fire was started when two metal balls got jammed between two pins, closing the circuit and causing the machine to overload. The hot, oily air, a meteorological rarity, enhanced the spread of the flames with disastrous results. The flames, Wun posited, must have caused the star-shard to melt, vaporize, or explode. As part of a star, it must have contained incredible heat.

I agreed with him. I had to agree with him, even though I knew he was wrong.

Nowadays I often go to the crater at the side of Thuggle's Tor, usually alone, since Wun has lost his taste for the wonders of the heavens. I go to view the constellations, the god-charts in the sky. And I go to ensure that no one digs in the grass-covered remains of the crater, that no one has unearthed the deadly treasure buried there.

Sometimes I nap at the site of the crater, and I have dreams. The dreams are of a multiheaded dragon, snarling and trying to escape its misshapen, greenish egg. I hold the egg in my hands, as I held the star-shard the night after the fire. In the dreams the dragon heads call to me, promising riches and wonders and discoveries beyond my imagination. The dragon heads call to me, as the shard called to me the night I took the statuette from Wun's lab. I buried it there on Thuggle's Tor, in a black box.

In the dreams I bury the egg as well, and as I bury it the serpents hiss and retreat back into their rocky lair, where they can no longer influence the lives of men and gnomes.

And when I wake, I feel like I've accomplished something. I have discovered one of the secrets of the heavens.

Master Tall and Master Small
Margaret Weis and Don Perrin

They called themselves Master Tall and Master Small.

We knew those weren't their real names, of course. We may be mostly farmers in Goodland, but we hadn't just fallen off the hay cart. We knew those names had to be made up. We had no idea what their real names were, however, or why they chose to hide them. That was their business. We're pretty easygoing in Goodland. So long as the strangers didn't cause any trouble, we didn't trouble them.

Master Tall was the taller of the two and he was extremely tall, probably the tallest man that any of us had ever seen and there's been many of us that have traveled out of our lush vale on either business or pleasure, though we never stay long. I'm Lord Mayor of Goodland and so I admit that I may be prejudiced, but of all the places I've been, I've never found one to equal to my valley homeland.

Master Tall was so tall that he had to stoop not only his head, but his shoulders and half of his back to get in through the tavern door and Goodland's tavern was not some ramshackle dive. The only tavern I've seen to match it was one in Solace whose name escapes me.

We assumed that Master Tall had some elf-blood in him. We have nothing against elves in Goodland. We have nothing against anybody in our sunny valley, so long as they're good-humored, good-natured, and don't mind taking a glass of ale and smoking a fine bit of pipe-weed. If they happen to be chess players on top of that . . . but I'm getting ahead of myself.

We call our valley Bread Bowl Valley. It's a large valley, with three towns: one at the north, called Fairfield; one at the south, called Sunnyvale; and our own, Goodland, at the west. In the east is Mount Benefice, named because of the crystal clear water which cascades down from that high peak and waters our valley. Due to the water and the fact that we have more days of sunshine in our valley than almost any other place on Ansalon, our farms are truly blessed by the good gods. We grow food enough not only to feed all the people in our valley, but to ship to lands around us.

This summer, we had heard terrible tales of a severe drought hitting other parts of Ansalon. I myself had traveled down to Northern Ergoth and back and what I saw dismayed me. Crops withering under a blistering sun, creek beds gone dry, grass fires everywhere. On my return, I gazed up at Mount Benefice and offered thanks to Paladine that we remained blessed. The water continued to flow from our mountain top. Our crops were doing excellently well this year.

They would be needed. We began to make plans to distribute our harvest to all those lands near us who would have no food at all this winter.

But it was not harvest time yet. The two strangers came to us in late summer. They entered the tavern in Goodland, bought ale, requested pipes, and very politely drank to the health of the innkeeper. She returned the favor. Next the strangers turned to me. I was wearing my gold chain of office, of course, and so they knew who I was.

"Lord Mayor," they said, "we drink to your fine town and its people."

I raised my glass, more than happy to return the favor. "To your health, friends," I said.

I meant that, too. Outside of the strangeness of their names, which we took for a joke, the two were well dressed and well-spoken, though they were certainly odd looking.

One man was, as I said, inordinately tall, with sharp features that came to a point around his nose, which is what made me think of elves. He was mostly human, however, somewhere around middle age, with silver-gray hair, dark eyes, and a sad, almost wistful, smile. His hands were fine boned, the fingers long and thin.

Master Small was human, too, but I guessed that he had dwarf-blood in him. He was the shortest human I'd ever seen. I've known kender who might top him. He had a chest like an ale barrel, though, and arms that looked as if they could punch through solid rock if he took it into his head to do so. He jingled when he walked, which meant that he was wearing chain mail under his clothing. That wasn't as peculiar as it sounds, since we'd heard rumors of war way, way off to the northwest, somewhere around the Khalkists. Seems like they were forever fighting wars in that part of the country.

Being not only the lord mayor, but the owner of one of the largest grain mills in the valley, I felt it behooved me to make the strangers welcome, and so I made a little speech, welcoming the two to the valley, and then ended by asking if they were on business or pleasure.

"Business *and* pleasure, my Lord Mayor." Master Small rose to his feet and bobbed from the waist. He climbed up on a chair so that all of us in the tavern could see him and continued, "You good people of Goodland are no doubt wondering why we have come to pay your bountiful valley a visit. We've heard that your children are beautiful, your ale superb, and"—he paused with the timing of a thespian— "that you consider yourselves to be the finest chess players in all of Ansalon."

"What do you mean 'consider'?" called out Farmer Reeves, and we all laughed heartily.

As I started to say earlier, if we have one passion in Bread Bowl Vale, (not counting farming), it is playing chess. There was a chessboard on every table in the tavern, a chessboard in every home in the valley, and even a giant chessboard in the town square, which was used for the annual inter-valley match. We had children's chess clubs, the League of Women Chess Players, the League of Men Chess Players, the League of Men and Women Chess Players, the Chess Association, the Chess Guild, and many more. Our chess players traveled throughout Ansalon, wherever there was a tournament, in order to compete. We had to build a hall to house our trophies. We not only knew we were the best, we had carried the proof of that home with us from tourneys all over the land.

Master Small bowed to us to acknowledge this fact, then continued, "For that reason, Master Tall and I have come to

Goodland to admire your children, drink your ale, and to challenge each and every one of you to a chess game with Master Tall, who considers himself to be the finest chess player on all of Krynn."

"We'd be delighted to play Master Tall," I said, pulling up a chessboard. "As the lord mayor, I'll go first."

Master Small raised his hand, which, I noted, was callused and sun-browned and seemed more suited to holding a sword than a chess piece. "Ah, a game in a tavern—while enjoyable and friendly—is not quite what we had in mind. Master Tall and I have to eat." Master Small said this in apology, as if this were a weakness. Master Tall nodded sadly. "Chess is a way for us to earn our living. If you will come to where we have pitched our tents, out in the Midsummer Fair grounds, we'll show you what we have in mind. I think you'll find it worth your while."

I said that I'd be out the next day to take a look. The next day, several of us tramped out to the Midsummer Fair grounds, where the strangers had pitched their tents.

The tents were of rich material, made up of panels of red, white, and gold silk sewn together. There were three tents—two small and one large. The two small ones were where Master Tall and Master Small slept. (I couldn't help but wonder if Master Tall slept with his feet sticking out the front, because it didn't seem possible that this tent would hold him.) The big tent was open on all four sides and inside the big tent was a table and two chairs.

The table was round, about three feet in diameter, with four legs. Inlaid in the center of the tabletop was a checkered playing board, the squares made up of light and dark wood.

There sat Master Tall in a chair on one side of the table. The chair in front of him was empty, waiting for an opponent. On the table was a chess set and a small brass dish.

I only saw the small brass dish later. At first, I couldn't see anything but the chess set.

It was simply the grandest, most wonderful, most valuable, most beautiful chess set any of us had ever set eyes upon.

The chess sets we played with were mostly carved of

wood, though some of us had brought back sets made of stone from Thorbardin or steel made in Palanthas. We had kings and queens, and knights and castles. This chess set was different. This chess set was made up of dragons and it *wasn't* carved of wood or stone or steel. If there was a precious metal or a rare gem on Ansalon, it was in this chess set.

The golden dragon Paladine ruled the side of light. The chess piece stood at least eight inches high and was carved out of solid gold, crafted with such skill that I could pick out every single one of the dragon's thousand scales. The piece shone like flame in the summer sun. Next to it, where the queen would have customarily stood, was a female dragon. It was carved of solid silver and was so delicate and beautiful that it brought tears to the eyes just to gaze at it.

Across from these was the side of darkness, represented by a five-headed dragon of many colors. This dragon was encrusted with gems. It sparkled with a myriad of colors that dazzled the eye. Next to the five-headed dragon on the board was a black dragon carved from a rare black opal.

The rest of the pieces were equally valuable and equally gorgeous. The rooks were dragon-guarded keeps, with dragons twined about them, made of precious metals on one side and diamond on the other. The knights were dragons mounted with riders, the pawns were smaller brass dragons on the side of good, draconian warriors on the side of darkness. Every piece was made of precious metal—gold, silver, and platinum, or precious gems—diamond, emerald, sapphire, and ruby.

I have heard it said that certain objects are "worth a king's ransom." The Kingpriest of Istar himself may have been worth the price of this chess set, though I doubt it.

I stood and stared at the chess set and was not ashamed to wipe the tears of admiration from my eyes. More than one person around me was doing the same.

Master Small waited until we had all seen our fill of the wondrous dragon chess set, then he announced, "Here are the conditions. You will pay one steel coin for the privilege of playing chess with Master Tall. If you beat him, you leave here with this magnificent chess set."

I couldn't believe my ears. I shifted my stare from the gold and jewels to Master Small and Master Tall.

"Are you gentlemen serious?" I demanded.

"We are serious, Lord Mayor," said Master Small.

I dug my hand into my coin purse, as did everyone else standing around the tent. Steel coins rattled in the brass dish. We put lots into Master Small's hat, to see who the first player would be—Bommon. I groaned in good-natured disappointment. Bommon was one of our champion players. A wing of the trophy hall belonged to Bommon alone.

"Well, friends, we might as well go home," I said to the rest. "Bommon here will win the chess set."

But none went home. Everyone stayed to watch.

Bommon took the side of darkness and, for a moment, it was all he could do to force his attention to play—he was so fascinated by touching and admiring and exclaiming over all the details of the wonderful chess pieces. But, eventually, he settled down and the game began.

For nearly three-quarters of an hour, Bommon and Master Tall exchanged moves. The rest of us watched, with the exception of Master Small, who apparently had no interest in the game. He gathered up the steel coins and carried them into his tent, then replaced the brass dish on the table. Then he puttered about, polishing up a very handsome sword, which hung in a shabby leather harness outside his tent, and arranging several very fine chessboards and pieces on display for sale, though none as fine as those his partner used.

In the end, Master Tall moved his silver dragon forward one space, smiled, and leaned back in his chair as if to signify the game was at an end. It occurred to me then that I'd never heard him speak a word, not since the two came to town.

Bommon studied the situation, then shook his head.

"Aaagh! You are right. Check and checkmate. You have me, Master Tall," Bommon conceded. He sighed deeply and smiled. "That was, however, the best match I've ever played. I'll remember that combination of moves. I was particularly impressed by your move of your knight to my denied flank. It proved to be brilliant!"

Master Tall bowed slightly in his chair and waved his hand toward the brass dish, as if to invite Bommon to deposit another coin.

Bommon shook his head regretfully.

"I cannot today, I fear! I must get back to my work. I thank you for the game, though. Perhaps tomorrow?"

"Tomorrow, anytime," said Master Small, bustling forward and rattling the brass dish.

Bommon cast one final, longing look at the beautiful chess set, rose and departed.

The rest of us exchanged glances. We'd met our match. That much was obvious. Rubbing my hands in satisfaction, I sat down to play.

It took Master Tall only fifteen minutes to finish me off. One by one, the rest of us fell to Master Tall's unparalleled skill. But none of us considered our steel wasted. We left that day, but only to go home to practice our moves and prepare for the morrow.

Word of the challenge, the valuable chess set, and Master Tall's skill spread quickly throughout the valley. When I arrived the next day, I had to stand in line behind fifteen people: men, women, and children, eager to try their skill. By the end of the week, there were so many people clamoring to play that Master Small was forced to hand out numbered tickets and schedule appointed times.

Large crowds gathered around the main tent, watching in a breathless silence that was broken only by the ring of steel coins in the brass dish. More tents had sprung up, the business-minded of Goodland not failing to take full advantage of this opportunity. The Widow Peck was doing a brisk business selling fresh fruit to those who grew hungry while waiting. Alderman Johannson was offering to impart guaranteed winning strategies to anyone who would pay him three steel. The crowd was in a good humor.

"Today's my big day, eh, Master Tall?" called out Goodwife Bacon.

Otto Smithy behind her shouted, "You'll only need to play as far as me, Master Tall! After that, you won't have your fine chess set anymore."

The first match for the day began. It was clear by the sixth move that Master Tall had won. His opponent, a short man from the Tailor's Guild, stood up and shook Master Tall's hand.

"I fear I am not at my best today. You are truly the best chess player I've ever come across, with one exception."

Master Tall looked startled, lifted his head.

Master Small strode up, his interest piqued at last. "And who would that one exception be, good sir?"

"The man we call Blackshanks, Master. We don't know much about him. He hasn't been here long, or at least if he has we haven't seen him before this summer. He lives somewhere up in the mountain, and he comes down to the valley every now and then for a game of chess. He's a loner, sort of a rough fellow and not very friendly. But he's a fierce lover of chess, and as good as Master Tall here or better, if you'll excuse my saying so."

Master Tall did appear extremely put out by the remark. He frowned down at the chessboard and pushed the pieces back and forth with his long index finger.

Master Small smoothed things over with a smile and a clap on the back. "Well, then, perhaps this Blackshanks'll come by and give us a match, eh, Tailor? Then we'll see."

Perhaps he would. I myself had played a game with the mysterious Blackshanks and, though he was far from being a genial opponent, he was certainly an excellent player. He had demolished me in three moves, using a gambit I'd never seen before nor have I seen it since. From that moment on, we in Goodland began to talk of what a great game that would be, and we started looking out for Blackshanks, hoping he'd make one of his rare visits to our town.

"Next player," called Master Small.

A tall woman in well-worn boots and fighting breeches took her seat. Master Tall stood, bowed slightly, and reseated himself. By twenty moves, Master Tall had proven himself again. Without a word, the woman rose and stalked out of the tent.

The day continued on with match after match. Master Tall never took a break, not even to eat. Master Small busied himself around the area, occasionally darting into his own tent to restock his supply of chess sets. Sales were brisk, with many a potential challenger purchasing a set for playing while waiting—practicing against the other players.

By the end of that day, Master Tall had defeated seventeen opponents. The line outside the tent had not diminished. Master Small went out to address the fifty players waiting.

"We will continue the matches until sundown. Those who have not yet played are welcome to return in the morning. If you cannot play tomorrow, then please be good enough to return your tickets and let someone else take your place. For a full refund, of course."

The wonderful chess set glowed and sparkled in the late evening sunshine that filtered through the tent. Everyone who sat down to play with those marvelous pieces longed to see them shine in his or her own dwelling place. Master Tall's phenomenal skill amazed and delighted all who watched and all who played against him.

No one turned in a single ticket.

The next day was a repeat of the one before. People arrived at the tent long before the two men were even awake, sitting quietly on the grass outside the big tent, practicing their moves.

Master Tall set to work immediately. By noon-sun, he had defeated eleven players, and his pace seemed to be accelerating. His eleventh player, Toby Wheeler, one of our more inquisitive ten-year-olds, asked, "Why is it that the human kings and queens are dragons on your set, Master Tall?"

Master Tall cast a sad-eyed glance in the direction of Master Small, who hurried over to reply.

"A wise question, son. Master Tall and I believe that the forces of good and evil are far more influenced by dragons than by any human. The power, intelligence, and wisdom of dragons make them more appropriate for the primary pieces on the board, wouldn't you agree?"

Toby shrugged, not much interested in the philosophy, far more interested in winning. He made his move. Master Tall neatly countered, and within four more moves had the game decided in his favor.

"I don't suppose I could take home just a pawn?" Toby said, fingering a jewel-encrusted draconian with longing.

Master Tall shook his head. Toby set down the pawn and ran off to rejoin his playmates.

Two more days passed, with Master Tall defeating all who came before him. He had just passed his one hundredth victory mark early on the fifth day, when the line of people waiting to play and those standing around watching began to buzz and whisper and point. I had been over visiting the Widow Peck and, turning, looked to see what all the fuss was about. A man dressed in black, with black leather pants and long black boots, came strolling up the hill.

"Blackshanks!" The excited whisper went about.

Such was the nickname we'd given him, since he never volunteered to give us a name of his own.

Blackshanks quietly took his place at the end of the line. Master Small hurried over and offered the brass dish. Blackshanks dropped one steel coin into it. A ripple of anticipation passed through the crowd. Several small boys dashed into town to spread the news, and soon most of the population of Goodland had left their crops and their washing, their blacksmiths and their innkeeping to watch what we knew would be the chess match of the century.

Master Tall was obviously looking forward to this game as much as the rest of us. He kept glancing down the line at Blackshanks, and finished off the next players rapidly, with what seemed absentminded skill. Even Master Small appeared to be excited at the prospect of a match. He ended the sale of his chessboards and, settling down to polish his sword, rubbed it with such fervor that it gleamed.

Blackshanks waited and watched and spoke to no one. He was not a likable fellow. In fact, most of us always felt rather uneasy when he was around and were generally extremely glad when he left. He had cold black eyes, cold pale skin, and cold, clammy hands. I myself had hinted that there were other valleys just as nice as ours in other parts of the world where I was sure he would be more comfortable, but he always maintained that he liked Goodland best.

Which was quite flattering, so how could I argue?

Still, I had to admit that I was glad Blackshanks hadn't left quite yet. Not before he played chess with Master Tall.

At last, it was Blackshanks's turn. He strode up to the table, stood and looked at the wonderful chessboard. A faint tinge of color rose into his cold pallid cheeks. He gazed at the chess set with a longing that, truly, I don't believe any of us had felt—and most of us wanted that chess set pretty badly. Blackshanks didn't just want it. He coveted it, lusted after it. He reached out a hand to touch the five-headed dragon made up of different colored precious jewels. His hand shook with his longing and I heard him breathe a soft sigh.

"Is it true," he said in a sepulchral voice that set the teeth on edge and made goose bumps chase themselves up my back, "that you will give this fine chess set to anyone who beats you?"

"True enough, sir," said Master Small.

Blackshanks silently took his seat. Master Tall sat forward. Master Small actually ceased polishing his sword and, elbowing his way through the crowd, stood beside his partner to watch, something he'd never done before. He had an anxious expression on his face. Master Tall looked grim.

Undoubtedly, they feared they might lose their valuable chess set.

Blackshanks made the opening move, a bold jaunt forward with a knight. Master Tall nodded, then looked over at Master Small, something he'd never done before. Master Small nodded back. Master Tall looked to the board, thought for a long, long time, then made a counter move with a rook.

Blackshanks grunted and settled down to serious play.

The game continued for thirty moves with neither side gaining an advantage. The crowd gathered around the board was as silent as if they had all been watching from their graves.

The game reached fifty moves, and the advantage was beginning to sway to the challenger. Master Tall appeared nervous. His hand trembled as he touched his golden dragon king. Master Small was sweating and looking even more anxious than before. Master Tall nodded once again to his partner, then made a move with his gold dragon.

Blackshanks laughed slowly, and moved his own five-headed dragon into a winning position. "Check and check-mate, Master Tall."

A collective sigh swept through the crowd. We had just witnessed a chess match that we would be talking about for the rest of our lives, but it wasn't that. It seemed a terrible shame to us that the cold and unlikable Blackshanks should now be the owner of the exquisite chess set.

Master Tall sat back in his chair, pale and broken. Master Small appeared to be in shock. His mouth opened and shut, but he had been robbed of speech.

"It looks as if I've bested you, Master Tall," said Blackshanks, leering. "I'd be obliged if you'd hand over the prize now."

We all waited, hope against hope, for Master Tall to make some brilliant move that would yet win the day. He stared at the board, shook his head, then, slowly, he rose to his feet. He bowed to his opponent.

"It is true that you have beaten me, sir." He motioned for the crushed and quivering Master Small to come forward. "Bring the box, Master Small. We must pack up the chess set."

"Pack it well," ordered Blackshanks in a nasty tone. "I've a long way to go and I don't want it harmed."

Master Small stifled a sob, walked with feet dragging into his tent. Master Tall sank back down in his seat, as if his legs had gone weak and could not bear his weight. He touched each piece lovingly, saying good-bye. I had to turn away. I could not bear to see the pain on his face.

Long moments went by. Master Small did not reappear and Blackshanks began to grow impatient.

"Not thinking of trying to back out on our deal, are you, Master Tall?" Blackshanks said, his face paling in anger. "Keep your box. I don't need it."

Reaching out his hand, he picked up the golden dragon and was about to thrust it into his pocket when Master Small emerged from his tent.

Those standing near him gasped and drew back, while

people in the back of the crowd strained to see what was causing all the commotion.

Master Small wasn't carrying a box. The only object he carried was his sword. He was dressed in full plate mail that shone silver in the sunlight and over the armor he wore the tabard of a Knight of the Rose.

He marched up to Blackshanks, who was regarding him with suspicion and disdain.

"What's this?" Blackshanks demanded, with a harsh laugh. "Dressed up for the Night of the Eye, are you?"

Master Small slid his sword from his scabbard and held it in front of him in a knightly salute.

"I am Sir Michael Stoutbody, Knight of the Order of the Rose. The Holy Writ of Paladine requires me, as a Knight of Solamnia, to counter evil wherever I find it. It is my duty, therefore, Blackshanks or whatever it is you call yourself, to best you in combat. Prepare yourself, sir."

Blackshanks stared, then he began to laugh. Sir Michael came to Blackshanks's waist. "You little runt!" Blackshanks snorted. "Better put that sword down before you hurt someone."

I looked at Master Tall, hoping he might intervene to save his partner from further embarrassment. He merely watched, a half-smile playing about his mouth.

As lord mayor, I would have to take things into my own hands.

I made my way forward. "Here, now, Master Small," I said. "Blackshanks won fair and square. It was a great game. It's a shame to lose your valuable chess set, but you were the ones who offered it, you know."

Sir Michael bowed to me. "Lord Mayor, if you will take my advice, you will warn your people to leave this area and return to their homes."

"But, really, my dear sir—" I stopped.

Blackshanks was glaring at the knight with such hatred that it made me wish I was well on the other side of Mount Benefice with a good horse and a clear road. I began to back off, away from the tent.

"Ladies and gentlemen," I called out, "I think it would be a good idea if you did as advised. Especially those of you with small children."

A feeling of dread, of danger, spread over us like the creeping of a dark, dank fog through our sunny vale. Children began to whimper in fear and I must admit that I felt as if a whimper or two might be in order. As Lord Mayor of Goodland, it was my duty to remain on the scene, as did some of the aldermen. The rest of our townspeople ran down the hillside in a panic that seemed to grow and spread like wildfire.

All the time, Blackshanks had not moved. He stood, holding the golden dragon in his hand, his gaze shifting from Master Small to Master Tall and back again.

"You have been challenged, sir," said Sir Michael in cool tones. He drew his sword from his scabbard. "Fight or perish where you stand, Evil One."

Blackshanks suddenly hurled the golden dragon piece straight at Sir Michael. The knight lifted his arm; the piece struck him on the shoulder and bounced off.

"Evil I am, little knight," Blackshanks snarled, "but not as you might suspect. I have a surprise for you, Sir Michael."

Blackshanks placed his hand on a ring he wore and suddenly the man's appearance began to change. He started to grow. He'd been about my height, maybe a bit more, but within a minute he was taller than the center pole holding up the tent. His clothes seemed to melt from his body, and in their place glistened black scales! Wings sprouted from his back. His jaw thrust forward, his nose stretched out to meet it, and became a snout over a mouth filled with hideous fangs. His eyes were red as the rubies in the chess set. Claws curled from his fingers. A black tail lashed savagely.

"This is my true form!" he announced, enjoying our terror.

Quivering in the air around Blackshanks was the transparent image of a black dragon. He had not completed his shapeshifting yet, but that is what he would be when the transformation was finished.

The dragon was enormous. It loomed over us with snapping maw and deadly acid breath and a wingspan that banished the sun, shrouded us in darkness.

At the sight, some of the people who had remained with me shrieked and began to flee down the hillside. I would have liked to run away, but I was paralyzed from the shock of it all.

A black dragon!

We'd been harboring a black dragon in our peaceful valley!

"You are doomed!" Blackshanks hissed. "How can a runt like you battle a powerful creature like me?"

In another moment, he would be taller than the tallest oak trees, his acid breath would come raining down on us. In another moment . . .

"You should have fought me in your man-form," advised Sir Michael. "I gave you that chance."

He jumped to attack the half-man, half-beast. Had the sword encountered flesh, it would have finished Blackshanks. The knight's sword hit scales, however, and the blow glanced harmlessly off.

Blackshanks kicked out with his dragon-haunch leg, struck Sir Michael in the chest, and sent the knight reeling backward. Sir Michael crashed into the table holding the chess set. The table smashed. Sir Michael tumbled down and lay dazed amid the wreckage. The wondrous pieces fell over him, like rose petals scattered over a grave.

Master Tall knelt beside his friend, looking anxious, and checked to make certain he was all right.

"I'm not hurt!" Sir Michael gasped, already struggling to get back on his feet. "You must . . . stop him! Don't . . . let him grow. . . ."

Sensible words. The dragon was growing larger by the second. His wings were starting to unfurl, his neck snaked out in a sinuous curve. More and more scales covered his body, rapidly closing up all areas that might be vulnerable to attack.

Master Tall sprang to his feet. Holding up his right hand, he spoke a single word. The word sounded among us like the call of a silver trumpet bringing an army of knights to our rescue. I did not understand the word, but it brought faint hope to my heart and, for a moment, lifted my fear.

Whatever it meant, that word seemed to be one of arcane

309

power. It struck Blackshanks as if it had been a spear. He gasped, quivered in rage and gnashed his teeth.

The shapeshifting spell came suddenly to an end. Now Blackshanks was caught in between two forms: half man, half dragon.

The beast howled and gibbered and lashed at Master Tall with a lethal claw, but Master Tall kept carefully out of range. Slowly, Master Tall, chanting more strange words, began to circle around Blackshanks, who was endeavoring to follow the man's movements with his snaky head.

As he circled, Master Tall made twining motions with his hands, as though he were braiding a chain, a chain that he alone could see.

The man-dragon was caught in mid-transformation, like a chick half in and half out of its shell. Enraged, Blackshanks lunged with snapping jaws at Master Tall. The man-dragon couldn't move with the speed of a black dragon, however, and the deadly fangs closed over air. Master Tall began racing around and around the infuriated dragon, winding fast the great invisible chain he was weaving.

"Hurry, lord knight!" Master Tall shouted. "I can't hold this spell for long!"

Sir Michael was on his feet, his sword in his hand. Puffing beneath his heavy armor, he dashed forward at the furious, spitting and clawing man-dragon.

Sir Michael thrust his sword. The man-dragon parried the strike with a swipe of its claw, or at least Blackshanks would have parried it, had the blow actually been struck. As it was, Sir Michael's attack had been a feint. He held his blade until the dragon's lethal claws had swiped past, then Sir Michael lunged forward, stabbing with all his strength, aiming for a part of the chest that had not yet been fully covered over with black scales.

The blade passed through the chest of the half man, half dragon and emerged, covered with blood, out the back of the beast. Blackshanks roared in pain and tried to free himself from the sword. Sir Michael held on gamely, though he was lifted clean off his feet by the efforts of the pain-maddened beast.

The dying dragon whipped back and forth. Blood and its acid breath rained down on Sir Michael, burning the knight's flesh wherever it touched. At length, Sir Michael was forced to let loose. He fell heavily, groaning in pain.

The black dragon plucked the sword from his chest, but it was too late. The wound was mortal. Blackshanks began to slump toward the ground. He gazed with fury at the two who had defeated him, particularly the tall, skinny chess player.

"Who?" he managed to gasp. "Tell me! Who are you who has slain me? No ordinary human, as you pretend!"

Master Tall stepped forward. "This is for my family and my clan. In the name of Vloorshad the Swift, and of Huma the bravest of them all, it is my honor to end the line of Basalt Blackdragon, his stain upon Krynn finally at an end. You are his final progeny, and with you dies great evil in Ansalon."

Blackshanks looked up with his dying gaze. He saw, as all of us saw then, rippling around Master Tall, the transparent outline of a silver-scaled body, the graceful shape of a large silver-scaled dragon's head. Silver wings lifted over Blackshanks. He snarled, turned his face away, and died.

The image of the silver dragon faded, leaving only Master Tall, chess player, behind.

Master Tall helped Sir Michael to his feet. The rest of us stood staring at the two of them in wordless and somewhat wary amazement.

Sir Michael smiled reassuringly. "Don't be afraid, my friends. This is Sheen Vloorshad, youngest of the silver dragon clan of Vloorshad. We are sorry to have deceived you and the fine citizens of Goodland, my Lord Mayor," the knight added, turning to me, "but we had to lure Basalt from his lair in order to slay him, and this was the one way which we were certain would work."

Master Tall gazed down at the twitching black carcass. "It is well known—Basalt Blackdragon could never resist a game of chess."

* * * * *

And so ends the story of the greatest chess game for the highest stakes ever to be played in our valley.

We carried Sir Michael into town, where the two were celebrated as heroes. Our cleric attended to his injuries and he was well enough to have dinner as my guest, along with Master Tall.

"How were you so certain that Blackshanks was a black dragon?" I asked.

"Because he was the only one who defeated me," said Master Tall, with a smile. "No offense, Lord Mayor, to you or your fine townspeople. You are skilled chess players, no doubt of it. But you're only human, after all."

I must admit that rankled a bit. "I'll play you right here and now," I said, reaching for the chessboard.

Master Tall rose to his feet, smiling and shaking his head. "I'm sorry, Lord Mayor, but if I never in my next thousand years play another game of chess, it will be too soon."

Sir Michael also rose. "Farewell, Lord Mayor. We must return to make our report and take up the fight against Lord Ariakan. If you people of Bread Bowl Valley will take my suggestion, you will put aside the chessboards and start preparing to face a real enemy."

"We will do it. I can't begin to thank you two enough," I said, giving them each a parting handshake. "May Paladine guide your footsteps."

Sir Michael and the silver dragon left the tavern, amid shouts and cheers from the populace.

I was just about to call a meeting of the town aldermen, when a young boy came dashing up to me. He held, in his hand, a large wooden box.

"What's this?" I asked.

"Them two strangers said I was to give it to you, my Lord Mayor," said the boy.

On top of the box was a note:

> We leave this with you, Lord Mayor. We think it would make a fitting addition to your trophy hall. May it bring you and your people good fortune.

I opened the lid to the box.

There, glittering and sparkling in the torch light, was the magnificent chess set.

It was missing only one piece: that of the black dragon.

Icewall

Douglas Niles

Keristillax awakened slowly, a stirring as imperceptible as the
creeping progress of the nearby glacier. A puff of frosty air
wafted from his broad nostrils, and then a year passed. A
leathery membrane, white as pure snow, inched upward,
and over the course of a hundred days revealed an eye of
slitted pupil and pale, ice-rimmed blue. Wings crackled,
breaking free the shards of ice that had formed during the
past . . .

How long had it been?

The first question emerged from a fog of whiteness, from
a place where the searing heat of the world was held at bay,
where ice needled through the air in whipping, wind-driven
assaults.

Keris pondered the question while another year fled by.

I am the white dragon Keristillax. This was the first truth,
emerging from the haze of pale white to form a mantle for
his thoughts.

This place . . . this place is Summerbane Island . . . Summerbane Castle.

The second piece of knowledge came forth, and now
Keris had a memory.

The rocky, barren isle lay below the southern coast of
Ansalon. It was a treeless and fog-shrouded place, icebound for fully half the year. Once, long before, the ships
from Tarsis had put in here, and a human lord of great
wealth and exalted status had been master of this castle.
Then Keristillax had come. The lord and his subjects died,
and, after the first few, the ships from Tarsis had ceased
their visits.

A great war had followed, and the white dragon had
flown to the summons of his queen. The chromatic clans
gathered at Sanction, and the whites suffered a sweltering

campaign, flying through hot, fire-scorched air in search of violence and glory. Sweeping toward the enemy, Keristillax sneered to see the good dragons burdened with lancers. Like his kin-dragons, the white wyrm brazenly challenged the tiny pins those riders carried into battle.

And he had watched the white dragons die, driven from the air by the pricks of those lethal pins. He saw his queen, rising like a mountain over Krynn in her moment of glory, pierced by a lance borne by the knight, Huma. She withered and then simply faded away, abandoning Keristillax and his surviving kin-dragons.

He had no awareness, nor would he have cared, that after the war he had been fortunate to be granted a return to his lair. Most of the queen's dragons, those who were still alive, were condemned to the Abyss upon her defeat. Yet Keris and a few others, as reward for bold service during the war, were allowed to become dormant in the forgotten corners of Krynn. And so he had returned to Summerbane Castle, on its spire of rock and ice that jutted above the stormy waves. Creeping into the lower catacombs, he had lapsed into a long sleep.

But still, how long had it been? His first question remained cloaked in the surrounding whiteness of the unknown, for there was no measure of days, winters, even centuries within that hibernation.

It was curiosity more than the hunger that had begun to gnaw at his belly that finally drove Keris, over a period of many hours, to raise his weight onto his four taloned feet. Moving at last, he took a long, patient step, then another. The activity brought returning vitality, feeding itself until he padded gracefully along—an alabaster snake of rippling motion.

His memory led him through the maze of corridors below Summerbane Castle, dark caverns that had been slick with chill mist when he had first come here. Now, he noticed with a little thrill of pride, they were thick with ice. No doubt his own frigid presence had lowered the surrounding temperature enough to create this beautiful rime.

Abruptly the passageway ended in a dark blue plug,

where snow had condensed, packed over many years into solid ice. This was no barrier to a white dragon, and with a few scrapes of his claws Keris pushed through the frozen mass to emerge on the cliffside below his castle. This cave mouth faced south, he remembered, where the chill waters of the ocean swept away until they merged with the distant realm of ice.

An expanse of still whiteness greeted him, a vast sheet of glorious snow that seemed strangely out of place on the ocean. He must have awakened in the midst of a very cold winter, Keris realized. But he was surprised, too, that the surface of white was so close to the level of his cave. He remembered this perch; it was a ledge a thousand feet above the sea. Yet now the snowy surface had risen to within a tenth of that distance, merely a pounce or two below.

Keris was still unready to spread his wings, so instead he traversed around the snow-covered slope of the island's steep hill. As the view to the north, where a stormy channel separated Summerbane Island from the Tarsis coast, became clear, Keristillax was further unsettled: There was no water to be seen! In the white dragon's long memory, even when the ice pack had fully encircled Summerbane, it had never encroached upon the open water that lay to the north.

In the clear, pristine daylight he should be seeing the coast of Ansalon, but instead there was only the ice blanket that, so far as Keristillax could see, might be expanded to cover all the world. Like the frost within the Summerbane dungeons, this was a fantastic change—though now the dragon was forced to admit to himself that he hadn't caused the alteration. It made him queasy to think of the powerful forces that must have been at work in the world as he slumbered.

Now he flew, arching wings that, for all their stiffness, bore him easily into the air. He circled the castle on its spire, and saw that the entire place was caked in frost. As his spirals took him higher, he saw that the island of Summerbane had become a pale white cliff in the midst of this glacier.

This place is Icewall—and it is still my lair. The thrill of pride was stronger now, disquiet overwhelmed by sheer delight at the prospect of this great, frozen realm. What stronghold could be more perfect for a white dragon? Flying ever higher, he saw that the glacier continued for many miles to the north, into the place that had been Ansalon. Far away, there was a hint of brown, dusty plain.

Then he saw the other dragon. Also a white, the strange wyrm marked a straight course toward the promontory of Icewall Castle. Keris urgently veered back, landing on the high tower before the other serpent had drawn very near. When the wyrm finally spiraled about the pinnacle in a long, lazy bank, Keristillax saw that the intruder was larger than himself—great enough that it could probably usurp this splendid lair, if it desired to do so.

But not without a fight. Keris spit a blast of frost in the air, a gust that didn't come close to the flier, but insured that the creature would think twice about a headstrong attack.

"Peace, clan-dragon," declared the other, his voice the boom of an iceberg calving from a glacial cliff. "I am Terrisleetix—and I bring news of glory!"

"What glory?" growled Keris, certain that this dragon called Sleet was trying to trick him.

"The return of our queen! She has brought us forth from the Abyss, has summoned her dragons from across the world. We gather at the Lords of Doom!"

"Go back to your glory and your fire mountains!" Keristillax roared. He well remembered the Lords of Doom, where the whites had suffered for several years before winging into the disastrous war. He intended to never again lay eyes on those volcanic summits.

"I go, but not until I have summoned the others . . . those, like yourself, who served Takhisis well in the Human War, and now lie dormant beneath the snow."

Sleet swept closer, his tone level, his azure eyes fixed upon Keristillax. "That is, you *must* have served her well, old dragon, for her to have gone to the trouble of preserving you. I believe this, or I would not tolerate your ill manners."

"I flew against the metal dragons—I killed a brass, and even a silver. But then the dragonlances slew my clandragons and kin-dragons in great numbers. And if you fly against them again, they will do the same to you!"

"Bah—the metal dragons will have no part in this war." Sleet's tone was contemptuous. "I myself led the whites to the Dragon Isles, where we found the eggs of the silvers in the high glaciers. We bore those eggs to Sanction, while the blacks took bronze dragon eggs from the brackish swamp. And reds ventured into the golden city itself, where the foolish metallics slumbered—until our queen awakened them."

"Why did she do that?" Keris growled, his skepticism overcome by curiosity.

"Takhisis has exacted an oath from the dragons of Paladine! Their eggs will be spared, so long as they remain on their islands. There will be no metal dragons in this war!"

Sleet bellowed with a force that rattled powdery snow from the slopes of the castle walls, a reminder that Keris would be overmatched in battle.

But the venerable white had begun to believe this intruder, at least enough to feel reassured that Terrisleetix had not come here to steal his lair. And the strange dragon's words had brought forth the question that above all teased his mind.

"You say that the queen has preserved me? For how long . . . how many winters have passed since the Human War?"

"You have slumbered here, Ancient One"—the honorific was heavy with mockery as Sleet maneuvered in a tight circle—"for more than thirteen hundred winters. In that time, the world you remember has been smashed by Cataclysm, wracked by the gods themselves. And finally our queen gathers her forces, prepares for her return."

Once again, Sleet roared, twisting in the air and soaring away toward the southern ice. His final command was delivered with neck swept forward and thrust down so that the mighty wyrm spoke almost from beneath his own belly—a further mockery. "Fly to the Khalkists, old dragon— or the queen will exact her obedience in another way!"

Trembling with fury, Keris watched the white shape dwindle into the southern distance. He felt a momentary and prideful urge to hurl himself after Sleet, but this desire he easily held in check. Instead, he curled more tightly about his spire, glaring, huffing ice, eyeing the intruder until Terrisleetix had vanished.

Only then did he glide down from the tower, spiraling into the spacious courtyard. He was no longer afraid. He did not know whether or not he believed Sleet's words about the dragons of Paladine and the Oath. No doubt some of it was truth, though he could not imagine a mere promise binding the vainglorious metallics for long.

But the real truth was that he was here, master of his lair; he had no intention of ever flying to the Lords of Doom.

* * * * *

More than two score years waxed and waned upon Icewall Glacier with little measure save that the winters were dark for long months, until they finally brightened into short, twilight days. Ultimately each summer was illuminated by a sun that seemed, for a time, as though it would never set. Yet in seasons of light and dark the cold remained constant, the blanket of glorious snow an apparently permanent fixture upon the land.

During that time, Keristillax became the scourge of the glacier, unchallenged ruler of the arctic wastes from Ice Mountain Bay to the frozen coast of the Southern Courrain Ocean. He saw no other dragons of white or of any other color. It was not long before the encounter with Sleet became a foggy memory that had no meaning.

In the early years Keristillax encountered a few tribes of ice barbarians encamped in the vicinity of the castle. These he swiftly eradicated, or forced to flee. He also met the tusked Thanoi, brutal warriors attuned to the arctic wastes, and they paid him gifts of homage and food. In return, he let them live, allowed them the honor of serving him.

His favorite food had always been the blubbery carcass of a freshly killed seal, and thirteen centuries of dormancy had done nothing to dull his hunger. For the most part he stayed near the castle, but often he flew as far as the coast of Ice

Mountain Bay to hunt and devour the plump coast-dwelling delicacies. Like all white dragons, he needed to eat only rarely . . . so when he did, he preferred to take nourishment that was pleasing to his palate.

In the midst of a gray spring, some forty-three winters after Sleet's unheeded summons, Keristillax decided to fly far from his castle, striking out toward the coast with uncommon urgency. The preceding winter had been long and dark, as always, and he had slept through the greater part of it. Yet the hunting in fall had been poor, and he had awakened to this cold spring with a gnawing hunger.

Shaking off the lingering light-headedness within a few hours of awakening, Keris took to the air, winging in a straight line toward the nearest promontory of Ice Mountain Bay. There would be seals there, in great numbers, and the prospect of feasting drove his wings to even greater urgency.

Until a spot of darkness caught his eye.

The shape was smooth, and it resembled a seal—but why would the animal be so far from the water? With an irritated puff of frost from his flexing nostrils, Keristillax banked into a shallow curve, circling the object that stood out in such sharp contrast to the perfect whiteness of the frosty glacier. As he drew closer the white dragon perceived that this motionless object was in fact a seal—a great, fat male, apparently dozing on the ice.

Now his wings settled into a still, nearly soundless glide as Keris dropped toward the unsuspecting creature. All questions about the animal's unusual location were buried by the eager, trembling anticipation of an imminent meal. He imagined the warm fat flowing over his jaws, the blood running down his throat, and he had to suppress a moan of pleasure. Time for the final plummet, then, the tuck of the wings, the telltale lash of wind through the icicles of his mane.

Close now, he spotted the hole, the black circle that was the seal's escape into the chill waters of the icebound sea. Hypnotized by hunger, he didn't notice that the rises of a low valley marked this place as land. Keris saw the seal make a sudden lurch toward the hole, and his white wings pulsed hard. The dragon took no note of the fact that the creature's fins and tail trailed limply, that it was pulled by the force of a line snapped taut around the seal's neck; all his focus was on killing, and the slaking of his hunger.

The animal vanished through the black circle, but the hunter was not yet thwarted. As he had done countless times before, Keris stabbed his head forward, ready to brave the frigid waters for the chance to snap down on a thrashing fin or tail.

But there was no water here, only a cold, dark cave walled in blue ice and rock. The seal tumbled down a long chute, and even as it fell, Keris caught the scent of death—this was mere carrion. Still he ignored the proof of a trap, desperately straining his supple neck, striving for a bite that would save his illusory meal.

A clamp of hard metal jarred him out of his frenzy. A steel band had clapped inward from the rim of the hole to encircle his neck, and Keris whipped his head back in outrage. Thrashing from side to side, he tried to cast the collar away, but it was clamped tight.

He broke free of the hole, squatted, and then lowered his snout to the opening, spreading his jaws, and blasting an eruption of lethal frost. As the vaporous fog dissipated he tried to stare into the darkness, sniffing for some clue as to the nature of his enemy.

"Greetings, Keristillax."

The voice came from behind him as the white dragon whirled, his tail lashing. But he saw that the speaker, a human, stood just out of reach.

"You are a mighty dragon, but you are impulsive. You should allow me to speak." The man's voice was frank, his face unemotional except for a hint of admiration.

Keris was surprised enough to hesitate before his next attack. His instinctive fury against the unexpected events began to settle within his breast. He could afford to examine this person for a moment or two before destroying him.

"Who are you?" Keristillax demanded, as, with feline grace, he settled his four clawed feet firmly onto the ice. Blinking lazily, he studied the man, who was garbed in a tight-fitting suit of black leather armor. Only the man's face was visible, for a cap of his suit rose to encircle his scalp, while supple gloves and boots seemed to be part of the single skin.

"My name is Lord Salikarn, but you shall call me Master— and together we will fly for the glories of our queen."

Salikarn's breath frosted in the air. His face was squarish and swarthy, his dark eyes startlingly gentle. The strong chin was framed by carefully trimmed whiskers, and his voice had a smooth, almost disinterested quality—he might have been discussing a matter of complete insignificance for all the passion in his words.

Instinctively Keristillax breathed, spewing a white wave of frost that roared like a hurricane, burying the black-garbed man in a deadly cloud. Only when his lungs had been emptied, when a layer of frost completely masked the black armor and face of the interloper, did Keris allow himself to inhale. The white dragon realized that his entire body was taut; nervous tingles of alarm shot through him. He blinked and lowered his mighty jaws, carefully inspecting the rime-cloaked shape.

Before his astonished gaze, the dragon watched the ice melt away from the black leather, steaming into vapor, settling downward in the still air. Now Lord Salikarn raised one of his arms, lifting a hand as if to ward off another attack of dragonbreath.

Yet even then Keris understood that there was nothing defensive, or at least nothing fearful, in the response. His instincts called for another blast of frost, yet the mighty dragon held back.

And jaws of fire clamped around the sinuous white neck, burning through his scales, searing his blood and flesh and mind. Keristillax collapsed, writhing in the snow, howling aloud. With a supreme effort he moved his foreclaws, frantically striving to clutch the awful metal collar. When his talons touched the ring of steel, fire lanced through his legs and shoulders, and the white dragon could only arch his back, tumbling over, painfully smashing the bony frame of his wing in the grip of paralyzing agony.

The fire vanished as suddenly as it had begun. With a hunch of his shoulders and wings, Keris rolled back to his feet, body taut, trembling between fury and fear. Fury prevailed, and he lunged, jaws gaping. If his breath would not destroy this warrior, then his size and power would prove more than enough.

But once again that ring of steel seared away his will in an embrace of fire. Crushed to the snowy ground, Keris reeled with an agony that should have numbed his mind, but didn't. And when the horrific burning at last ceased, the white dragon drew a deep breath before he rose onto trembling legs. He was certain that the next burst of pain would, no, *must*, kill him.

"Why should you try to attack me?" Lord Salikarn argued calmly. "You cannot succeed, and each time the painful consequences will inevitably be repeated."

Suddenly Keris was more afraid of this man than he had ever been of anything in his life. How could Salikarn be so dispassionate, even polite, as he inflicted unspeakable torture?

"I do not choose to attack you again, now," the white dragon finally replied, grudgingly.

"Your spirit is strong. That is good—you will make a splendid mount when you have learned discipline."

And then Keris knew: the Dark Queen's war, the armies gathering beneath the fiery Khalkists, had reached out to claim him. As if in reply to a mute question, Lord Salikarn continued, "This is the face of your master. When you learn the truth of this, when you accept me, then together we will form a mighty team."

"I am already a being of might—without a human to burden me!" barked the serpent.

"Ah, yes, but in ways you are foolish, too. Look how you fell into my trap—here, in the hills. You thought that a seal had come to rest on an ice cap! I knew that your hunger would blind you; by simply pulling the seal into the hole, I knew that I could draw your head into the collar."

The urge to attack returned as the white dragon stared down hatefully at that calm face. Yet this time Keristillax reared back, recoiling instinctively from this bizarre human. He wanted to pounce, to breathe injury, to tear this insolent intruder to shreds—but not as much as he dreaded a return of the crippling pain.

The dragon reminded himself that he was a patient creature, a mighty being forged over long centuries. He would take the time to learn his enemy, to come to know his ways. Ancient lessons whispered in his ears, and he forced his rage—and some of his fear—to recede.

"How did you come here?" Keris asked, lowering his head in a gesture that, he supposed, the man might take as a sign of acquiescence.

"I was carried by magic, teleported by the will of Takhisis herself."

"For what purpose?" Keris feared that he knew the answer, and the man confirmed this with his reply.

"I was sent to seek you, to show you the rightness of returning into your queen's favor." Lord Salikarn spoke with some warmth now, and Keristillax sensed that the man was sincere in his desire to make the dragon understand. "There will be war . . . and you are a bold and mighty wyrm. Fly with me to glory!"

"What glory is there in dying at the end of a lance?"

"We will win this war—it is the metallics who will die!" declared Salikarn, with the most vehemence Keris had yet heard from the man. The white noted, with a twinge of respect, that at least the human didn't try to convince him that the dragons of Paladine would remain aloof from this war. "Takhisis has found a mighty emperor—and already he assembles great armies."

Keristillax remained silent. He remembered great armies from an earlier era, and he, too, had flown under the auspices of an emperor of the Dark Queen's. And still his clandragons had died.

Then another thought occurred to the pensive wyrm. The collar had burned when he attacked the lord, but suppose Keristillax was simply to take wing and fly away? It would vex the prideful wyrm, of course, to leave this arrogant interloper unpunished . . . but it might be his only chance.

"Do not try to escape me," declared the man evenly. "Her Dark Majesty's might will reach you wherever you fly. That collar will be your bond so long as I am alive—and you have already learned that you cannot kill me. You should know, too, that next time, your punishment shall not be so mercifully brief."

Keristillax felt a deep chill at the lord's words—not only because of the threat of additional pain, but because the man had somehow intuited what the dragon was thinking before Keris had even had time to act.

He decided that he would go along with this warrior, for now, at least. Perhaps a chance to escape would arise at a more opportune time, when Salikarn wasn't so alert to the possibility of treachery.

"What is it that you desire me to do?" asked the dragon, once again lowering himself into an easy, four-legged crouch.

"Take me into the air." The lord stepped forward and Keris hastily lowered his heard, touching his shoulder to the ground just in time to meet the man's soft-soled foot. Salikarn scrambled upward, clutching both at the dragon's neck bristles and the spikes of his back.

"You have done this before," noted Keristillax, with a swivel of his long neck that allowed him to meet his rider's gaze.

"Never upon a wyrm so large as yourself," allowed Lord Salikarn—though Keristillax was still too resentful to be flattered.

Salikarn settled into the hollow between the white's shoulders, straddling the base of the neck with his leather-armored legs. Even through his hard, thick scales, Keris could feel the unusual warmth of that armor. He immediately guessed that the heat within the suit was magical, and that this was how the man was able to survive in Icewall's harsh clime.

With a snort, Keris leaped upward. The snowy ground swept past, while his shadow, cast at a steep angle by the low sun, rolled silently across the undulating terrain. The man was a leaden weight dragging him down, but Keris stroked harder, straining for altitude, sweeping forward with increasing speed.

Finally the ground began to fall away, and the white dragon allowed himself a measure of relaxation. He had to pulse his wings in powerful strokes, but for now, at least, he could climb gradually, without the worry of slamming into an outcrop of ice or one of the steep hills that flanked the shallow valley.

He pulled higher, banking gradually, angling toward the coastline where, he at last remembered, the plump seals would lie in wait. With that thought, pangs of hunger returned, and Keris renewed his determination to eat.

"Back to the right . . . carry me to Icewall Castle," declared Lord Salikarn.

"I must hunt and eat! This is the way to my prey!"

"You will eat at my pleasure. Now, turn!"

The lord's hand, as warm as the rest of him, came to rest on the scales of the white neck. Keris imagined little prickles of heat rising to merge with the steel collar, and he could not bring himself to disobey. Grudgingly he veered, rising higher in his flight until the vast swath of glacier was a blanket of featureless white below.

The idea came to him, beautiful in its simplicity, irresistible in its quick accomplishment. He did not have to *attack* the man to cause him harm! If Keris dived into an upside-down loop, the rider couldn't possibly hope to hang on. And the dragon would again be free.

Immediately Keristillax ducked his head and went into a steep plunge. Before he could continue the loop, rivers of fire shot through his whole body, wracking him with agony. A shrill bellow escaped his jaws as Keris thrashed helplessly, waiting for the fire to curl him up, to consume him.

But instead his wings jutted firmly to the sides, and his neck uncurled. He raised his head as his back and tail arched into a curving spear. Responding to commands that came from some distant, untouchable place, his body smoothly pulled out of the dive, returning to level flight even as the pain continued to twist and distort his senses.

And then the agony dissipated, gone like steam vanishing

into dry air—though the memory of it lingered on the fringes of his awareness. He soared for a long time, unable to find the strength to pump his wings. And then he heard the calm, reasonable voice of his rider, seemingly coming from far away, as if the man spoke as a detached observer instead of one who had just made an attempt on his life.

"You see, there really is no escape. Your intent was clear—and your punishment, once again, surprisingly merciful."

Keris shuddered, accidentally sideslipping for a moment, then instantly pushing hard, leveling himself and his rider.

"You are a good flier. You have nothing to fear." Salikarn clapped the dragon on the neck in a gesture that might even have been affectionate.

"Why are you not angry?" Keristillax was baffled and frightened by the man's cool reaction. "Does not my treachery drive you to fury?"

"This is your way, and your strength, my mighty wyrm. But know that in my way there is also strength. Together we will be invincible! We shall be awarded a captaincy, at least, in the White Dragonarmy. I wonder if you can even begin to imagine the conquests we will lead!"

Keristillax had no desire to make conquests, or to fly in the lead of any wing. He knew the value of an oath, and he was certain that no mere pledge would hold the metal dragons, and their deadly lances, back from the war. Sooner or later they would come, and the chromatics would die. But he remained silent.

"It would please me to see you kill," declared the rider, leaning easily forward so that his fingers intertwined in the spiky bristle of the dragon's mane.

"I . . . may I fly to the coast?" Keris dared to ask.

"No. Our destination lies to the east. But I give you leave to take whatever game we see."

This time Keristillax felt little resentment of the command. Even here on the wastes, they would eventually come upon a caribou, or bear, perhaps even a wandering ice barbarian. His gut growled in wholehearted anticipation of fresh meat, and he almost convinced himself that his pale wings sliced the chill air in pursuit of his own purpose now. Hundreds of feet above the shelf of the glacier, the dragon and his black-clad rider soared in the full, crystal light of the sun. Keristillax felt keenly aware of his own majesty, the pure, gleaming whiteness of his scales, the great spread of his wings, and the power of his scaly flesh.

"There." Lord Salikarn's voice was accompanied by a clap on the dragon's right shoulder.

Dipping a wing, the dragon banked toward the cliff. Immediately he saw the ice bear, though the mighty carnivore was pressed belly-down on a snowy ridge, colorless fur all but invisible against the wintery backdrop. Keris felt a glimmer of admiration, impressed that the rider had spotted the well-camouflaged animal.

The dragon's shadow rushed across the face of the cliff and, seeing at last that it was discovered, the ice bear broke from concealment to sprint wildly along the ledge. Powerful wing strokes closed the distance between predator and prey, and the bear howled in panic, knowing doom was near. With a desperate pounce the lumbering creature tried to spring upward to reach the imaginary safety of the upper shelf.

But the distance was farther than the animal had imagined—or else terror had driven reason from its mind. The bear clawed at the brink, gouging chips of ice but finding no purchase for its massive bulk. Toppling backward, the creature skidded off the ledge, then bellowed frantically as it tumbled down the long cliff. The cry ceased with brutal suddenness.

The animal was quite dead as Keristillax settled beside the white-furred shape at the base of the precipice. Lord Salikarn dismounted and seated himself on a rock as the dragon settled down to feed. Ignoring the toughness of the meat, Keris tore away great chunks, swallowing massive bites.

The human lord produced a small brazier from his kit. Filling the iron grate with bits of peat, he struck spark into his tinder and soon produced a small blaze. The man sliced several steaks from the carcass. He grilled and ate these while the white dragon polished off the bulk of the meat.

The warm flesh and rich blood filled the dragon's belly, and a soothing contentment spread through his body. He regarded his companion, saw that a ring of snow had melted around the man. More questions rose in the dragon's mind, and he felt emboldened to speak.

"How do you stay warm here? Most humans must be clad in many layers of fur to survive Icewall."

Salikarn smiled benignly. "This armor is a gift from Takhisis herself. I need merely to be exposed to sunlight during the day, and the magic will keep me warm through a long night."

"And so you survive here?"

"Aye, until we travel north."

"Do we journey to the Lords of Doom?" Memories of those fiery summits, of the stifling blasts of hot air that surrounded the city of Sanction, rose in the dragon's gorge like bile.

"Aye." Perhaps Salikarn sensed his thoughts, for the man chuckled and shook his head. "Don't worry—her Dark Majesty has given the white dragons range on the southern heights. There is sometimes snow there, and volcanoes are rare."

"I remember those mountains," Keris said without enthusiasm, scorning the tiny swaths of shady snowfields as compared to the majesty, the vast perfection of his glacier.

"And in any event, the war will come soon—within five or ten winters. Then we may reveal our presence in the world. We of the White Wing will surely come south."

"I could return to my castle?"

Salikarn shook his head. "That castle will be the lair of Terrisleetix, you can bet. He will be the mount of our high-lord."

Keris was not surprised by the news, but he could not suppress a surge of rage. Sleet, who had scorned him and flown away, would inherit his splendid lair!

"You spoke of revealing our presence. Do you mean that for now we must hide?"

"Aye. Our flight to the Khalkists must take a circuitous route, avoiding realms of human and elf alike."

"Flying over the ocean, then?" The gray waters of the Southern Courrain held no fear for Keris. He had claimed many a walrus, and even whales, from that turbulent sea. And now in early spring there would be ice floes and great bergs, floating frost-islands that would dot the vast seascape.

"Yes. We will skirt the Plains of Dust, making landfall somewhere to the west of Silvanesti. From there it will be night flying, until we reach the ogre realms and the Khalkist foothills."

"A long flight." The Plains of Dust, Keris had recently learned, was the brownish swath north of his glacier. Now he considered the route, trying to piece it together from his memories of pre-Cataclysmic Ansalon. "Yet we will stand a good chance of keeping our presence secret."

"And your old wings will make it, I trust?" asked Salikarn with an easy grin. "Or we can put in to shore once or twice for rest, if we need to, although that's a pretty barren coast."

"The ocean flight will be tiring, but perhaps I can come to light upon an iceberg halfway through the journey. That way we can be sure to remain concealed from observation."

"Very well. Now I shall sleep—and I suggest you do the same. We commence our flight at the first sign of dawn."

Lord Salikarn made a bed on a flat rock that he had brushed free of snow. Within minutes the warrior's breast rose and fell in the rhythmic cadence of sleep. The dragon crouched nearby, immense and reptilian, unblinking in the frigid night air. For a time Keris considered the temptation of a sudden attack—and squelched the notion even before a prickle of heat ringed his neck. Instead he sat, motionless as the ice beneath his talons, and waited.

He examined his problem with a patience attainable only by one who has lived for many centuries. There was a way, there *had* to be a way, to avoid this doomed journey, to stay away from the fire mountains and the metal dragons and their lancers that would, inevitably, fall upon him.

He reflected on his steel collar, and on the man he was bound to protect. Strangely, he could not bring himself to hate Lord Salikarn. He even admitted to a certain respect at the way the lord had tricked him into sticking his head into the loathsome collar. Keris sensed that Salikarn was not inordinately cruel; but the lord was a very inconvenient presence. The dragon's thoughts churned, seeking a weakness in the man, a flaw in the web that spun ever more tightly about him, drawing him toward a fate he abhorred.

With a sudden return to wakefulness, Lord Salikarn stood up. The man washed his face in the snow, and announced that they would once again take to the air.

As Salikarn approached, Keris noted that he clapped his arms around his chest, shivering in the fashion of one who is cold.

"Did your magic armor fail you?" asked the serpent, blinking lazily.

"The enchantment lasts only for so long—I'll be fine as soon as we get into the air, when the sun can reach me."

Keris bowed his head, allowing the lord to straddle his shoulders. And when Salikarn ordered him to fly, the white dragon spread his wings and pounced into the air without any thought of defiance. This time he was ready for the additional weight, and climbed steadily away from the glacier. Soon they emerged from the haze into daylight, and almost immediately Keristillax felt the uncomfortable warmth of the lord's magic armor. Though this was the beginning of the warm season, the skies were a pale white overhead, blanketed not by cloud but by tiny particles of ice that diluted the light of the sun and washed out the pure blue of the heavens.

Only after he had circled upward to a height of a thousand feet did the dragon even think to ask a question.

"Where should I fly, Master?"

Though the words grated within him he spoke them smoothly, still fearing the stinging force of the steel collar.

"Take me along the Icewall, but ever toward the east," declared the man.

Dutifully Keris pulled through the chilly air. Gradually the misty frost gathered into pale clouds, ultimately forming an overcast that obscured the sun. The white dragon relished the frigid blast of wind, and—though Keris sensed that the black-armored rider was not fond of the cold—Salikarn made no complaint as the hours stretched on. Still the dragon flew swiftly over the snow-covered expanse.

They passed an abandoned village of ice barbarians, a place Keris had raided so many times that the hardy humans—those who survived—had finally been forced to flee north to the trackless tundra. The lord bid him to circle the ruin, asking questions about the shattered lodges and the savage, hardy folk who had dwelled within. Salikarn was particularly intrigued by the wreckage of one of the great ice-riggers that was now little more than a splintered hull, though the dragon figurehead and long mast still jutted from the ruin with a suggestion of the ship's earlier grace.

For more hours they flew through polar skies. Lord Salikarn remained active and interested, swiveling easily in his seat, remarking about this or that feature of Icewall Glacier. His armor, having been touched by sunlight, maintained its enchantment throughout the day.

Finally they reached the remote and windswept coast—cliffs of black rock framed by immense icicles, relentlessly hammered by raging surf. Waves assaulted the craggy cliffs, hurling up great sheets of spray, showering rocks and shoals, coating everything with slick ice. Beyond, the ocean, gray as cold steel, churned to the eastern horizon. Great swaths of whiteness interrupted that slate surface, and Keris knew that these were sheets of ice that had broken free from the glacial coast. Some were mountains of the sea, towering icebergs rising to jagged peaks a hundred feet or more above the surface, while others were flat, raftlike floes ever collapsing amid the roiling tempest of the arctic spring.

"Now to the east, we fly."

"It has been many hours already," Keris noted. "Perhaps we should stop here for now, allowing me to restore my strength."

"You said that you could rest on an iceberg, and I see many of them before us. No, we will keep flying until dusk."

Resolutely the white dragon left the storm-wracked shore
behind. The sea was a vast blanket, and that very vastness
was comforting, no threat to the great, leather-winged flier.
Out here, Lord Salikarn truly needed him, depended upon
Keristillax for life itself.

The man was almost forgotten as Keristillax forged
through blustering winds. Pinpricks of ice dotted his scales,
brightening his eyes and tickling his cavernous nostrils with
sensations of tingling pleasure. This icy sea was no more than
an extension of the glacier—of *his* glacier—and the dragon
was as comfortable here as over the sweep of empty ice.

And he felt confident, his own master again. When dusk
shrouded the gray sea he began to look for a place to land.
He chose a large iceberg with a long, rectangular summit
and a surrounding precipice of glacial frost. The top was
flat, divided into two sections by a deep crevice.

"It has a large area on top, there—it won't break up for a
long time," the dragon pointed out, to Lord Salikarn's agreement, as he banked toward the larger of the two segments.

Making his approach in a steep glide, Keristillax reared
back, ready to drop lightly to the frozen surface.

But suddenly his low approach revealed a smaller crevice
below him, a steep-sided cut that intersected the central
chasm. Partially concealed by a cornice of snow, the shorter
gap was nevertheless wide and deep. With a powerful
thrust, the white dragon tried to pull up—but now the
weight of his rider dragged him down. Keris skidded onto
the slick surface, felt his forepaws slide over the edge, while
his rear talons ripped and gouged into the ice.

Thrown forward by the momentum of his flight, the
dragon skidded into the crevice amid a cloud of powdery
snow. Keristillax twisted, and his right wing cracked into
the edge of the chasm. With a roar, he tumbled into the
steep chute, careening downward as Lord Salikarn clung to
the fringes of his mane. Talons extended, the serpent tried to
arrest his headlong plummet; chips flew as his claws
gouged into the hard blue ice.

And then at last they were motionless, perched at the
brink of the iceberg. Below them the sea surged against a

curtain of ice, fingers of foam exploding upward, clutching toward the victims who had so narrowly escaped.

Gingerly, Keristillax backed away from the edge. He came to rest on a fairly wide shelf of ice at the base of a steep, ice-walled notch.

The dragon collapsed weakly to the ground. His wing was a crumpled membrane, and pain stabbed through his flank like blasts of lightning.

Salikarn slid down from his scaly saddle, watching grimly as the white dragon tried to move. The man blanched visibly when Keris moaned and quickly drew his wing tight against him.

"The bone is broken," hissed the serpent, twisting, shaking his head in tremors of agony.

Grimly, Lord Salikarn spun on his heel. He stalked to the edge of the ice cliff, looking to the left and right. There was no hope, nothing but angry ocean to the limits of the foggy horizon. Turning back, the man looked at the dragon appraisingly.

"Is there any way that wing will bear your weight?"

Keris tried to extend the membrane, then groaned and drew the flap back to his side.

"I cannot straighten it."

"Very well. We will remain here until you can fly."

Night fell, and the human made himself as comfortable as possible. To the dragon, the lord looked weak and small. Droplets of water slicked his leather armor, and Keris knew that Salikarn still remained warm—for now.

By dawn, however, frost had formed on the man's arms and legs, and he was shivering. Pale daylight provided sign of neither land nor ship, nor even, at first, the sun. After a time the fog burned away, but the horizontal rays remained high on the walls of the ice gorge, and dappled the sea with their sight, but not their reach.

Lord Salikarn stared longingly at the distant brightness, but the precious light could not penetrate into the depths of the chasm. Keris was strong enough to rear back, hoisting the man in his forepaws—but even then the rays struck the crevice wall too high overhead. Eventually the shifting tides and winds spun the iceberg around, but by then the sun had disappeared behind the growing murk, and the two castaways huddled in shared pain in the shadows.

"Will the current carry us to shore?" asked the man, as his teeth started to chatter.

"We drift southward," Keris declared with a shrug. "We can only wait and see." He looked into the distance, catching the scent of a faraway seal. The spoor triggered no growl from his belly; he was a white dragon, and it would be long before he needed to eat.

Night arrived in a blustery assault of wind and snow. The world was nothing more than this raging storm, the crippled dragon, and the man who was by now convulsed by shivering. By midnight, the snow was freezing on the black leather armor, and Lord Salikarn's skin had grown pale with frostbite.

Drained by the frigid assault, the human struggled to speak. "We would have made a good team," he declared, his voice barely audible above the crashing waves.

"I think you are right," Keris agreed. "Even the fire mountains wouldn't have stopped us."

Even in the midst of ice and darkness, he could not speak of those mountains without a twinge of horror. Yet Salikarn was weak; he barely took notice of the dragon's words.

The next morning the human lord did not awaken. Keris leaned over, saw the blue flesh, the open eyes that could no longer see. At last Salikarn had yielded to the cold.

With a snort of satisfaction, mingled with a curious twinge of regret, the dragon shrugged, and felt the steel collar break and fall away . . . the collar that had bound him, so long as his master lived.

He looked again at the stiff figure of the dead man, saw that frost had begun to coat the leather-clad limbs and pale, lifeless face. Of all the agents the Dark Queen could have sent for him, this one had not been bad. Keristillax was vaguely saddened that the fellow had been doomed by the task. Still, there were many willing to serve Takhisis, to wage her war.

And there was only one Icewall.

Huffing, Keristillax turned toward the edge of the ice cliff. The wind blew through his bristling mane. It might be hundreds of miles away, but that no longer mattered.

The white dragon spread his crumpled wing, felt the strong, unbroken bone support his weight.

Finally, he took to the air with easy, powerful strokes. Setting his sights toward the glacier that, for now, belonged to him, Keristillax flew.

To those familiar with it, Krynn is a world that evokes images of mighty dragons and powerful magic set against the ravaged landscape of the War of the Lance. It is a land where the wizards are distinguished by the color of the robes they wear and the type of magic they practice. But the lives of the peoples who inhabit Ansalon are not so easily categorized. Good and Evil are not white and black, but many shades of gray. As the lands are torn asunder by war and strife between the races, heros are born and legends are made.

These are the heroes and legends of the DRAGONLANCE® saga: warriors, mages, and clerics; ordinary folk who struggle in their day-to-day existence to do what is right, though it brings them no glory and may well result in violent and sudden death; reluctant heroes, who find fame forced upon them; brash, young knights who consider only the glory of war and none of its horror. These are but a few who find their places in the annals of the world.

Not all are human. They may be elves, or dwarves, or gnomes, or even—gods forbid!—kender. Heroes come in all shapes and sizes, in either gender, and from many races.

They have but one thing in common: action.

They act, to the best of their abilities, when others would only sit and let the conquerors come. The evil dragons, the mutant draconians, the Dark Queen Takhisis, who with her minions would take Krynn and make it her own. With the help of the gods or without it, it is the individuals who stand up against Evil, whether bravely and of their own free will or because they are left with no other option, who are the true heroes of the DRAGONLANCE saga.

It is of them our stories are told.

If you enjoyed reading *The Dragons of Chaos*,
be sure to read these other DRAGONLANCE® saga
short story anthologies:

DRAGONLANCE authors showcase their talents in
The Dragons of Krynn (ISBN 1-56076-830-4) and *The Dragons at
War* (ISBN 0-7869-0491-7). These short story collections con-
tain tales of good and evil dragons (and those some-
where in between) as well as gnomes, gully dwarves,
kender, minotaurs, knights, wizards and draconians.
Authors include Jeff Grubb, Mark Anthony, Richard
A. Knaak, Roger E. Moore, Douglas Niles, Linda P.
Baker, Nick O'Donohoe, and Margaret Weis.

In *The Second Generation* Margaret Weis and Tracy
Hickman tell the stories of the children of the Heroes
of the Lance. Selections include "Kitiara's Son" and
"Raistlin's Daughter" as well as poetry by Michael
Williams. Many years have passed since the War of
the Lance. Krynn is peaceful, but the future is uncertain. It will take a new generation of heroes to continue the struggle against evil—a darkness that was
defeated but never completely destroyed.

(ISBN 0-7869-0260-4)

DragonLance®

FIFTH AGE®
Dramatic Adventure Game

GAMES Magazine's 1996 Best Adventure and Role-Playing Game

The DRAGONLANCE® : FIFTH AGE®
Dramatic Adventure Game is a new
storytelling game that emphasizes **creativity**, **action**, and **heroism**.
It's **easy to learn**, and **fun to play**.

The Heroes of Krynn need you. You can join
them—find the DRAGONLANCE: FIFTH AGE game at your local
book, game, or hobby store.

® and ™ designate trademarks owned by TSR, Inc. ©1997 TSR, Inc. All rights reserved.